For Ted H

A Kin..., ...
I'm so glad we met.

No Other Medicine

by Gail Hallas

Second Edition 2015
Copyright © 2011, 2015 Gail Hallas
All Rights Reserved

Feedback welcomed on
GailHallasBooks@gmail.com

The miserable have no other medicine,
but only hope.
– William Shakespeare, 1604

Wishing you lots of
sunshine smiles
and bountiful heats.

Gail
2·12·17

In loving memory of Jack.
You are a big part of the story,
and I miss you every day.

~ ~ ~

1

Long Island, New York

August 1968

The last time Vincent Fossari saw his father alive was the moment before the explosion, when the older man's eyes froze in the space between his surgical cap and mask. Julian Fossari's life ended in a green flash from the lights that hung above the four-year-old boy who lay draped and unconscious on the operating table.

From the observatory's first row seat, Vincent Fossari felt his body jar in the deafening blast. He saw that the force had severed the wires glued to the child's small chest, disconnecting them from the cardiac monitor chirping in erratic fits near the outlying wall. The cauterizer whipped its narrow rubber body like a snake trying to shake loose from a trap. The instrument's heated end glowed in the now-dim room. Then it cooled off and went out.

Above, Vincent Fossari could hear the steady hissing of gas as it escaped from the detached facemask that had been held over the child's nose and mouth a moment before.

Fossari ran for the telephone next to the teaching theater's exit door and impatiently waited for the operator's voice. "Dr. Fossari here," he screamed. "Get the crash team. Stat! Explosion in OR 12."

Almost before he finished, he heard the overhead speakers spring to life. "Code Blue and Code Red. OR 12. Code Blue and Code Red. OR 12."

In a panic, Vincent Fossari stood by the door, the telephone still in his hand. He watched the crash cart push into the operating room, followed by three nurses and a doctor. One of the nurses took the fire extinguisher off the wall and sprayed the flames that licked at the child's surgical drape. Another woman ran to turn off the switch controlling the anesthetic gas filling the room.

The doctor kneeled on the floor next to Julian Fossari, and leaned his ear on the surgeon's chest. Vincent saw the blackened face of his father roll to one side and then stop. From where he stood, Vincent Fossari knew his father was dead – along with the child, the scrub nurse, and the anesthesiologist. Two others, the circulating nurse, and an operating room technician sat dazed in opposite corners of the room. Stretchers arrived and the two survivors were wheeled away.

Vincent Fossari didn't hear the conversation below, but he saw the doctor cover four people with clean white sheets in the soot-laden room.

2

For his entire life, Julian had strong ambitions for his only child. It was the same drive that moved Julian to leave his own parents in Italy as a young man, working day and night to graduate top in his class at Columbia University's Medical School. Then Julian drove his son, and since Vincent's mother died three years before, resentment toward his father's push intensified. Vincent didn't want to be a doctor in the first place, and hated the way his own academic skills paled in his father's shadow.

"You will make me proud," his father had said so many times. "You be respected physician like you Papa, you understand me, Vince? Mi senti?"

A mixture of fear and awe prevented Vincent from defying Julian, and the younger man shrouded his anger in self-pity and emotional isolation.

In 1968, Vincent Fossari was thirty-two years old, unmarried and just finishing his residency at Northfield Medical Center, the largest facility in eastern Long Island where his father was Chief of Surgery. In secret contempt of Julian's wishes, Vincent was preparing to set up practice in pediatrics. He planned to move into the new medical complex they built near the hospital. Vincent saw that mistakes with children, unlike adults, were often concealed.

The day four-year-old Joel Paulter came to the emergency room, it was Vincent Fossari's final rotation in the ER. Joel and his older sister had been playing on the pool deck of a motel where their parents vacationed. Joel slipped, fell, and injured his arm. After studying the X-rays of Joel's left ulna and radius, Vincent Fossari had applied a plaster cast to the child's arm from mid-palm to an inch above his elbow.

"Thank you for taking care of Joel," Amy Paulter told Fossari, saying the child's name in a one-syllable echo, as if the letter J was stuck in a hole. Fossari admitted the boy to the orthopedic unit for the night so the cast could dry.

Right away Joel complained of pain in his arm. He cried for an hour before Dr. Fossari gave him a sedative.

"Let him sleep for a while," Vincent told Joel's parents. "Kids always cry when they come to the hospital." Finally, Joel slept. His parents went back to their motel and Vincent Fossari drove home.

The next morning when Joel's parents returned to the hospital, they found Joel lying in bed with the sheet pulled up over his head. Sitting on the edge of the child's bed, his mother eased the covers from Joel's face. His eyes were swollen, and the pillowcase under his ear was wet. "I'm sorry, Mommy," he said. "Don't tell Sissy I'm crying."

Looking at her child, white-blond hair tousled and wet against his head, Amy Paulter felt her heart break. "It's all right, Joel," she said. "Daddy and I will take you home soon. Would you like that?"

Later that afternoon, as Vincent Fossari sipped coffee in the hospital cafeteria, he heard his name paged, along with an extension to call.

"Dr. Fossari, I'm afraid it's Joel Paulter again," the nurse on the orthopedic unit said. "He's been complaining of chronic pain in his left hand, Doctor. I thought you'd want to know."

"Did I order a sedative for the child last night, nurse?" Fossari said, sounding annoyed.

"Yes, Doctor, you did," she said. "Phenobarbital sodium, 30 milligrams IM, PRN."

"Do you know what PRN means, nurse?"

"Of course, Doctor. Give it as needed."

"Well, then," he blasted into the telephone. "Give the damn medication to the kid!"

"But Doctor . . ."

Ignoring the nurse, Vincent Fossari said, "And write up an order for acetaminophen 100 milligrams, P.O., every four hours. I'll sign it later." He hung up.

By mid-afternoon rounds, Joel didn't wake up as Fossari examined the cast on his arm. The child's small fingers, dark gray-blue, felt cold as they extended from the end of the plaster.

Rushing from Joel's room, Fossari ran down the corridor to the nurse charting at a large U-shaped desk. It was the same nurse he had spoken with earlier.

"Who's watching the fracture in 224?"

Looking up, the nurse frowned. "I beg your pardon, Doctor?"

"Goddamit. I can't turn my back for a few hours without something going wrong. Why didn't you tell me the kid's arm was swelling?"

"You mean Joel Paulter? I tried to tell you, Doctor. That's when you ordered the painkiller. By the way, here's the order for your signature." The nurse slid the form on the desk in front of Fossari.

"I didn't order a pain killer," he said. "Not for a fracture patient." He shoved the form back at the nurse. "And who the hell was on duty during the night? I want an incident report filed. And every goddamn person who went into that room is going to sign it." Fossari leaned over the desk and picked up the telephone. To the operator he barked, "Find Dr. Julian Fossari. Have him call the nurses' station on Two North."

Joel was scheduled for surgery that evening. Amputation of his left extremity above the elbow was documented on hospital records as secondary to complications resulting from Monteggia's fracture.

Just before the explosion, Vincent Fossari watched from his seat in the observation room as his father

7

removed the child's left arm. "Damn those nurses," he said to his reflection in the slanted window in front of him. A stocky man with thick glasses and dark curly hair, Vincent Fossari squirmed in his seat as he watched his father operate on Joel. The vertical crease between his small eyes deepened as he peered ahead. He ran his fingers nervously over the top of his head. A habit had that increased lately, and was one of the last movements he made before the blast.

3

St. Petersburg, Florida

September 1968

Isolated clouds swelled against a turquoise background high above palm trees that waved their fronds outside the hospital windows.   Part of the cumulus mass pointed upward, coming around to the bottom edge abruptly, like ice cream cones severed with a thin-edged knife.

Below, the building's exotic beauty ribboned its windows around each layer of floors, with shiny black metal in between.   The corners of the eight-storied tower were rounded, and from a distance the building stood proud, taller than most of the others nearby.   Its upper level housed the doctors' lounge, dining room, and sleeping quarters.   Executive offices were one story below.   On the sixth floor were the operating and recovery rooms.   Cardiac intensive care, medical intensive care and other specialty units occupied the fifth level.   On floors 3 and 4 there were patient rooms for post-op surgery and medical care, including both private and semi-private accommodations.   A tunnel connected the south end of the third floor to a three-story twin structure beside it.

One fourth of the second floor was separated by sterile doors that led to nine orthopedic rooms, outside of which opened to a huge central atrium with hollow

9

glass tubes running from floor to ceiling and flared at the top. The remaining area of offices and clinical space housed laboratories, respiratory therapy, physical therapy and the computer room, outside of which there was a circular corridor, railed off in bronze to prevent workers and wheelchairs from falling to their deaths. The outpatient clinic and the main lobby took up the ground floor, with the morgue beneath.

The smaller building had been completed three months prior, to accommodate additional pediatric patients. Since Federal accreditation as Florida's only Cystic Fibrosis Center, the need for additional rooms at St. Petersburg's Parkwest Pediatric Hospital had been great; and although two corridors were still unoccupied, the census rapidly grew.

Inside and out, the entire structure demonstrated rhythm and proportional grace. A creation of the finest architects in the country.

With the temperature in the low nineties, the air promised to bake sidewalks by noon, until the season's predictable showers cooled things down. Inside the air conditioning, Vincent Fossari's Canali jacket collected sweat along the underarm seams and down the sides of his pinstriped vest. With his hand resting on his knees, the wool absorbed perspiration from his palms. A mammoth mahogany desk separated Fossari from Arthur Lowndes, the administrator of Parkwest.

Arthur Lowndes moved slowly in the large chair, its velvet upholstery restricting his movements. When plans for his new office were developed, Lowndes had been eager to work with the architects and interior designers. From a catalog of pictures and rectangular swatches stapled to glossy pages, Lowndes selected rich velvet furniture for his office. Now he hated his choice.

Vincent Fossari watched the other man as the administrator silently read Vincent's three-page resume. Then Fossari's eyes moved toward the clouds rolling past the window in an effort to relax.

After his father's funeral, Vincent had taken leave of absence from Northfield Medical Center before his official staff responsibilities had ever begun.   He claimed a full refund on his deposit for the proposed medical office space.   Joel Paulter's parents shipped their child's body to their hometown in Bayside, New York, for the burial.

Vincent turned his father's affairs over to an attorney. "Put Julian's house up for sale," he'd told the lawyer. "As far as I'm concerned, get what you can. I'll send you my address when I have one and you can mail me the check." Then he was alone. Free.

Vincent had spent a long time in the medical library searching   through   Biomedical   Communications magazines for job vacancies at hospitals in the south. He filled two pages of possibilities with his sloppy scrawl.   Then a blurb in a week-old publication had caught his eye.

DR. LOUIS COCUZZO,
HEAD OF PULMONARY UNIT
PARKWEST PEDIATRIC HOSPITAL,
SUFFERS HEART ATTACK

Dr. Louis G. Cocuzzo, M.D., director of the Pediatric Unit at Florida's first Cystic Fibrosis Clinic, suffered a myocardial infarction at his home on Bellaire Beach over the weekend.   Hospital authorities reported that Dr. Cocuzzo was admitted to the cardiac intensive care unit on Sunday.

Cocuzzo, 62, a nationally recognized pulmonary expert was appointed the first director of the Pediatric Pulmonary Disease Unit at St. Petersburg's Parkwest Pediatric Hospital last year by unanimous vote of the Board of Trustees. Arthur Lowndes, administrator of the hospital, called Cocuzzo, "one of the premier pediatric pulmonary specialists in this country."

A graduate of Columbia University Medical School, Cocuzzo is the medical director for the

children's Medical Services, District 12, Pinellas and
Hillsborough counties, and a clinical associate
professor at the University of Florida Medical School.
He is a fellow of the American Academy of Pediatrics
and a fellow of the American Academy of Pulmonary
Diseases, as well as a board member for the Pinellas
county Medical Association for the past 16 years.

By the time Vincent had arrived at the hospital, Dr.
Cocuzzo's condition had stabilized. Vincent found the
man finishing lunch in a private room on the fifth floor.

"Well, I'll be damned," Cocuzzo said when Vincent
introduced himself. "Yes, Julian and I were pretty close
for a while. Most paisanos med students were. We
formed a small club, you know. Two dozen maybe," he
said staring away and chuckling to himself. "Julian was
a better student than me. The bastard'd study day and
night when he wasn't working. Had a real knack for
blocking out the world – uncanny ability to concentrate
on whatever it was he was doing."

"I know," Vincent had said without emotion.

"I'm real sorry to hear about his death. Great guy,
Julian was. Great guy. I must say Vince, you look like
a chip off the old block. What brings you south,
anyway? Just want to get away?"

"No, sir," Vincent said. He cleared his throat, and
ran his palms forward, wiping them on his trousers.
"I'm specializing in children's diseases. Pulmonary
mostly. Thought, well, since you and Dad were friends
. . . well, maybe I could learn something from you. Sort
of in Dad's memory."

Louis Cocuzzo chuckled again, then turned to watch
the palm trees whipping in the wind across the street.

Vincent studied the other man's profile.

"It's odd you should come here today, Vince,"
Cocuzzo said, still looking out the window.

"Odd?"

"Yes." He had turned toward Vincent. "During these past few days, lying here in bed, I've had a lot of time to think about my options. I know that much of my ticker problems have to do with my workload. It's all been a tremendous responsibility, trying to justify the clinic's existence as the first CF center in Florida. Takes up most of my time. Seeing patients, studying lab reports, X-rays. The whole nine yards. What I'd really like to do is research on CF. Instead of hands-on practice, if you know what I mean. I'm hoping to present a paper at the next International Conference in '71. In Switzerland." Cocuzzo tipped his head in the direction of the window where several file folders sat in a perilous heap on the sill.

"I've tried to catch up a little on paper work since I've been here. Seems, though, that this room is an excellent medium for reproductive growth of paper, not thoughts." His laugh came from deep in his gut and shook the blanket over his belly.

Vincent started to relax. Then Cocuzzo looked at him through squinted eyes. "You serious about helping me?"

Vincent tensed. "Yes," he said, and then added, "sir."

"Serious enough to move here and work with me full time?"

"Absolutely."

Settling back on his pillows, Cocuzzo reached across his chest for the bed control and elevated his head six inches. He stared at the ceiling, waiting for the motor's grind to stop. "Julian was a good man." He put the control back on the bed, tucking it under his pillow. For a long time Cocuzzo studied Fossari. Fossari, the answer to his dilemma. The neophyte doctor who dropped into his lap. A man he could mold to his way of thinking. Toss the other candidates who'd applied for the Assistant Director's job. It'd give the sons-a-bitches something to talk about – bringing in a newbie wop

13

doctor from up north. A wave of enthusiasm lifted Cocuzzo's spirits higher than they'd been in years. "It'll be a pleasure showing you the ropes around here, young man."

Cocuzzo pointed to the telephone on the table next to the bed. Vincent handed Cocuzzo the receiver.

"This is Dr. Cocuzzo, the hospital's patient of the year," he said to the hospital operator. "Call Sally at my office and have her get back with me in Room 502 as soon as possible. Yes. Thank you."

"Give me a few days to put my thoughts together," said Cocuzzo. He waved his hand in dismissal. "Oh, and by the way, for the record, Vince, I'll need a formal introductory letter and background information on your residency history, and detailed curriculum vitae. Standard résumé stuff."

"Yes, sir. I can have . . ."

"And, Vince . . ." Cocuzzo stared at Fossari. "This is a tremendous opportunity for you. I want you to recognize that. Learn things my way and you'll do good here in St. Pete's medical climate." He paused again. "Mi senti? You understand me, Vince?"

Vince cringed, hearing his father's words. He nodded slowly. "Yes, sir. I do," he said, as he walked out of the room. By the time he reached the parking lot, Vincent Fossari had started plans for his move.

4

". . . before we can give you our decision," Arthur Lowndes was saying. "And so I'll refer your application to our research committee for their recommendation to the hospital's board of trustees." The administrator pushed back his chair, stood, and leaned across the desk. Extending a soft palm, "I'll contact you next week. Good day, Dr. Fossari."

Within three weeks Fossari's office adjacent to the cystic fibrosis clinic overflowed with sick children and scared parents. Ailments from myelophthisic anemia to common croup. As Fossari inserted his thick fingers into tiny throats and rectums, he learned Louis Cocuzzo's ways and deposited the checks. Soon he reigned over four staff physicians, seven pediatric interns, and numerous wide-eyed nursing students they sent in groups from the local nursing school.

Relieved of former burdens and proud of his cookie-cutter protégé, Cocuzzo wandered the clinic once or twice a week now, to discuss rare conditions with the staff or to present mini-lectures on the diagnosis and care of autosomal recessive aberrations in children.

In December, when Cocuzzo died from a second heart attack, hardly a child or parent noticed. Hearing the news from an excited intern, Fossari nodded and continued to stitch lacerated tissue back onto the hand of a twelve-month-old girl who had toppled onto a broken drinking glass in her back yard.

Fossari was king of the children's jungle now. His five-year contract passed him the crown in the event of Cocuzzo's death. Rest in peace, Louis Cocuzzo. Your work shall carry on without you. Maybe not exactly as you wanted, but carry on nevertheless it shall. Fossari relinquished the bandaged baby to her mother. "Make an appointment with the nurse at the front desk, Mrs. Arnold. I want to see Jeannie in three days."

Fossari was leaning against the examining table with his arms folded across his chest when a nurse popped her head through the doorway. "Oh, there you are, Dr. Fossari," she said, startled to find him alone. "Wanda Jones is in Exam Room 3. Bad shape. Could be another flare-up of her leukemia, Doctor. Vital signs are weak, and the child is not alert. Do you want to see her next before . . ."

"I'll see who I want to, nurse," he snapped. Then he glanced at his watch. "Start the child on the usual protocol for leukemia crisis and then call Dr. Wyman to handle the case. In fact, tell Dr. Wyman to take the rest of my afternoon appointments."

"Excuse me?" said the nurse. "Do you mean Craig Wyman? The intern who helped in the clinic last week?" Fossari nodded absently, washing his hands at the sink.

"Are you sure, Doctor?" she said, frowning.

"Do it!"

Incompetent bastard, she thought. But the nurse had no intention of doing anything about it. Too many good nurses had already quit to start other careers because of shitheads like Fossari. Professional nursing magazines called it burnout. Hell, nurses weren't burned out. They were just plain sick of the bullshit. Few stayed with any hospital long enough to get benefits. Why, one of her best friends was fired two months ago for a trumped up charge of insubordination just before retirement, losing everything she'd invested in the job. Well, that wasn't going to happen to her. She had decided long ago no one really cared about the plight of nurses, and since she wasn't willing to join the exodus, she'd just put in her eight hours, then go home every day and forget the whole damn thing.

"Yes, Doctor," she said, and went to find the intern.

5

He knew the facts. And the facts were that nobody gave a damn about Vincent Fossari. Yanking his sports jacket off the rack, he tossed his lab coat, still warm with the sticky blood from Jeannie Arnold's wound, onto the peg. He headed for the door and then stopped, his hand on the knob. He turned and surveyed the small room, realizing his ownership at last. Then he walked through the waiting room at a pace not too fast to take in the dull faces of mothers in various stages of anguish. Some had waited two hours or more – arms fatigued from holding children, fevered, infectious, and squirming. Some of the children had given in to their illness and slept.

He didn't need these people. They came here because they needed an expert. Him. Let them wait for Wyman. Right now, his head throbbed and he felt a longing deep in his gut.

The new Chief of the Florida Cystic Fibrosis Center didn't see the nods or silent pleas from mothers wrapped around fidgety babies as he walked past.

Inside the womb-red interior of his Mark V Lincoln Continental, Vincent felt safe. He turned the car west and headed for the beach. Then he remembered the cat and the throbbing in his head became a dull ache. At first, he enjoyed the images for what they were. Remembered fantasies. Toying, teasing the corners of his mind. He'd had creature fantasies since as far back as he knew. It gave him a feeling of sexual power over the animals.

Why not? Wasn't he the only living survivor of Julian Fossari, great white high priest of surgery?

Benefactor of Louis Cocuzzo the CF great? Besides, he needed to know. And she was just about ready. If he waited, it'd be too late.

Just past the dry cleaners, he crossed the last bridge to the island and swung left into the parking lot under the billboard proclaiming Carter's Hardware to be the oldest operating store on St. Petersburg Beach. He believed it.

He walked out with a shopping bag containing four toilet plungers, a ball of heavy twine and a few odds and ends. After luring the cat with the leftover fish in the refrigerator, he'd set up his worktable. The damn cat came around every night anyway. But he wanted to be sure.

In his kitchen, he poured three ounces of Jim Beam into a glass of ice cubes and gulped it before refilling the glass. Then he put a sheet of thin metal over the burners on the electric stove and turned on the overhead light. Too dim. He replaced the bulb with 200 watts. It took some doing for Vincent to suction the four plungers to the Formica counters on either side of the stove. The loosened twine sat ready, next to Ward's Best Dissecting Set and his glass of bourbon.

Sea oats swayed in the same breeze that carried the fishy smell to the cat's nose. The cat crept closer to the house as Vincent waited on the lower deck facing the Gulf of Mexico. The cat's sagging belly rested on the sand as she nibbled the food. She didn't see his hand until too late.

In the kitchen, Vincent tied string around the pregnant cat's four paws and turned her over onto her back.

"RReeerrowrrr . . ." The cat wiggled desperately, trying to get free. Her vulnerable belly moved independent of her will, animated bumps under her fur. Fossari tied the cat spread-eagle between the plunger handles and slid the twine down toward the rubber cups so the cat lay supine. Vincent didn't notice the

18

temperature rising from the metal sheet. Nor did he realize that he'd pushed the number three button that cooked at moderate heat. The cat bellowed in another high-pitched rage, but only her head moved now.

The patient needs something for discomfort, he thought, reaching for his glass and pouring bourbon over the cat's face. He squeezed her mouth with his fingers and dribbled the last few drops down her twitching throat. He never saw the ice cube lodge in the cat's windpipe, nor did he notice the cat's body fall limp in his hands. He was a man with a purpose now and his mind sorted out only what it needed.

Taking the scalpel from its leather case, Vincent sliced a Y-shape cut from the cat's chest down to her genitals. The cat's blood spurted onto the metal shield over the stove, down Fossari's pants and onto his shoes, mixing with the dried serum from the child he had sutured just a few hours earlier. The gash deepened under his knife until the fibrous muscle tissue of the cat's uterus appeared through the opening. Deeper he sculpted until the amniotic pouch gave way and semi-clear fluid poured out.

Vincent used his fingers to rip the opening wider. Gently he removed the rudiments of an unborn kitten. He stepped to the breakfast bar and sat on a stool staring at the dying fetus curled in his palm.

In another room, a telephone rang. Outside the kitchen window, if he had looked, Fossari would have seen the orange blaze that settled in streaks across the sky to the west, reflecting on the sails of three catamarans. The only light in the room came from the glare under the stove's hood when Fossari placed the dead kitten back inside its mother's belly and carefully, delicately sutured the wound.

6

St. Petersburg, Florida

1980

"And they all lived happily ever after." Emilie Creighton raised her stemmed glass and felt a drop of wine trickle between her fingers. She brought her hand to her mouth, and like a frog after an insect, caught the liquid with her tongue before it stained the ruffled lace at her wrist. Emilie didn't go to parties often. But this one was special. This party celebrated attorney Michael Sutherland's legal victory last week. "You were terrific, Mike. Really terrific. F. Lee Bailey'd be proud."

A willowy brunette with expectant blue eyes, Emilie Creighton had a posture that gave her the appearance of being taller than her five feet seven. She was single and chose to remain that way. Right now though, Emilie sensed that Ross was watching her from a few feet away. Granted, Ross Manchester, M.D., was the most fascinating man she knew, probably ever met. But as far as Emilie was concerned, outside of a simple acquaintance, she wasn't available or interested. Besides, Ross had all he could do taking care of Karen. And with his interest in research, he probably didn't have time for women anyway. That's a laugh, she thought. Fact was, he probably didn't even know she was alive. She was thankful for her job as county social worker. It kept her busy, distracted and out of trouble.

"To attorney Michael Sutherland and his successful trial. May there be many more," Emilie said, smiling at the group.

From her place at the end of the couch, Barbara Sutherland watched her husband's face. She laced long fingers in an arc and gently laid them on the curve of her round middle. At a hundred and fifteen pounds and still two months to go before the baby was due, Barbara outweighed her husband by three pounds. She worried a great deal about Michael and the baby, but she had promised herself that tonight she'd concentrate on the victory party. Nothing else. So she settled back on the cushions and tossed her thick auburn braid so it hung over her breast. Tiny copper freckles spotted Barbara's skin, beginning lightly on her face and spreading to cover her arms and legs. The effect gave her a natural and wholesome beauty that was magnified by her pregnancy. Large brown eyes surveyed the living room in the small apartment that was filled with people.

She'd always loved the home she and Michael shared since they were married eight years ago. Both Barbara and Michael had been students at Stetson Law School, Michael preceding her by one semester. After they were engaged, Barbara quit law school and took a job at the county clerk's office. It was only last month when she began to feel sluggish that she quit work altogether. Since then, with not much to do but wait for the baby, Barbara's thoughts concentrated on how much Michael's health had deteriorated since she first knew him.

At 33, Michael still looked like the poet she thought he was when they met. She had often wondered why such a delicate and shy man would choose the legal profession as a career. With his dark brown hair, well-trimmed mustache and beard framing his classical features, Michael gave the impression of polished artistry that would never survive the courtroom wolf packs. So far, she'd been wrong. In the courtroom, the small man grew. The combination of his boyish charm and sincere representation of clients was a winning touch that his opponents couldn't seem to match.

Two years ago, Michael had developed a persistent cough and began to lose weight. With no history of illness, except for the usual childhood diseases and a bout with pneumonia when he was six, the family doctor said he probably had the flu. Then, as an afterthought, the doctor suggested Michael see a pulmonary man at the pediatric hospital. "I can set up an appointment for you tomorrow as an outpatient if you want," the doctor had said. "Don't worry about it being a clinic for kids, Michael. We've got the best medical minds in the area there."

The next day, following a brief physical exam, Michael was admitted to the hospital with a diagnosis of cystic fibrosis, and although both Michael and Barbara were shocked to learn of Michael's disease, they were more outraged at the hopeless attitude of the doctor at the clinic. Now, sitting here watching her husband enjoy the attention of his legal success, Barbara's mind went back to that day. She remembered how she had waited in the plush consultation office, and she still heard Dr. Fossari's words.

"I'm sorry, Mr. and Mrs. Sutherland. Cystic fibrosis is a deadly disease. We will do what we can to slow down its course, using respiratory therapy and antibiotics. But you will not improve, Mr. Sutherland. You will only get worse."

For almost a year, the doctor's predictions came true. To Michael, it seemed as if he were driving through a tunnel that narrowed, smaller and smaller, until it would zoom in and close off his future. Michael's frustration steadily grew. Questions went unanswered as he spent six months of that first year in and out of a hospital bed, tied to IV needles. Nothing to show but repeated injections and mounting medical bills. And his condition continued getting worse. At one point, the cavity surrounding his heart filled with fluid and he nearly died.

Then a friend of Barbara's told her about a physician, Ross Manchester, whose small practice specialized in allergies and pulmonary diseases of adults and children. In his spare time, Manchester did research on the cause and treatment of cystic fibrosis.

From their first meeting, Michael Sutherland and Ross Manchester became friends. Ross explained that Michael had inherited cystic fibrosis from his parents, and that the disease took its main toll on his lungs and digestive system. "Parents don't usually know they're carriers of the CF gene until their child is diagnosed," he said. "It's a recessive trait and shows up about once in every four children when both mother and father are carriers. And there's no way to test for carriers beforehand. Not yet anyway." Ross told Michael that his childhood pneumonia was most likely an incorrect diagnosis. It pleased Michael to know that Ross' philosophy of the treatment and prognosis of his illness was far different from the attitudes prevalent at Parkwest. Ross told Michael that statistically Parkwest had much higher death rate from the disease than most other cystic fibrosis centers. "That's why I applied for a staff position at Parkwest Hospital." Then he mumbled something about medical politics, which neither Michael nor Barbara understood.

"Hello, beautiful lady," said Michael, breaking into Barbara's reverie. "Haven't we met somewhere before?" Michael took Barbara's hand. "I'm a famous lawyer here in Florida, who's celebrating my latest conquest, winning another war in the battle for justice and human rights in our society. And you, little lady, are sitting this one out."

"You are inebriated," Barbara said. "And therefore I shall forgive your 'little lady' comment." She reached for his glass, took it, and after smelling the drink, placed it on the end table. "But I love you anyway, counselor." Barbara stood up and put her arms around him, pushing her belly against his flat stomach. "You, my love, have the finest mind of them all, you know," she said. And meant it.

"For your information, Barbie," Michael said, "Ross has invited us, you and me, to visit his garage next week to meet with his house. No. Wait. He's invited us to his house to see his garage." He squinted, thinking hard. "Does that sound right?"

Just then, Ross approached and stood by their side. A head taller than Michael, he smiled and motioned for them to sit down. "I think what the counselor is trying to say, Barbara," he began, "is that I think you and Michael would be interested in what I'm doing in my lab."

Michael slid a hassock over to the couch sat down. The three of them sat, knees in a circle, bending close to shut out the background noise of music and happy chatter.

"As you both know, I've been doing a great deal of research on cystic fibrosis," Ross said. "At this point, I'm beginning to draw conclusions on the possibility of an improved treatment. Maybe even one-time therapy to induce long-term remission of CF."

Ross stared at his palms. "Unfortunately, because of the controversy of my proposed treatment with humans, I'm afraid my methods would be labeled quite risky by some."

Barbara watched Ross, feeling an inquisitive hope. Ross' silver-white hair crowned his six-foot four-inch frame and gave him an air of sophistication that evaporated into a boyish grin, exposing perfect teeth.

"I'm always in trouble with one medical group or another with this idea." His smile lingered as he nodded his head. "But I know I'm right. I believe in my hypothesis deep down into my gut. Damn it, something's got to work. We can't just sit back and watch people with CF continue to suffer and give up."

It was Michael's turn to nod.

"I'm not going to give up on this," Ross said. "If I have to do the research from jail, well . . ." He paused. "I'm right and I intend to prove it."

"We're with you, Ross," Barbara whispered.

"Until now I haven't shared much with anyone," said Ross. "I think, though, that maybe you two should know what I'm doing." He looked at Michael, then Barbara. "Think about it."

In a quick movement, Ross stood and began to smooth unwrinkled creases from his slacks. "Well," he said, "I guess it's time to leave you good people. I've got an early date with an alarm clock." Ross bent over and kissed Barbara on the cheek.

"Give my love to Karen if she's still awake when you get home," Barbara said.

"I will." Ross turned and saw Emilie Creighton standing alone in a corner looking across the room at him. He started in that direction, stopped, then waved to her, turned and walked to the front door, followed by Michael.

Making his way through the crowd, Michael saw Patty McClelland, one of his clients, move towards him.

"Michael, Don and I will be leaving soon. We both really appreciate everything you've done for us. We know how difficult we've managed to make your life at times."

"You're very welcome, Patty. "I'm just glad we won," said Michael. Then he smiled. "You won't thank me when you get my bill." The woman grinned, then stepped back into the crowd to collect her husband.

7

Karen Reo sat on the floor leaning against the front of the refrigerator, letting the machine's vibrations comfort her. Her throat hurt and she wanted to sleep. From the voices by the front door, Karen guessed her stepfather was in trouble again.

"Look," he was saying, "the old lady is senile. She has called you people at least three times this month with some cockamamie story or other. Why do you listen to her?" He sounded annoyed and tired as he spoke to the police officer.

"I'm sorry, Dr. Manchester, but we have our orders. It's not just the old lady this time. Anyway, I've already told you your rights. Let's go."

"You've got to be kidding." Ross stopped. Then, "Wait a minute. What did you just say? Who else?" Anger overwhelmed him. "What are the charges against me, exactly?"

"I should've made this clear to you before, Dr. Manchester. Your arrest is on a charge of attempted murder of your ward, Karen Reo. The victim was reportedly seen being forcibly held under water by you in your backyard pool for long periods of time this evening at approximately . . ." he looked at his notebook, "at approximately 6:15." The man licked his thumb and flipped through several pages. "The allegations were reported by two witnesses. One Dorothy Cassel, who resides in the house next door . . ."

"I know where the woman lives, officer. Please, go on," Ross said. "Who was the other person?"

"The other person is a man by the name of Vincent Fossari. He says he was a visitor at the home of Miss

Cassel at the time of the incident." The officer snapped his notebook shut. "The witnesses say they are prepared to support the allegations with evidence."

"What'd they do, take pictures?" Ross snapped.

"I don't know, sir."

"Well, I'll be god-damned," Ross said. "Fossari's a real SOB," Ross whispered to the air. Then in a motion, he reached for the telephone on the wall nearby. "Just a minute."

Karen was glad to hear her father call Emilie. "Then you'll come over and stay with her? No, you'll both be fine. It's me they're after." He started to hang up, then, "Oh, by the way, Emilie will you do me one more favor and call Michael Sutherland? Ask him to meet me at the police station. Yes. Thanks."

Usually Karen was proud of her stepfather. He was different from the other kids' dads. Smarter. And he was the nicest man in the whole world. But tonight he had scared her to death. It was after supper when she started coughing. He didn't seem to notice at first, reading his journals and all. Then he went out to the garage to check on the animals he studied and she went to her room and sat in the closet for a long time. At first, she coughed into her pillow. That usually worked. Not tonight. She considered calling Emilie then. Now she wished she had. Probably would've kept everything else from happening. The police and all. But at the time, she didn't want to bother Emilie.

8

When Ross Manchester's parents died in a car wreck six months before he graduated from high school, Ross dropped out and joined the Army. A miserable year later, after a combat fire, Ross woke up in a military hospital with third degree burns across his back. For over a year, he lay on his belly in the VA hospital as bed sores deepened on his hip bones and chin. Depression hit hard. When the 17-year-old soldier in the next bed died, Ross thought he would go crazy. He swore if he made it out alive, he'd honor his roommate's death.

Soon they gave him a medical discharge, with a packet of papers wishing him luck. He took the high school GED test and passed, then Ross met with the veterans' counselor to sign up for college on the G.I. bill.

"I want to take pre-med courses," Ross said.

The counselor laughed, said he guessed Ross earned the right to fail out if he wanted. With a reason to challenge himself – and his rebellious attitude under control – Ross stayed a loner, studied hard, and made good grades.

In graduate and post-graduate school, no one asked about his GED. He was accepted into the brand new University of Arizona's pre-professional science division, taking upper-division lab courses, where he double majored in animal science and pre-med. His postgraduate work focused on a combination of animal culture and habitat and medicine, with an interest in genetic disorders. Then, finishing his residency in pediatric pulmonary diseases, Ross moved to New York and began his training under Eric Hamilton, the brilliant and legendary physician from Long Island

Teaching Hospital. Ross' new mentor gave him the confidence he needed to follow his dream in medicine, combining humane research with conquering cystic fibrosis, the deadly disease of children. Hamilton also taught Ross the controversial lung-flushing procedure that saved the lives of children.

In a modified form, that's what Ross had done this evening when he came in from the garage and found Karen lying in the closet. Her gray color told him to move fast. He rolled her over on the floor, and after clearing a mucus plug from the back of her mouth with his fingers, forced his breath down her throat. Ross knew he had to clear the rest of her lungs quick, though, or she would die. He scooped her up in his arms like a rag doll and headed for the swimming pool.

Japanese lights illuminated the patio when he jumped into the water with Karen still in his arms. With her face down, Ross had pushed her head under the water. Within seconds, he felt her small body jerk, and he pulled her out of the water as she choked and gagged. The mucus came spurting from her mouth. Standing in the water, dripping, Ross held Karen in his arms for ten minutes, rocking her back and forth close to his chest. That's when heard Mrs. Cassel's voice shout from the house next door. He ignored it.

Later when Ross put Karen to bed, she breathed easier and her color was pink. His clothes smelling of dried chlorine, Ross collapsed and was sleeping on the floor next to Karen's bed when the police knocked on the front door.

9

When Emilie arrived, she found Karen still sitting on the floor pressed against the refrigerator. She put her arm around Karen and led her to the living room. Together they sat in a large overstuffed chair holding tight to each other. Emilie hummed softly with Karen's head on her chest, as the child slept.

After a while, Karen stirred, raised her head. "Is Daddy finding my real mother yet?" she said.

Emilie smiled. "I don't know, honey. People can go pretty far in nine years." Then she asked, "You miss her, don't you?"

"Not her," said Karen. "Not really. I don't know her. But I think about her a lot. And Michele. First Michele. Then me."

"Yes, honey. Your parents were just kids themselves," Emilie said. They must have been scared out of their wits when they took you to the hospital that day."

"I'm a big problem to people, aren't I?"

"Oh, Karen, no. Don't say that. So many people love you. You're no trouble at all."

Karen felt her heart flip in her chest. She squeezed her eyes shut. She wasn't anybody's kid. Now. Or ever. She might as well get used to the idea.

Soon Karen fell asleep again. Curled in Emilie's lap she could see an angel hanging from bare tree limbs covered with snow. The angel whispered to her, over and over, "Hello Karen. I am your mother . . ." The angel smiled at first. Then the angel looked scared. And when Karen looked closer, she saw that the angel's face was turning blue. Then black. Then Karen coughed and woke herself up.

"Hold me," she said, burying her face in Emilie's neck.

10

By the time Michael got to the police station, Ross was preparing to leave. "Don't ask me what happened," Ross fumed as he held the glass door open for Michael. "All I know is that the witnesses decided not to press. And the officer said, quote, another doctor called to say that what looked like a cruel act on your part, meaning my part, was actually a life-saving procedure in this case, unquote. Oh, and the police wouldn't give me the calling doctor's name."

Michael shook his head without saying anything.

"God, I'd like to know what the hell is going on," Ross said.

On the sidewalk, Ross stopped and faced Michael. "It was exactly the same thing I did nine years ago to save Karen's life. Shit, she would have died if I hadn't jumped in the pool with her tonight. I love that child, Mike. What the hell is all my research for, if not for her? I guess that bastard Fossari is trying to tell me to lay off applying at Parkwest. Son of a bitch."

Michael shook his head slowly. "Car's over this way." He pointed to the far end of the parking lot.

Ross continued as they walked. "Ever since I put in an application at the hospital, for a staff doctor position, that damn Fossari has niggled me a hundred ways." Ross took a deep breath and let it out. "The board of trustees knows damn well that I'm qualified. They care more about their damn electioneering than they do about the kids they're supposed to treat, for god's sake."

"Look, Ross, the guy's wacko," Michael said. "And you have every right to be mad. But you need to cool down so we can make a few important decisions. Like what you want to do about Fossari, if anything. Let's face it, the guy's got the whole hospital behind him. You may be right that this is their way of averting you. They don't want you there at Parkwest. Whatever their reasons."

In the car, Michael started the engine. He shifted into reverse, then reached over the seat with one arm, checked the rear window, and backed out of the parking space, spinning the wheel to the right. The movement triggered a coughing attack, and Michael hit the brakes. He coughed repeatedly, then inhaled a shallow breath, trying to control the spasms.

In the passenger seat, Ross studied Michael's behavior, his anger now concern for Michael. "I hope you'll make our date Sunday," he said when Michael's coughing stopped. "There are many things I want to tell you about."

"I'll be there." Michael rolled the car onto First Avenue North. He wanted to know more about Ross' research. And new treatment maybe. Whatever it was, the risk would be an improvement over Fossari's doctoring style. Every cell in Michael's body cried out for health. Inside was a sick man who wanted to live. To see his child born. And grow. He wanted grandchildren and retirement. But there was more. Michael was afraid of dying in the slow, agonizing way CF patients experience. Often in his sleep, he saw a giant pillow hovering an inch above his face. As he tried to push it away, the pillow grew heavier and heavier, weakening his arm muscles, until he couldn't push anymore. Michael knew he'd been more fortunate than most folks diagnosed with CF. But still, he felt cheated. He had so much to live for. So much to do. Whatever it was that Ross wanted to discuss, if there was one chance in a million it'd give him more time, he'd do it. Gladly. Screw Fossari and his rotten attitude. He'd love to prove the bastard wrong, and live to be a hundred and ten.

"Just tell me one thing, Ross. Do you want to take action against Fossari? Or the whole hospital for that matter? They never did get back with you on your application, did they? That might be a start. Might be able to work it into an employment rights violation."

"I don't know, Mike. I called Lowndes five times after I applied. He never took my call. Always out. In a meeting or some other excuse. Secretary said he'd left word to tell me there hadn't been a formal decision yet. Decision my ass. It's just a ploy. They're hoping I'll give up and disappear into the woodwork."

Michael looked ahead at the road and nodded.

Ross thought for a moment. "Right now I'd really rather spend our time looking for Karen's parents. Finalize the adoption proceedings. Plus, I'm at a point in my research that I honestly think I can start using some of what I'm learning." Ross looked ahead without seeing. "No, we can go after Fossari later if we have to. Maybe if we leave Fossari alone for now, he'll give us rope for a real case later on. That would do everybody good. Keep him away from those sick kids at Parkwest. With your streak of trial wins, who knows, Mike? But that's for on down the road."

Michael sighed. "I may not have much time later, Ross. Remember?" Michael forced a laugh. "Besides, it's only been three wins in a row." He paused, then grinned. "Hey, you know what, old buddy. Three wins in a row. Not bad. Not bad at all." He glanced at Ross. "Seriously, I should have a little more time now that Patty's case is over. I doubt if the other side will appeal her case. Settlement's not that big and the insurance company's paid more in cases like hers. What do you say about starting to trace Karen's parents next week?"

"I'm ready."

The two men rode in comfortable silence for a long time, each one lost in his own thoughts. As the car's motor calmed him, Ross let his mind drift back to the night that changed his life. It had been a crisp October evening when the call came. Just as he returned home after working 16 hours straight. He arrived back at the emergency room to find an infant girl in the throes of acute suffocation. Her belly was bloated and her spider-like arms jerked in spasmodic movements as she gasped for air. Beneath the baby's emaciated ribs, Ross watched her heart as it fluttered in vain to pump oxygen to her tiny body.

At first, he'd thought it might be respiratory distress syndrome, so common in premature births. She weighed under five pounds and looked like a recent home birth.

Examining her mouth, Ross saw that a mucus plug blocked her throat, causing the immediate problem. He cleared an airway by suctioning the child's windpipe, only to have more of the thick mucus rush to fill the same space. That's when he made a decision. He had assisted Dr. Hamilton with the bronchial lavage operation several times, although never alone. Unable to reach Dr. Hamilton, Ross had an operating room readied, and directed the ER nurse to notify Hamilton as soon as she located him. Then he ran to the waiting room to talk with the baby's parents.

He found Janet and Tom Reo huddled in a corner of the small room. Both looked like children. Their faces were bloated from crying.

"I'm Dr. Manchester," Ross had told them. "As you probably know, your little girl is in bad shape. "Not much time to confirm a diagnosis yet, but our first task right now is to clear the baby's lungs. I need to know if she's had these symptoms before.

It took a long time for Janet Reo to answer. "Karen's going to die, too, isn't she?" she choked. Then she started to say something else, but began sobbing out of control.

"I'm sorry, Doctor," Tom Reo said, holding his wife. "What did you say your name was?" Tom Reo's eyes were wet, but he seemed in control.

"Manchester."

"Dr. Manchester, my wife's very upset," he said sounding older than he looked.

"I can understand that, Mr. Reo. Any mother would be."

"You don't understand, Doctor," Tom said, shaking his head. "You see, both Janet and I know what's going to happen to Karen. Five months ago, when Janet was pregnant with Karen, we lost another baby. Michele. My wife and I tried so hard." He tightened his hand into a fist. "So hard." He stopped in an effort to stay composed. He sighed. "But nothing worked. Nothing. We watched Michele suffer for a long time." He nodded toward one of the curtained cubicles. "She died in that room over there one week before her first birthday."

Ross felt something sour come to the back of his throat. Will I ever get used to all this, he thought. Then: if I ever do, I'll get out. "What was Michele's diagnosis, Mr. Reo?"

"You mean what did they say she died of?"

"Yes."

"First they said it was cystic fibrosis. But after she died, they said they couldn't be sure, because . . ." He hesitated. "Because we wouldn't let them do an autopsy on her." Tom Reo bowed his head. "We just couldn't let them cut her up like that. You know? She was just a tiny baby. Our baby. We didn't want her to die like that." Tom Reo turned toward the wall and covered his face. His body shook, still holding onto his wife with his other arm.

Ross reached out and touched the boy's shoulder, then went out of the room. He knew it would be a long time before he could forget the mewling sounds the two young parents made as he hurried to try and save the infant.

That night he had performed the bronchial lavage procedure alone. Eric Hamilton had gone to a football game and never heard his page. With the help of the on-call anesthesiologist and several nurses, Ross rushed Karen into the operating room and carefully inserted the bronchoscope through her mouth, gently slid it deeper and deeper into her tiny lungs. Using a liquid solution, he flushed deep into Karen's fluttering chest. Soon her body started to gag. Then the baby jerked until great gobs of dried mucus from the inside of her lungs projected from her mouth. Although Manchester wore a plastic faceplate, several clumps of the sticky mass spattered onto his cap and surgical gown.

For twenty minutes, Karen Reo tolerated the procedure. Then the anesthesiologist raised his hand signaling changes in the cardiac monitor connected to the baby's chest. Quickly Ross slid the pliable tubing from her throat.

Nurses wheeled Karen from the operating room to recovery. Ross removed his gloves and surveyed the area around the table where the baby had been. Nodding with satisfaction, he said, "From what I see of the mess around here, I'd say that little lady has been given a ten percent lung recovery. At least." Not bad for his first time. He'd grinned, threw his operating clothes into the dirty linen bin, pushed through the double doors, headed for the waiting room and Karen's parents.

Karen had stayed in the hospital four months. Ross had hovered over her every moment he could spare. During that time, she tripled her weight and appeared healthier than most babies her age. After one month, Janet and Tom Reo stopped visiting their daughter. By the time Karen was ready for discharge, her parents couldn't be found.

For weeks, the hospital social worker tried to locate Mr. and Mrs. Reo, and when the baby was discharged, there was no place for her to go. Ross Manchester found only one place that would accept Karen. The state home for mentally retarded children.

"It's entirely possible that this child has an IQ of thirty points more than you or I do," he screamed at the social worker. Then he suggested he take her home with him until her parents were found. If no one claimed her, he'd said, he would legally adopt her.

The social worker said all that would be quite impossible because "in the first place, Dr. Manchester, you're a man. And in the second place, why you're not even married. I really don't see how you can possibly take care of this child. What kind of institution would place a child with a single parent, Dr. Manchester? A bachelor, no less."

Ross tried not to yell. "My requirements, madam," he said in a hoarse voice, "are that I did, and do, in fact, and in the first and second place, one, save the child's life, and two, have a strong interest in seeing that my efforts haven't been in vain." The social worker blinked and opened her mouth to speak. Ross cut her off. He raised his voice, pointing at the air with his index finger. "I want this little girl to live the longest, healthiest life that she possibly can. And having her moved to a mental hospital will not, by any stretch of the imagination, give her an opportunity for health." By the time he finished he was shaking with anger. His final words to the social worker that day were spat as he towered over her, balled fists waving in the air. "The only way you will ever take Karen Reo to a state institution for mentally retarded children is over my dead body."

He'd won.

After a lengthy battle with the Department of Social Services and other assorted agencies that operate in the best interest of children and others, Ross Manchester gained temporary custody of Karen. The agreement had been that he would care for her as her father until her real parents were located, and then the parents would be presented with papers for permanent adoption if they so chose. Or, they could choose to take her back.

In Ross' home, Karen had thrived. So did Ross. He'd watched closely for symptoms of her condition and stayed ahead of the disease. He prescribed and gave her medications, and performed clapping procedures to clear her lungs on a daily basis.

Now, at nine and a half years old, Karen Reo was the picture of health. Only an expert could detect the slight clubbing of fingertips, the result of chronic oxygen shortage. It was the only visible sign of the disease.

After three years, the Department of Social Services gave Ross permission to take Karen with him when he moved to Florida. Then the agency closed their files and their efforts to find Karen's parents. So Karen and her temporary stepfather hung out drying in limbo. To Ross, however, she was his child. She was also his patient. Now, she was also the reason he experimented with marmots in his garage.

"Did you want to stay in the car all night?" Michael stared at Ross.

Struggling out of his thoughts, Manchester opened the door, stepped outside and stretched. Then he poked his head back inside the car. "Sorry, old buddy. Guess I must have dozed off for a minute." He reached across to shake Michael's hand. "Thanks for the lift, Mike. And about looking for Karen's parents? Let's do it. It's time that little girl had an honest to goodness real dad."

11

The wide-mouth bass curved from side to side, weaving in slow motion through a bed of floating grass attached to the bottom of the lake. Beneath the old rowboat, noiseless minnow shadows darted in and out among the tangles, like costumed skaters gliding across a rink floor. Above the water, morning fog rose. The bass spotted a new movement in the water ahead, and followed, tail fin flipping now close to the bottom, sending loose mud to float in spirals then settle on the bottom again. The fish trailed behind, watching the black and chartreuse object break the water's surface, and then disappear.

In the boat, Michael separated strands of grass from the plastic bait with patience and skill. He held his fiberglass pole secure inside his elbow as his fingers pitched residue over the side, watching it drop onto the surface of water and expand into widening circles. He cast the line again. The startled bass turned toward the movement, jerking, fanning its tail to inspect the area. Seeing nothing unusual, it continued to circle under the boat, moving cautiously, fins fluttering in soft whiffs against its side. It stayed deep now.

Once more, Michael lifted his rod high, this time on the fish's blind side, watching the curled nylon line straighten and snap as he flipped his wrist, yanking the lead weight in mid-air, sending it into the water. The bait landed in sparse weeds near the edge of the lake and sunk to the bottom. The fish lunged, opened his jaws, then popped them shut in the exact instant Michael snapped his pole into an arc, piercing the pointed metal hook through the soft flesh of the bass' mouth.

Skimming the last few feet toward shore, Michael swiveled the oars and threw the anchor line onto the muddy grass. On shore, Barbara waited. "You sound wheezy, Mike," she said as Michael stepped out of the boat. "Maybe we should call Ross when we go in." She took the boat cushions from Michael, tucking them under her arm.

"I'm okay, Barb," Michael said. "Here, if you'll take the poles into the cabin, I'll go clean the fish." He turned and took the cushions from her, tossing them, one by one, onto the ground. He moved closer and touched Barbara's cheek with the back of his fingers. "Honey, you worry too much. I'm a strong guy, remember? So far I've outlasted the statistics." He reached for her hand. "I'm a winner, Baby. Remember?" Then he kissed her on the mouth.

"I love you," he said. "And we're going to make it. Honest."

"Just let me call Ross," Barbara said. She rested her head on Michael's shoulder, turning at an angle to accommodate her protruding belly. "He'll know what to do."

"Tell you what," Michael said. "Let's wait ten minutes. If I'm still wheezing, we call. If not, we don't. That's logical. Right?"

"I don't know, Michael . . ."

"Besides, we've already got a date with Ross in the morning."

Barbara sighed. She squatted, gathered the cushions, and headed for the path to their cottage.

The fish house sat beneath moss-laden oaks near the edge of the water. Michael and Barbara had come to the lake on their honeymoon. Since then, they made it their special place to get away. Five miles from the main highway, the 60-acre lake was surrounded by seven rustic cottages, most of which stayed empty except for peak tourist seasons. It was an ideal place for Michael to chill – and think – whenever he was deep into a particularly trying case. This weekend he studied adoption proceedings for Ross and Karen's case. Something told Michael there was more to finding Karen's parents than Ross suspected, and Michael wanted to learn what it was.

In the fish house, Michael had a brief choking fit, but cleared an airway by coughing deep from his diaphragm. The second time, it lasted longer, and he felt a sudden sense of doom settle on him. Was it for the fish he carried – or himself – he wondered. The room smelled musty and damp and reminded Michael of the times he'd gone fishing with his father when he was a child, and the older man demanded that Michael snap his wrist just right to pop the hook into the water. "Or you're just wasting your friggin' time sitting here all day while the fish are laughing their guts out their ass at you." Michael had been repelled then by the sight of dying fish – their suffocated faces, flapping bodies. But his father didn't want to hear any of his blubbering.

"You gotta cut the fish's head off last," his father had said. "Keeps them living and energetic longer. That way's the meat's sweeter."

Michael didn't agree.

The razor-sharp blade came down fast as Michael de-headed the bass. What did it feel? he thought. Was pain reflected in its mute struggles? Blood poured into the sink and mixed with water streaming from the faucet. Slimy liquid slid down the drain and splashed into a bucket under the sink. Michael held the bass with the tail facing him, scraped the scales off using a metal spoon. Then he sliced the underbelly, pulled out the guts, and tossed them onto a stack of old newspapers. When he was finished cleaning the fish, Michael picked up the three severed heads and balanced them on the drain board. Propping his chin on his hands, he examined the cloudy marbles staring at him like black headlights.

Michael remembered the last time he had come to the lake. He'd thrown the fish back into the water after removing the hooks with great care. This morning he'd sat in the boat for a long time, letting his body sway with the water's gentle rhythm before he baited a line. He wondered how it would feel to suffocate from too much oxygen.

Now, he pushed the fish heads off the end drain board and into a large plastic bag. Then he dumped the bag into the bent metal can outside the fish house door. He wiped off the sink, tightened the faucets, and rolled the cleaned fish in fresh newspaper.

As he walked to the cottage, Michael felt a deep burning inside his chest. Suddenly, he dropped the package of fish pieces onto the grass and toppled to his knees a few feet from a large oak tree. On hands and knees, Michael crawled to the tree and wrapped his arms around the trunk to spread out his lungs. He gasped. Then collapsed.

12

The ambulance screeched to a stop behind a parked truck that blocked the double doors to the hospital Emergency Room. A man and a woman jumped from the rear of the vehicle, a man ran from the cab. All three pulled the stretcher to the ground, released the metal legs, and wheeled Michael toward the building. Michael's head rolled on the hard gurney mattress. He heard muffled voices and tugged at the oxygen mask covering his nose and mouth.

"My head," he whispered. "Raise my head." He heard metal on metal as a crank turned, and he felt his back tug in a rubbery slide, as his head went up. Before him, he saw two automatic doors separate as the EMTs pushed the gurney past a crowd of people lined up in chairs. He heard a child wail. Inside a cubby, the gurney was parked next to a similar bed, and Michael heard the scrape of a privacy curtain being yanked along the ceiling track around his bed. He heard jagged murmurs being shouted from faces fluttering suspended above him, his body absorbing dozens of hands, touching, stretching, pulling. A cold swipe inside his left elbow, the sharp sting of a needle. There was a loud hiss of forced air as an aerosol mask pressed against his face, followed by the snap of elastic behind his head. For a while, Michael slipped in and out of consciousness. Then he woke up with a start to the sudden sound.

"Dammit," a voice barked. "I want isoproterenol in with that mucomyst. Why in hell'd they give you a license to nurse, anyway?"

"But, doctor, I – "

Then a third voice from farther away. "Dr. Fossari, there's a stat page from your clinic that says they – "

"Jesus Christ, are you all incompetent?"

Neon sounds bounced inside Michael's brain. Fossari? No. When he opened his mouth to speak, all that came out was a bubbling sound from deep inside his chest.

Around the edge of the plastic oxygen mask, Michael saw the outline of a nurse up close. Cold fingers touched beneath his earlobes. She removed the oxygen mask and he saw the nurse swipe something shiny across the tip of a floppy rubber tube as she made an angry comment about the apparatus and Vincent Fossari's anatomy. Michael felt the nurse force his head backward on the hard table, arching his neck. Grabbing the bedrails, he shut his eyes to close out the sight of the tube as the nurse snaked it into his nose and pushed it down his throat as he hacked. His entire body twitched.

"Start the oxygen. Three liters," the nurse said over her shoulder. "Keep it there until we get his blood gases back from the lab." The nurse put her face close to Michael's, separated his jaw and peered down his open mouth as she aimed a small flashlight inside. Michael gagged when she pushed the wooden blade hard against the back of his tongue. Then he felt a sharp crack on his right hand and someone shoved his wrist down over the edge of the gurney rail.

"Veins don't look so hot," a voice said. "Where the hell's the I.V. team when we need them?"

Michael felt the rubber tube slide up in his throat then as the nurse tugged the portion still sticking out of his nose. The start of a sneeze became a prolonged gag. The sound of bandage tape ripping. Thumbs pressed and slid across both sides of Michael's face, securing the tube to his cheeks.

That's when he started to cough. Great spasms gripped him. Gasping, Michael choked and spit. Again and again. His belly ached. The people around him stared, unmoving. Then suddenly it was over. He went limp, exhausted. But his lungs were open now and he breathed easier than he had in weeks. Michael sucked in air and blew it out. In. Out. Over and over again.

13

Inside Parkwest Hospital's tiny ER admittance booth, Barbara sat on a hard metal chair, answering rapid-fire questions as the clerk flipped through a packet of forms. "Insurance carrier?" said the clerk, perched over a large typewriter. A cigarette bounced between her lips as she spoke, one eye closed as a stream of smoke drifted up.

The clerk grabbed a pile of papers, wheeled it around, and slid it across to Barbara. Then snapped a pen on top of the heap. "Sign all the pages marked with an X," said the clerk. "Be sure to read them first. There's fourteen places I need your signature on."

Barbara's heart raced. "You don't understand," she said looking around. "My husband has a severe case of cystic fibrosis. He can die in there any minute." She stopped and took a deep breath. "Please, won't you contact Dr. Manchester?" Her voice sounded shrill in her own ears.

The clerk opened a drawer on her desk, reached and thumbed through a small booklet. "I'm afraid I can't do that, ma'am," she said, returning the booklet, and closing the drawer. "Dr. Manchester's name does not appear on our list. One of our staff doctors will handle your husband's illness. He's probably in with your husband right now," she said. Now, may I please see your insurance card?"

Barbara ruffled through her purse and handed over a plastic rectangle. "Excuse me," she said standing up. "I need to use the ladies room." She turned and scampered into the side hall. At the end of the corridor, she saw the door marked *Women*, and moved passed it in a near run until she entered the front lobby. She stopped at the high counter, and spotted an elderly woman in a pink striped apron reading a magazine. The woman looked up and smiled as Barbara approached.

"May I borrow your telephone directory?" Barbara asked.

The woman laid a thick book on top of the counter, glancing around in both directions. "Just don't keep it too long," she whispered, leaning forward, her hand cupped at her mouth. "Supposed to be for hospital staff only."

Barbara wrote down a number and glanced at her watch. Almost midnight. She hurried to a booth on the far wall, wondering if Ross was asleep as she counted three rings.

"Hello?"

Barbara explained Michael's crisis. "I told them to call you," she said. "They won't listen."

"Let me think a minute." Long pause. Then, "Barbara, go back to the ER and cooperate the best you can. I'll be right there."

By the time Barbara finished filling out hospital forms, Michael's condition had improved, and they were preparing to admit him to one of the unoccupied rooms in the new the Cystic Fibrosis Center next door to Parkwest Hospital. Michael, alert, sat up on the gurney as Barbara trotted alongside, holding his hand. On their way to the elevator, they passed Vincent Fossari talking on the phone at the nurses' station.

"Put the new admit in the East Wing away from the kids," he was saying. "I know it's been closed off. Open it!" He hung up and spun around, knocking into Barbara as she passed.

"Well, hello, Mrs. Sutherland," he said, backing up. "It's been a while, hasn't it?" He glanced at Barbara's large middle. "How's your pregnancy coming along?"

Barbara hesitated, watching the attendants continue to push Michael toward the elevator.

"Hello, Dr. Fossari," she said, her tongue feeling thick as she spoke. Then, forgetting Ross' advice, she said, "I'm sorry you've been called in to see Michael, Dr. Fossari, but there's been a mistake. Apparently I didn't make myself clear to the ambulance driver . . . and we would prefer – "

"And you'd prefer that your husband's current doctor take the case. Is that right, Mrs. Sutherland?"

"Yes."

"Mrs. Sutherland," Fossari said through a wry smile. "Your husband is a very sick man. Aside from the fact that I'll be surprised if he makes it through this crisis at all, I've made arrangements to have him transferred to a room next door at the Cystic Fibrosis Center, so that I will have at my disposal the expertise of the staff and the necessary equipment for his care. I don't believe his current physician can say that."

All Barbara heard was *disposal*.

Fossari continued. "It is my opinion that to move your husband now would be a grave error and would only exacerbate his disease. I feel certain that we would lose him even sooner." Fossari squinted at Barbara through his horn-rimmed glasses. "You do have the option of removing your husband from the premises against medical advice if you wish. However, I'm sure that your insurance carrier will not allow payment if he is moved from our care."

Barbara bit the inside of her lower lip. She hated this man, this doctor, who let her husband's condition deteriorate under his care. And who, for the moment, was controlling whether Michael lived or died. She couldn't do that to Michael. But at the moment, she had no choice.

"Have him admitted," she said.

48

14

Marilyn Pelletier, R.N. muttered under her breath. She slammed the telephone receiver down so hard that the bell inside it chimed. "Damn that Fossari," she said to another nurse sitting nearby writing in a chart. Marilyn frowned and pushed a few hairs away from her face. Then she reached to the top of her head where her shoulder-length hair was pulled into an elastic band and twisted into a knot. Light brown tendrils hung near her cheeks. She removed a bobby pin and rearranged a few wisps of hair in an attempt to use up the extra energy brought on by her anger.

The other nurse looked and smiled knowingly. "Hey, Marilyn, you want the kids to pick up that language?" she teased. Then she swiveled her chair to face Marilyn. "What's Fossari up to now?"

Marilyn exhaled, letting her breath out slowly so that her cheeks billowed. "Some of these doctors are the pits. They really are. But that damn Fossari takes the cake. God, Sue, I'd like to see him knocked down a rung on his ladder of supremacy."

"Who'd be crazy enough to try that?" Susan said, closing a chart and slipping it back into a rack. "Fossari's big cheese around here. I've heard it said in the surgeon's lounge that *the shit rolls downhill*, and I'm afraid you and me, Marilyn baby, are at the bottom of that hill." Just then they heard the gentle ping of the elevator a few feet away and turned toward the sound. The doors slid open and Fossari lumbered out.

"Speak of the devil," Susan muttered softly before Fossari got to the counter.

"You get the orders on Dr. Burton's tonsillectomy patient yet?" he said.

"No sir, I don't think so," Marilyn said, flipping through the work sheets on the nurses' station counter.

"Well, make sure you get them before the kid arrives from Recovery. Her name's Tina or Tanya, or something. Thomas. Had surgery this morning, and from what I gather she's doing okay. Vitals, color – " He reached into the pocket of his lab coat, and read from a rumpled slip of paper.

Marilyn's forehead creased. Why would he admit a post-surgery patient to the medical unit? "This floor, Doctor? Or did you mean three?"

"She had elective surgery," Fossari said, staring at the paper in his hand, as if he didn't know how it got there. "She's Dr. Burton's patient."

"Yes, sir, but protocol has surgical patients admitted to the surgical floor. I know the census on three is high today, but two kids were discharged yesterday, and their beds are empty."

"Dr. Burton needs to catch a plane in Tampa this afternoon. Surgical conference. Los Angeles. I'm taking the kid's case till he returns. She's stable, and I've already got a couple of my patients on this floor." Then, when Marilyn started to speak again, "Do it!" He strode to the elevator and jabbed rapidly on the call button several times.

15

An hour later Tracy Thomas arrived by stretcher, along with her mother and the otolaryngologist, Dr. John Burton.

"I think there's been a mistake on this patient's admittance sheet," Burton said to Marilyn. "Tracy needs to go on the surgical floor. I've got to leave right now or I'll miss my plane. Dr. Fossari's taking the case. Please contact him, and have this straightened out before she gets settled up here on four." Abruptly he turned and shouted, "Hold the elevator," and then he was gone, leaving Marilyn, Tracy, and Mrs. Thomas all staring at each other.

After having Vincent Fossari paged, Marilyn relayed Dr. Burton's message to him. Fossari politelessly informed Marilyn that he was now in charge of this patient, and that if, and until, she was licensed to practice medicine, she would follow his orders and admit patients to the unit as she was told.

Marilyn shivered. She moved to a cabinet inside the nurses' station, reached into the drawer and scooped up the blood pressure cuff and thermometer to take Tracy Thomas' vital signs.

"Come on, Tracy," she said approaching the child and her mother. "How about a room with a view? There's a girl in the same room who's been getting a little lonely lately. Dr. Fossari thinks maybe you can cheer her up."

Tracy wanted to say, "or she can cheer me up," but her throat hurt too much to talk, so she nodded instead.

Irene Thomas hadn't said much since her daughter's arrival on the unit, but as they passed by a room marked "Library," her face brightened. "Look, Tracy," she said. "A piano." She stopped, pointed. "In there." She peeked through the door. "Looks like just an old spinet vertical, but once you're out of bed, you can practice on it." Then Mrs. Thomas looked at Marilyn. "Would that be all right, Miss Pelletier?" she said.

"Of course," Marilyn said. "As a matter of fact, you'll be interested to know that this is the only piano in the whole hospital. Maybe you were meant to be on this floor after all, huh, Tracy?" She winked at the child and Tracy gave her a timid smile. "Well, let's get you checked into this fine hotel," said Marilyn.

Marilyn pushed Tracy's stretcher into a room. "Hi, Alyce," Marilyn said, looking at the child in the bed by the window. "Here's a roommate for you. Alyce, meet Tracy." Marilyn bowed low. "Tracy, meet Alyce. I'm sure you two will have a great time together."

By the time Irene Thomas left for the day, she was confident that her little girl was in good hands. After thanking an unfamiliar nurse who had replaced Marilyn on the evening shift, Irene Thomas left the hospital.

16

Michael lay in bed with the head raised high, staring through the open door, and taking in as much of the corridor as he could see. His nose held a nasal cannula that pushed oxygen down into his lungs. A needle taped to his right hand dripped fluid from a plastic tube draped across the bedrail and up to a bottle hanging from the portable IV pole. Ross Manchester had arrived just after midnight when the nurses' station – the daytime hub of activity – was dim and deserted. Towing Karen by the hand, Ross was undetected getting on and off elevator, and had snuck into Michael's room without awakening him. Soon Karen climbed on the vacant bed, curled up and fell asleep. At two a.m., when Michael opened his eyes, he saw Ross sitting in the visitor's chair near his bed.

"It was easy," Ross said in answer to Michael's confused look. "This is the CF floor. That part was easy to figure out. The hard part was finding your room. As you can see, we did."

Michael blinked, trying to clear his head.

Ross looked around the room. "Interesting. Not one person has come into this room the whole two hours I've been sitting here."

Michael nodded. "I'm just glad Fossari went home," he said. "Couldn't take a confrontation with him in the night." Looking around the room, Michael asked about Barbara.

"She was exhausted, Mike. I told her I'd stay with you until I was sure you were out of the woods. She finally gave in and went home to sleep. I figure we're all going to need it."

Ross stood up, stretched his arms toward the ceiling, arching his back. He knew he was stalling, awaiting courage to talk serious. "I'll take Karen home soon and see you later this morning, ole boy. Looks like you'll manage till then."

Michael sensed something was wrong. Barbara had never left him like that before. "You've told Barbara something, haven't you, Ross?" he said. "Is she okay? When is she coming back?"

"She's fine. Just tired, as anyone in the last trimester of pregnancy would be. She and I plan to meet back here at eight this morning. Right after your breakfast. Your physical therapy treatments should be over, too. And yes, I did talk with her. Enough to convince her to go home for a while." Ross knew Michael didn't buy it.

Michael wanted to ask Ross a few more questions, but he didn't have the strength. He sunk in a heap onto the pillow and murmured, "Ever think of becoming a lawyer, Ross? You'd convince an Eskimo to buy ice cubes."

Ross went to the other bed and gathered Karen, still sleeping, into his arms. "Not on your life," he said. "The medical profession is bad enough. We both know there are some pretty shifty lawyers out there making a fortune on other people's troubles." Ross looked down into Karen's face and his mind flashed to a poem he had read. *Men too gentle to live among wolves.* "Come on, little lady," he whispered, "Let's go home."

Karen stirred and settled herself in Ross' strong grasp. As they stepped into the hallway, Karen waved her hand toward the room. "'Night, Mike. Hope you feel better soon," she said, then closed her eyes.

As Ross passed the nurses' station, he saw a gray-haired woman leaning over a paperback book. Ross and Karen passed and she continued to read. Just before he stepped into the elevator, Ross turned. "Mr. Sutherland in 412 needs his IV changed," he said.

17

Michael thought he was dreaming. Suspended in a post-sleep limbo, he allowed the music to wash over him like warm waves on a summer beach. Reaching for Barbara, Michael suddenly recoiled as the IV line tugged at his hand. When the music continued, Michael wondered if he was having a reaction to a hallucinatory drug.

One side rail was up. Using it for support, Michael swung his legs over the other side of the bed. The action triggered a vital reflex neuron in the center of his brain. His chest convulsed and he choked on thick secretions deep in his throat. The double lumen tips of the oxygen cannula fell from his nose and drooped under his chin. Trying to calm himself, Michael tightened his abdominal muscles and forced air through his windpipe in a controlled cough. Then he pulled the overbed table close and leaned forward on his elbows. The coughing slowed, then stopped. Michael rested his head on his arms, breathing with care.

The music went on, a brilliant piano solo performance.

When Michael's pulse rate calmed and his breath slowed down, he pushed the overbed table to the side and stood by the bed. With his bare feet, he found his slippers. Then, using the IV pole for support, he walked to the foot of the bed, removed his robe. He slipped his left arm through the sleeve, and draped the other over his shoulder and scuffled to the bathroom. He splashed water on his face and ran a comb through his hair. Then he guided the IV pole back through the bathroom door, past his bed, out to the hallway, following the music.

Michael stopped at an open door. He saw dozens of kids' books lined up on shelves and scattered on child-size tables and chairs. In the far corner of the room, sitting on a piano stool, back to the door, sat a little girl. Her hospital gown had parted in the back showing pink lace panties. From where he stood, Michael saw the child's fingers move across the piano like an accomplished musician. The tones from the worn keys sounded smooth and deliberate. He rested his shoulder against the open doorway and watched the child play.

"Okay, okay, let's close this here, folks." Michael turned and saw a young woman in a nurse's uniform. "Some people around here are sick," said the nurse, gently prodding Michael into the room. Then the nurse closed the door and was gone.

Startled, the child spun around on the piano bench. She stared at Michael with intense gray eyes. A scrambled ponytail the color of shiny coal hung off center on her head. Brown freckles sprinkled her nose.

"You play very well," Michael said, wishing the nurse had been more subtle. The child smiled, and Michael saw there was a bottom tooth missing.

"Would you like me to leave?" he said.

"Uh. I play better for a aud-i-ence," she said in a whisper so low he almost didn't hear.

"Your voice sounds scratchy. You okay?" Michael pushed the pole closer to the girl.

"I had a oper-ation. Hurts to talk."

"Okay, then. Play more of your beautiful music for me. Okay?" Then he reached out his hand. "My name's Mike. What's yours?"

"I'm Tracy," she whispered, letting Michael shake her limp hand. She sat unmoving as Michael dragged a tiny wooden chair close to the piano and sat down.

Tracy turned and touched the keys. Michael watched her cubby fingers glide across the dirty keys, fascinated by her talent. She played for ten minutes, without stopping or looking his way. Then she suddenly stopped.

"Thirsty," she said, rubbing her throat. She slid off the stool and started for the door. Then she stopped, looked back at Michael. "Want to meet my friend? She's Alyce." Tracy said. Michael nodded and Tracy reached for his hand. Pulling his IV pole, he followed the child, opened the door and they marched into the hall.

The best therapy a guy could get in this place, Michael thought.

Alyce Hobbs sat up in bed, reading a book that was four inches thick. In her hand, she held a tattered white rabbit. The animal's checkered vest was torn where the chain from the pocket watch had pulled apart. At 12, Alyce was small boned and emaciated. Her delicate face showed tiny blue veins through pale skin at her temples and around her deep chocolate eyes. Eyes that seemed older than her years. Eyes that reflected intelligence, caution, and something else Michael couldn't identify. Sadness? Defeat?

When Michael and Tracy entered the room, Alyce looked up once, then lowered her eyes, flipping pages in her book. She flattened the open book to her chest and coughed several times. Michael watched her fine hair shuffle in straight lines around her face as her head jerked. He waited till her coughing stopped. "Hi, Alyce," he said. "Pretty heavy reading you've got there."

"She reads boring stuff all the time," Tracy whispered. Then she grinned. " 'Cept when she reads stories to me."

"It's not boring," Alyce said. "I'm trying to find out if mucomyst will hurt my nose after I have surgery."

Michael wrinkled his brow. "What kind of surgery? he said.

"They're gonna take the polyps out of my nose."

"What's that?" Tracy asked.

Alyce closed the book. As she did, Michael saw her fingertips. Gray-blue, flattened and clubbed at the nails. Like his. Alyce picked up the rabbit and placed it on the center of the heavy book still on her lap. She picked at the rabbit's fur. "They're polyps, Trace," she said. "Little lumps growing inside my nose. Don't bother me much, really. But the doctor says they're getting big, and get in the way when I breathe."

Alyce looked at Michael, pointing to the book. "All I can find so far in other books is that polyps form because of the inflammations in my nose, and has something to do with the bioelectricity of sodium when I breathe. What I think it does is pulls in the sodium, and that pulls in water, and that's what causes me to make polyps in my nose. But I can't find anything in here about it. Doesn't matter, now, anyway," She started to sigh, but it caught in her throat and she coughed in long spasms, hugging the book until she was under control. "They won't take them out until my infection's gone. And that could be for weeks. According to them." She flipped her hand in the general direction of the nurses' station.

"You have CF, don't you, Alyce?" Michael said.

Alyce squinted at Michael. "Yeah. How'd you know? You a doctor or something?" she said, petting the limp rabbit.

From the day she was born Alyce's parents fought, blaming each other for giving birth to a sick child. By the time she could talk, Alyce knew she had an incurable disease. By then, her father was gone. After a bitter divorce, he moved to California, sending short notes to Alyce on holidays. But what Alyce treasured most, was the white rabbit with a chain made of real gold that was attached to its pocket watch, that her father gave her on her first birthday, in honor of her storybook namesake.

"Nah," I'm not a doctor, Michael said. "It just so happens, that you are looking at the oldest living survivor of cystic fibrosis in this entire city. The state maybe. That's how come I know."

"Really? Wow." Alyce said. Then she frowned. "Wait a minute. All survivors are living, silly."

Michael laughed. Bright kid. "Well, I may be the oldest CF patient, but you're one up on me. I know what mucomyst is, but never had polyps in my nose. So I can't help you in that department. It sounds like you're doing okay, though. You really know your stuff. What does your doctor have to say about your medical wisdom?"

"Yuck." Alyce wrinkled her nose. "No thanks. He doesn't like kids." She settled back and picked up the rabbit, petting its fur. "And the feeling is mutual."

Michael squinted. "Fossari, huh?"

Before Alyce could answer, Ross stuck his head in the room and knocked on the open door. "There you are," he said. "Should've known I'd find you with a couple of beautiful women."

Ross had met Alyce when she and her mother came into his office for the first time several months ago. Although her mother preferred Ross as Alyce's doctor, she was forced to use the Cystic Fibrosis Clinic at Parkwest, so Alyce's treatments and care would be paid for by the state-funded Children's Medical Services. With medical bills for Alyce adding up to more than fifty-thousand a year, she had no choice. As it was, she worked two jobs just to make ends meet.

"Good morning, Alyce," Ross said, smiling a generous grin. "Who's your new friend?"

"Hi, Dr. Manchester. This is Tracy. She had her tonsils out yesterday. Says she can't talk, but she's doing pretty good if you ask me." Tracy giggled and jumped onto her own bed.

Ross saluted Tracy. "Very glad ta meet'cha, Miss Tracy," he said. Something is wrong, he thought. What is a post-op tonsillectomy patient doing in a room on the medical floor? *Note to self: Scrutinize the facts later.* Then he turned to Michael.

"Well, old buddy. There's a meeting about to begin in your room. Let's not miss it."

18

In Michael's room, Ross, Michael, and Barbara sipped watery cokes from the hospital coffee shop. At first, they made light talk. All three of them eager, yet wary of getting to the topic they needed to discuss. Ross wondered what the impact his story would have on these two young people. He also knew that the outcome of his experiment – if he were to test it on this dying man – could possibly add years to other CF patients' lives. Like Karen's. And, it could possibly change the type of treatment for all cystics.

"Well," Ross said. "End of weather report. Let's get started. The gang at the office has been pretty good today. They rescheduled my morning patients for me. But if I don't make it in there by noon, they'll have my head."

Barbara, fidgeting in her chair near the window, moved to sit on the bed beside Michael. She reached for his hand. "Ross thinks he can help you with a new treatment," she murmured.

"What kind of treatment? A lung transplant?" Michael blurted. "Because that's what it'd take." He poked at his barrel chest with his thumb.

"If you'd've kept our date," Ross said, "then you'd already know what I'm going to say." Michael started to say something, but Ross put up his hand. "I know, I know. You got sick and wound up in the hospital. That's what they all say." He smiled then cleared his throat. "Seriously, kids. We've got to come up with something. Some alternative to the treatments you're getting now. Especially here at Parkwest. It's not just that the damn disease is wearing you down, but there's

Karen I'm thinking of, too. I'd like to see that little girl grow up. And Alyce, too. She's certainly suffered enough." Ross stopped, nodded, thinking. For a moment, he watched tiny puffed clouds roll past the window as if they were running away from what he had to say. "That Alyce. She's a fighter. Great kid."

Ross sipped his coke, arranging his thoughts. Michael and Barbara sat rigid, mute.

Then Ross crumpled the paper cup and his eyes followed it as he tossed it in the direction of the wastebasket. It fell two inches short, and he stared as it lay on the floor. "What I've been working on in my garage this past year hasn't been shared with anyone," he said in a near whisper. "I didn't dare. But then, that's another story." Ross stood, picked up the cup, and placed it in the trash. "To say that the research I'm doing is unconventional would be an understatement. But, it's working."

"Unconventional?" asked Barbara.

"Yes, Barb. Seems my work goes against the grain of a whole bunch of others in the health care profession. But I learned a long time ago, that sometimes neither *health* nor *care* are the motivating factors for my profession. Especially when it comes to research and experimenting with animals. Mostly, I stand at opposite poles of the big gun corporations and scientists who are willing to exploit sick children and hurt defenseless animals to pad their own bank accounts. If you doubt what I'm saying, pick up a copy of *Animal Liberation* by Peter Singer. It's just a small paperback, but it talks about how Americans casually accept animal slaughter as a necessary way of life. Without a tinker's damn as to the inhumanity and illogic of the behavior. As I see it, leaders in medical science and pharmacology are some of the worst offenders. I mean, come on, putting monkeys in restraining chairs for a year's time to test the effect of electric shock and anxiety on the growth of ulcers is unconscionable.

"So, yes, I've got to be careful to keep my work under wraps. Watch out for spies." A grin wavered on his face, then he frowned. "Though I'm already seeing signs of professional intimidation and stopping blocks."

"Sounds serious, Ross. What do you mean?" said Barbara.

"It is serious, Barb. To me, it's somewhat terrifying. You see, although we docs swear to follow the Hippocratic Oath in the beginning, our *Do No Harm* intentions fall by the wayside when it comes to inflicting pain and suffering in animal testing. Scientists call it research. I call it torture. And the government funds the pharmacies, teaching schools, and corporations who conduct the experiments. I see this going on all the time. It's hard to sit back and watch. It gets me in trouble within my profession, but I am compelled to do something." Ross snickered. "That's why I'm trying to organize a group. Loosely, I call it the *Institutional and Research Animal Protection Committee*, but I'm still just laying the groundwork for the idea. It's for those of us who accept animals as sentient beings, not merely chattel put on earth for humans to use at their whim. There are a few others who think like me. Not many, but some. And this organization could be a means to share ideas. Who knows? Maybe one day the group can lobby our legislators on the importance of inspecting and monitoring how experimental animals are treated. So far, though, I've had to keep my efforts underground."

"What's your legal support on all this, Ross? I mean, have you incorporated or taken any measures to protect yourself if those big shooters start firing their Glocks?"

"Hey, I'm a doctor, Mike. You're the lawyer. You tell me what I need."

"Okay. But first let's finish the current topic. Your controversial animal-lover work."

"All right. I might as well share my dirty little secret." Ross leaned forward in the visitor's chair, elbows on knees, steepling long fingers under his chin.

"Somewhere into my residency, doing pediatric pulmonary work, it occurred to me that the kids coming into the ER and who survived near drownings had two things in common." He ticked off on his fingers. "One, the kids were retrieved from water that was salty. And, two, the weather at the time – and the water they were taken from – was cold. The children who didn't make it were those who fell into a lake or backyard pool. **And** the weather was warm. The time the kids spent actually in the water, the time they couldn't breathe, showed no significant difference between the two groups. I saw this over and over again, and started recording my findings. There was a definite pattern. Then my question was: *On a cellular level, does the body's need for oxygen decrease when the body's temperature drops below a certain point?*

"Slowly, I started watching for more and more evidence of my hypothesis. I even bought property in the snowy mountains of North Carolina, thinking I'd have a place to test my theory someday if my research ever got that far. Then the idea of hibernation came to me, and I began to pull my hypothetical ideas into a firm research plan. I conducted my first trial using marmots here in my – "

"Hibernation?" Barbara asked. "I thought that – "

"What the hell's a marmot, for God's sake?" Michael said. "Wait, wait a minute." He wrinkled his brow and looked toward the window. "I know. They're small monkeys that live in South America. Right?"

"Close. But not quite," Ross said. "You're thinking of marmosets. Not the same." Ross studied Michael's sudden behavior change. Then he walked to the wall oxygen control, switched it on, unkinked the tubing, and handed Michael the cannula end. He returned to his seat.

"In essence, the theory is to temporarily convert a warm-blooded animal to a cold-blooded one, which is exactly the same thing that happens naturally when mammals hibernate. Technically, it's a latent ability that all mammals have. Possibly – likely even – humans. So far, with my work, I have proven that I can turn the hibernation state on and off on demand.

"My current research is carried out in my laboratory sequestered in the garage. It is designed so that it's entirely non-invasive to the animals. Actually it turns out the marmots have fun. And so far, every one of them has been cured of their disease symptoms. My study is different than other research with animals, in that I don't jeopardize the health or wellbeing of any of them. The only animals I treat are those who were already sick, and would have died. The runts of their litters. Specifically, I look for those with general symptoms of cystic fibrosis. In children, we call it failure to thrive, and it can be caused by countless conditions, so sometimes it's hard to tell at first. Right now, I'm treating seven animals in my lab. Three are cystics. Four had symptoms indicating the metabolic equivalent of CF, but turns out it's not CF. Their anomalies were slightly different, such as other pulmonary, autoimmune, or digestive problem – like asthma or systemic lupus erythematosus. These marmots were my control group. And they were treated for their individual conditions as well. Most researchers use animals that start out healthy, and the experimenter makes them sick, or inflicts them with some adverse condition. I will not experiment with healthy animals. Nor will I remove a baby from its mother. That's inhumane. My animals are those who would have died if I didn't treat them. They get the best medical care possible to help them live long and happy lives later, among their own kind.

"I bring these newborns home with me, make them comfortable, and then – this is key – I try my darnest to

65

avoid having them imprint me as their mother. Which is really difficult for me, because they really are appealing. But for the animals' sake, this non-imprinting, this non-attachment to me, becomes very important later, when it's time to return the animals to their natural habitat and live among other marmots.

"Immediately I put all of the animals into a state of torpor, a reversible metabolic hibernation. This is done with a substance found in the blood of hibernating animals. It's called HIT, or hibernation induction trigger. I found a great veterinarian who I work with. He checks the animals once a week, then he does follow-up after the animals are back in the wild. During this state of torpor, oxygen deprivation depresses metabolism, slowing cellular activity to a near standstill. In turn, that cellular reduction substantially shrinks an organism's need for oxygen. That's the hypothesis I developed from my documentation of kids with cold-water near-drownings."

From behind the oxygen cannula, Michael nodded his head.

"My theory is that if we can replicate this hibernation state in humans, it would buy time for a person with cystic fibrosis to be given antibiotic and other therapy to rid the body of the disease-destroying actions – hopefully permanently. Or at least send the symptoms into remission for long periods of time. Which should extend the time between postural drainage treatments – "

"I'm for that," Michael muffled.

" – antibiotic therapy, and so forth, with possible repeat of the torpor state when symptoms reappear. Now to the importance of imprinting. In their natural habitat, marmots mate shortly after they emerge from hibernation, and their babies imprint only with their natural mother. Never with humans."

Barbara squinted. "What's imprinting, Ross?"

"Imprinting is when an animal – or a person, for that matter – attaches itself socially to a stimulus. And then recognizes that stimulus as their mother. It's a phase-sensitive learning period, which determines the behavior for the rest of the animal's life. Simply put, an imprint means to leave a mark. Or, say, an impression. So you can see why I need to avoid having the marmots call me Mom. It would destroy them when they went back to their natural habitat."

"That makes sense," said Barbara."

"So at the end of the experiment, and the animals are strong, I quickly have them moved to Montana where – "

"Montana?" Michael and Barbara said together.

"Yes.   I release the marmots into the rocky mountain slopes. Hillsides or alpine meadows. They're carefully placed just inside the mouth of an underground burrow.   But the timing has to be just right. It has to be during the weeks adult marmots are coming out of their own natural hibernation.   That's when they start giving birth to their litters. Ordinarily marmots are territorial and chase other marmots from their feeding range. Which initially was a big concern I had. I mean, I didn't want to heal sick baby marmots, make them strong, and then have them be turned away to die because their species rejected them. But the good news is that the adults accepted the babies and allowed them to imprint on them.   When they were placed between February and April. With that timing, so far, every one of the animals who were released from my previous treatment experiments, have all been accepted by surrogate mothers. My healthy babies spent their first month in the burrow, and lived with their new family for the first two years. Then they were adults themselves."

"Wait. Hold it, Ross," said Michael. "How can you be sure that the baby marmots survive with their new families?"

"Good question, Mike. Very good. While the animals are in the torpor state, I fit them with a tiny soft collar containing a micro-transmitter. The transmitter emits signals that can be read with a radio receiver kept in the vet's office. A vet tech monitors the signals, and documents the findings once, maybe twice a month. I still get ongoing reports from the vet. A couple of times the vet had a colleague in Montana send me photographs of one of the ranges where the marmots were placed." Ross chuckled. "It's probably my eyes playing tricks, but I swear I see a collared animal in one of the pictures. Anyway, that's how I know."

"That's incredible," said Barbara.

"And what's so gratifying to me, Barb, is that I know these marmots would've died if they hadn't gone through the experiment in the first place. To me that is mind boggling."

Michael removed the oxygen cannula from his face. "But I still don't get it. Why it is that the other scientists – the ones who are doing research to find a cure for CF – why do they have a problem with your method, Ross? Why would they keep hurting animals in their research? That doesn't make any sense."

"Well, Mike, we're back to money. And power. On the surface, their argument is that it's a matter of choosing what's best for humans. Their mindset is that if it's going to help humans, then animals have to suffer. But ethically, we humans don't have the right to inflict suffering on another being. Period. There are ways to conduct research that's a win-win situation for both humans and animals. And preserve the physical, psychological, and social well-being of both." Ross spread his palms. "My small successes so far are an indication of that."

Suddenly, Michael started coughing. He pulled the pillow across his face to muffle the spasms. Ross and Barbara watched, ready. Soon, Michael flopped, exhausted, on the bed.

Ross looked at his watch. "Your postural drainage treatments are late," he said.

Barbara pressed the call button and spoke into the intercom.

"I'll give Respiratory Therapy a call right away, Mrs. Sutherland," a woman's voice said.

"Mike, one question before I leave," said Ross. "How old were you when they diagnosed you with CF?"

"About nineteen," said Michael. "I'd been sick maybe once or twice as a kid, but they always said it was the flu or pneumonia," Michael shook his head.

Barbara stood and moved to the window where she sat on the wide sill. "Ross, how long before your work with this group of marmots is done?" she said.

"Ideally, I'd like to stay at it another week or two. At least. Just to be sure the animals stay strong as they are now. Anything after that might be a risk. There's a physiologist in California who's kept mice in a state of hypothermia for as long as fourteen weeks. But then he maintained a temperature control warmer than I do. His was between 5 and 7 degrees Centigrade."

Michael frowned. "Translated, means . . . ?"

"Forty, forty-two degrees Fahrenheit. Sorry."

"Tell me one thing, Ross," Michael said, hunching forward on the bed. "Are you suggesting that I go into hibernation?"

Looking at Michael's face, Ross inhaled deep, then exhaled slowly. "Yes." He said. "I am."

"Ross, you can't be serious. I'll freeze to death. I thought the hibernating part of the experiment was for the animals. Not me. Good God. I'm a bikini-weather man. Why do you think I live in Florida?"

"You're not going to freeze to death," Ross said with a confidence he wasn't sure he felt. "Just hear me out. That's all. The decision is up to you and Barb."

Barbara reached over and touched Michael's hand. "Go ahead, Ross. Tell us the rest."

"Well, after flushing out and clearing Michael's lungs to get rid of the mucus, I'll start altering the environment. External and internal. Wind velocity and illumination shouldn't matter much. But climate control does. There's a close correlation between relative humidity and attempting to induce a torpid, hibernating state. That's why the property in North Carolina is ideal. It's in the Blue Ridge Mountains. Banner Elk area. Old log cabin I fixed up. Quiet – nobody'd intrude. Winters get pretty cold, so I should be able to lower your body temperature without any problem."

"You've really covered everything, haven't you, Ross?" Barbara said. From the corner of his eye, Ross saw Barbara shiver.

"I can't afford not to. This experiment has to be successful, Barb."

"I don't know. Still sounds like I'd freeze to death," Michael said.

"That's something we'll try to avoid," Ross said. "I'll monitor your vitals to see that doesn't happen. And you'll be comfortable during this state, Mike. From what I can tell, my animals have been completely relaxed during the hypothermic period." He paused. Both Michael and Barbara looked expectant.

"Well, there're a few other things you need to know if you decide on the treatment."

"Like what?" Michael said.

"Weight, for instance. You'll lose weight during the hibernation. So, you need to put on a few pounds first. Add a some fat to your body."

Michael looked down at himself. "Yeah, right."

"A small animal can tolerate losses of one-third their body weight. But for you, 8 or 9 pounds would be your limit. I'll give you a diet to follow. Put a thin layer of fat on you between now and then. You'll need more vitamins, too. Both before, during and after the sleep state is over.

70

"How long would this treatment take, Ross?" Barbara asked. If Mike agrees, that is."

"It depends on the results of his blood work and cultures. That'll be the key. The presence or absence of bacteria for one thing. I'll keep an IV line open and give digitalis and a diuretic prep, slow drip, and HIT solution to begin with. To help induce the hibernation. This slows the heart and lowers blood pressure. Once the appropriate temperature is reached, Mike's compensatory mechanisms should keep the temperature at that level. Later I'll increase his temperature with the antagonist drugs."

Michael started to say something, then changed his mind. His mouth hung open for a second then slowly closed with a sigh.

"During hibernation, I'll use an antibiotic in large doses. Directly into your lungs, Mike. This part of the study with the animals shows the most promise, actually. I have no reason to believe it won't work the same for you. Maybe even more so."

"Why is that?" asked Mike.

"Well, at a normal body temperature of 98.6, infection can spread rapidly. We don't want that."

"That's for sure, said Mike.

Ross stood and pushed the chair back against the wall. "Okay, folks. I've given you plenty to think about. The rest we can talk about later."

"What? No other goodies we should know about, Ross?" Michael said.

Ross shook his head grinning. "Nope."

"In that case, I'll just take a little nap before the R.T. guys come to whack on my chest." He settled his head on the pillow. "God, I'm tired," he said.

19

"*Look, Mommy. Look at that little girl playing the piano up on the stage. She looks just like me.*"

"*Yes, darling, I know.*" *The child's mother smiled.* "*That's because that little girl is you.*"

From high in her rear balcony seat, the little girl watched herself perform while the other members of the Boston Symphony Orchestra sat mute, lifeless hands resting on instruments or in empty laps. Their blank faces matched the stares of the people in the audience, none of whom moved or breathed, only watched the tiny figure in the center of the gilt-framed stage playing Samuel Baker's Pulitzer Prize-winning Piano Concerto Number One.

"*A genius,*" *someone whispered, breaking the hush. Everyone in the audience stood then, and the girl heard muffled flaps as their velvet cushions smacked against the soft seat backs. The people were in her way now. She couldn't see the girl on the stage anymore. She climbed up on her seat, and still she couldn't see the girl.*

"*Mommy.*" *The little girl pulled her mother's sleeve. I can't see me anymore,*" *she said. "Make everybody sit down.*"

A bright light filled the room for an instant and all the people in the audience started clapping with a sound that burst in the little girl's ears. "*Bravo, bravo,*" *they shouted. "Encore.*"

Then, as if on signal, the crowd sat down in one movement, and the little girl heard a delicate applause, that turned into a wet, slapping sound. Looking down in front all that she saw was an empty stage. The girl was gone. The orchestra, too. All she saw now was the piano. The moist applause continued from around her as she watched four men walk onto the stage, pick up the piano, and carry it to a door on the side of the stage. They loaded the piano into a large truck outside the curtained window near the front side of the stage. The piano was a 5-octave just like Mozart would have played Beethoven on. She had wanted to touch it when she went with mommy to the New York Metropolitan Museum of Art. It was one of the oldest piano in the world.

Cymbals. Drum roll.

The flood of raindrops struck the window near Tracy's hospital bed with a force that woke her. She heard sounds, but couldn't open her eyes. Her heart pounded in her chest and spread down around her entire body as she lay flat against the mattress, hands pressed to her sides. She felt heat rise around her body, like waves on summer pavement. Her left foot was tucked under her other knee in the position she liked best. Daddy called it a figure-four. But she wasn't comfortable now. Nothing felt good on her body, especially the deep space inside her throat. It was like someone had sandpapered it. Like Daddy did once to the plastic pipes under the kitchen sink to roughen them for glue.

Someone was shaking her, but she still couldn't open her eyes.

"Breakfast's here, Tracy."

She rolled her head to the side. Cool fingers touched her cheek. Then she heard muffled voices and people moving around her. The rain was so loud. If she could only see what was happening it would make sense and then when Mommy came to visit they could practice a while on the old piano in the library before she got dressed and went home from the hospital to her own music room and the piano she hadn't touched in four days. And didn't Mommy say that she had another surprise for her today? Two surprises, not just the one

about going home from the hospital after she said good-
bye to all of her new friends –

*One hundred and four degree temperature, shaking
and chills, inappropriate behavior, peripheral cyanosis.*
Marilyn Pelletier jotted rapidly in Tracy's chart, then
picked up the telephone at the nurses' station.

"Carol," she said when the hospital receptionist
answered. "Page Dr. Fossari for me, please. Ask him to
come to the medical floor, peds, right away." When
Carol protested that the doctor didn't like to be
interrupted when he was in clinic, Marilyn's anger
pushed at her chest. "I know he's busy in clinic, Carol,"
she said. "But one of his kids here looks real bad. Tell
him it might be symptoms of septic shock." Was she
trying to convince the receptionist that the child's
illness was more serious than Fossari's personality
quirks? "Get him, Carol," she said firmly. "Please."

Marilyn hung up the phone and saw Irene Thomas
standing at the nurses' station. She didn't seem to have
heard Marilyn's talking on the phone.

"Oh, Marilyn," Mrs. Thomas said. "Tracy's going to
be so excited." She flashed two yellow tickets at
Marilyn. "Did she tell you I had a surprise for her
today?"

Marilyn stood up. She tried to smile at the woman,
leading her up the hall to Tracy's room. Irene continued
her chatter. "Tracy and I are going to see the Boston
Symphony Orchestra on Friday at the Bayfront Center."
A Julliard-trained pianist, Irene Thomas had eight
years earlier written the score for the award-winning
movie, *California Fires*. When Tracy was two years old,
she had given up her career with the orchestra to
dedicate herself full-time to guiding the child's musical
future. All Irene wanted in the whole world was to see
her daughter become a successful concert pianist.

"Tracy's never seen this orchestra in person. She'll
be so – "

Marilyn stopped abruptly outside Tracy's room. "Mrs. Thomas," she said gently, "I'm terribly sorry, but I really don't think Tracy will be going home today as we thought. Tracy seems to be awfully sick today."

The words slapped Irene in the face. "What? What do you mean, she's awfully sick? She's supposed to go home today. She was fine when I left her yesterday afternoon." She stormed behind Marilyn into Tracy's room. Seeing Tracy lying motionless on the bed, she turned to Marilyn.

"What's happened to my baby?" she screamed. "All she came here for was to have her tonsils out. Why does she look like this? Oh, my God." She pushed her fist against her teeth.

"I've called Dr. Fossari," Marilyn said. "He should be here any minute, Mrs. Thomas." Marilyn bent over Tracy's bed and pushed dark hair off the child's forehead. "Tracy, honey," she whispered, "your mother's here to see you." She removed the blood pressure cuff from its place on the wall near the head of the bed and wrapped it around Tracy's upper arm.

Irene sat next to Tracy on the opposite side of the bed from Marilyn. She felt the heat of the child's body under her hand. The concert tickets fell to the floor. Irene leaned over and picked them up without interest, and tucked them inside her purse.

By the time the orderly and two nurse's aides rolled Tracy's bed out of the room, Irene was disoriented. A simple tonsillectomy, she thought. That's all it was. Why is my little girl unconscious?

"Wait here, please, ma'am," Vincent Fossari said to Irene when they got to the elevator. "Fifth floor, intensive care," he said to someone inside. Then Irene stood helpless as the elevator doors clicked shut in her face.

20

"Monitor pulmonary artery and systemic pressures. Watch blood pH, gases and lytes." Fossari spoke rapidly while two ICU nurses gathered supplies. A third nurse started an intravenous line on Tracy's left hand. A short male technician drew blood from the child's other arm into a syringe.

"I and O every hour, CVP and start nasal O2," Fossari shouted to the team in general. "Watch this kid closely, dammit. I don't want to deal with metabolic acidosis here."

The telephone rang, and when the older of the nurses handed Fossari the instrument, he shot her a scorching look and turned away.

"It's pharmacy, Doctor," she said. The woman had survived doctors for 43 years, and wasn't about to let this one kink her style. "They're double checking your antibiotic order." She placed the receiver on the counter in front of Fossari and walked away. His face reddened and he picked up the phone.

"Paul, I'm waiting for that drug order. This kid's in a goddam coma. The IV line is open and waiting for the medication. And you want to chat. What gives down there?"

Fossari listened briefly, then he said, "Goddamit, yes, it's Garamycin. No, there's been no culture. No time. Sixty milligrams Q 4 hours – " Pause. "Because I know what the fuck I'm doing, that's why." Fossari breathed in two loud puffs. "The kid's sick, Paul, so fill the goddam order. I want it now." He slammed the receiver down and went back to Tracy's bed.

Gram-negative pseudomonas aeruginosa, Alyce Hobb's infection, had invaded Tracy Thomas' body. The postoperative site had been warm and moist – an ideal medium for the microorganisms to gather and multiply. And now, Tracy's defense mechanisms progressively weakened her small body.

For the first 72 hours, few people at the hospital suspected post-op complications on such a healthy child. Now they all knew the deadly trap Tracy was in.

Once the antibiotic was delivered and its potent liquid entered Tracy's bloodstream, it started its work in a steady drip, drip. Fossari sat at the medical desk dictating Tracy's condition into a small machine, ignoring the nurses hustling around Tracy's bed on the other side of the large glass window. Clicking off the tape, Fossari stared at Tracy's body as the nurse repositioned the child to her side. It was Joel Paulter's face Fossari saw.

He had never been implicated in the mass operating room accident in 1968, and Vincent Fossari had put the matter out of his mind. Now he remembered a scene just before Joel's surgery. He was walking through the surgical waiting room then, accompanied by a technician new to the hospital. He had stopped at three nurses' stations before he found a technician who would go with him to see Joel's parents. Just tell them, he had said to himself that day. No one could blame him. Joel would be all right.

"I'm sorry, Dr. Fossari," Joel's father had said to him then, "but our child is not going to be all right." Howard Paulter was close to tears. "When this place is through with our son, he won't have an arm anymore. And you say it's all right?"

"Calm *down*, Mr. Paulter," Fossari had demanded. Several people in the waiting room looked up at Fossari's words, and one older man sitting in the corner of the room who was waiting to hear the results of his wife's heart surgery, and was visibly shaking from worry, stood and left the room. "I am not accustomed to being spoken to in that tone of voice," said Fossari.

Howard Paulter stepped one foot back, bumping into his wife who was silent. Fossari continued. "I am your son's doctor. I am doing everything I can for that child. These things happen and they are nobody's fault. If you wish, I will discharge your son immediately. You may take him and his arm somewhere else if you prefer, he had said. "What do you say, Mr. Paulter?"

Defeated, Howard had shaken his head. "No, Dr. Fossari," he had said. "Go ahead with the operation as you have it planned." He absently wiped his forehead with the back of his hand. "I'm sorry, doctor."

"Fine." Fossari pushed the technician into the hall. "Mr. Paulter, wait here. I will see you when it's over."

Amy Paulter disappeared into the ladies' room then and her husband slumped on the couch where the old man had been. Howard Paulter thought he couldn't feel any worse. He was wrong.

21

"Good morning,. Pinellas County Department of Social Services. May I help you?" The woman suppressed a yawn. Then she sat up straight. "Yes, ma'am," she said quickly. "I'll certainly find out if Ms. Creighton is at her desk. Hold, please."

After making one wrong intercom connection, the operator buzzed the telephone on Emilie Creighton's desk, and watched the blinking light of the holding party. "Emilie, there's a call for you on line three. It's Congressman Sauers' office calling from Washington."

While Emilie waited for Senator Sauers' secretary to put him on the line, she rummaged through her notes and found the questions she wanted to ask the man. Emilie knew Sauers made it a point to publicly announce his interest in the lives of adoptive children and parents in the United States, particularly those children who had a physical or mental handicap. Well, we'll just see, she thought.

"Yes, Miss Creighton," Senator Sauers was saying now, as Emilie wrote in her modified shorthand style. "My Senate Bill S4084 was passed into law in last year's session. It amends Social Services Law, and authorizes public welfare officers to enter into a contract with adoptive parents of children with handicaps for payments of medical and other expenses until the child is 21 or to make payments of those expenses without contract, without regard to financial ability of the adoptive parents." It sounded as if the man was reading from a script. Or had rehearsed his lines well for spontaneous promotion of his future candidacy. Emilie had stopped writing a long time ago.

"That sounds like a very important piece of legislation, Senator Sauers," she said. "I'm sure it'll have a strong effect on the lives of many adoptive families in our – "

"Well, of course, young lady. That's the purpose of all my child-related bills that are introduced in each session of the legislature. Most people don't realize that in order to get even one small legislative change around here, numerous bills must be presented, lobbied, argued on, and voted in. At that, one must always be willing to settle for compromise. It takes many years before any congressman can even hope to be effective." He chuckled and Emilie pictured his wide belly shaking under his desk. "I guess that's why us long-timers do the most good for the people of our great country here in this judicial jungle in that – "

In her mind's eye, Emilie saw the man leaning back in a thick leather chair, feet up on his desk, cigar smoke settling on a picture window, clouding his view of the capitol city.

When Sauers paused (leaning forward to relight his cigar?), Emilie asked about laws governing the rights of single foster parents in temporary custody of a child they wish to adopt on a permanent basis.

"Of particular importance in this case I'm working on right now, Senator, is a child whose parents abandoned her almost nine years ago. Neither the foster father, nor anyone to our knowledge, has been contacted by either of the biological parents." Before he could interrupt her, Emilie quickly added, "I was sure that you, Senator, would be able to help me in this dilemma. What are the rights of this child and of her foster father?"

"Well," he said. Emilie heard a cigar-sucking sound. "I have Federal legislation pending right now that amends the Internal Code of 1954 to allow deduction of adoption expenses for – "

"Yes, Senator, that's a much needed law for many families. But in the interest of your time, please, that is not the case in this case. The doctor who wants to adopt this child is not asking for financial assistance. On the contrary. He is only interested in finding the child's parents."

"Does this man's wife work? Sometimes income from the little lady of the house can help out when they have another, uh, another mouth to feed, so to speak. Heh, heh."

"I'm sorry, Senator, I must not be making myself clear. The adoptive parent in this case is a single man. He has never been married." Emilie felt a twang in her stomach picturing Ross as someone else's husband.

"It's a rather unusual case," she said. Keep it simple, Emilie. "The foster father is single, Senator. He is a physician who has had temporary custody of a nine-year-old girl with a chronic and terminal illness, cystic fibrosis. The child's chances of surviving to adulthood are very slim. That's why time is so important to both the child and her foster father. The father, a medical doctor, saved the girl's life when she was an infant. She's been with him since that time. Now, everyone interested in this child's welfare feels that a situation of permanence through legal adoption would be best."

Sauers didn't speak. Emilie wondered if he was still on the line. "My question to you, Senator, is: Can you help this little girl? What law would open a door for her? For the foster father to legally adopt her?"

Another silence. Then, "Well, my dear, that certainly is an interesting case you have there. And I'm glad you called me for assistance. I always try to help children in need." Puff. Puff. "I'll certainly do what I can to study the matter here with my colleagues," he said. "Perhaps in the next legislative session we can draw up some notes taken from our constituents when we go back this summer. You realize, of course, that 1982 is an election year, and all of us will be

81

campaigning, but as my constituents know, much of my platform is based on the health, welfare and safety of our country's children, especially those who need lawmakers like myself, who – "

"Senator, I'm sorry to have taken so much of your time today." The right side of Emilie's head ached, and her shoulders felt stiff. "One more question. Do you know of any current law to protect my clients in this case?"

"No."

22

Michael shook his head as he listened to Emilie's story. After a week, he was still in the hospital, dodging Vincent Fossari. He was also troubled by his impending decision about the proposed radical treatment by Ross Manchester to cure his disease. And now, Michael welcomed the distracting new challenge Emilie was presenting to him.

"I keep running into governmental red tape that leads me nowhere, Mike," Emilie said, as she paced back and forth at the foot of Michael's bed. "If you don't hurry up and get out of this place soon and help me with this case, I may lose my mind. I've spent four days straight on the phone with government heavyweights, and haven't found one person willing to help."

"Be nice, Emilie," Michael said, smiling. "Remember, you're an employee of the government."

"I know. All the more reason they should help me, don't you think?" She moved to the window and sat on the sill. "I'm really discouraged, Mike. Come on. You're the expert. Not me. Help me."

Michael asked the next nurse's aide who came in the room to bring him a telephone directory, and while they waited, he asked Emilie what information she had collected so far.

Referring to the folder on her lap, she said, "I've gotten information on Karen's birth from Mary Immaculate Hospital in Jamaica, Long Island. The Department of Social Services for Queens Borough, thank heaven, has been helpful anyway. Said they'd call the Bureau of Vital statistics at the Health Department and have them send Karen's birth certificate." She continued, "Let's see, a Dr. Harry Berstein, Bernum – " Emilie flipped through papers, "Here it is. Dr. Harry Berlin delivered Karen. But I haven't been able to reach him yet. Secretary says he's out of the country till next week. Medical seminar or something. He may be helpful. Oh, and here's the stuff from Karen's parents' marriage certificate. I took it over the phone."

"And that's being sent, too?" Michael asked.

"Yes."

"What else?" Michael wrote in a yellow legal pad propped up on his knees.

"Michael, did you know that Karen's mother was just sixteen when Karen was born? And it was her second delivery. We probably should spend more time with Ross on this. I bet he's got plenty of information he could tell us about those two kids. After all, he was there when they brought Karen to the hospital. Want me to set up a meeting with him?"

"Yes, as soon as I'm out of here," he said, staring at the pad in his lap. "One thing bothers me, Em, is the lack of records you mentioned. What you said about there being that don't fit. I feel that way, too. What's your sense on why it doesn't stack up?"

"I'm not sure, really," Emilie said. "It's just a feeling I have. A hunch. But when I follow my hunches, every once in a while they pay off."

The nurse's aide came into the room and wordlessly handed Michael a thick telephone directory.

"Well, we'll find out soon enough," he said, flipping through the white pages. *Fossari, Vincent, residence . . .*

23

"The best thing about it is that it won't hurt anymore," Alyce said. "That's how I'll know when I'm dying, you know."

Alyce Hobbs and Tracy Thomas stared at a silent television attached to the wall past the foot of their beds. The screen flickered in green and red as animated characters spoke without words. Tracy didn't react to Alyce's comment. They were waiting for the food cart to arrive in their hall, and they both kept an eye on the doorway.

Alyce went on. "I'm sorry for the way I smell, Tracy. But I think it'll be over soon," she said with a sigh. "Does it bother you, Trace? The way I smell?"

Alyce stared at Tracy, waiting for a reply. "I'm hungry," said Tracy. "Are you? You hungry, Alyce?" Then Tracy wrinkled her nose at Alyce. "Wha'd you say?"

"I said I'm sorry for the way I smell." Alyce said in a loud voice.

Tracy picked through a stack of music books on the nightstand next to her bed. She selected one and thumbed through the pages, pulled the over-bed table across her legs and laid the book flat on the table. Then she began pumping her fingers on an imaginary keyboard in front of her.

Alyce jumped from her bed and pulled a chair to a spot under the television. She coughed several times, bracing herself on the chair back, then stepped up on the seat. She reached and snapped off the picture on the television. "I never knew a kid to play the piano as much as you do. Even without a piano, you play the piano." She eased down off the chair, walked to her bedside stand, and removed a large worn book from the top. "Want me to read you a story until our breakfast comes?" she said, walking around to Tracy's bed. She sat at the foot and opened the book. Tracy rolled her table closer to her belly to make room for Alyce. She continued playing her mock piano.

"My smell brings ants around me, you know," Alyce said, leafing through her book. "Next thing you know, they'll be crawling all over this room."

"Huh?" Tracy said.

"It's true. They come out more and more all the time. I was scared at first. They made me think of the Queen of Hearts." Alyce giggled. "That's funny, don't you think? Here, here she is." Alyce pointed to a page in the book. "There's the deck of cards all around her. Look at her. She's got her queenly arms folded across her big queenly boobs."

Tracy looked at the picture as Alyce pointed and continued to talk. "The queen's saying, 'who stole the tarts?' Then Alice really gets it. All those weird things crawling around her. Just like me and the ants."

"What's that?" Tracy asked, pointing to the picture of the queen. "Will you read it to me? I'll stop playing the piano if you read to me."

"Why is a raven like a writing desk?"

"Huh?"

"Two days wrong! sighed the Hatter. I told you butter wouldn't suit the works. I can't have much butter either, you know that, Tracy? It makes my stomach hurt and I fart a lot." Alyce glanced at Tracy and frowned. "Then the March Hare said – "

"What?"

"Tracy, why do you keep saying *what?* for? You getting sick again?" Alyce stretched across the bed and touched Tracy's face. "You're not hot. What's the matter, anyway, Trace?"

"What'd you say?" Tracy squeezed her face together and leaned closer to Alyce.

Alyce fumbled beside Tracy's elbow and found the plastic nurse-call device. She pressed a button, and looked up at the speaker on the wall between the two beds waiting for the red light to come on and the nurse to respond. When nothing happened, Alyce slid off the bed and went out of the room. "Be right back," she said.

Moving down the hall, Alyce saw Marilyn Pelletier carrying two food trays into a room at the far end of the unit. By the time she caught up with Marilyn, Alyce was out of breath and coughing.

"Oh, hi, Alyce," Marilyn chimed. "Want to help deliver breakfast trays this morning? Or are you just hungry?"

"No. But Marilyn, something's wrong with Tracy," Alyce said between coughs. "She's not listening to anything I say."

"Not listening," Marilyn said. "Don't worry, kiddo." She touched the tip of Alyce's nose lightly. "That's really no big deal. Nobody listening. Happens to me all the time." She reached into the food cart and removed two trays. Alyce followed Marilyn into the next room. "Why I've been ignored by the best of 'em.

Marilyn spoke to the   six-year-old boys eagerly waiting their food. "Hi, kids, she said, as she placed trays on each of the overbed tables, and hurried out the door, with Alyce on her heels.

"Doctors.   Nursing supervisors.   Assorted men. Everybody. Nobody ever listens to what I say." Marilyn grinned at Alyce.

"I think it's important, Marilyn.   Tracy's really acting weird. Please come talk to her." They had gotten closer to Alyce and Tracy's room, and now Marilyn carried their trays into the room. She slid Tracy's tray on her make-believe piano. "What's the concert today, Tracy?"

"Boy. I'm almost tired," Tracy said. She struggled to open the top of a red and white milk carton. Just as she poked the straw into the milk, the carton slipped and fell on the floor. "I wonder if Clara Schumann liked milk when she was a little girl," Tracy said, staring at the widening puddle on the floor near her bed. She didn't move.

"See?" Alyce watched Tracy. "It's like we're invisible."

Marilyn stooped, picked up the milk carton, then stepped to the paper towel dispenser. As she yanked out four sheets, she said over her shoulder, "Tracy, you feelin' okay?" Then she returned to Tracy's bedside, squatted and sopped up the liquid.

Marilyn tossed the wet papers into the trash by the sink, and washed her hands. Then she moved across the room and sat on the edge of Tracy's bed. "Tracy, you okay?" She put her hand on Tracy's forehead and looked into her eyes.

"What, Marilyn? What'd you say?" Tracy leaned back against her pillow and pushed her hair away from her face. "I'm so tired," she said.

Marilyn stood up and looked down at Tracy. She felt her heart race as she jammed her hands into her uniform pockets, thinking. *First Tracy gets an infection and goes into a coma because Fossari puts her on the wrong floor. Then, after taking his good old sweet time, the bastard finally decided to give her an antibiotic. But she's over it. Why's she acting so strange? Couldn't be another infection. Lord knows she's been taking enough meds to kill an army of childr–* Marilyn froze. "Oh, my God," she said out loud.

Marilyn ran to the door, then stopped, motioned for Alyce to get in bed. "Eat your breakfast honey, before it gets cold," she said. "I'm going to try something." She turned her back to the girls and shouted Tracy's name.

Tracy didn't respond. She lay unmoving on her bed. Marilyn called again. Again, Tracy lay still.

"No, please. No. Let me be wrong." Marilyn said under her breath. "Just when she's getting better." Later, she would thank the heavens that last Wednesday had been her day off.

Marilyn ran to the nurses' station and grabbed the telephone. On her first try, she got a wrong number. On the second try, she heard a familiar voice. "Doctors' offices. Can I help you?"

"This is Marilyn Pelletier, nursing supervisor on Four North at Parkwest. I need to talk to Dr. Fossari right away."

"The doctor's in with a patient right now. I'm sorry, but I can't bother him. Can I have him return your call?"

"If you don't mind, I'll wait. This is about one of his patients here. And it may be an emergency."

"Hold, please."

Marilyn flipped through Tracy's chart while she waited, looking for something to prove her theory was wrong. Six minutes passed before she heard the telephone come back to life.

"This is Dr. Fossari. What is it?" he demanded.

"Dr. Fossari, this is Marilyn Pelletier at Parkwest. I'm sorry to bother you, but I'm calling about your patient, Tracy Thomas. She's been acting unusual today. I think sir, well . . . it seems that Tracy can't hear very well today, sir."

"What do you mean, *can't hear today*? Miss Pelletier, I'm a busy man. And you are taking me from my patients."

Marilyn flinched, suppressing the urge to slam the phone receiver in Fossari's ear. "Sir, Tracy's still on Garamycin for her infection. It's been more than ten days, and – "

"Goddamit, nurse. I'm fully aware that my patient is on Garamycin. Who the hell do you think ordered it?"

"Yes, Dr. Fossari." Marilyn hesitated. "Did you want me to order lab work on her, maybe? Or an audiometer test, Doctor?"

"Young lady, when you get your license to practice medicine in this state, you let me know. Until then, you are just a nurse. I'll give the orders." Vincent Fossari's voice turned from the phone and was muffled in Marilyn's ear as he spoke to someone in his office. Then he returned to the telephone. "What's the dosage on that kid?"

"She's getting 60 milligrams. Every four hours."

"What are her other symptoms? Nausea? Headache?"

"I'm looking at her chart, Doctor. The three-to-eleven nurse wrote that Tracy threw up her supper last night. I don't see anything else here, but she seems lethargic this morning."

"Discontinue the goddamn antibiotic. I'll see her this afternoon during rounds." Marilyn heard the phone go dead.

After writing a long paragraph in Tracy's chart, Marilyn hurried back to Tracy and Alyce's room. Alyce's plates were empty. Like most cystic fibrosis patients, she had a voracious appetite in spite of her small size. When she had entered the room, Marilyn saw Alyce at Tracy's bed, stealing a piece of Tracy's toast.

"I see what I eat and I eat what I see," Alyce said, looking sheepish. "At least I mean what I say. That's the same thing, you know."

"It's all right, honey," Marilyn said, moving next to Alyce and giving her a hug. "You need it, and by the way, did you take your enzymes before you ate? I forgot to remind you."

Alyce nodded and Marilyn went to Tracy. She was still shaken from the confrontation with Fossari.

"You okay, Tracy?" she said.

Tracy rolled her head to look at Marilyn. "Marilyn," she said in a whisper. "Do I have to eat this stuff? I was hungry before. Not anymore. My head hurts. Sounds like a water hose is squirting in my ears. It's so noisy. I want my mom."

Marilyn sat on Tracy's bed. "Your mother should be here soon, honey. Dr. Fossari is coming to see you too. Probably this afternoon. I told him you didn't feel good." Understatement, thought Marilyn as she stroked Tracy's forehead. Tracy closed her eyes.

"Woo-hoo. Lucky yooo," said Alyce. "A visit from Dr. Fossari," Alyce rolled her eyes. Marilyn tried not to chuckle.

Later, when Irene Thomas visited, she watched her daughter sleep and suspected nothing. Marilyn managed to avoid Mrs. Thomas for the rest of her shift. What could she say? Let Fossari face his own mistakes. She'd covered for him for the last time.

After she clocked out, Marilyn grabbed the *Physician's Desk Reference* from the nurses' station and carried it into the employee lounge. Sitting alone, she balanced the large medical book on her lap and cursed everything she read.

24

At three-thirty in the afternoon, Tracy woke up feeling sick to her stomach. Alyce had joined two other kids in the library down the hall, and Irene Thomas was sipping coffee downstairs in the hospital cafeteria.

Finding herself alone in the room, Tracy hobbled out of bed, went to the bathroom and threw up. Then she sat on the toilet and stared at the floor tiles, each one looking just like the other, except for the way the lights reflected up into her face. The lines and squares. A game she played, but she couldn't remember which one it was. She continued to stare at the floor, and felt her head start to vibrate and swing. Like it was going around in circles. Or somebody was pulling the floor out from under her feet. She looked at her hands and wondered if she should wash them. Soon she felt prickly pins shoot up her legs. She was afraid to stand up. She turned sideways and slid up close to the wall. The movement made her dizzy, so she leaned her shoulder against the wall, closed her eyes and rolled her head until her nose flattened on the plaster. Her ears roared. A tiger in her head. She opened her eyes and took a deep breath, letting it out in a shout. Her neck veins bulged and she felt warm air bounce off the wall in front of her face. But she didn't hear anything. She wanted her mother to come back. "Mommy," she screamed. "Mommy, Mommy, Mommy." When she tried to stand up, she fainted, hitting her head on the sink.

25

"Look, Fossari, you do what I tell you, and there won't be a fucking problem." Arthur Lowndes, Administrator of Parkwest, opened a gold box of cigarettes and offered it to Vincent, who took one. Then Lowndes laid the box on the desktop along side a lighter and an ashtray. The remainder of the desk was bare.

"For years I've been running this place my way," Lowndes said. He leaned forward and lit Fossari's cigarette. "I intend to continue that way." He sat back and looked at Fossari. "Do you understand?"

Fossari's head dipped once.

"Good. You take care of the front line image down there in the clinic, Doctor, and I'll handle the big stuff up here." Lowndes stood up. "Just stick around tomorrow in case we need you. Now go."

26

Standing in the hallway, between the conference room and his office, Arthur Lowndes heard pieces of conversation bouncing back and forth among several board members. As soon as the elevator doors opened, Lowndes approached and greeted Harry Krause, President of the Pinellas County Savings and Loan Association. "Afternoon, Harry," Lowndes said, offering his hand.

"What's up, Art?" Krause said, as the two stood in the hall. Krause was a local attorney who dabbled in hometown politics. He was the current chairman of the board at Parkwest Pediatric Hospital, and had been since the mayor cut the ribbon on opening day.

"Manchester filed a complaint," Lowndes said gesturing for Krause to follow him into his office.

"We have complaints against the hospital every week, Art," Krause said. "You don't usually call a board meeting for them. On such short notice. Jesus, I just found out about this meeting last night. Had to cancel — never mind." He waved his hand in the air and then sat on the large sofa in Lowndes' office. "Who's this Manchester, anyway? Some kid's father?"

"He's a father all right." Lowndes sat his bulk on the corner of his desk. "He's also a doctor, Harry. A doctor who's specialty is pediatric pulmonary diseases. Trained under Eric Hamilton."

Krause whistled low. He poured a glass of water from the thermos pitcher on the coffee table. "Probably a damn good doctor, this Manchester."

"I'll say. I've had people checking him out for weeks. Ever since he applied to come on staff. He's done over 23 bronchial lavage procedures without one hitch, as best I can tell. In fact, the record shows that since he's started his practice nearly six years ago, he hasn't lost one cystic fibrosis patient yet. That's unbelievable." Lowndes folded his arms and watched the other man. "You know what our record is with Fossari?"

"As I recall, he tried the bronchial lavage procedure twice."

"Both kids died, Harry. I know they were real sick, but, God, what a record."

"Art, I still don't see why the meeting. There's really no question here. Manchester's your problem, not mine. Take care of it. You know as well as I do that the Cocuzzo estate pays the hospital endowment only if Fossari runs the clinic. Or he dies. So we keep him. Open and shut. Give me a drink, will you?" he said, reaching for a glass. "What's the complaint? Get to the point, Art. I can't stay all day."

"Manchester wants to replace Fossari in the clinic. He applied twice and is pushing for answers. We're running out of bullshit."

"So? A lot of guys want that job."

"You don't understand, Harry. Manchester's a kook. Unpredictable, patient-goddamn-advocate type. That kind of shit."

"You want him gone?"

Arthur Lowndes stared out the window and absently watched an ambulance drive down the street. "We don't need him, Harry. This place runs just fine without him. That's the story. You decide what to do. Fossari's bad. So what. He does what he's told. No one reads statistics. And he brings in the bucks."

The two men shook hands and then walked out of the administrator's office and into the boardroom.

27

Barbara stood in the bathroom doorway with a towel wrapped around her protruding middle. Water glistened on her shoulders and her skin was pink from the heat of the shower.

They rarely took showers together anymore. Michael said that since she was pregnant, Barbara confused herself with a tea bag, some kind of pregnancy gotta-have. Like pickles and ice cream. But the brew was too hot for him. That, and the fact that there was barely enough room in there for all three of them. Him, Barbara, and the belly.

Michael lay on his back on the bed, watching Barbara's heavy breasts rise and fall beneath the towel. Her hair hung in wet curls at her cheeks. She looked so healthy and ripe, he thought, and wondered if the baby would come early. Or late. Michael envied Barbara's ability to carry a child. He knew her smooth sexiness would soon return, and wondered how long he could satisfy her needs. A vision of her as an old woman, wrinkled and gray, flashed in his mind. He envied that, too. Old was something he knew he wouldn't share with his wife. Or anybody.

Barbara waddled to the bed with a glint in her eye. Soundlessly she stood near Michael and let the towel drop to the floor. Then she crawled clumsily onto the bed, carefully kneeling, legs spread on each side of Michael's hips. She leaned down and kissed him on the mouth.

After they made love, they held each other for a long time. When Michael fell asleep, Barbara crawled out of bed, slipped on her gown, and tiptoed into the living room. She curled up in a large easy chair in the dark.

The ache in her back started out slow. Then it grew until it felt like someone with a giant shoe was pushing against her spine. She felt a tingling just below her shoulder blades that radiated down her buttocks and into her thighs. A numbness crept around her legs and forward into her groin. All of a sudden, she felt weak, as if she would never move again. Maybe having sex this close to the due date wasn't such a hot idea, she thought. The baby moved, pushing forward with a leg or arm. She laid her hand on her belly and felt a slick roll under her palm.

Her mind wandered in a semi-sleep state. In her dream, her body was thin. She was in a field of yellow columbine flowers, wearing a chiffon dress, white, that flowed in the breeze as she ran. And ran, and ran. Then she tripped, fell, hurting her belly.

She awoke to the sound of her own voice. Slowly she got up, went to her bed, and lay down next to Michael. She rolled to her side and pulled one leg up. It was the only position she found comfortable in the last few weeks. Michael stirred.

"The baby," she said.

"Mmmm."

"Really."

"Next month, Barb. You're dreaming."

Barbara nodded sleepily and settled her head deep in the pillow. A gripping sensation crept around her navel and moved down toward her crotch. At the same time, she felt a tight crawling move up the inside of her backbone with precision, one vertebra at a time. Inside her pelvis, the baby flipped.

"I think it's now," she said. She was conscious of a space between her legs that felt vulnerable, wide, exposed. She stood and felt a heavy pressure, as if a bowling ball would fall from her, and immediately sat back down. Michael shook his head, sat up. and turned on the light. He reached for the telephone beside the bed, his hands shaking, and dialed Ross.

"I know we're not due yet," he said into the receiver. "Tell her that. Or the baby." He listened a moment longer, nodding, then hung up.

"Ross says to time the pains and head for the hospital now, but to be careful and take our time. He says we have plenty of time."

"Contractions, Michael," Barbara said through a grunt. "They're contractions. Not pains. It's all in the interpretation." She grimaced and screwed up her face.

Michael pulled on a pair of wrinkled jeans. Here's your robe. Let's hurry, Babe." He grabbed her hand to help her stand up, and as she did a gush of fluid spilled down her legs, wetting her gown but releasing some of the heavy pressure.

Within thirty minutes, Barbara was settled in the labor room. "Looks good so far," Ross said after he examined her. He wrote down the baby's heart rate and then pressed Barbara's belly with his fingertips.

On the way to delivery, Michael trotted alongside the stretcher. Barbara saw a nurse in a green shower cap, and felt the wheels bump into the delivery room. Cold air touched her skin, stung her nose. She saw green tile everywhere.

Let's get you onto this table, Barbara," said the nurse.

"Wait. Wait a minute, please," Barbara said. *Oh, God. It's too much. Forget it. I want to go home. Michael, where are you?*

Michael kissed Barbara's forehead and reached for her hand.

Too quick. "Can I rest for a few minutes? Can I go home?"

Barbara felt them lift her sheet and thought she was falling. A metal bar passed under her shoulders. No, someone's arm. A hug. How nice. She felt so heavy. Helpless. Like a giant turtle turned on its back.

Someone put warm blankets on her and wrapped them around each of her legs. Then her legs were spread and placed in two rain gutters. Comfortable in that position. Maybe she could take a nap. Her gaping crotch seemed far, far away. She could see it through somebody else's body. Numb there. Good.

She stretched her neck to see the progress between her legs. Nothing was visible past her belly, which pointed up now in an irregular shape. Was the baby standing up? She needed to get it out. Push it out.

"Don't push," a woman's voice said.

"Pant, Barbara. Puppy dog." A man this time. Familiar. Close to her ear. Michael. Oh, Michael.

Have to push. She felt her lips stick together when she tried to tell them she had to push. *It won't stop. I can't stop it. It's splitting me in half.*

"Face approach." Was that Ross? "Hold on Barb. Baby's coming out wrong."

Wrong. How? Can't move.

"I'll do it for you, Barbara." She felt something slide into her vagina. *It's going the wrong way.* She heard her breath catch as she pushed harder this time. *It's too big.* Her voice flung upward and hung under the ceiling in moans, pants, and wails.

Michael heard Barbara's sounds and smiled. Familiar sounds. A giant orgasm. Ecstasy to make this child. Ecstasy to bring it out.

"Look at that dark hair."

"Rest a second, Barbara."

Rest. Yes. Rest. But it's almost over. Here we go agaiiiiiiii . . . Barbara didn't think she could stand it. She moved her head from side to side. Sweat ran from her face into her ears. *Michael?* "Michael!" she screamed as shoulders, belly and legs slid out in one motion.

"Right here, Barb."

Ross pressed down on her abdomen and the placenta slipped out.

"It's over," the nurse said.

"The baby." Barbara tried to sit up. "I don't hear the baby." Ice water spurted through Barbara's veins. No, she thought.

"Waaa . . . ahhhh!" The infant's voice filled every corner of the room, bouncing off the tiles and multiplying the sound. Barbara fell back, flaccid. Now there were tears pooling in her ears. She felt Michael's warm breath as he came close to her and licked a wet droplet from her cheek. "It's a boy," he whispered.

Ross lay the wiggling infant on Barbara's abdomen. Muffled squeals as Ross aspirated the baby's nose. "Sounds great," said Ross. "Good lungs."

"Thank God, thank God, thank God," was all Michael could say. Then he kissed Barbara and got in the way as she reached for the baby lying across her middle, still red and slimy.

The infant wrapped his tiny hand around Barbara's finger. "Hello, Jeffy," she whispered.

"Reflex. Good reflex," said the nurse in a crisp voice, picking up the infant, and placed him on the scale. "Six pounds, nine ounces of healthy baby boy," she declared.

28

"Tracy is profoundly deaf." Vincent Fossari sat behind his desk facing Irene and Wayne Thomas. Fossari's fingers were laced in a double fist that rested on a thick manila folder. Beside the desk sat a small, bespectacled man wearing a lab coat.

"This is the hospital's otolaryngologist, Dr. Vorderman here," Fossari said, nodding toward the man. "Dr. Vorderman performed the diagnostic evaluation on Tracy. He did her hearing examination." The man tilted his head once.

Irene Thomas sat in silence, watching the doctor's words flow from an expressionless face, opening and closing his mouth, wooden. Flat. A ventriloquist's puppet whose only movements were artificial eyelids, up and then down.

"I will let Dr. Vorderman explain Tracy's condition." Fossari twisted his wrist, palm up. "Dr. Vorderman?"

"Ahem. Yes. Mr. and Mrs. Thomas. I am so sorry for Tracy's hearing loss." To Tracy's parents, the man sounded sincere. "In Tracy's case, there is no involvement of the conductive apparatus of the ears. Her outer and middle ear structures are functioning in a normal manner." Dr. Vorderman reached for the file beneath Fossari's hands. "May I?" he said.

Thumbing through a few pages, Vorderman removed two sheets that were stapled together. "The problem is that Tracy is unable to interpret sound vibrations because of damage to the eighth cranial nerve, which is the hearing center linking with the brain." He tore the pages apart and handed one of them to Wayne Thomas, who stared at it a moment before

101

reaching out his hand, then held it between himself and his wife.

AUDIOGRAM. Large block letters. Someone had filled in the form using fine handwriting: *Tracy Thomas, age 5 years*, along with date of admission to the hospital for her tonsillectomy, hospital code number, and the date of the hearing exam. Yesterday. Centered on the page was a square block with smaller, equally divided lines that formed rectangles, wider than they were high. Scattered on the lines, someone had drawn small circles, triangles and other shapes that symbolized Tracy's hearing score, and had no meaning to Mr. and Mrs. Thomas.

In the lower left-hand corner of the page was a chart labeled AUDIOGRAM CODES. Wayne Thomas saw that many of the markings on the graph corresponded with the *no response* code symbol. He continued to study the chart as Vorderman talked.

"As you can see, Mr. and Mrs. Thomas, the increments of hearing frequency go from one hundred and twenty-five to eight thousand, and there on the side of the audiogram, the hearing threshold levels are indicated in decibels. He flipped his paper over, and pointed. "There is an explanation of the audiogram on the backside of this form.

"The pure tone audiometry hearing threshold level for a person with normal hearing is zero to twenty-five decibels. According to the examination made yesterday, Tracy's hearing threshold level exceeds ninety decibels. To a point that can no longer be measured. Again, I wish I had better news to report. I am so sorry."

"Thank you, Dr. Vorderman. That will be all," said Fossari. Vorderman stood, nodded to the Thomas', and left the room.

Fossari placed the manila folder back under his fists. "I know it must be difficult for you as parents of the child. But with proper training and instruction, she will be able to adjust. We may even be able to locate a hearing device that will help her some, although I doubt it, because as you heard Dr. Vorderman explain this type of deafness, even in cases where it is not as complete as it is with your daughter, children who can hear some sounds find it difficult to use a hearing aid because of the intense amplitude of all sounds received, and the scrambling of multiple noises causes the patient to be unable to distinguish one sound from another."

With Fossari's words, the nightmare that Irene and Wayne Thomas were experiencing continued to go on and on, evaporating the tiny drops of hope they had been holding onto throughout the six days that Tracy remained on the critical list in the Intensive Care Unit. And then when their child seemed to get well again, the future that they had so carefully mapped out for their child – the future that Tracy herself wanted as badly as any gifted child ever wished to achieve – was being wiped away with the stroke of Fossari's words. Words that welded together the bars of a silent prison for their daughter, their baby, their Tracy. For the rest of her life.

" — and the third component of rehabilitation for your daughter will be speech therapy." Vincent Fossari rose from behind his desk, circled around the side, and perched in a half-sitting position, one thigh resting on the desk, the other leg standing on the floor. He folded his arms across his chest. "Since Tracy is no longer able to hear her own voice, it is important that she begin this form of therapy in order to maintain the habit of speech." Fossari paused to remove a small spiral notepad and gold pen from the chest pocket of his jacket. "There are several dozen fine schools with programs for deaf children in the United States, which you may want to consider. You might also want Tracy to attend one of the summer camps for the deaf, so she can work and play alongside other handicapped children like herself. That way she won't feel so different from the other children who are normal, and who may want to ridicule — "

Irene Thomas, who had been staring wide-eyed at Vincent Fossari for the last ten minutes, felt a cold numbness creep into her body. It started as an ice cube somewhere deep within her middle, then flowed in frozen chunks toward her fingertips and down into her legs. Now her head was spinning, and she could endure his words no longer. She jumped from her chair and fled out of the room.

Startled, Vincent Fossari wrinkled his brow in disapproval. Then, shaking his head from side to side, he spoke to Wayne Thomas as if he were a secret pal. "Women have such a difficult time with news such as this. I probably should have discussed this with you first, Mr. Thomas, and let you tell your wife."

Wayne Thomas glared at Fossari. "You piece of shit!" He spat, standing up and knocking his chair to the floor. He walked to the far end of the room, and then back to the desk, facing Fossari. Wayne Thomas placed both hands firmly on the back of the chair his wife had vacated just minutes before, holding his elbows stiff to stop his body from shaking. He looked directly into Fossari's eyes.

"Doctor Fossari, you are really a piece of work," his look piercing the space between them. Vincent Fossari blinked once and his body tensed. "My wife is a well-known and extremely talented pianist who has played solo and also with the best orchestras in this country and abroad. Her whole life has been dedicated to the art of music – something I doubt you, with all your powerful potions and disease, will ever understand. Doctor. And my wife was at the peak of her career when she saw that Tracy had an even greater gift than she did. My wife felt that Tracy could give the world a musical sound that comes along maybe once in a hundred years. And so my wife has sacrificed . . . no, my wife willingly gave up . . . her own musical career to dedicate her own talent to teach Tracy. To teach her and encourage her to surpass even the greatest musicians of today." Wayne Thomas reached into his hip pocket and removed a white handkerchief. He wiped the sides of his mouth.

"Tracy's whole life revolves around the piano music she loves. And you, you son of a bitch, have the arrogance, the . . . the gall to sit there and tell us – as if you were discussing yesterday's football scores – that our child's whole future is not going to be the way we planned it. That the training and musical talent my child has, is all gone. Down the drain. A silly pipe dream. Is that what you're telling — " Wayne Thomas choked on the last words. He turned away from Vincent Fossari and took a deep breath. Then he stood up to his full height and leaned closer to Fossari.

"I am going to find Irene, now." Each word came out with careful deliberation, Thomas' anger replaced by exhaustion. "And then we're going to stay with Tracy for a while. And somehow we're going to tell her what this is all about. Although, God knows I don't know myself."

Thomas walked to the open door, wheeled around to say something else, but stopped. No words came out. His thoughts were packed in dry cotton that stuck to the inside of his throat, soft fibers that refused to move upward or down. He marched from the room to locate his wife.

29

They found Tracy in the library sitting on the piano stool. "I can't hear it," she said, and it was up to Irene and Wayne to tell the child that she would never hear her music again. They tried to explain, but she just looked at them, puzzled. When Tracy pivoted on the stool and began fingering the black and white keys, Irene and Wayne Thomas gave up. By the time Alyce came in with two chocolate milkshakes she'd made in the small kitchenette off the nurses' station, she saw Irene Thomas brushing Tracy's hair in a rhythmic trance. Wayne Thomas sat in a small wooden chair, his knees poking up like mountain summits, long arms hugging his own waist.

Halfway across the room, Alyce stopped, turned, then rushed back out into the hallway, her rubber-soled scuffs slapping against the linoleum floor. As if on cue, Tracy leaped off the piano stool and ran to catch up with her friend, leaving her parents in a whirlwind of emotions.

30

"When I was eighteen, I thought I'd live to be at least forty. But now that I'm twenty-one, I think my forty has dropped to thirty."

Kevin Douglas flipped through the pack of cards and shuffled them one more time, then dealt the next hand. He and Michael sat facing each other on the side of Kevin's hospital bed. They both had been admitted to Holt Memorial that morning, and were scheduled for the bronchial lavage procedure to be performed in the operating room the next day. It was their choice who went first, and Michael insisted Kevin be number one on the schedule, since Kevin had gone through the procedure twice already, and was eager to be done, impatient to get back to work as cook at Hobo Herman's, the most popular outdoor party place on the west coast of Florida.

Tall and lanky, Kevin wore his sun-bleached hair loose at his shoulders. His two hundred and twenty-five dollar a month medicine bill ate up most of his take-home pay, but Kevin managed to make ends meet. And still have a few bucks left over for gas and insurance to keep his second-hand Vespa putt-putting down the highway. While other men his age sported expensive three-piece suits and designer haircuts costing more than he could ever make, Kevin went to work dressed in ragged cut-off jeans and thrift-shop sandals. Shirts not required. When he could afford it, he paid his parents for the small beach apartment he kept over their garage in Beach Pocket Park. Kevin hoped to enroll back in school to get an education and better job, but the Division of Vocational Rehab, the folks who help with things such as that, said they couldn't help unless he was unemployed. When he asked the welfare department for help, they told him there was nothing they could do. Ongoing hospitalizations, once paid for by the Florida Division of Children's Medical Services, had stopped last year on Kevin's twenty-first birthday. When the St. Petersburg Independent printed a story about Kevin four months ago, the Knights of Pythias had organized a local project to raise money for Kevin's plight. The $1,462.23 barely dented his annual medical costs. His balance with the hospital right now added up to more than $18,000.00, and increased on a monthly basis. Before the donation from the Knights, Parkwest had refused to admit him for lack of money on two occasions, even though he had been in respiratory crisis.

Michael loved Kevin's laid-back style right away, keeping at bay his own self-pitying mood that often took over when he faced a medical ordeal. Under the dietary cahooting of Ross Manchester – and urgings of his own wife, Barbara – Michael had gained sufficient weight for the unusual therapy that would take place in a few months. That is, of course, if it were to take place.

"Ever had this kind of procedure done?" Kevin took a card from the top of the deck, and slipped it into the fanned display in his other hand.

"Nope," said Michael, "But I hear it does wonders for the breath."

"It does, it does," Kevin said. "It's hard to believe, but afterwards, it's as if someone has removed the plastic bag from your face and blown up your lungs an inch or two. You can actually breath a few times without choking. It's great."

Michael squinted at Kevin. "Scared?"

"Nah. If I stopped to think about it, I probably would be," said Kevin. "But, you know, after what I've been through – and I'm sure you have, too – the way I figure is that being nervous a few hours before I go to the O.R. ain't much to pay for the relief I feel later.

Besides, Dr. Manchester is the greatest guy in the world in my book. Knows more about cystic fibrosis than anybody." Then, "Well, cept'n us, of course."

"Of course." Michael studied Kevin. "How long does the tube stay in your throat? That's the part I hate the most. All those tubes and needles coming at me." Michael looked out the window. "It's so undignified. Unmanly. You know?" Kevin nodded and Michael continued. "I've defended rape victims a few times, and their out-of-control-helplessness, their being invaded, sort of describes the trapped, caged feeling I get. I can understand why so many women who've been raped need counseling later on, or have problems adjusting to married life. It makes plenty of sense."

"You know, Mike, I never really thought about that before. Been so wrapped up in my own self pity-party world. But you're right. It's the feeling of helplessness and out of control that's the bummer. Must be tough on women." He paused, nodded. "Life can be the pits. Makes you wonder what it's all for, doesn't it? Does me, anyways.

"It's funny. When you're a kid, you figure everything'll always turn out okay. You love everybody and everybody loves you. You don't even stop to think about it. You just know it. And then one day, somebody comes along and knocks the hell out of that theory."

"Don't I know what you mean," said Michael.

"I remember being in the sixth grade," said Kevin. "There was this kid. Name of Henry, as I recall. He had Down syndrome. And even though he was three years older than the rest of us, he looked younger. Because of his retardation, I guess. They had put him in our school with the normal kids because he'd been doing so good in his special school. The teachers wanted to reward him, so they promoted Henry to the *big* school. The *normal* school. Some promotion that was.

"One day, not long after he started, it was maybe a day or two after Christmas holiday was over, several boys were gathered in the school cafeteria, clowning around. And this kid, Henry, was sitting alone minding his business, eating his lunch. Happy as a pig in shit, as they say. A few of us spoke to him a couple of times and he always smiled back, his thick tongue working up and down over his lips. He'd smile and you could hear him laugh deep in his throat, unusual like. Well, this one day, a group of guys from fourth period, Shop One, Mr. Barrington. These guys come in and sit down next to Henry, pretending to be his friend. They handed him a note they'd written, and baited Henry into carrying it over to Cindy Englehart, the head cheerleader for Junior Varsity."

Michael watched Kevin talk.

"Well, Cindy read the note. Then she jumped up and smacked Henry, and yelled 'ugly retard' in his face. This poor kid, he just sat there with an expression on his face that I've never seen before. Or since. He was confused, destroyed by that girl's treatment. A couple of us got up to help him. Try to comfort him. But Henry bolted from his chair, screaming, when we came near. They admitted him to the psych ward for several days after that and medicated the hell out of him to get him to calm down." Kevin laid his cards on the rumpled bed. "God, Mike. Kids can be really cruel." He stared ahead.

"The worst of it all, Mike, was that when the whole thing happened, every kid in that cafeteria just watched. Grinning and enjoying the whole thing. They actually enjoyed that boy's suffering and humiliation."

Kevin stopped. He hadn't thought about the incident once since it happened. Just pushed it to the far corners of his mind, where he stored things that were painful, like outgrown clothing you packed away in an attic to decompose and crumble until you couldn't recognize them anymore. It was all so complicated, ambiguous and without justice. Like that little girl Michael told him about. Tracy. She was having it rough. And it'd get rougher as time went on.

Kevin looked at Michael. The spell was broken now, but a bond had formed between the two. "So, my man," said Michael. "Tell me how it's done. First, they stick this tube down your throat. Then what?"

Michael and Kevin spent the afternoon and evening engrossed in conversation and intermittent challenges of Poker and Scrabble. By the time the nurse came in and hung up N.P.O. signs over each bed, Michael and Kevin were old friends. Two people who shared part of their lives. They had no way to know that their friendship would soon end.

31

The next evening Kevin Douglas, sprite, feisty, and bored, paced the hospital room. He breathed strong and was eager to leave the hospital. "I need to get back to work," he said, plopping down in the visitor's chair, and unfolding the St. Petersburg Times from the volunteer cart that had rolled in ten minutes ago.

Michael, who'd slept most of the day in preparation for the procedure, remained in the *monitor-closely* window of time that follows an O.R. stint. And now, as nutrition and enzymes flowed through Michael's I.V. tube, and the nursing staff hovered, Michael was eating his post-op meal. Due to the high-risk of inflammation, infection, and the tendency for his lungs to return to the pre-bronchial-lavage state, trying to refill with thick mucus, Ross had ordered high-alert infection control signs posted at the doorway, and put Michael on 30-minute watch, looking for labored breathing, elevated temperatures, and shortness of breath.

"You're right," Michael said, then slid a forkful of scrambled eggs into his mouth, and washed it down with bites of coffee-dunked toast.

"Huh?" Kevin looked up from the sports page.

"You're right."

"About what?"

"It's great, Kev. Gotta hand it to you."

"I'm listening."

"I can breath. I can actually open my mouth, or flare my nostrils, and take a gust of air without coughing up my guts. And hey, look at this chest when I inhale. Big as a kids' balloon. Don't you think?"

"Hey, man, let's enter you in the next Winter Olympics. Alpine ski racing, say. I'll enter the weight lifting competition. Arnold Schwarzenegger, outta my way."

"Good idea," Michael said. "You do the muscle-man event." Michael leaned back on his pillow, flexing his arms. "Not much there yet. But, hey, just you wait. Baseball may still be a demonstration sport in the Olympics, but if I practice my pitch, by the time the '84 games roll around, you might just see me up there on the platform, with a gold — " Michael stopped mid-sentence, eyed his pillow, and pushed his overbed table aside.

"You crack me up, Mike. But it's great to feel so good, ain't it? I may just join you in — " Kevin felt a soft blow on the side of his head. " . . .what the — ?

" . . . medal dangling from my neck."

"You are feeling your oats, man. And so am I." Kevin yanked the pillow from his own bed, gripped it in a tight fist, then hurled it across the room.

By the time they spotted Barbara and Karen standing in the doorway giggling behind sterile face masks, most of the feathers had already settled onto the floor. "Oh, wow," said Karen, kicking the fluffy spines.

"And at the '84 games, Jeffy will be old enough to appreciate his father's illustrious talents," Michael said.

Barbara moved across the room tiptoeing among the feathers. "Good to see you and Kevin are doing well," she said, kissing Michael on the cheek. "When's Ross pulling down the infection control signs, so Jeff can visit his dad?" Then she turned toward the door. "Come on, Karen, let's go find a vacuum cleaner and clean up this mess before the nurses kick us all out."

"Wait, wait. Karen, don't go yet." Kevin stepped to the windowsill, scooped up a fistful of feathers with one hand, and turned the window crank. As Karen approached, Kevin placed his hand just outside the screenless window. "Now, blow," he said. Delicate

113

flakes sifted out the window and into the sky, several floors above the main hospital entrance. Then a gust of air blew into the room stirring up the feathers on the floor, sending them into the hall.

"Oops," said Kevin. "Time to snitch the housekeeper's vac and destroy the evidence. Then we start some serious party-planning to celebrate our upcoming Olympic victory party at Hobo Herman's, the most popular outdoor party place on the west coast of Florida."

32

Marilyn shifted on the low wooden chair as she waited in the library for the other seven-to-three nurses and aides to arrive for the incoming report.

Except for a middle-aged woman in the far corner taking notes from a new Burn Patient Protocol sheet, Marilyn was alone in the room. In the elevator up, she'd overheard an assistant from Respiratory Therapy telling a lab tech that two pediatric admits had been caught in a tent fire while camping at the Hillsborough River State Park last week. By the time they got the kids out of the emergency room and beds ready in Intensive Care, their doctor had changed his mind and ordered the children to be admitted directly to the pediatric medical floor, since isolation precautions were unattainable in a crowded I.C.U.

Now that Tracy was gone, Marilyn sensed a dull emptiness in the library. For a short time, the child gave new life to the room. Spirit and zest and a touch of class. Staring at the silent piano, its role reverting to the practice of holding up books, dust, and debris, Marilyn remembered the day that Alyce had patiently removed books from the stool and piano top, walking back and forth, back and forth, one volume at a time, and then sliding each book onto shelves in neat rows, like soldiers standing at attention during roll-call. So Tracy could play the piano. While Alyce read. Now, all the walls heard was bickering staff nitpicking about the habits of patients and doctors during shift-change colloquy. The room could be shut down as far as she was concerned.

Marilyn gazed at the book in her lap. Worn hardcover. Turquoise background. Wide black letters. *The Old Man and the Sea*. *Ernest Hemingway*. That's all it said. She picked up the book, hefting its weight, remembering all the times driving to work that she'd take the long way around and pulled into the side lot of Haslam's Book Store, dash inside and then stand for twenty minutes struggling to select just the right book for Alyce. The child was incredible. Devouring literary works most kids read only as an assignment from the teacher of an advanced humanities class. Although Alyce preferred the more liberal-minded writers like Edith Wharton, Alyce had, in a weak moment, admitted to Marilyn that she had a strong interest in Papa Hemingway, if, for no other reason than to study his womanizing, male chauvinistic style and prose. Not only did Alyce read this stuff, thought Marilyn, but she also examined authors' techniques and philosophized on their intent.

Yep, Alyce was a marvel all right. At least Marilyn had never met another child like her before. Her heart dropped when she thought of how really sick the child was, and forced her mind to focus on the upcoming Christmas Party Committee she chaired. Most nurses on the wing predicted this would be Alyce's last Christmas. Marilyn disagreed. But it certainly wouldn't hurt to make this the biggest and best holiday season for Alyce anyway. Besides, she needed a boost herself, in spite of the fact that this was her first day back to work after a four-day break that she'd requested in order to recuperate from the emotional roller coaster of Tracy's up and down condition. And today she'd deliver the turquoise book to Alyce.

Marilyn twisted her wrist to check her watch. With six minutes before report was scheduled to start, Marilyn dashed out of the room to deliver *The Old Man and the Sea* to Alyce, and finding her asleep, left the book on Alyce's overbed table so she'd see it when she woke up. She was back in the library a full minute before she heard the elevator ping, followed by laughter and chattering voices, as nurses came spilling through the door, individually and in groups, ready for today's report. Marilyn propped a spiral pad on her lap and removed the multi-colored pen from the vest pocket of her uniform. Red for 3 p.m. to 11 p.m. shift. Green, 11 p. to 7 a. Black for 7 to 3 – or, sometimes blue ink could be used in a pinch on days. Oh, the legal mandates they drilled into a nursing student's skull. Marilyn clicked, and the black point appeared.

"Let's begin," said a tired-looking nursing supervisor who was ending her shift, and the other voices hushed. In the middle of the low table sat a black cassette player. The nurse pressed *Record*.

"Report for pediatric medical floor, Tuesday, December second, nineteen hundred and eighty. Ruth Gastmeyer, R.N., eleven-to-seven supervisor, reporting."

Just then, a girl wearing a tight black sweater, who Marilyn had seen down in the records room, poked her head in the doorway. "Excuse me," she said. "I have a message from Dr. Rominger. His office is on the north side. He just called, and — "

Marilyn heard Gastmeyer swear under her breath as she pressed the recorder's *Stop* button.

The girl at the door managed a nervous grin. "Dr. Rominger is sending a new intern – I forget his name – over from his office. Dr. Rominger wants you to hold report until the intern arrives."

Gastmeyer glowered at the girl. "Look," she sighed. "I'm tired, and I'd like to go home at a decent hour. Dr. Rominger probably wants this guy to work with those two burn kids, and since they're at the end of the report anyways, I'll just go on like nothing happened, if you don't mind." She looked down at her notes. "Let's see, where was I?"

"Was me, I'd wait," said the girl, her former politeness replaced with a tone of brusqueness triggered by the possibility of answering to Dr. Rominger's ire. "Dr. Rominger specifically said for you to hold the entire report." Then, having done her duty, she wiggled her fingers in the air. "Tah," she said, disappearing down the hallway.

Gastmeyer waited. The other staff waited. By the time the intern arrived, report given, and keys transferred from off-going nurses to on-coming nurses, a report that should have taken under eight minutes, ended a full thirty-five minutes later.

Marilyn was pleased to see that she was not on the assignment sheet to care for the two burn patients today. She wanted some quality time with Alyce. See her reaction to the Hemingway book. She snapped her note pad shut and raced the other nurses to the scant supply of blood pressure cuffs and Thermovacs. With the hospital census up, Marilyn's patient load was heavy, but at least she was familiar with most of the kids on her hall. Except for the boy with sickle-cell anemia who had his leg in a cast, the other kids should be easy today. Marilyn wanted to take time with the boy, get acquainted, then hurry through vital sign procedures with the others, so she could save time for Alyce, who usually hung out in the hallway outside the library, waiting for shift report to end so she could borrow more books. But right now Alyce was probably engrossed in a world of words, Hemingway style.

Ten-year-old David Honeycutt argued with his mother the whole time that Marilyn wrapped the sphygmomanometer cuff around his wiggling arm; and, after pumping the sleeve with air for the third time, Marilyn still couldn't hear – or sense – the child's pulsing blood pressure in her ears. She pressed her thumb on the compression screw, slid the stethoscope earpieces to the back of her neck, and looked at the boy. "Okay, hold it," she said. "Time out for vitals."

The child, nicknamed Bear by his schoolmates for reasons much more significant than the sound of his last name, tried to dart out of Marilyn's grasp.

"Ow!" he whined. "Get that thing offa me, will ya?"

Bear had juvenile diabetes, diagnosed shortly after he was admitted to the hospital four days ago, and this was normal behavior for an active kid obliged to spend his playtime in a boring hospital room, poked and probed and tested. Now that he felt better, Bear Honeycutt let loose with his spirit. Good sign, thought Marilyn. But if she didn't get his vitals and out of the room soon, she'd go bonkers.

"Tell you what, Bear," she said. "you count to fifty and hold absolutely still while I take your blood pressure, and I'll come back in here later and show you how to give an insulin shot to an orange. Okay?"

"Promise?"

Marilyn nodded and started moving the earpiece from behind her neck.

"Say, 'I promise.' "

"Geesh," Marilyn said. "Yes, Bear, I promise." As she plugged the stethoscope's rubber tips into her ears, she hear Bear's mother mumble for him to mind his manners. *Now, concentrate, Marilyn. Tha-rump, tha-rump. Ah, good-sounding blood shifting inside this li'l guy's arteries.* Disconnecting the earpieces, Marilyn heard Bear's counting become shouts, louder and louder with each number. Then, "Fifty!" at the top of his lungs.

With expert precision, Marilyn inserted the Thermovac into Bear's mouth, "Temp time," she said, gently squeezing his chin and nose to close his mouth, then stroked his cheek with the back of her fingers, and looked over at the boy's mother. "It's important that both you and Bear learn how to give him his injections when you get home," she said, holding the thermometer still. When Mrs. Honeycutt grimaced, Marilyn added, "There's really nothing to it, once you get the hang of it.

Don't worry, we won't send you guys home until you're both comfortable with giving the shots."

From the bed by the window, six-year-old Patrick Jacobson sat cross-legged and silent, watching the scene with Bear. Patrick held an ice pack against his nose. From inside the pack, a tepid solution leaked through the interlocking ridges at the top of the plastic, and trickled down the child's arm, falling off his elbow, and leaving nickel-sized drops on the sheet. Marilyn made a mental note to try and persuade a lab tech to deliver the remainder of Patrick's test results to the nurses' station before his doctor called at ten o'clock this morning. No easy task, since the lab staff was accustomed to delivering their findings on a schedule convenient to them. Maybe she'd run to the lab herself. During break. Or get the information verbally, and listen to the doc's rhetoric rant on proper procedures and written documentation. But, hey, there was only so much she could do.

Marilyn wrapped the stethoscope around her neck and pushed the tattered BP cuff into her pocket. Then she washed her hands at the wall sink, and moved to Patrick's bed.

"Hi, Sport," she said, taking the warm ice pack from the child's hand. She stepped to the plastic pail under the sink, and dropped the pack. "You 'bout ready to go home?"

Patrick nodded, and Marilyn rearranged his hospital gown, wrapped the blood pressure cuff around his boney arm. She arranged her feet in a precarious posture, around an empty I.V. pole that stood in front of the bedside cabinet, iron legs jutting to threaten her ankles. Rubber tubing hung in circles around the rusty T-bar on top. Last she'd seen, the pole held a bag of fresh frozen plasma to compensate for Patrick's nosebleed. Now she saw a dirty bandage strip taping a hand-written note to the pole. She yanked. *Do not remove this message or IV equipment until patient is discharged.* Okay. She removed a small roll of fresh bandage tape from her uniform pocket and stuck the note back in place.

"Be right back, guys," Marilyn walked out of the room and returned moments later with a new cold pack filled with ice. She gave it to Patrick and helped him get settled in bed with a pile of toy trucks and the TV remote controller. Leaving the room, she saw that Bear's bed was empty. Mrs. Honeycutt sat in the corner near her son's bed reading a *Redbook* magazine. "Bear's gone to the playroom," she said. Then she smiled in a sheepish way. "I'm enjoying the quiet."

The next hour was a jumble of thin arms, open mouths, giggles, and drippy tears for Marilyn. Her hefty patient load – from three-year-old Lisa Huff diagnosed with failure to thrive and being kept in the hospital until her parent's story about her falling out of bed could be proven or not, to the toddler healing from esophageal burns from accidentally swallowing a yet-to-be-confirmed caustic solution she found under the kitchen sink – Marilyn was done-in when she finally entered Alyce's room.

Happy face, Marilyn, she reminded herself as she slipped into Alyce's room, expecting a faceful of thank-you's and chatter cheer, as Alyce called it. The kids deserved Marilyn's smiles, at least. Even if, now and then, she had to put on those smiles with great effort. After all, it wasn't the kids' fault that she burned out sometimes. And, besides —

Was Alyce's position in bed the same as when she'd dropped off the book an hour ago?

Marilyn slid the tousled bedclothes away from Alyce's face, down past her shoulders, and off to the side. She inhaled audibly. The child, who ordinarily slept on her side, one knee flexed in a way that made it easier for her to breathe, was lying flat on her back, hands clutching a stuffed rabbit under her chin. The thick volume of Physician's Desk Reference was pressed against Alyce's left thigh. Protruding from the book was a sealed envelope with *To Mommy* scrawled in Alyce's familiar handwriting. A vise-like glove seized Marilyn's heart, filled her veins with ice. *Wonderland* . . . she heard Alyce's voice whisper from somewhere above her own head. *I'm in wonderland.*

Although the next actions took less than thirty seconds for Marilyn, it seemed to her that time had stopped. She moved as if she were walking through water up to her neck. With one hand, she reached to palpate Alyce's neck for a pulse. The other hand groped for the nurse-call device hanging on the wall grate. It dropped on the floor. Without taking time to pick up the instrument, Marilyn punched at it with the toe of her shoe, and at the same time she slid the PDR toward her, opened it to the center page and laid it flat. Then, with her left hand and arm, Marilyn lifted Alyce's frail body between the little girl's shoulder blades and slid the open book under Alyce's back. The intercom blared to life.

"Can I help you?" said a static-filled voice from the nurses' station.

"Cardiac arrest," Marilyn screamed at the wall. "Alyce Hobbs. Get help. Crash cart. Stat!"

By the time Vincent Fossari arrived to declare the patient dead, Marilyn and the rest of the nursing team had been trying to resuscitate Alyce for sixteen and a half minutes. Perspiration and tears ran in streams down Marilyn's face.

When he first stood in the doorway to Alyce's room, Fossari's demand to Stop! took the nurses by surprise. In one silent move, they all backed away from the bed and stared at the doctor. All except Marilyn, who froze, unable to leave the blurred figure of the child she dearly loved. Fossari pushed Marilyn aside with a rough hand, and before she bolted out of the room, Fossari's words echoed and bounced off the ceiling, hitting Marilyn's ears like shots from an M2 machine gun. "Can't you see she's dead," he said in an angry bark. "Clean up this mess and prepare the body for the morgue."

33

Millie Hobbs had read the note they gave her when she first arrived at the hospital and learned that her daughter was dead. At the time, her shock and disbelief had overshadowed her ability to process the message.

"We found it in the medical book she carried," Marilyn had said.

Now, two days later, Millie Hobbs sat alone in a small side room at the funeral home. How long had it been since the man told her to wait? Someone would be with her soon, he had said.

Millie Hobbs fumbled in her purse until she found the envelope folded once and torn in a ragged edge where she'd unsealed the flap with her shaking index finger. She spread the opening wide, and with great care, slid the note from its enclosure. Several flecks of the blue-lined paper came loose along the side where Alyce had torn it out of her spiral notebook, and landed on the funeral home carpet, like confetti settling on the sidewalk at the end of a parade. For the sixth time that day, Millie Hobbs read her daughter's message:

Dear Mommy,

Please don't worry anymore that we don't have all the money we need. All the money in the world can't buy me what I really want, and that's a healthy body and for me to grow up strong. I'd even settle for a plain-looking figure, a lot bigger, of course, and for my ribs to be covered with more fat. And two soft breasts like the other girls.
I had a beautiful dream last night. I was strong and healthy and you took me to the beach. We swam

*together, you and me, under the sun. And then I turned
into a gray and white seagull and my bird wings
flattened and protruded as I flew above the gulf, away
from you, and into the arms of Jesus.
I guess that means that I'm going to die pretty soon.
And the truth is, Mommy, that we'll never have enough
money. And I will never grow up.
Love,
Alyce
P.S. It isn't your fault. None of it.*

Dry-eyed, Millie Hobbs re-folded the note, returned it to the envelope, which she then bent in half and inserted into the lining of her purse.

" — Ma'am?" A different man approached with quiet steps and told her she could go in there now. Following his dark shoulders, she smelled mothballs from the fabric he wore. They walked in silence down a hall twenty feet long, and when he opened the door to a large foyer-like room, Millie Hobbs didn't recognize the people who stood in small groups and drifted in and out of the room, talking in the hushed way that people who were shampooed and polished for such a solemn occasion usually speak. Whatever the trouble was that they had gone through to be there, Millie Hobbs wished they hadn't bothered. Alyce was all she wanted. How could these people know the grief she had been going through these past twelve years. Watching her little girl die. Such a beautiful child. Such a brilliant mind. Such a sweet personality. Such a terrible waste. And now, why didn't these people just leave her alone?

A small woman with freckles and long auburn hair smiled, took a step toward Millie. The woman carried an infant, sleeping, in her arms. Oh, God, Millie thought, and then turned away. She hurried into the next room and sat down on the front row of folding chairs. Through her cotton dress, the cold metal stung Millie's legs. Gripping both hands into tight fists on her lap, she stared through glazed eyes at the coffin five feet in front of her.   Then she felt the warmth of people surrounding her, one on each of her sides, and the woman with the baby laid a soft palm on Millie's clasped hands. It was warm, too. She was surprised that it felt good.   That's when Millie Hobbs took the lace handkerchief from the woman and wiped away tears she didn't know were there.

Sitting next to Barbara, Michael reached out to take his child.   The baby was a comfort to him, and he wondered why he'd been so blessed with this gift. That last time in the hospital, with Kevin, had been a turning point for him, and he was beginning to take on a new and positive view of his future.   In spite of the odds, Kevin always looked on the good side of things. But it was more than that. Michael felt physically better since the bronchial lavage treatment. Just as Ross predicted. And even though it had been four weeks since the procedure, he was still taking in more air and holding it in his lungs longer than before. He could breathe.

Barbara turned toward Michael then, and seeing that the top of Jeffy's ear was folded under as his head rested on Michael's shoulder, she eased the infant's head into a more comfortable position. Michael patted Barbara's hand.   Thank God for you, my darling, he thought. And thank God for this bundle in my arms. Little Jeff Sutherland.   Michael knew that this child was truly a miracle. There had been only two chances in a hundred that Michael could have hoped to conceive. Back when he first learned he had cystic fibrosis, Michael had read everything he could about the disease. One of the facts he'd learned back then depressed him for a long time: Almost all males with cystic fibrosis are sterile because the vas deferentia, the tubes that carry sperm, are missing. But then, so few cystics lived to adulthood anyway, that it usually didn't matter. It was nearly impossible for researchers to collect data on parenthood. Genetic counseling had helped both him and Barbara adapt to a childless future. So when Barbara missed her period last year – and then the rabbit died – they were both elated. And scared. All during Barbara's pregnancy, Michael had prayed for a healthy child. And so far, his prayer had been answered.

A long note rose from the organ at the back of the room, signaling people on the front row to rise. As the music droned softly, Michael followed Barbara, watching her steady Millie Hobb's elbow as they led the procession to the front of Alyce's coffin. Then Millie dropped, one knee at a time, onto the velvet railing. Michael and Barbara and three others, Irene and Wayne Thomas and wide-eyed Tracy, stood behind Millie. Then they, too, took turns offering silent prayers for little Alyce's soul. As Michael looked down at Alyce's body, Jeff wiggled in his arms, and Michael shifted the baby to his other shoulder.

In her coffin, it was as if Alyce had become part of the pink lace blanket that tucked across her flat chest. The pale grayness of her flesh was a shade lighter than it had been yesterday, but neither the chemical solutions, nor makeup could add natural tones to the girl's dainty features that had been devoid of color for a long, long time.

Beside the coffin stood an easel with tiny sweetheart roses of yellow and silver, which had been arranged into the shape of a rabbit. Two flowers stood out, white, as the animal's buck teeth grinned back at the solemn spectators.

Michael tried to pray, but all he could do was stare at the delicate face before him. Then the line moved him along, and he returned to his seat to wait for the service to start. As the last mourner sat, the minister entered the room from a door near the foot of Alyce's coffin. He carried with him a small upright podium that he placed off to the side in the front of the room.

"Ladies and gentlemen. Boys and girls. We are here today to celebrate the short life of little Alyce Hobbs. Today's service will not consist of the usual lengthy dissertation that is so common in funeral services today." No one spoke, and except for the moist sound emitting from deep in Michael's lungs, the room was quiet. Michael wished he could cough.

Then the speaker's voice burst through the silence. "I have been asked by the mother of the deceased child to forego the routine eulogy and any reading of the Bible. Also, you are asked that any prayers offered for the deceased be carried out individually after the end of this service. Unaware of it, Michael nodded to the man.

"Instead, ladies and gentlemen. And boys and girls, I have been asked to read to you excerpts from a poem found in the story *Alice's Adventures in Wonderland*, a tale so cherished by the deceased Alyce Hobbs." The minister picked up a large legal pad on which Michael saw had handwriting in dark blue ink. Then the man started reading in a rich, velvet voice.

> *All in the golden afternoon*
> *Full leisurely we glide;*
> *For both our oars, with little skill,*
> *By little arms are plied,*
> *While little hands make vain pretence*
> *Our wanderings to guide.*
>
> *Ah, cruel Three! In such an hour,*
> *Beneath such dreamy weather,*
> *To beg a tale of breath too weak*
> *To stir the tiniest feather!*
> *Yet what can one poor voice avail*
> *Against three tongues together? . . .*
>
> *. . . Anon, to sudden silence won,*
> *In fancy they pursue*
> *The dream-child moving through a land*

Of wonders wild and new,
In friendly chat with bird or beast –
And half believe it true.

And ever, as the story drained
The wells of fancy dry,
And faintly strove that weary one
To put the subject by,
"The rest next time – " "It is next time!"
The happy voices cry.

Thus grew the tale of Wonderland:
Thus slowly, one by one,
Its quaint events were hammered out –
And now the tale is done,
And home we steer, a merry crew,
Beneath the setting sun.

Alice! a childish story take,
And with a gentle hand
Lay it where Childhood's dreams are twined
In memory's mystic band,
Like pilgrim's wither'd wreath of flowers
Pluck'd in a far-off land.

The minister balled his fist, expelling a choked cough. "In closing, I will share one more thought with you," he said. "It is from the same story. Although this is taken just as it was written in the year 1865 by the story's author, Lewis Carroll, I have been told that it in many ways describes the generosity and love that young Alyce Hobbs had felt for other children, even though she, herself, was only a child. This excerpt is dedicated to Alyce Hobbs' make-believe sister – her former roommate. It's for Tracy Thomas, who I understand cannot hear my words." The man flipped a yellow page as he spoke.

"Here goes," he whispered to himself.

"*Lastly, she pictured to herself how this same little sister of hers would, in the after-time, be herself a grown woman; and how she would keep, through all her riper years, the simple and loving heart of her childhood: and how she would gather about her other children, and make their eyes bright and eager with many a strange tale, perhaps even with the dream of Wonderland of long ago: and how she would feel with all their simple sorrows, and find a pleasure in all their simple joys, remembering her own child-life, and happy summer days.*"

The man looked up from his papers. "The End," he said.

Later, at the cemetery, no one noticed the man who stood at the far end of the graveyard, too far to be seen, one foot propped up on a bench made of gray cement, his right forearm resting on his knee, his head hung low. The man was hidden by the cluster of palm trees, leaves rustling above him. He clutched a worn-out photograph of a round-cheeked baby who sat in front of a cup cake with one pink candle on top. The child wasn't looking at the cake. Her eyes focused on the object in her tiny hands held over her head. Her mouth was open in a wide smile. Two bottom teeth reflected light from the camera's flash. In the child's fist was a stuffed animal, it long ears bent over a bunny's face, and one of its eyes hung from a thread. The animal's checkered vest was torn where the chain from the pocket watch had pulled apart.

The man remembered taking the picture a split second before the child smashed the toy into the candle. He remembered that he had almost dropped the camera, laughing himself silly at the time, looking for a place to situate the sticky rabbit. He wasn't laughing now, as he stared at the old photo of his child.

The man stayed after the other mourners had gone, watching the graveside workers roll a heavy green and white canopy around thin metal poles until it looked like a giant peppermint stick. Just like the ones he left for Santa on Alyce's first Christmas Eve. The workers moved quick now as rain fell in quarter-sized drops on top of their pinstriped shoulders. With the coffin gone, the open door of the hearse looked obscene to the man. He thought it resembled a deep gaping hole like the one the dentist left behind in his mouth once after his tooth had been pulled. Flower arrangements brought for a child who couldn't see them fell as heavy as the man's heart as he watched the workers lift armfuls of blossoms and toss them into the hearse. The man held his breath inside of his chest until that hurt, too.

The man walked to the fresh grave. He kneeled by his child. For a long time he stared at the rain hitting the soft earth above Alyce, the heavy drops plopping onto the brand new puddle and bouncing up, fountain-like. The man couldn't hold it any longer. Bursts of hysterical tears materialized on his face. Alyce Hobbs' father cried until the rain stopped and the sun pushed the clouds farther south. He cried while the sky changed from bright blue to pink, then to black. Finally the man stood. Made the sign of the cross. Then he turned and walked away from his daughter. The daughter he couldn't bear to watch die. Maybe in a week or so he'd call up Millie and try to explain.

34

"All right. All right. I'll stop."

"Michael, the room is so full of toys right now that one of us is going to break our neck just trying to walk from the front door to the couch."

"Then let's move the tree. No big deal."

"Come on, little papa, we've moved the tree twice already. Remember? There's just no room for you to outfit Jeff in a complete football uniform. The shoulder pads alone weigh more than you and me and him all put together." Barbara folded her arms. "I'll tell you what. Get him a football. One ball. That's it. No more stuff." She swung her arm wide in the direction of the presents under the pine tree that touched the eight-foot ceiling. "Do you realize how ridiculous all of this looks? There'll be nothing left to get for Jeff next year. Or when he's seven. Or twelve, or — "

"Um. Excuse me, ma'am," interrupted Michael. But did you forget that we have a little pact with each other to remember not to forget to remember that we will only plan for the immediate future." Michael emphasized the word *immediate*. "So I get the baby too many Christmas presents. So arrest me. What's the big deal? I'm having fun. And, besides, I love that kid." Michael tugged Barbara's hand and pulled her over toward an easy chair and onto his lap. With his weight gain and her loss after the baby's birth, she was twenty pounds lighter than Michael. "And I love you, too," he said. "Forever and for always. In all ways." He kissed her gently on the lips. Then, his fingertips traced the profile of her nose. "And we'll keep our promise to each other," he whispered. "We'll think only of the good we can do in our lives. For you and for me and for our little Jeffy there. And for anyone else who wants to get in on our sweet and wonderful natures."

They stood and Barbara wrapped her arms around Michael's shoulders. "You're right," she said. "Michael Sutherland, you are always right."

"Right."

They heard the stove timer ring, and Barbara ran to the kitchen. "Oh. The banana nut bread. I almost forgot."

Michael stepped to the portable crib, picked up his son and sat on the couch. The baby wriggled his arms and legs, and stared up into Michael's face. "Man to man, I love you." Michael whispered.

Barbara emerged from the kitchen carrying silverware and four cups and saucers, and placed them on a rolling table in the dining room. "Michael, the Thomas' should be here in about ten minutes, hon. Would you change Jeffy's diaper while I get things ready?"

When Michael answered the doorbell, he greeted Irene and Wayne Thomas. Tracy stood back, one arm wrapped around her mother's leg.

"Hello, Michael," said Wayne, extending his hand. "Thank you for seeing us on a Sunday afternoon. And in your home. I know it's unusual, but we felt for Tracy's sake that would be best."

"No problem, Wayne. I understand," Michael said. "Actually, I'd prefer to see all my clients in my home. It's so much less stuffy than downtown. Here, come sit. Hello, Irene." Then, Michael squatted and reached out his hand. "Hi, Tracy," he said. "Come on in. Come see the baby."

"Ma," said Tracy. It was almost a grunt. Irene Thomas followed Michael and Tracy, then stooped down on one knee next to the crib. She held Tracy around the waist and pulled the girl close to her own body. Tracy looked at her mother and frowned. She used her finger to draw a question mark in the air.

Irene guided Tracy directly in front of her, so the child could watch her mother's hands and facial expressions. It was a technique Irene was trying in an effort to teach Tracy the beginnings of sign language and lip-reading at the same time. Irene looked at Michael. "Since Tracy had already learned to speak before she lost her hearing, we're starting off with simple words that are familiar to her."

Folding her arms across her chest, Irene made a rocking motion, from side to side. "Ba-bee," she said, exaggerating her mouth movements.

Tracy watched, then repeated the motion. "Bah-bah," she said.

"Good girl," said Irene, smiling in Tracy's face. Then she stood up and stared out the window, her hands nervously fingering Tracy's ponytail. Then she blinked, and hurried to the kitchen.

"Hello, Barbara. Anything I can do to help?" she said."

By the time the sliced cakes were served, Tracy Thomas and Jeff Sutherland were good friends. Tracy sat on the large hassock next to the crib, shaking a rattle above Jeff's head, as he waved his arms and legs trying to reach for the toy. Every once in a while, Tracy pulled the rattle close to her face, shook it, and laid it against her jaw.

"Quite a team we have here, wouldn't you say?" Michael scooped up the last crumbs from his plate and dropped them into his mouth.

Irene Thomas sat at the far end of the sofa watching Tracy play with Jeff's rattle. Barbara looked from Irene to Tracy. "Irene, Michael and I will never eat all this leftover cake. Let's you and me go in the kitchen and wrap it up for you to take home later." As the women left the room, Barbara turned and spoke over her shoulder. "Wayne, ask Michael about his

Santa role this year. Especially his football ideas for our son."

"Well, what do you expect, Barb?" Michael piped. "The kid's going to be pumping iron by the time Santa arrives."

There was a brief strained silence. Then Wayne spoke. "We've been reading a new Bible lately, Mike. Called *Sign Language Made Simple*, and we're all three trying to learn the art together." He leaned forward on the couch. "Since Tracy had already learned to read, and since her vocabulary is – was – rather extensive, that at her age, learning American Sign Language and lip reading should be fairly easy for her. She's regressed a great deal in her speech, though. Pronunciation's way off because she can't hear herself talk. But I know she'll improve. I just wish my wife shared my optimism." He sighed. "All she hears is the way Tracy's words are distorted when she speaks.

Barbara and Irene returned to the living room. They both had heard the end of the Michael and Wayne's conversation. "I don't know," said Irene, sitting next to her husband. She shook her head from side to side and looked into space. "I don't think that Tracy is interested in her piano like she used to be." When she saw the confused silence from the others, she added, "I know that sounds odd to you because Tracy can't hear. But her whole life has been wrapped up in music. Now it's as if it didn't exist."

"It's still so new to her, Irene," said Barbara. "There's bound to be a way she can continue to enjoy music. I mean, I saw her holding Jeff's rattle to her face to sense vibrations. That seems encouraging."

Michael opened his palms. "Irene, Tracy is going through a rough adjustment. But you know she's a genius. I'm believing she'll find a way." Michael looked over at Tracy, who was still feeling the rattle's sounds with her jaw. "She's probably working out the formula as we speak."

"I hope you're right, Michael," said Wayne. He saw Tracy looking his way, and crooked his finger. She came and sat on his knee. Irene watched.

"I just read an article about the pianist Gary Graffman," Irene said. "We know him vaguely. He was only nineteen years old when he won the Leventritt Award for movements of Rachmaninoff and Prokofiev concertos. A great musician." Irene looked at her hands. "Just last week he was at Carnegie Hall playing Schubert's *Trout* for a full house when his fingers collapsed on the keyboard." She blew out a delicate sigh. "What a terrible thing that must have been for him. And the audience. His four string players sat right there and watched it happen."

"What was the matter?" asked Barbara.

"Papers say they don't know yet. He's supposed to have tests done to see if it's a nervous disorder. Apparently, he's had this trouble before. At practice. But never during a concert. I can't imagine it. Such a wonderful musician."

Wayne nodded. "There was a short clip in yesterday's *Times*, said there's some speculation that Graffman has the same disorder that another pianist had just before his death in the thirties. I've forgotten his name." He slid Tracy off his knee and stood up, rearranged the fabric of his trouser legs, sat back down. Then he scooped Tracy up, and sat her next to him on the couch. "Well, Michael, what do you say we get down to serious talk? The real reason for our visit today."

Barbara rose from her place on the armrest of Michael's chair. "I can take the kids across the street to the park if you want." She looked at Irene. "It's nice and sunny — "

"Please stay, Barbara," Wayne said. "I'd really like to have both of you ladies in on this. When Michael and I talked on the phone the other day, we discussed the importance of a woman's input into a situation such as this. We both agreed that your insight can be valuable

135

in deciding on strategies should we go ahead with litigation."

"Sure," said Barbara, dragging a dining room chair to sit close to Irene.

The afternoon passed in a flurry of words. Ideas, brainstorms, and dialogue meant to determine whether they had strong enough grounds to take legal action. Wayne wanted to convince Michael that not only would their daughter suffer a grave communication loss for the rest of her life, but also through the very real absence of enjoying her God-given musical gifts. They also discussed the fact that Tracy's losses were preventable, and that they were caused by the medical negligence of one man. Michael scribbled notes on a legal pad, frequently stopping to ask key questions.

When Irene took Tracy down the hall to the bathroom, Wayne watched until they were out of earshot. "I don't know if Irene is going to hold up through all of this, Mike. I mean, she's had her whole life wrapped around Tracy's musical career. And Tracy's shown so much potential. She really has." Wayne rubbed his forehead as if it hurt. "Did Irene tell you that Tracy had won the Southwest Regional Competition in her age category? Her point score was far above the runner up. And she was competing with pianists up to age twelve, more than twice her age. We already had Tracy entered in next year's nationals, knowing she'd make their list. And if she'd won there, she'd've been eligible for a scholarship to New York's legendary Manhattan Institute of Piano Arts. Tracy's bedroom is already full of ribbons and trophies. But the dream ends there, Mike." He stood up and grabbed his hair in both fists. "God, what a mess, Mike. What a friggin mess."

From his seat, Michael sat unmoving, his brain analyzing, evaluating, and sorting through possible case facts.

"Fossari's to blame for this, Michael." Wayne began pacing back and forth across the living room floor. "That bastard has maimed my little girl. He's as guilty as if he had reached into her head and pulled out her ears, Michael. And the son of a bitch is down there, right now," he pointed in the direction of the hospital, "treating other kids. Tampering with someone else's child."

When Irene and Tracy returned from the bathroom, Wayne settled into the easy chair across from Michael. Holding his head in his hands, he whispered to the carpet. "What are we going to do, Michael? What are we going to do?"

Michael nodded, then looked over at Irene and Barbara sitting close, holding each other's hands, tears streaming from their eyes. "I can answer that question once we start putting together our legal strategy," said Michael.

Irene fumbled in her purse, removed a handful of shiny colorful pamphlets, and handed them to Wayne. He held them up, their top edges fanned. "Brochures we've collected from schools for the deaf." He laid them in a stack on the coffee table. "We'll probably start out taking a course for parents of deaf children at this clinic in Los Angeles," he said, pointing to the brochure on top. "It's a correspondence course, and will at least help us become more familiar with what we're up against."

Michael nodded. He leaned to the side, reached down and opened the briefcase at his feet. He removed a thick portfolio and laid it on the coffee table. "I've done a little homework myself, Wayne. There's an excellent school in D.C. that operates a preschool, an elementary and a secondary school for children who are deaf. It's also a liberal arts college with courses leading to bachelor, masters, and even doctoral degrees."

"A liberal arts college for deaf people? I never realized," said Wayne.

137

"Gallaudet University. Been around over a hundred years. They're set up specifically to teach people who can't hear. Classes are small and the teachers, many deaf themselves, use sign language and voice to communicate. I've talked with a man on the board of directors. Went to high school with Barbara's grandfather, would you believe?"

Wayne turned to Irene, then back to Michael. "Promising," he said.

"I've requested more information from them. Plus other schools. Course catalogs, and so forth. Should be here soon. I'll give you a call."

"Okay," said Wayne. He bent forward, leaned on one elbow, looking at Michael. "Okay, Mike. We've talked. And we've beat this thing around all afternoon. I think you have most of the facts. The known facts, anyway. What do you say? Do we have a case against Fossari? Or do we not?"

Michael gathered his paperwork and organized it in his briefcase on the floor, snapped the lid shut, and stood it upright. "Wayne, I don't usually like to take malpractice cases," he said at last. "Most people respect me for that. There's so much garbage coming down the pike on these things that malpractice insurance rates are bound to continue to skyrocket. And right behind them will be the steady rise in hospital and health care costs." Michael stopped. He wanted to be absolutely sure that he would have no regrets on whatever route he took. Malpractice was a hard thing to prove. And nobody really ever won. Michael watched Tracy playing on the floor beside Jeff's crib. With one hand, she was knocking Jeff's rattle against one of the crib's wooden legs. The other hand gripped a crib rail higher up. Every once in a while, Tracy pressed her cheekbone against the rail near her hand. She seemed faraway and lost.

Michael rose to his feet in a slow, confident move, as if to dismiss his clients and call in his next appointment.

Wayne stood. Then Michael hesitated, looked over at the crib again. This time he studied his son, belly down, head to the side. Sound asleep. Bulky diaper raising his buttocks high up in the air, chubby knees tucked under him. Content. Full and warm. Dry pants. Ready to wake up to any sudden noise. Because Jeff Sutherland could hear.

Michael approached Wayne, offering his hand. "Yes, Wayne," he said. "You bet I'll take this case." The two men shook hands. Then they embraced.

35

For two weeks, Michael spent every spare moment researching Vincent Fossari's life.

Like an obsession that grew with each bit of information, Michael struggled to pull together a puzzle that was made up of scattered facts he hoped would turn into evidence, arguments in the Thomas case. Facts that started Michael on a voyage into Vincent Fossari's heritage, from Italy to America. He collected facts on Fossari's childhood, his school days, formal education, hospital residency, and medical milestones weaving through rule and control of the pediatric pulmonary department and all the people, so it seemed, who touched the lives of unsuspecting families and children who lived – and died – within a 3,000-mile radius of St. Petersburg, Florida.

On Christmas Eve, Michael developed a bad cough. Fatigue enclosed him and slowed down his progress on the case. At Barbara's insistence, they spent Christmas day alone and quiet. Just before bed on Christmas night, Michael hid in the bathroom, back flattened against the locked door. The thermometer jutting from his mouth read 102 degrees Fahrenheit. That's when he called Ross Manchester.

"I'll be right there, Mike. Just give me time to check with Emilie, see if she'll come stay with Karen."

"No Ross," said Michael, just call in an antibiotic. Barb will go pick it up. I'm upping my vitamin C intake to eight thousand milligrams, and Barb's doing an extra postural drainage. That should work. Just call in the prescription — " Michael coughed " — and I'll call you in the morning."

"I don't like it, Mike. You're working too hard. Let me come over and check you out. I'll bring the script when I come."

"No, don't come, Ross," said Michael. "I've got a million things to do on Tracy's case. Tonight I just want to go to bed. Sleep it off. Tomorrow, I'll be fine."

"Mike, you know how important it is you stay in good shape. You need to be ready for the hibernation therapy soon."

Michael grimaced. "I'll let you know, Ross. Right now, I'm facing a tight deadline to file papers with the court." Michael heard a muffled groan at the other end of the line.

"You win, this time," said Ross. "Just remember that I'm ready at a moment's notice. My lab's closed down. All the equipment and supplies are packed and ready to go. Whenever. Just don't wait too long." Then, "Oh, while I have you. One quick question: Emilie tells me you're hitting a wall on finding Karen's parents. In ten words or less, what's the story on that?"

"Not sure, Ross. Lots of red tape to wade through. And dozens of gaps on Karen's legal history."

"I hear you, Mike."

"It's funny, though — " said Michael.

"What's funny?" said Ross. "I hate to sound pushy, Mike, but I'm getting antsy. If we don't get this adoption finalized, at some point isn't there a statute of limitations staring us down? I mean, the kid is practically middle aged, and she has no legal father."

"Ross, you said you wanted her biological parents contacted no matter what. Does that still stand? There are some . . . some . . . um . . . a few legal loopholes, shortcuts I could — "

"What do you mean?"

"Well, there are some developments that are taking place, some glaring assumptions that come through the fragments of data. Turning out to be more questions to questions actually. Could be these assumptions are in our favor. Maybe not. If not, I could stretch things with legal jargon if you — "

"No short cuts, Mike. Sorry to put this pressure on you. But no negotiating with ethics. Something else, maybe. Not this time. This undertaking needs to be done right. Full agreement from her parents. No risks when it comes to Karen's future. Okay, Mike, follow the doctor's orders, and call me – any time, day or night – if your condition changes."

A fit of coughing hit Michael as he dropped the telephone receiver onto its cradle.

36

By December 31st, Michael thought he was going to die. Moving between couch and bed, every breath was an effort. After a week on antibiotics, and Barbara's postural drainage treatments on him, Michael still kept bringing up hunks of green mucus.

When his fever spiked to 103, Michael told Barbara to call Ross. As he waited, propped up in bed and shaking from chills, Michael forced his mind to think about Tracy's case. About the new pattern to the facts he'd discovered yesterday. What did the pattern mean? Think, Michael. Think. The notes. The facts are all there, Mike. All you have to do is organize the little gems in the correct order and the case is another win.

Lying in bed staring up, Michael wondered why the ceiling was turning in lopsided circles like that. As his eyes followed the circles – around and around – Michael saw the pattern he was looking for. Yes! Yes, that's it. That's the answer. Then, everything went black.

37

Ross Manchester's Buick headed north on Interstate Highway 77. He drove just above the legal speed limit, cruise control on the steering wheel set at fifty-eight.

Concentrating on the order of things that he needed to do when he arrived at the cabin in Banner Elk, North Carolina, he mentally ticked off his list. He knew that was the paramount test of his life. An ordeal that he had been preparing for, for a long time. A test of survival that could end in disaster for himself. Or the death of his friend. Where would it end? Inside the Buick, the temperature was in the low 50's as Ross wiped sweat from his eyebrows.

It wasn't just Michael who stood to gain – or lose – from the outcome of the hibernation therapy. First, there was Tracy Thomas and her parents, now struggling through their losses with little hope that their child would lead a productive life. Michael needed to be there for them at the trial.

There were the other children in the CF clinic at the hospital. The kids who occupied beds at this very moment. And the kids who'd be admitted in the days and weeks and months to come. Delivered into the hands of Vincent Fossari. How many would end up like Tracy? Or Alyce?

Then there was Barbara, thought Ross. Michael's courageous and tormented wife, who had the increasing burden and fear of watching Michael's condition plummet, then rise only to fall deeper the next time. Yes, Barbara seemed stronger than any woman he'd known, but Ross wondered how long she'd hold up under the stress she faced day after day.

And the infant, Jeff Sutherland, who showed no symptoms of inheriting the CF trait that was crippling his father. Would Jeff always be free of visible signs? Even if the boy remained healthy himself for the rest of his life, what were the odds that his developing sperm would one day pass this horrible disease to a child of his own?

And Karen. Ross' heart flipped. Karen. Asleep now and safe there with Emilie. Ross had hastily packed a few of Karen's belongings, and Emilie agreed to take Karen to stay with Barbara and Jeff until Ross delivered Michael home strong and well and in a state of permanent remission from his disease.

Remission. That's how Ross prayed for the treatment to end. If not, and the hibernation therapy had a tragic end, not only would he lose his license to practice medicine, but Fossari's power and medical clout being what it was, no doubt he'd be tried for manslaughter. Or worse.

But what were his options? Sit back and conform to society's persuasive prejudices toward those who are helpless or sick? Allow legislative mandates and mistakes that were written in smoke-filled rooms hide the tyranny in layers of smiles and handshakes, like a virus frosted over with thick, sweet chocolate? Let Michael die according to the hospital's plan? Along with the dashed hopes and dreams of children like Alyce and Tracy and Karen. And Jeff. And the parents with hopes for their kids. Other Michael's and other Barbara's. Other Irene's and Wayne's.

Futures. It's all about futures, and if this experiment with Michael fails, then none of us has a future. Even me, he thought. Part of this is for me. Because if I buckle to society's pressures, cave under professional intimidation and threats, if I watch Michael die on schedule, at the hospital's convenience, just like Alyce died . . . then I deserve to —

A raspy cough from the back seat broke into Ross' thoughts. He glanced in the rearview mirror and saw a dark silhouette as Michael sat up, hair tousled from sleep.

"Hey, man," said Michael in a hoarse voice. Keep the car on the road. Give me a chance to get there alive first before you do your number on me."

"Sorry, Mike," Ross said over his shoulder. "Been sitting in this seat a long time now. The old tush is getting numb." He shifted his weight under the seat belt and opened the window an inch. A sliver of cool air rushed past his ear.

"Time for a pit-stop. For both of us. What say?" said Michael. "Anything up ahead?

Deep in his thoughts, Ross hadn't paid much attention to the signs along the road. He thought there'd been something a while back – near an overpass? – about crossing the state line. But that seemed like a long time ago. Hours, maybe. Just then, his headlights flashed on a green and white road sign affixed to a bridge railing. *Highway 901 – six miles.*

"Should be coming to an exit soon, Mike. Can you hold out another few miles?"

"Sure, Ross. In the meantime, I'll be praying for our safe arrival, if you don't mind." Michael settled back on the pillow propped against the back window. The emergency flushing Ross had performed yesterday had opened some airflow, and with it oxygen. Just as it had after the procedure he and Kevin had in the hospital. Other than exhaustion and trauma to his throat, he felt okay.

After Michael had passed out yesterday, Ross examined him and told Barbara of Michael's critical state. If he didn't have an emergency bronchial lavage, then and there, he would not make it through the night. So, with Barbara's help, Ross set up a makeshift OR where Michael lay unconscious. Since Michael was already out cold, but with his cough reflex still intact, it was not necessary to anesthetize him. In order to decrease Michael's fever, and rid his lungs of the progressively thickening secretions, Ross had to remove the germ-laden mucus that was blocking Michael's breath and pushing his fever up. Ross told Barbara there was a risk of postoperative lung obstruction after bronchial lavage. Often after the lung-flushing takes place, around the second or third day after the procedure, the body overcompensates and begins reproducing mucus secretions at a rapid rate. It was a calculated chance Ross thought both Michael and Kevin had overcome. However, in Michael's case, Ross explained, what had happened was the post-op reaction was delayed.

He had watched for it in both Michael and Kevin, and when neither of them showed signs of this adverse effect, they were sent home with instructions to call him at the first indication of trouble. In Michael's case, the secretions began to build up after three weeks, not three days as expected. To add to the complications, because Michael had been working so hard, he had neglected to watch for the symptoms of deterioration, and the bacteria reproduced on the sticky mucus lining inside his chest before Michael realized. That's why Michael took so long to call, and caused his swift decline, shortness of breath, fatigue and high fever.

Yesterday, in the crude operating room, when Ross had inserted the double lumen fiberoptic bronchoscope down Michael's throat, Michael didn't react or flinch. So Ross continued pushing the scope deep into Michael's lungs, then forced a saline solution, mixed with bronchodilator and mucolytic agents. The effort soon paid off. Deep within Michael's ribcage, the stubborn mucus began to bubble, causing his intercostal muscles to contract, in a diaphragmatic cough that sent globs of venomous glue out of Michael's nose and mouth. Onto the bed linens. The walls. The floor. Stepping back out of the way, Ross saw Barbara's panic-stricken face.

"Quick, Barb, go get a dishpan of warm water from the kitchen," he'd said to get her out of the room. Unable to monitor Michael's cardiac changes, Ross knew that he'd have to discontinue the procedure earlier than usual. He had removed only enough mucus to give Michael breathing space in his lungs, and to halt some bacterial growth. The procedure would have to be repeated anyway if Michael agreed to go through with the hibernation therapy.

Barbara had come back with the water basin just as Ross slid the rubber tube from Michael's mouth, its end curling when Ross threw it on top of the scattered newspapers on the floor. As if on cue, Barbara wrung out the facecloth, leaned over her husband, and began wiping his face.

That's when Michael woke up yesterday. His belly was sore, and his throat felt like a balloon on fire, but in the deep brown infinity of Barbara's eyes as they caressed his soul, Michael sensed nothing but comfort and love. When he could talk again, Barbara convinced Michael to go to the mountains with Ross. To give the hibernation treatment a chance.

Ross hit the blinker switch on the steering wheel and eased the car into the exit lane veering left onto Highway 421. The first open station was a Kwik Mart just east of Wilkesboro, North Carolina. Ross had driven straight through from St. Petersburg, stopping only for gas during the last 14 hours. His back felt like an army tank had rolled over it, and the cramp in his right thigh sent shooting pains down into his foot.

"Headin' up the mountain, are ya?" The man behind the counter took Ross' money for the gas, two refrigerator-stale tuna sandwiches, and a quart of orange juice. Ross had what Karen called sleepwalker brain. He joggled his head.

"Yes," he said, hugging the brown paper bag to his chest. "But I can't seem to get the radio to pick up a station. Any idea what the roads are like between here and Boone?"

"Ain't no wonder," said the man, showing a missing tooth. "Only got A.M. radio station up thar. One in Boone. One in Blowing Rock. WOIX's yer best bet. But only soon's you clear the Piedmont, though."

"Has it snowed in the last few days?" asked Ross. He'd experienced a snowstorm the winter he first bought the property, and respected the black ice that spun 18-wheelers off the edge of the steep cliffs that appeared too late around the narrow mountain curves. That's why tonight he planned to take Highway 105 to 194 into Banner Elk, instead of the convoluted hills.

"Yep. Had a little weather. Mebe last week. Reckon five inches. Roads been plowed, though. Shun' be no trouble. Less'n mebe yer drivin' wun'a 'em Zuki's." The man guffawed as Ross stepped through the glass door waving a hand in the air.

Inside the car, Michael lay sprawled, snoring in the back seat, pillow propped between his shoulder and cheek. Ross rubbed his hands together, removed the orange juice from the bag, took a swig, and then placed the carton next to him on the seat. Fifty miles left to go.

38

Like the other three houses dotting the two-mile steep mountain section of Avery County, Ross Manchester's cabin had been built just after the turn of the century by proud mountain farmers whose only income was the tobacco leaves they sold in the fall. But the crop growers were long gone. The last inhabitant was an old man who'd found the house vacant, then froze to death in it during a late March storm.

Ross had found the five-acre property at a reasonable price when the estate went up for auction. During the first summer he'd had the place either repainted, repaired or replaced. Inside and out. He had converted the old outhouse into a supply shed that became Karen's personal project, a coat of lemon-colored enamel the backdrop for cartoon sunflowers and insects drawn on all four sides. Farther away, sat a run-down barn with a doorless opening, in which generations ago someone had parked a farm wagon, then walked away, leaving the weathered wood to tilt in the direction of a missing wheel.

The cabin itself was large, an almost perfect rectangle, with step-up porch running the long width of the house in front, holding a wooden swing and a rebuilt antique rocker. Inside the front door sat a square wooden eating table that the last farmer had built the summer before he died. He had used old barnwood slats that matched the gray timber benches attached to the wall by thick pegs.

A pot-bellied stove dominated the far side of the room, and faced a second-hand daybed Ross picked up from a thrift shop in Crossnore to benefit foster children. In the kitchen was a long counter, a sink, a Coldspot refrigerator with a humidrawer food crisper, and the original cast iron cook stove that Ross had repainted.   Beyond the kitchen, a narrow hallway divided the shower bath from a combination linen closet and six-drawer dresser built into the wall.   Farther down the hallway, a door opened to the cabin's only bedroom, which occupied the entire side of the house. It was furnished with twin beds, two nightstands, a dresser, bureau of drawers, and a chair.

As Ross unpacked his medical supply box, he checked each item for any travel damage, arranged individual equipment on an open shelf, then crossed through his list, one by one. Portable cardiac monitor, microscope, two large wall thermometers, disposable and reusable syringes, needles, electric sterilizer, bronchial lavage kit, bandages, tape, sutures and miscellaneous surgical supplies. There was a separate document box containing six folders with Michael's recent hospital records, including nurses notes, doctors' orders, X-rays, lab reports, cardiograms, and other assorted graphs and charts, previous hospital admissions in chronological order, and a four-inch thick binder labeled *Artificial Inducement of Realistic Winter Torpor Using Hibernation Induction Trigger (HIT) in Hoary Marmots Born with Symptoms Indicating Metabolic Cystic Fibrosis*, from Ross' current and previous research, along with massive notes on how to replicate the hibernation state in humans by temporarily converting a warm-blooded animal to a cold-blooded one using a similar reversible metabolic hibernation procedure.

Ross opened a thick Styrofoam carton. Referring to the *Drugs and Interactions Form* attached to the inside of the lid, he moved items around the carton and matched their labels with the form. Then, one by one, Ross placed each item in the top drawer of the wood dresser across from the bed. Multi-dose vials of digitalis to slow Michael's heart rate and bring on and maintain dormancy within his body during the torpid state. Dehydration-inducing diuretic medication: fact-acting Furosemide, potassium to prevent electrolyte imbalances; and slower, maintenance dosages of the less dangerous Aldactone diuretic. Antibiotics to kill off any stubborn microorganisms inside Michael's respiratory system, if there were any that could withstand the cold environment of his body. An indwelling Foley catheter, and a spare, to control the small amounts of dilute urine output from Michael's bladder. Two rectal thermometers to monitor Michael's body temperature. Hyperalimentation supplies for nutritional intake. Pancreatic enzymes, vitamins, saline.

While Michael rested in bed, Ross made three trips to the car to carry in the remaining boxes, two suitcases, and the I.V. pole.

"Damn, that metal's cold," Ross said, as the T-attachment from the I.V. stand tumbled to the floor in the bedroom. "I need to rig up a better lighting system for this room, too. Also, warm up a place so your medications don't freeze."

"Medicines, hell," said Michael. "What about me? I know your wicked plans include unplugging this toasty electric blanket."

"Enjoy it while you can," Ross said. "At 4 a.m., we start cooling things down." He glanced at the thermometer he'd nailed to the wall above Michael's bed. "It's 52 degrees in here now." He ambled to the bedroom door, pulled it shut, and sat down on the vacant bed. "I'll watch the temperature in here until it gets to 43 degrees. We'll hold it there before we turn in for the night. In the meantime, stay comfy under that blanket for a while. I'll describe each step in the morning before we get started."

Michael looked at Ross. "Do we really have to go through this, Ross?" he said. "God, my insides are shaking from the cold already. I'm a Florida-weather kind of guy. You know? Anything under 85 degrees, I'm cold. Look at it out there," he said pointing to the cold, gray shadows beyond the glass window.

"Up to you, Mike," said Ross. "I know this has got to be hard for you, and if you really want to give it up, just say the word." He saw Michael scrub his face with two hands. "To be honest with you, old pal," said Ross, "I doubt if I'd've had the wherewithal to go through what you have already." He shook his head. "You're really one tough guy."

"Ho, no, you don't," said Michael. "You're not pouring all that emotional stuff on this manly man," poking a thumb at his chest. "Seriously, Ross, it's beyond tempting for me to want to make a mad dash for the car, and demand you return me to my warm home in the south. To go home to Barbara and Jeff and my work. Disease free. But the reality is that ain't never gonna happen. Not unless and until we fight this thing with our bare hands. You and me. Now. Here in this place. Only then can I move on with my life. I believe in you, Ross. And everything you stand for. That's why I'm putting my life in your hands. Besides, I won't know I'm cold when I'm hibernating, will I?"

"No, Mike. Once this procedure has officially begun, the only ones suffering'll be Barbara and me."

Michael kicked off his shoes, wrapped the blanket closer to his body, and curled up on his side like a child. "Tell me what's going to happen, Ross," he said.

39

Vincent Fossari inserted the plastic credit card between the frame and the lock, pushed, and opened the door. He stepped inside the dark garage and waited for the gray outlines of objects to appear.

There was a strong chemical smell in the room and he stifled a cough. Removing a penlight from his chest pocket, he shined it in front of his feet, and followed the beam as it moved up, exposing a laboratory table with an array of utensils on top. Standing in front of the table, Fossari ran his hand along the surface until he touched the corner of a bulk of papers in a stack. He focused the light on the cover. The blue carbon ink was smeared, and there were brown stains bleeding through the top pages. But he could still read the words. *The Analytical Study of the Effects of Hibernation in Warm-Blooded Animals with Cystic-Fibrotic-Like Symptoms, and the Implications of Remission Control of the Disease in Humans, by R. Manchester, M.D.*

Propping the penlight on a pile of books nearby, Fossari leafed through the pages of the report, nodding his head and sensing the familiar neural joy run through his body. He pointed the light in a slow circle, moving it around the room. At the door to the house, he saw a note taped to the wood.

Mrs. Jordan,
Thanks for coming on such short notice. I expect to return in about a week. Not much for you to do, just the leftover laundry and a dusting or two. I'll see you when I return from the cabin.
Regards, Dr. M

Already Vincent Fossari's plan was taking shape. He turned and shuffled back to the side garage door, locked the knob, stepped out, and slammed the door. If there had been more lights in the yard, and if Dorothy Cassel had been standing at her second-floor bedroom window with the blinds bent just enough to peek, like she stood not two hours earlier, she would have spotted the thick man in horn-rimmed eyeglasses as he closed the door to her neighbor's garage, then move along in hurried steps to a womb-red Mark V Lincoln Continental parked two blocks down under the street lamp that burned out yesterday, darkening the corner, so that even if someone stood right there leaning on the cast iron post they wouldn't be seen. But no one was around for miles anyway, and the only movement came from a seagull that had drifted in from the beach and stood vigil on top of the luminaire post.

Two hours later Vincent Fossari turned right onto Highway 693 on his way to Banner Elk. In the back seat of his Continental was a pile of sweatshirts, his London Fog slicker and a pair of rubber wading boots. Inside the trunk, a gray wool blanket was neatly wrapped around an 11-inch steel cook's knife and a long-handled axe.

40

"You want ketchup on your scrambled eggs?" Ross shouted from outside the bedroom door. Michael's muffled answer sounded like a yes to Ross, so he turned the glass bottle upside down and gave it a hard whap with the palm of his hand.

Pushing the door open with his foot, Ross laid the tray of food on top of the nightstand next to Michael's bed. "Sorry about the plastic fork," said Ross. "Not much in the way of luxury at this hotel."

The two men ate in silence. Then Ross stacked the dishes and slid the tray onto the high dresser. "Okay, time to get serious again, Mike. Here's the plan." Ross sat sideways on the bed opposite Michael, arranging his notes on his lap.

Michael relaxed into his pillow, hands under his head.

"First, I'll do a light lung-flush to remove more of the remaining secretions. Then, through an I.V. line, I'll start the antibiotics. At the same time, to prevent future growth, the room air will be reduced and maintained at a very low temperature, low 40's, to make it difficult for microorganisms to survive. It should give your body a chance to replace the diseased lung tissue with a healthier environment, and start a network of growth present normally in people without cystic fibrosis.

"Next, as your metabolism slows in the cold room air, your insulin secretions, and the rest of your digestive system, should start to regulate themselves and compensate for the malfunctioning mess going on in your gastrointestinal tract. You've got just enough egg juice in there right now to stabilize things in that department. In a sense, Michael, this initial therapy is like going to square one on the health meter. Hopefully, for a more normalized digestive and respiratory system at that point."

"Hopefully," Michael said. He was getting sleepy, and didn't realize his eye lids had been closed for a while.

Ross watched Michael for a moment. When he heard soft snoring sounds, Ross set a low-noise alarm for five-thirty in the morning, and muffled the ticking under his pillow. He removed his shoes and slipped them under the bed. As he pulled on his wool robe, Ross watched Michael's labored breathing. Then he crawled under a thick pile of covers, and turned out the light. Within three minutes, he was asleep, too.

41

Barbara sat up in bed nursing Jeff. She hadn't slept all night, and when her infant was full and content, she settled him close to her side. Still she couldn't sleep. Her mind was far up in a cold mountain cabin, a place she had never seen, a place that would decide Michael's future, and Jeff's, and hers. A shiver ran through her body as she lay flat on her back staring into the dark. Then she heard a child cry from another part of the house, and remembered that Karen and Emilie were sleeping on the sofabed in the living room.

"Mama," Karen wailed for the third time.

"Wake up, Karen," whispered Emilie. "Sweetheart, you're having a dream."

"No, mama. I'm not dreaming," Karen said, eyes still closed. "I see you next to me." Then she rolled onto her side and laid an arm across Emilie's waist, burying her face in the woman's neck. Emilie stroked the child's hair until she felt Karen's steady breaths against her skin. So precious. Ross is lucky to have this child to love. Then Emilie eased her head back to look at Karen's face. And she's lucky to have him, too. As Emilie drifted off to sleep, she pictured Ross in the tiny cabin, alone with Michael, trying to save the man's life. Alone. Could he do it alone? All by himself?

At 7:30 Wednesday morning, Barbara's kitchen hummed with activity. Karen was dumping spoonfuls of sugar on top of Frosted Flakes that had been piled to the top and flooded with milk.

"Know why they call those flakes frosted?" Emilie said.

"Yep. 'Cause the sugar's already on top." Karen dipped her spoon into the bowl and turned it in circles.

"Would you rather have eggs and toast?" Barbara carried the percolator to the table. Then she sat down next to Karen. "You really should eat something, honey," Barbara said. "You've already taken your enzymes, and they need some food to work on." The toaster popped. Barbara laid the bread on a plate, spread butter and jam across each slice, and pushed the plate toward Karen.

"Who's gonna do my treatments while Daddy's gone?" Karen asked. She poked two fingers into the jam, then into her mouth.

"Guess I'm in charge of that." Barbara smiled at Karen. "Since your Dad's looking out for my guy, the least I can do is look out for your Dad's girl.

Karen shrugged one shoulder, then glanced at Emilie.

"Sounds about right to me," Emilie winked at Karen. "Well, look at that, will you. Karen, you've got Barb, and Michael's got Ross. Sounds about right, don't'ja think?"

"Right," said Karen. "And Jeffy's got Barbara, and Barbara's got me."

"Thanks, kiddo." Emile gave Karen's shoulder a soft punch. "You just helped me make the point I was getting around to."

"Which is?" said Karen.

"Which is: who's looking out for your Dad?"

Barbara frowned. "Huh?"

Karen blinked. "Daddy doesn't need anybody to look out for him. He's the biggest man I know. And the smartest, too." Karen stopped. An image appeared in her mind. Two policemen leading her father out the door and into a car that had bright lights flashing in his face. "Yeah, well, maybe you're right Emilie. Maybe Daddy does need somebody sometimes." She stared at her plate of toast. "I wonder if he's okay up there in the mountains. It's really dark outside at night."

The previous night, Emilie explained to Karen that for the next week her father would be treating Michael at the cabin. That Michael would be unconscious most of the time.

"How's Daddy gonna see what he's doing?" Karen said.

"I saw him pack a box with extra lights, Karen."

"Okay, Em," Barbara piped. "You're up to something. Let's hear it."

Emilie laced long fingers around the base of her cup. What *was* she up to? She'd had her own bad dreams last night. "I don't know, Barb," she said. "I'm not really sure what it is, but I've got this nagging feeling that Ross shouldn't be up there alone with Michael." She looked deep into her cup, swirling it in the air. "When you stop and think about this whole thing, it's not quite right somehow."

"What do you mean?" said Barbara.

"Well, backup. Ross has no backup. No help. I mean, he's always so organized and on top of things. Ordinarily. But with everything happening so fast. Michael's crisis and the urgency to make so many decisions, then having to pack up and leave in a hurry like that." Emilie shook her head. "It just doesn't feel right to me."

Barbara watched Emilie. "Ross has done this alone in an emergency before. But, I see what you mean."

"I realize that Ross is an extremely capable man," Emilie said. "He's the best when it comes to medical skills, dedication, endurance. No question about that. Heaven knows, if anyone can send Michael's disease into remission, permanently, or otherwise, it's Ross Manchester. And, I also recognize that the whole experim . . . procedure must be kept secret. At least till it's over. But, my God, Barbara, the man is miles from anywhere. With no phone." Her voice went up an octave. "And we can only assume that the electrical wires didn't freeze last week, or whatever it is that happens to electrical wires when it snows. And the car. What about that? The Buick, right?"

Barbara nodded.

"He needs a four-wheel drive. Front wheel, at least. Mountain roads. Ice." Emilie's words were coming faster. "How do we know if they even made it up there safely? We don't." She stood, walked across the kitchen and leaned against the sink. "The more I think about it, the more it makes sense. I need to — "

"What?" said Barbara. "What do you want to do, Em?"

"We need to get someone up there with him. He's only one person. Even the best doctor on the planet needs help sometimes."

"My Daddy *is* the best doctor on the planet," said Karen.

"That's right, Karen. He is." Emilie returned to the table, sat down, and stroked Karen's hand.

"Daddy says it's hard to take care of a patient alone."

Barbara frowned. "We're the only ones who know where they are, Em. What they're doing. I don't think Ross trusts anyone. He wouldn't want us to send — "

"Oh, God, no. I don't mean tell anyone."

"Then what do you — ?"

"I mean I need to go there. Now. Today. This morning. Yes, I should go to Ross." Emilie stood.

"Daddy'd like that, I bet. I can stay and babysit Jeff. Then Jeff and Barbara and me, we'll all have each other." Karen said. "And Daddy will have you. He'd like that."

Emilie searched Karen's face. Then she looked at Barbara.

Barbara moved to Emile and put both hands on the taller woman's shoulders. "Go," she said. "It feels right to me, too."

By late afternoon, as the baggage handler threw Emilie's Samsonite duffel onto the conveyor belt, Emilie studied the overhead monitor at Tampa International, and Vincent Fossari had long ago driven past the entrance road to Charlotte Douglas Airport where Emilie would deplane after a one-layover stop in Atlanta.

42

Michael hardly felt it when Ross palpated for a vein in his right hand. His fingers were limp at his side, and when Ross slid the needlepoint into his unflinching skin, Michael opened his eyes.

"Thought you might wake up, counselor."

"Good thinking, my man." Michael shifted, tried to sit up.

Ross reached out and pressed his shoulder. "Hold still a minute, will you. Old buddy, old pal."

Michael flopped back on the mattress. "Should I be awake?" he said.

Ross taped the I.V. line onto Michael's wrist, and then stood up to adjust the drip rate of the fluid as it moved through the tube. "After I get this thing going and the meds in it, you'll make night-night for a few days."

"Okay to move now?" Michael said. Ross nodded silently. He sorted through various ampule solutions and began filling syringes. Michael rolled to his side and studied Ross' skilled hands, large fingers grasping the tiny glass bottle and snapping off the tip with his thumb, then tilting the open end of the bottle at just the right angle to insert the beveled needle without spilling a drop. A gifted artist, brushstrokes quick, easy and sure.

"The timing of these meds is critical," Ross said pulling back on the plunger and drawing fluid into the barrel. He raised the syringe vertical and flicked it twice with his middle finger, and expelled an air bubble from the needlepoint. Then he placed a plastic cap over the end of the needle.

Ross opened a pill bottle, dropped one yellow tablet into a miniature paper cup with pleats around the side, and handed it to Michael, along with a glass of water. "Take this Mike." He reached to the control knob on the electric blanket. "I'll turn this down a notch for now. Then when that Valium hits home, we'll start getting serious about dropping your temperature."

"I'm quite comfortable with it as is, if you don't mind, my good man," razzed Michael.

"Just relax, Mike. Go with it. I'll be right beside you every minute." Ross patted Michael's arm. "In a few minutes I'll begin the I.V. digitalis to lower your heart rate and start to slow down your metabolism. After you're in the full torpid state, I'll insert the Foley, then start the diuretic to speed up dehydration," said Ross. "Try to keep up a little chatter with me so I can evaluate your initial responses, okay? Just until you go under."

"Okay." Michael had been through this before, and understood the routine. As he started to feel drowsy, he could only respond with a slight nod or head roll. Soon his hearing started to fade. By ten o'clock that morning, Michael was completely out.

43

Night flurries added an inch and a half of snow to last week's layer outside the cabin. Inside, Ross kept close watch over his sick patient who had vanished into a dormant state.

The cardiac monitor ticked off his vital signs, while an indwelling catheter dripped urine through tubing into a rubber bag hitched to the foot of Michael's bed. Ross performed his labors with proficiency, documenting procedures and progress, and recording dosage, time, routes and frequency of each medication he gave Michael, along with observable reactions.

Forms checklist:
Furosemide, digoxin, antibiotics, ascorbic acid, HIT, O₂.

Column checkoff:
Enteral. Parenteral. Topical. Intranasal. Epicu.
Infu. SubQ. Inhal. I.V. I.M. P.O.

Vital signs Q15minutes:
BP. P. R. Temp.

By 9:30 in the evening, when Ross recorded Michael's temperature, his body was sixty-seven degrees Fahrenheit. Great, thought Ross, unwrapping a sandwich and settling in the chair beside Michael.

At the same moment that Ross took the first bite of his tuna on rye, Emilie Creighton was locking the seat belt across her hips in coach class, as the Boeing 747 lifted off on its way to Atlanta. And the man at the Longvue Motel on Blowing Rock Road, Boone, North Carolina, was signing the guest register as Vincent Fossari.

44

Ross finished flushing Michael's lungs for the second time in three days, hoping it would be the last time – or never again – that Michael needed bronchial lavage.

Folding the clear plastic sheet around residual mucus splatterings and rolling it into a ball, Ross placed the bundle inside a plastic garbage bag labeled CONTAMINATED. Now he could focus on the next phase. First, put Michael into a deeper state of torpidity, reduce his oxygen need, further depress his metabolism, and slow his cellular activity to a near standstill. Until Michael was in full-blown hibernation.

He removed the electrodes connected to the cardiac monitor, coiled the wires and stored the machine close to the bed. A thorough check of Michael's vitals – blood pressure, pulse, respiratory rate, and body temperature – told Ross that all was going well. Michael's systolic blood pressure reading of 60 over 40 diastolic gave indication the pressure was on its way down to the expected low of 50 over 30. At that point, Michael's oxygen consumption should remain approximately half the normal amount.

Already the room air had dropped, and Ross was beginning to see his own breath vaporizing in front of his face. Now for the first test. Ross knew that with the decreased moisture in Michael's lungs, plus his internal temperature plunge, there should be no vapor visible as Michael exhaled, as it did with the warm, moist air from his own lungs. Ross glanced at the wall thermometer: the room air was 39°F. Then he watched the slow rise and fall of Michael's chest. No vapor. Michael's internal temperature was the same as the room. Yes! Michael had moved into the hibernation phase.

Outside, the snow flurries increased. Large flakes began falling in a steady rhythm, dancing in zig-zag motions in mid-air, and then were blown to the ground. When a loose cluster of snow and wind jarred the glass pane above the head of Michael's bed, Ross shivered under his heavy sweater. He opened the bottom drawer of the dresser, removed a small radio and fiddled with the dials. "Should have done this a long time ago," he mumbled. Through loud static, Ross heard Olivia Newton-John sing. Then a man's voice sputtered incoherently behind a fireworks of crackles and pops.

". . . *wind-chill . . . below zero . . . Asheville northward . . . tonight and tomor . . . mountains . . . ten degrees lower . . .*" Ross adjusted the volume, hoping the updates would soon come through clear.

Ross gave Michael a complete head-to-toe exam. Vitals were good. The bedroom wall thermometer read 38 degrees. Time to assess the conditions outside, he thought, slipping on a pair of woolen gloves. Ross left the bedroom door ajar, and jogged through the living room, opened the front door, and stepped onto the porch. A blast of snow whipped under the porch eave and smacked him in the face. Above the storm's roar, he heard the old swing bang against the porch rail, its chains frail as kite strings bending in the wind. Ross spotted the thermometer. It was thick with rust, but the glass bulb was still clear, and Ross saw that the red line stopped at minus 9 degrees. He moved back inside the cabin. Dropping his gloves, Ross stood by the woodstove's warmth, rubbed his palms back and forth, then returned to the bedroom. Michael's rectal temperature read 64 degrees.

Ross pulled the space heater closer to the bed and set it to low. Then he discontinued the piggyback flow of medications in Michael's I.V., leaving the slow, steady drip of dextrose five percent. Now, the hibernation effect should continue on its own, with the help of routine antibiotics and vitamin therapy. Before the 15-minute vital sign check was due, Ross dashed into the kitchen to perk a new pot of coffee.

45

Vincent Fossari pulled his car to the side of the road, stopped and turned off the engine. He used his shoulder to push open the car door against the powerful wind. Bursts of snow and sleet bit at his face.

He stumbled as he walked toward the rear of the car. With every step, he felt the deep snow suck at the bottoms of his wading boots, and by the time he reached the trunk, his feet ached from the brilliant cold that attached itself to his feet through two layers of socks.

His thermal gloves were soaked as he pulled open the trunk lid. He reached in and removed the blanket, shaking out the knife and the axe. Then he used the sharp point of the knife to rip the blanket fabric lengthwise, tearing it into a six-inch strip, which he wound around his neck and ears. Then Fossari placed the knife and the axe inside the toolbox, set the toolbox on the ground, and closed the trunk lid.

Hefting the toolbox, Fossari trudged into the blizzard, leaving behind what looked like just one more unidentified vehicle stalled along Highway 194 in Banner Elk, North Carolina.

46

Emilie stood at the car rental booth across from a tall man in his late twenties, whose teeth and pockmarked complexion were both an off shade of green.

"Look lady," he said, "I'm not gonna argue with you all night. Like the sign says." He pointed to a hand-written sign taped to the counter. "There are no cars available right now." He folded his hands on top of the counter. "Come back in the morning when the holiday rentals are back. I'm sure we'll have something for you then."

I should be long gone from this place by tomorrow morning, she thought. It was after midnight already, and she had wasted forty-five precious minutes here at Douglas Airport trying to lease a car. She was tired and her stomach was burning acid. The last three rental agencies had told her the same thing. No cars.

Emilie reached near her feet and gripped her duffel bag. Then she flung the long strap over her shoulder and raced to the last booth at the far end of the terminal. A young girl stood alone in the corner of a cubicle, back to Emilie, tearing perforated paper from a computer track. As Emile stepped up to the booth and dropped her heavy bag, she had an idea.

"Oh, dear me," Emilie said. The girl looked up, dropped the paper, and moved to the counter. "Young lady, you have got to help me. I just came in on the plane and I have to drive all night long to see my parents," she said. "My father sent me a telegram this afternoon." Emilie covered her face with the palms of her hands and shook her head from side to side. Then she looked into the girl's eyes. "I have got to go up the mountain tonight. My mother is slipping fast, and if I don't hurry, it'll be too late. I'll never see her alive again." Emilie reached across the counter and patted the girl's hand. "Your mother's probably well, so you don't know what it's like. Oh, but it's not your fault. I know that. How could anyone blame you, you poor dear sweet thing."

The girl blinked back tears. "What can I do?" she said.

"I need a car."

"I'm so sorry," said the girl. "They're all out."

"They can't be all out. Don't you have even one stashed somewhere with a . . . a broken headlight? Or something? I'll take anything."

"They only deliver them to our lot after they're inspected," said the girl. "There's nothing out back right now. I just came on a little while ago and the lot was empty." The girl wrinkled her brow. "Well, except for the transport vehicle. But that's not a rental."

"The what?"

"The transport vehicle," said the girl. "We only drive it around the lot out back. To get from one flight to the next if we need to. The employees are the only ones who drive it."

"Good. Let me have it," said Emilie.

"I can't do that."

"Yes you can." Emilie reached into her pocket, removed a fifty-dollar bill. She folded it in half and slid it across the counter." The girl's eyes opened wide.

"Oh, I'd get in trouble for that," she said. "I just started working here, and the boss, he's a nice guy and all, but, I don't think he'd — "

"Think of it as a tip." Emilie laid another fifty in front of the girl. "They let you accept tips, don't they?"

"Well, yes, but — " The girl stared at the money. She'd been making minimum wage at the car rental, and certainly nobody ever tipped. And just last week she'd promised her landlord at the walkup apartment where she lived with three other students – some part-timers like her – that next month would be different, that she would pay the rent on time, definitely next month, but that this month she didn't quite have all of it just now. There was no money left in her checking account, and could he wait please one more week, and she really hated sneaking around trying to avoid the guy.

"It's a Toyota Land Cruiser," the girl said, snatching the bills. "Looks like a jeep. Three years old. Red. Tires may be worn. And if it's not back in two days, it's my neck." She motioned with her finger across her throat.

Emilie filled out the forms and paid for two days rental. "You go out that door. Lot C is on the right," the girl handed Emilie the keys. "God, I must be crazy," she said. But Emilie was already gone.

47

On any other day, the distance from Highway 194 to Ross Manchester's cabin – a stretch of no more than 700 yards – could be crossed on foot at an unhurried pace in ten minutes or less. On this night, however, Vincent Fossari faced unusual difficulties as he struggled to hold onto the toolbox, keep his body upright as he walked into the storm, and avoid frostbite on the tips of his ears.

A while back, his makeshift scarf had blown off. A few yards later, he'd fallen into a ditch and nearly lost his eyeglasses under the snow. Every few steps he took sunk his feet, filling his boots with snow.

Then he saw it. Lights from the cabin windows flickered erratically through the wind. Then he came to the Buick, its long body a thick layer of white. As he approached the car, Fossari dropped to his knees, throwing the toolbox and spilling the contents on the ground. Digging with both hands, he recovered the knife and gripped it in his numb fists. As he stabbed at the car's back tire, the point of the blade twisted against the icy rubber, flipped, and sunk deep into the glove on Fossari's left hand. He dropped the knife, and stared at his blood spurting onto the snow. Then he grabbed the axe with both hands, held it high over his head, and brought it down close to the rim of the tire. Forty pounds of pressure gushed into Fossari's face.

Breathing in gasps, Fossari rose from his knees and leaned heavily on the trunk of the Buick. His eyes searched around the outside of the cabin. He saw the electrical meter box attached to a pole near the back wall. He picked up the axe and headed in the direction of the pole.

Inside the house, Ross Manchester concentrated on the progress of his patient. At the moment Vincent Fossari was trudging toward the meter pole, Ross began irrigating Michael's Foley catheter bag. When Fossari removed the glove on his right hand to better grip the axe handle, Ross Manchester was unfolding the blood pressure cuff. And when the axe blade came down on the glass case of the General Electric unit installed six years ago by the New River Light and Power Corporation, sending hot sparks onto the snow and closing down 82,279 kilowatt hours of electrical power, Ross Manchester had just stuffed the rubber tips of his stethoscope deep into his ears, and all he could hear was the fwoof, fwoof, fwoof sound of air being pumped into the stiff belt wrapped around Michael Sutherland's bone-thin arm.

48

"Oh no . . . damn." Emilie held her breath as she braked, sending the rear wheels of the Land Cruiser sliding on the packed snow, and spinning her in a 180-degree turn in the middle of the road. Thankfully, there were no other vehicles close by.

Emilie put the jeep in reverse, backed it up, and steered hard onto Highway 421 on her way to Wilkesboro. Through snow flurries, she saw dim lights coming from a Holiday Inn sign. She drove into the lot and eased the jeep under the sheltered entryway. Then she peeled her aching hands off the steering wheel and shut off the engine. The temperature inside the cab dropped immediately, and cold air from the vents settled over Emilie's legs. There were two cars parked in the front of the building, and from where she sat just outside the front doors, she saw no one in the lobby. She got out of the car and entered the building.

"Hello?" she said, approaching the front desk.

"Well, hi." A woman about Emilie's age and height emerged from a back office. "Didn't expect anyone to be traveling this time of night," she said.

"I'm not sure exactly what I need most," said Emilie, smiling at the woman." A dry road, something hot to drink, or a good night's rest."

The woman laughed. "Pretty bad out there, huh? Guess that blizzard up the mountain is heading this way." When Emilie winced, the woman said. "Hey, you look bushed. How about joining me for coffee? This place is dead tonight, and if the weather turns out as bad as they predict, my replacement won't be able to get through. I'll probably have to do a double shift. At least till they clear the roads in the morning."

"Thanks," said Emilie. "Coffee sounds good."

"I'm Carolyn," said the woman. "And you are — ?"

"Oh, sorry. Emilie," she said.

Emilie and Carolyn sat at a table sipping coffee and watching snow fall on the other side of the picture window. "Lots worse than it was an hour ago," said Carolyn. "That road will be closed soon, that's for sure. By the way, which direction are you heading?"

"Up the mountain. Banner Elk," said Emilie.

"Oh, wow. I wouldn't if I were you. Not tonight. In fact, I wouldn't even try to make it up to Boone."

"I've got to."

"Not that bad you don't. It won't do whoever's waiting for you any good if you slide off down the side of the mountain. Likely no one'd even know it till the snow thaws. They always find people in the spring."

Big help she'd be to Ross and Michael if she got herself killed. "When do you think it'll be safe?" she said.

Carolyn stared out at the night, as if she were calculating the odds. And based on the four winters she'd seen, that's exactly what she was doing. "I'd say if you stayed till morning — got a good rest so your reflexes were sharp — and then called around to find a service station or hardware that's open. Pick up some tire chains." She paused, thinking. "Best bet's a service station," she said. "They'll install the chains for you. Probably no charge. Then you might make it in to Boone, around, say, noon, one o'clock tomorrow afternoon." She shook her head. "Now, mind you, I wouldn't do it. But whatever you're heading for sounds important."

"It is," said Emilie.

"By the time you get to Boone, you'll want to wait there for a spell. By then you'll need a break anyway. Road between here and Boone is steep and winding."

"If I'd known that before, I'd've taken another route," said Emilie. "I thought coming this way, I'd miss road problems. Ha!"

"Going up the mountain in winter, there's no such thing as no problems. No such thing as a better route, actually. Well, when there's snow, anyways. Or worse yet, ice. If you'd have come two days ago, for instance, it'd been clear for you all the way. Good visibility. You wouldn't have had to stop here I suspect."

Emilie nodded, feeling somewhat relieved that Ross and Michael were probably safe.

49

Vincent Fossari stood staring at the smashed meter and severed wires dangling from the pole outside Ross Manchester's cabin just long enough to know he had one hell of a throb in his left hand.

He turned and retraced his steps, walked to the Buick, picked up the knife and toolbox, and kept walking until he was back in his own car on Highway 194.

By then the storm had moved farther south.

50

The flame under a small pot in the kitchen heated the can of Campbell's Tomato Soup Ross cooked for himself. He watched the wood stove's glow light up the room as he poured a cup of coffee at the table. He had another twelve minutes before it was time to check his hibernating patient's vital signs again.

Inside the bedroom, Michael didn't know the night light had gone out. Nor did either man hear the ticking near Michael's bed as the space heater cooled down.

51

Emilie took the desk clerk's advice and spent the night at the Holiday Inn.

By the time she drove up the mountain, she felt the satisfying bumps and clunks of the tire chains gripping the ice and snow on the road. At 11:30 in the morning, when Emilie passed the Route 16 cutoff to Glendale Springs, she still had 47 miles to go.

Even with the snowplows clearing the road, the steady flurries kept a sheet of snow and ice on the road. With the Land Cruiser's wipers straining to clear the windshield, the only traffic Emilie saw were stalled by the side of the road, including an abandoned fifth-wheel RV that had jack-knifed and hung trailer-end down over the side of the cliff. She had to swerve to miss a highway patrol car and two men in heavy overcoats and earmuffs waving her to the other side of the road.

An hour and a half later, Emilie pulled into the Gulf station at the intersection of 421 and 321, diagonally across from the site where signs promised to build a new Boone Mall. At the station, she filled the gas tank and verified her driving directions on a map. Walking toward the ladies room, the air was clear and dry. The snow had stopped. On the way back to the car, she read the thermometer on the outside of the building: Five degrees above zero.

Two miles up the road, the engine stalled on an incline, and each time she tried to start the motor, the car rolled backward, down into oncoming traffic. She turned the steering wheel to the right and managed to move to the narrow shoulder at the edge of a deep cliff. She yanked the emergency brake and activated the car's hazard lights, before exiting. Then she started the walk back to the Gulf station two miles away.

52

Ross placed the dirty dishes in the sink. He'd let them soak. For now, it was time to get back to Michael and move on to the next phase of the treatment. He reached for the faucet with one hand and squeezed dish detergent with the other. Then he realized the water wasn't running.

He turned off the faucet and moved to the bathroom, the glow from the wood stove lighting his way. Although he'd left the water running in the bathroom sink to keep the pipes from freezing, that faucet was dry, too.

Well, right now, he needed to examine Michael's blood-smear slides under the microscope. First things first. Two previous specimens, each one hour apart, showed a significant reduction in the number of leukocytes circulating in Michael's body. A sign his infection was clearing. If the rate of decline of the white cells continued, then this afternoon he could gradually increase Michael's temperature and start bringing him out of hibernation 24 hours later. Great. He wanted to reverse the hibernation process as soon as possible. Too long in that state and the cold temperatures would begin to damage other parts of Michael's body.

Ross sat at the microscope and adjusted the focus. It was difficult to see in the dim room, but once he had the slides mounted, and magnification was set on the scope, the objects would be easier to see. With one eye on the slide, Ross reached up and flipped the light switch attached to the microscope to send a beam from underneath the stage and view the specimen up close. Nothing happened. Bulb's loose, he thought. Ross groped for the tiny bulb and pressed it in place. Again, he flipped the switch. Nothing. He hunkered down under the table and checked the wall socket, and as he did, he bumped the table, knocking the toaster on its side. Aha. The toaster. Ross pulled the small appliance toward him, pressed the rack down, and waited for the coils to heat. The toaster remained cold.

"Oh, my God," he yelled and dashed into the bedroom. The room was cold and dark. And there was a buildup of frost forming on the inside of the window near Michael's head. Ross snapped the electric blanket off his own bed and laid it on top of Michael. He removed two sheet blankets and a quilt from the closet and spread them on top. He rolled Michael onto his side and fumbled to locate the rectal thermometer under the blankets, but in the dark, he couldn't find it. Then, just as he felt one end of the glass tube, it slipped through his fingers, fell, hit the metal bed frame, and broke.

With one arm supporting Michael's upper body, Ross eased him back onto the mattress. He knew that excessive movement while in the dormant state could put Michael into shock.

Ross sat down on his own bed across from Michael, fists balled into knots on top of his thighs. He looked over at Michael. In the dark room, all he could see were gray shadows. Think, dammit. Think of your options, Ross. Michael is in a very cold state. He may be freezing to death. You don't even know his body temperature right now. You don't know what in the hell is going on with the water and the electricity in this place. It may be too late already. Think.

Okay, what are the possible sources of heat? The wood stove in the living room. Too far away. Can't move Michael. Maybe. But only as a final resort. Propane gas stove. I can heat water and fill the hot water bottle, and — No. No water.

As he whispered the word water, Ross ran for the kitchen and seized two saucepans from over the sink.

In seconds, he was outside, down on his knees, scooping snow into the pans. Then he saw the car. If he could stabilize Michael's temperature, he could take the car; go to Cannon Memorial for an ambulance. Ross knew that most farmer-neighbors didn't have telephones. The hospital was only three miles away, sitting off Highway 194, just past the second curve. Ross turned and saw the Buick's odd tilt and the drifts that had formed in unusual shapes around one of the back rims. He kicked snow around, exposing the tire. Flat.

What the hell? Was this a dream? Was sleep deprivation getting to him? Or was someone trying to kill Michael and him? Ross leaned against the car, looking up at marshmallow clouds floating in the turquoise sky. "Dear God," he whispered. "Please help me." Then he hiked back to the cabin.

Ross found a battery-operated lantern and two flashlights inside the bottom drawer of the built-in dresser. One flashlight worked. He located the second rectal thermometer, gathered his stethoscope and sphygmomanometer, and began examining Michael. His blood pressure, respirations, and pulse rate had all dropped since the electrical outage. His temperature had plunged to 57 degrees, and fell two-tenths of a degree with each of the following three inspections.

Ross measured the heated water and added handfuls of snow until the liquid reached exactly 105 degrees. Then he filled a hot water bottle and placed it between the layers of blankets on top of Michael. For the next four hours, Ross worked on Michael, recording his findings and described the implications. Michael's temperature continued to drop, and his urine output had stopped. Ross immersed a bottle of D5W in warm water, let it sit for 10 minutes, and then connected the solution to Michael's I.V. line hoping to reverse the dehydration effect. He carried a shallow bucket of simmering logs into the bedroom and placed it on the floor under the mattress. When Ross began rubbing

Michael's arms with his own hands, he immediately stopped, realizing his fingers were icy cold. By one thirty in the afternoon, Michael's temperature was 44.5 degrees, and Ross foresaw cardiac arrest soon.

53

Emilie tried to think of something else – anything else –
besides the shaking in her bones. During the trek back
to the Gulf station, the adrenalin rush kept her warm.
But when she entered the building, a warm carousel of
air blew around her face and ankles, and she started
feeling her body chill.

Just inside the door, six men sat around the bulge
of a pot-bellied stove. A bearded man wearing a
camouflage cap glanced at Emilie and tipped his head.
Fur lined flaps bounced against his ears.

"Howdy, ma'am," he said. "Can ah hep you?"

Emilie explained that her car had stalled two miles
up the road and she needed to reach a sick patient in
Banner Elk right away.

"Hey Sandy," the man hollered in the direction of an
open door behind him. "How 'bout hepping this h'yar
lady," he said, and spit into a Styrofoam cup.

Sandy emerged from the doorway pulling on a
quilted jacket the color of mud.

"Ya'll hep this nahs lady, y'hear? said the bearded
man, and without a word, Sandy walked toward the
front door. Emilie followed him around to a side lot and
climbed into the cab of a rusty Studebaker farm truck.

Arriving at Emilie's jeep, Sandy stopped his truck
diagonally behind her vehicle. They both got out of the
truck and walked to the jeep. "Keys, ma'am," said
Sandy.

It took three tries for the jeep's engine to start.
Then, leaving the keys in the ignition, the man headed
back to his truck.

"Wait," Emilie shouted. "Wait a minute."

"Ma'am?"

"What was wrong with my jeep?"

"Flooded, ma'am."

"But will it stall on me again? Before I get to Banner Elk?"

"Not likely, ma'am. If'n you don't pump the gas."

Emilie handed the man ten dollars. "Is this enough?" she said.

"Obliged," he said, climbed in the cab of his truck and waited. When Emilie got behind the wheel of the jeep, she felt a sudden jar from the rear. Sandy's truck was pushing her bumper away from the edge of the cliff. Then he backed up, made a U-turn in the road, and drove off.

At 3:35 in the afternoon, fog had already started to cover the tip of Grandfather Mountain to the south, as Emilie arrived at Ross' cabin in Banner Elk. She parked next to the Buick. As she reached across the front seat for her duffel, something caught her eye. There was movement from an electrical pole ten yards away. She stared. Wires dangled and swung in the air. Cut wires. In a swift move, Emilie pulled the duffel bag across the seat, and slammed the car door. "Ross!" she yelled, and ran to the house. Inside, the cabin was still. And freezing cold. She ran through the house and into the bedroom.

Michael was lying in bed, nose pointed up, eyes closed. An empty I.V. bottle hung from a stand beside the bed. Michael's flesh looked like freshly washed gravel, mottled in shades of gray and white. She saw no movement from the thick layer of blankets over his chest.

Across the room, Ross lay, uncovered, on his side in a fetal position, his hands clutching a silver and black stethoscope. A folder and pen were tucked between Ross' arms. When Emilie's foot accidentally jarred the bed, Ross didn't stir.

Emilie removed her gloves and palpated the side of Ross' neck. A faint pulse. "Thank God," she whispered, and reached for the stethoscope.

Emilie ran to the bathroom and turned on the hot water. Nothing. In the kitchen, both faucets were dry. Then she noticed a large graniteware pot on top of the antique cook stove. It contained partially frozen snow. She seized the wire handgrip and squatted down. On the oven door, above the Union Crawford label, there was a heat indicator gauge showing increments from 100 degrees, WARM, to 500 degrees, VERY HOT. The dial rested to the far left of the 100-degree mark. Emilie yanked on the drop-pull handle, and thrust the pot bottom deep into the cooling cinders. Then she dashed back to the bedroom.

With the palm of her hand, Emilie slapped at Ross' face, shouting his name. Ross remained still. She returned to the kitchen, grabbed the dry dishrag from inside the sink. She opened the stove door and dipped the cloth into the pot of melting snow, then wrung it out. As an afterthought, Emilie reached to one of the stove's upper shelves, unfolded several sheets of newsprint and stuffed wads around the pot of snow, where the embers were hottest.

At Ross' bed, Emilie began wiping his face with the wet rag. "Wake up, Ross," she begged. "Please wake up." When Ross didn't move, Emilie yanked the pillow from under his head and threw it on the floor. She rolled him onto his back, grabbed each of his shoulders, and using all of her weight, tugged up and down on his torso. His head bounced against the mattress.

His eyes popped opened. Emilie sat back, watching Ross stare up at the ceiling. Then he shifted his gaze to her face. "Em — " his lips stuck together. Emilie grabbed the wet cloth and gently wiped his mouth. "Emilie," he whispered. "Marshmallows . . . the sky. Snow." Then he jerked his head to the side.

"Michael!" he wailed in a mournful voice, scratchy and dry.

"He's frozen, Ross," she said gently.

"Oh my God! No!" He rotated to his side, but couldn't sit up. Emilie wrapped her arm behind Ross' back and pulled. "Emilie, quick, reach under Michael's covers and lay your hand flat on his chest," he said, propping himself up on his elbow.

Fumbling under Michael's heavy blankets, Emilie groped at Michael's body, forcing her numb fingers to obey. She found the curve of Michael's rib cage, looked at Ross and shook her head no.

"Hold your hand still and concentrate. If there's a heartbeat, it'll be weak and very slow."

Emilie closed her eyes, pressing down with her hand. She moved her hand higher up on Michael's chest. "Nothing, Ross." Then, she creased her brow. "Wait." Emilie nodded her head. "It's there, Ross. There's something there." She looked at her wristwatch and followed the hand for fifteen seconds. Seven beats.

"Emilie, help me sit up," Ross said.

Together, they struggled getting Ross into a sitting position, and then Emilie helped Ross stand up. He wobbled to Michael's bed and sat on the edge. Leaning over Michael's body, he spoke to Emilie. "We need coffee. Can you collect clean snow and — "

"There's a small fire going in the cook stove," she said. "I'll be right back."

By the time Emilie returned with two cups of hot coffee, Ross was unhooking the frozen I.V. bottle from the pole. He detached the line, clamped it off, and draped the tubing over one of the top hooks. Then he placed the bottle in the trash pail. He opened the dresser drawer and removed a fresh bottle of D5W. It was frozen. "Please take this and thaw it in a basin of warm water. Not hot. Just long enough to liquefy the solution," he said. Emilie nodded and carried the bottle into the kitchen.

When she came back into the bedroom, Ross pointed to the stack of notes still lying on his bed. "I need you to take notes while I dictate. Read to me where I left off."

"In the Vital Signs columns, you wrote *Respirations: 5. Comment: Cheyne-Stokes type, with long intervals of apnea. Spleen: Massive distension. Unable to measure erythrocytes or total hemoglobin level due to lack of microscope use.* Temperature column: *44.5 degrees.* Under comments, it says, *Poikilothermic reaction putting patient at high risk for heart block and cardiac arrest.* There's nothing more after that, Ross," she said.

"Okay," Ross said. "Be sure to check your watch and document the exact time you write each item down. Let's start with Michael's temp. In that column, put 43.8 degrees. Heart rate, 28 beats per minute. Blood pressure, 52 over 38 . . . "

For two and a half hours, Ross continued to monitor and evaluate Michael's condition, speaking in a droning monotone, as Emilie wrote it all down. Neither of them noticed the mountain shadows darken the sky, first gray then black, outside the bedroom window. At 6:30, when Ross removed the rectal thermometer, he said, "His body temperature is dropping. We've got to get him into the living room where it's warmer." Ross studied the arrangement of Michael's blankets. "I'll disconnect his I.V. tubing, and remove the top covers. Just till we get him settled on the day bed. He doesn't weigh much, but any sudden jarring, and Michael could go into shock. Then I'll need to restart his keep-open line and replace the blankets."

Emilie rushed into the living room and opened the couch. When she returned, she saw Ross had crossed Michael's feet at the ankles and had positioned his arms close to his sides. Now Ross was tucking the top flannel blanket around Michael's body.

"Watch how I tie the top corners of this under sheet together, Emilie. Then you do it there at his feet," Ross said. "Okay, now do a half-squat, and slide your shoulder under the knot. When I say *three*, we'll ease to a slow standing position, and you begin walking toward the living room. Move slowly. Very, very slowly."

It took them eight minutes to move Michael from the bedroom to the couch. When he was settled, covered with blankets, I.V. resumed, Ross and Emilie started moving medical supplies to the dining room table. Then they closed the bedroom door to keep stove warmth contained in the front of the cabin.

Into the night, they cared for Michael, with Ross beginning vital-signs checks over and over again. Emilie recorded the results, stoked the wood stove kindling, and prepared hot food and coffee. At 11 o'clock, Michael's temperature had risen three degrees. But his Foley bag remained empty. Ross knew that the hibernating animals he studied had stopped urine flow during periods of active hibernation, but during the process of awakening, which Ross expected to take approximately three hours with Michael, their urine flow resumed. When the second hour passed, Emilie suggested they get help from Cannon Memorial. But without a telephone, one of them would have to leave and drive the jeep down the icy mountain road.

Ross had another idea. With Emilie's help, he uncovered one of Michael's legs, lifted his foot, and began to rotate at the ankle in a gentle passive range of motion. Then Ross laid the palm of his own hand, flat against the bottom of Michael's foot, and pointed and flexed it. He moved to the other leg. Then to Michael's arms and hands. An hour later, Ross repeated the exercises, and began another full round of taking Michael's vital signs. Emilie was busy clearing dishes in the kitchen, so Ross recorded the numbers. Then he put the papers down.

"Emilie, can you come take my dictation?" She came and sat across from the daybed. "Let's go right to the comments section," he said.

"Latest vital signs indicate that there appears to be efficient and rapid warming of the patient's body."

Emilie looked up. "What did you say?"

Ross smiled, white teeth shining in the light from the cook stove. "Yes, ma'am," he said. "Keep writing. We need to get this down. Here goes.

"Certain indices of diastolic function appear to indicate that there is enhanced ventricular compliance . . . rise in heart rate and decreased peripheral circulatory resistance in the anterior portion of the body, and urinary output indicates recovery to full kidney function. All of which appear to be clear indications that the patient is entering the pre-awakening state."

By midnight, Michael's temperature had increased to 94 degrees and his catheter bag was full. At 1 a.m., when the air temperature was a comfortable 52, Ross opened the bedroom door again, and told Emilie to take a nap.

"If Michael's condition keeps improving, as I suspect it will, we can alternate two hour watches, while the other one sleeps.

As daylight appeared, a crusty ice layer covered the snow outside the cabin where the temperature stood at 39 degrees. Ross was sleeping in the bedroom. Emilie had just started a fresh pot of coffee. With her back turned to the daybed, she didn't see Michael's head rotate on his pillow. When she carried a tray of food toward the bedroom door, she tripped. Michael was staring at her.

54

"Stamp. You lick it. You stick it."

Karen giggled and tried to arrange her fingers in an appropriate configuration for American Sign Language. Then she raised her palm away from her face and swept her hand in a left to right movement three times. This told Tracy that she was erasing what she just said, and would start over.

It was their private signing, one they'd made up between the two of them because they didn't know the real thing.

The girls sat at the dining room table, ignoring two glasses of milk and a bowl of peanut butter cookies. A picture book lay open between them. *Finger Signing Dictionary.*

Karen pointed to a page and mouthed the word *stamp*. Then she attempted to sign the definition again. First she made a fist with her right hand, palm facing out, then she popped her thumb between her index and middle fingers. Next Karen folded her fingertips onto her palm, thumb upright. She held it for a few seconds, then tucked her thumb under the first three fingers and pressed her pinky into her palm. Struggling to bend her wrist down and point her thumb, index and middle fingers forward. Then she curled her ring finger and pinky into her palm.

"What'd I say?" said Karen.

"Mmmm. Tamp," said Tracy.

Karen frowned, unsure if Tracy missed the first letter. Quickly, she made an upright fist with her palm facing Tracy.

"Essss," said Tracy.

Karen grinned and touched her fingertips to her mouth, palm open and up, then moved her hand down to meet the flat palm of the other hand. "Good," she said, bobbing her head rapidly up and down.

Tracy bounced in the chair, clapping her hands.

Across the room, Barbara and Marilyn sat on the couch folding diapers, with Jeff in the playpen close by.

It had been Marilyn's idea. Bring the kids together on a regular schedule. Toss in a few basic signing books, make it a game with rewards, and let them play.

It was working.

Marilyn studied Karen and Tracy's actions. "Once they really get the hang of this, I'd like to see more children join in," said Marilyn. "I mean, have a larger group of both deaf and hearing kids play the game. Learning and teaching each other. There aren't any other programs like that around. All I've seen are the standard ruler-smacking teacher at the head of a class of children who are deaf." Marilyn shook her head. "Not my idea of the best learning environment."

"But this certainly is," Barbara glanced in the direction of Karen and Tracy.

"The advantage I see in teaming two kids together, one with normal hearing and the other with limited or no hearing, is that by them learning to sign together – to support each other – it would form a bond between the children. Rather than separating deaf children from those who can hear." Marilyn picked up Jeff and held him on her knees. "Every deaf child who I've ever cared for at the hospital seemed so isolated and scared in a world of voices they couldn't hear. When you can explain an upcoming procedure to a child – a shot, or even something like a physical therapy treatment – the child is much more comfortable and cooperative. Everybody wins. But too often the docs, and the nurses, too, assume that the deaf child won't get it, and just don't bother to explain. It makes me crazy."

"So, what are you thinking, Marilyn?" asked Barbara.

"Well, if we invited students from the college who are majoring in Special-Education -- even high school students who want to go into nursing -- it'd give them hands-on experience. They could learn a lot from the kids."

Barbara stared at Marilyn, nodding her head. "Yes, I see what you mean."

Marilyn remembered when she first learned about Tracy. It was the moment Fossari had burst into her unit calling Tracy *Dr. Burton's tonsillectomy.* Immediately she felt a strong sense of protection for Tracy, before she even met the child, and awaited her arrival on the unit.

She knew it was a glaring medical gaffe to admit Tracy to the medical unit. Even Dr. Burton ordered Tracy moved to the post-surgical floor as it should have been according to protocol. But Fossari's ego wouldn't budge. And that's when Tracy's problems began. Ever since that first day, Marilyn simmered inside, helpless to change what she saw coming at Tracy, just like in the story, *Libba Cotten and the Rumbling Freight Train.* And at about the same crazy speed. Marilyn remembered seeing Michael in the library watching Tracy play the piano that day. Later, she'd met Dr. Manchester and his nine-year-old daughter Karen. Marilyn remembered thinking that Manchester seemed more knowledgeable than most of the CF docs she worked with, and wished he'd been on staff.

The week after Tracy's discharge from the hospital, Marilyn had called to check on the child's progress, and was invited for a visit, which she did the very next day, running into Michael and Barbara, Ross Manchester and Karen, right there in the living room when she arrived. After that, Marilyn stopped to see Tracy often, and once she took both Tracy and Karen to Circus World in Haines City, where the girls rode the merry-go-round, cuddled baby goats, and had their faces painted like clowns. That's the day she decided what she wanted to do.

"I think it's a great idea," Barbara had said when Marilyn confided her plan. "I need to get involved in something, too, Marilyn. "I think I understand a little of the helplessness you must have felt watching Fossari's power take away something incredibly important to a patient.

Then Irene Thomas agreed to watch Jeff and suggested a church where they could hold classes once they incorporated their nonprofit *Pal Sign* finger spell program. Marilyn had made an appointment the following week with the minister to finalize a schedule for the weekly classes.

Now, in Barbara's house, Marilyn studied the girls as they giggled and signed. "It's funny how those kids keep right at it after we've fizzled out," she said.

"Yes, but in all fairness to us older women of the world, you have to admit we hung in there for almost an hour before our fizz fizzed out," Barbara said.

"I'm so glad the church is letting us use one of their classrooms. It's perfect," said Marilyn. "I just hope our living room lessons with two little girls will grow the way I'd like to see."

Barbara laughed. "If I'm right about you, Miss Marilyn Pelletier, you'll be a success at most anything you set your mind to. I'm just thrilled I can be a small part of this effort. I'm still not sure how I'll fit in, but I'm willing to give it a try."

"I'm the one who should thank you, Barb. You're probably right about my weird ideas that no one — "

"Wait a minute," said Barbara. "That's not what I said at all."

"No, but I can tell that's what you were thinking."

"Marilyn, c'mon. I admire your creativity. Hey, I couldn't come up with an original idea if my life depended on it."

197

"You're lucky," said Marilyn. "My mind never quits. Gets me in trouble sometimes. Creativity and spunk without power – or money – are not good things to have. I never know when to keep my brain, or my mouth, shut."

"What do you mean?"

"Well. Several years ago. Just after Dr. Cocuzzo died and Dr. Fossari took over, I opened my big mouth a couple of times. That was before I realized what I was up against. One time, I wanted to set up a mobile library program for the hospital kids who were blind. I tamper with writing kids' picture books. Illustrations. Large print. And Braille. I give them away at health care conventions for blind children, and slow readers. Because slow readers learn to love reading when they learn Braille. Anyway, the kids seem to like my books."

"That's really interesting. Yes, I bet the kids love your books, Marilyn," said Barbara.

"Back then, my idea was to create Braille lessons for both blind and sighted kids. Have them learn together. Like Karen and Tracy are doing over there. The way I saw it is that no matter who in the family is visually impaired, they could all read together. Less than ten percent of blind kids ever learn Braille. The rest, 90 percent, never learn to read and write. They grow up illiterate. Most people don't know this, Barb, and they're shocked when they find out. They should be. We all should be. And that's why I wanted to get the message out to people. That's all I was trying to do." Marilyn paused, sighed. "Barb, the sad fact is that, of the blind kids who *do* learn Braille, they excel in school. They go on to college. Become teachers, lawyers, social workers. There was a man at the turn of the century, Jacob Bolotin, a totally blind man. Lived in Chicago. He learned Braille and overcame social prejudice. Became a respected doctor.

"Kids are smart, Barb, if we would listen to them. When Louis Braille was three he became totally blind, and at fifteen, he made up a system of reading by using his fingers to feel bumps. But at his school for blind children, the teachers scorned his idea. It was only generations later that we came to appreciate his work. Yet Louis Braille's idea was magnificent. It's the system Helen Keller learned so she could graduate from Radcliffe University in 1904, the first ever deaf-blind person to receive a BA degree. Then when she met workers who had been blinded in industrial accidents, she recognized the gross unfairness of the Capitalist system, and for the next sixty years, she was a powerful voice for social justice. She couldn't have done any of that if a disabled teenager hadn't believed in his idea of reading with bumps. It's just sad we didn't listen to him.

"I mean, being blind – or deaf – or having cystic fibrosis, for that matter. Or any other health or physical condition. Being handicapped should not limit a person in what they can do. I've seen a lot of what goes on behind closed hospital doors, Barb. Sometimes I am so ashamed to be part of the health care structure. It's not about patients. It's about money. And power.

"Anyway, my idea started with one of my pediatric patients. A 12-month-old baby boy who was blind. Born with ONH, optic nerve hypoplasia. Cody's family didn't have money for the eye surgery he needed. I organized a rally to raise money. Did, too. Before Fossari stuck his nose in what I was doing. Parents brought kids from all over Florida. One mom came in all the way from Paducah, Kentucky. We were in the back lot near the park, hospital visitors making donations for Cody's surgery. Then, right in the middle of the rally, Fossari cornered me. Told me to get off hospital property with my childish games. I explained to him what my intentions were, told him about my idea for a *Good Bumps on a Roll* Braille mobile. Even wrote a song to the tune of Willie Nelson's *On the Road Again*. I told Fossari it would give the hospital exposure, that I planned to ask Dr. Hauser, our pediatric ophthalmologist, to donate an hour or so a month giving eye exams to inner city children whose families couldn't afford them otherwise. But no matter what I said to Fossari, he didn't budge. Made everyone leave the rally for Cody. I was so embarrassed and humiliated. Almost got fired over it. All I wanted to do was give that baby a chance to see."

"Oh my God, Marilyn. How cruel." Barbara said.

"And here's the kicker. Two months later, the hospital buys this brand new 45-foot candy-apple red motor coach. Plastered hospital advertising all over it, turn it into a mobile library for kids. Guess what kind of books were in it?"

"Braille."

"Yep. And it being an election year, Dr. Hauser, the staff pediatric ophthalmologist got his picture all over the news, giving eye exams to kids. Along with the legislative candidates who had the deepest pockets to pay the hospital to advertise the health care bills they planned to introduce to the governor – if they were elected. After the election, they sold the bus. Fossari was the leader of the pack.

"Well, thank our heavenly goddess, Fossari's been gone the last couple of days," said Marilyn. "Break-room grapevine says he hurt his hand or something. Won't be back until — "

"Gone?" Barbara whispered.

" – next week. All I know is it makes my job easier."

Barbara stood up. "Well, this time you've got a group behind you." Barbara looked at Karen and Tracy, heads resting on their arms, shoving cookies into their mouths. "We'll make Sign Pal work, Marilyn. For Tracy. And for all of those kids at your rally who Fossari sent away."

Then Barbara searched for the phone directory.

55

Michael's body felt disconnected from his head. And the room seemed miles away.

Was he dying? No, he thought. It's seems more like I'm coming back from somewhere else that I've been. Somewhere. Where was the somewhere else that I've been? Where was he now? He tried to focus his eyes, but the objects in the room were dancing in space, knocking into each other, and he couldn't make out the edges of things. Two blurred bodies floated above him, came close to his face, then moved away. He tried to reach out to pull the bodies back, but his arms were too heavy and the people were gone. There was a gluey taste in his mouth. Well, no wonder. Because his lips were secured together with some of that white paste he used to make in second grade, and it looked good enough to eat, and some of the kids did eat it. *Peter, Peter, white paste eater*, and he must be Peter because he has a mouthful of words stuck behind his teeth and his mouth is glued shut.

The air in his nostrils felt warm, and he gave all his attention to the smell. Hamburgers. Juicy and brown. A long-handled spatula, broad and flat. A grill. Are we having a party?

Michael's hand fluttered against his leg. He felt the blankets roll off from head to foot, then pressure on his belly between his navel and public bone. Someone was tugging his groin from the inside. Michael wet the bed as Ross glided the catheter tubing out of his penis.

The floating people want me to answer. *What?* God, he was hungry.

"Michael . . . "

The word sounds familiar, but the language is all wrong. If he could just sit up.

"Michael. Relax. It's over."

That's nice. He slackened his neck muscles and his head dropped back on the pillow.

" . . . do you feel? see? . . . her . . . me?"

A man in my room. Just take my money. Please . . . leave my wife alone. "Barbara!!!"

"Michael, she's fine." *Another man. Familiar this time.* "And so is Jeff."

"Jeff?"

"Your son. Your baby." *Soft voice. A face floating in space. Pretty face.*

A rough cat's tongue licked across his cheeks and around his forehead. *Can't see.*

"Michael." *A woman's voice. Soft. Gentle as a breeze.*

When Emilie slid the washcloth down Michael's neck, his eyes began to focus.

"What?" Michael wrinkled his brow. Then he remembered. Thoughts, real thoughts came rushing through his mind in a flood. He saw Ross' face again, and the two men locked eyes. Then with an effort, Michael spoke.

"Did we do it?" he said.

A wide grin crossed Ross' face. "Yeah, Mike. You did it," was all he could say.

It took Michael forty-five minutes to gain the strength to sit up in bed. He felt weak, and his muscles were flaccid, but as the morning turned into afternoon, Michael's temperature returned to normal, and his blood pressure was good.

Ross and Emilie sat on the floor in front of the sofa bed. Michael was propped up on a pillow, eating his first meal in four days. The reality of the situation was beginning to settle in on all three of them. Ross tried to hide his joy by planning ahead.

"First thing we need to do, Mike, is have you dictate in detail everything you feel. Your breathing, congestion, shortness of breath, et cetera. General overall sensations, mood. Anything you can think of, just let it pour out in words."

"That won't take long at all, Ross," Michael said. "In a word I feel great."

"Still weak?"

"Not bad."

"Hungry?"

"Starved. But if you'd leave me alone, I would take care of that." Michael dunked the corner of his toasted cheese sandwich into the chicken broth, and bit down on the wet bread.

"Slow down, Mike," said Emilie. "Ross says you'll get nauseated if you shovel it in too fast."

"Hey, Em, I've got pounds to make up for, remember?" He turned to Ross. "How much weight do you think I've lost during my little otherworld journey?"

"Hard to say, Mike. We need to weigh you, though, as soon as you're able to stand. As it is, we'll have to deduct the load of food you're eating right now. Hey, Em, what would you say this meal weighs?"

Emilie smiled and shook her head.

"You know, the two of you are a trip all by yourselves," said Michael. Then he stopped and looked at the man and the woman sitting on the floor at his elbow, Ross leaning against an end table, legs straight out in front of him, ankles crossed, and eating a sandwich. Emilie in a little-girl pose, Indian style, holding a tumbler of milk steady as it rested on the carpet in front of her crossed legs. Michael held that picture, locking it into his mind so he would never forget. Then he said, "Tell me. What happened when I was out? You must've been bored to death watching this marmot hibernate. And Em, how come you're here? That's no quick little jaunt. You can't just boogie on over here like you were going to the corner market. So, how come?"

At the same moment, Ross and Emilie looked at each other. There was a change in their relationship now. They both felt it. Like a warm breeze settling over them from the Gulf of Mexico. And they both knew they couldn't explain to Michael what happened during the past few days. Because they honestly didn't know.

56

"Marilyn! Barbara! Watch this!" Karen squealed. Her joy bubbled over. Karen pointed to Tracy, who stood prim and proper, ankles together, hands behind her back. Then Tracy burst out in a chortle, showing the gap where her top tooth was missing. Karen held the dictionary open in front of Tracy. She pointed to a page.

Marilyn and Barbara waited, afraid to breathe. The four of them were in a large classroom that belonged to the Fossil Park Church of St. John the Divine. They were doing their first dry run, to see if the room was suitable for their Pal Sign classes. The church was built in 1958, and had the original frosted glass strips in the jalousie windows. Years of polishing and dragging furniture across the terrazzo floor had dug tiny potholes in the mortar, and there were long cracks on the surface that went from wall to wall. Along one side of the room, there was a full kitchen with a long stand-up counter. On the opposite wall were two doors leading to the restrooms. The third wall supported four dozen orange stack chairs, and six folding tables, three of which were already set up. The room echoed at the slightest raise of a voice, but what Marilyn liked best was the wide expanse of solid white wall with four low electrical outlets, where she could present slide shows or use an overhead transparency machine.

"Tamp," said Tracy, looking at Karen. She held up her right hand in a neat fist, thumb bent over her fingers. "Essss," Tracy said. Then she manipulated the hand close to her chest and showed it to the group, last three fingers bent and her index finger wrapped over her thumb. "Teee."

Next, she folded all of her fingers flat against her palm and stuck her thumb up facing the ceiling. "Ay," she said.

Tracy hesitated on the fourth letter, and Karen walked to her, showed her a picture, and stepped back again.

"That one is really hard," said Karen.

Tracy bent her first three fingers over her thumb, and pressed her pinky flat onto her palm. "Emm," she said, holding her fist out to the audience. Then she pulled it close to her face, examined her fist, and turned it around again so the others could see. "Emm."

It took a long time for both Tracy and Karen to decide how to arrange Tracy's fingers in the last letter. Their concentration was intense. Then, they were satisfied.

"That's a P," Karen declared.

Marilyn and Barbara clapped and cheered, sending vibrations off all four walls. Then Marilyn caught Tracy's eye and motioned her over. "You did good," she said exaggerating her mouth movements. Marilyn did a slow finger spell for Tracy. *You did good.* She wrapped her arms around the child and tried not to cry. Then Marilyn reached out, placed her hands under Tracy's arms and raised her up, standing on top of the table. The little girl beamed. She placed chubby hands over her face and made giggling sounds in her throat.

"Let's hear it for Tracy," said Marilyn. "Hip, hip, hooray! Hip, hip, hooray!" and they all joined in.

"She can't hear us, you know," said Karen.

"I know, honey," Marilyn said. "But she can sure see everything we're doing. She knows, honey. She knows." Marilyn gave the tip of Karen's nose a tap with her knuckles. "Hey, she said. "You're the one who did all the hard work to teach this to Tracy. Let's give a little credit where it's due." She took Karen's hand. "Here, get up on the seat, kiddo, and take some of this glory." It was Tracy's turn to applaud now, as Karen took wide bows, not feeling embarrassed at all.

When the noise died down, Barbara became conscious of the new quiet that engulfed the room. "Good grief," she said. "I sure hope we're not disturbing the office crew in the other room."

As Barbara spoke, Marilyn looked up and saw two women standing in a doorway at the far end of the room. "Funny you should say that," Marilyn said. A middle-aged woman with a small round figure stood in the center of an archway, the hem of her one-piece dress unraveled at her ankles, and three-inch pointed shoes gave her the look of an inverted pyramid. Next to her, a tall woman leaned against the doorframe, arms folded across ample breasts, a hard-looking hairdo boxing in her large face that showed deep lines and shadows from her eyes to her chin.

Marilyn held up her index finger to Barbara. "Be right back," she said, then half skipped, half walked over to the women. The taller woman's expression changed from serious curiosity to a grin, friendly and wide, emphasizing her wrinkles.

"Hi," said Marilyn. "Sorry about the noise. Guess we got a little carried away." She held out her hand. "I'm Marilyn Pelletier, and the four of us," she turned towards Barbara, Tracy, and Karen, "are forming a program to teach sign language to children. We've gotten permission from Rev. Joe to use the room once a week for the classes. We'll try to be quieter next time."

The tall woman waved long fingers in the air. "Oh, my, no," she said. "Don't you worry about the noise. What's a church for if we can't serve those less fortunate than ourselves?"

The round woman bobbed her head, as the other woman seemed to be speaking for both of them. "Reverend Joe told us you'd be here today. We came to see the deaf children."

Marilyn's mouth dropped, but the woman didn't seem to notice. "Reverend Joe is just delighted with what you are doing, and we want to do whatever we can to help these poor children." Ms. Round continued her up-and-down head waggling.

"Thank you," said Marilyn, tonelessly, still trying to recover from the last comment. "Irene Thomas is the woman who suggested I call Rev. Joe. She's a member of your church, and said you'd be helpful."

"Mrs. Thomas is a lovely lady. So generous with donations. She teaches piano, you know. Matter of fact, she's the organist for our church. Such a talented lady." Then the woman leaned close to Marilyn as if sharing a secret. "Too bad about her little girl, don't you think? Why, if I were Mr. and Mrs. Thomas, I'd surely sue that doctor for what he did." Another nod from Ms. Round. "I just can't get over it. I really can't. Only the good Lord knows what this world is coming to. It's absolutely unforgivable." She pursed her wrinkled lips, closed her eyes, and rotated her head. "Unforgivable."

If you only knew, thought Marilyn.

For the first time, the short woman spoke. "Tell her about the newsletter, Mary."

"Oh yes, Gert. I almost forgot." Mary patted Gert's shoulder. "Thank you for reminding me." Then to Marilyn. "Reverend Joe thought you might want to help us write up a little article for our weekly newsletter here at St. Johns." Mary told Marilyn that they printed 1,200 copies of the newsletter for Sunday worship services every week, and another 300 were mailed to each of the local churches of all denominations, a practice that she herself had started just last year when she was promoted to the position of editor of the publication. Oh, and naturally the National Association of Divine Churches were sent a newsletter every week. They entered it in their annual newsletter contest that the national association held. Marilyn was informed that St. John's had taken third place four years ago.

"Seventy-seven, I believe it was." Mary frowned. "Or was it seventy-eight?" she said to herself.

"It was 1976," piped Gert, bobbing her head up and down, up and down, repeatedly. Marilyn stared, thinking the woman's neck must be getting sore from all the exercising.

"My how time flies." Mary looked down the short hallway. "Ms. Pelletier, if you can spare a minute, I could use your help. I've got space for about a hundred words left in the newsletter before I'm finished with this week's edition. Then we can get it to the printers and have it for this Sunday's service." Without waiting for Marilyn's answer, Mary and Gert turned in unison, like toy soldiers, and marched up the hall.

"I'll be right there," Marilyn called behind them. She dashed back into to room. Tracy and Karen were engrossed in finger signing something from a Bible they'd found. They all looked up when Marilyn approached. "Good news," she said. "Gotta meet in the office with the newsletter crew. Tell you about it later." As she wheeled around, Marilyn said, "Keep going without me." And she was gone.

57

"Oh, thank God." Ross heard Barbara suck in her breath at the other end of the line. He had just told her of Michael's recovery and early success from his torpid therapy treatment.

Ross had taken Emilie's rented jeep and had driven into Banner Elk. Once he'd found the Holiday Inn, the first call he made was to the New River Light and Power Corporation to get electricity back into the house. Because of his medical status, they promised immediate service. Then he tried to call Barbara, but there was no answer. He'd try again in a few minutes. In the meantime, the hotel lobby was comfortably warm, so he just stayed put until he could reach her.

Ross flipped through the yellow pages looking for the number of an auto towing service, turning his back on the small man in the adjacent booth who was talking way too loud.

Scanning the ads, Ross realized there were hardly any commercial listings for the Banner Elk area. Looks like everything's in Boone, he thought. Too far to travel now, though. He hoped that the fluctuating luck of the last few days – weeks, really – were well behind him. But he wasn't taking any chances, not on these roads.

As Ross thumbed through the pages, he came to realize the danger he and Michael had been through. He inhaled deep, then exhaled, felt his body relax. He became aware of his senses and glad to be alive as he leaned against the inside of the telephone booth and closed his eyes. When he opened them, he gazed through the glass at the room. The lobby. The restroom signs tacked to the doors just up the corridor. The fingerprints and scratches inside the booth. He heard the sound of dishes clanging somewhere close by. The feel when he touched the newsprint pages of the phone directory. It was as small as a sandwich, 163 pages thick, including the white pages. Banner Elk, Beach Mountain, Sugar Grove, and Watauga County, and in the fine print: Blowing Rock, Boone, Newland.

There, there's one. *Farthing's 24-Hour Wrecker and Towing. We Fix Flats. Banner Elk.* No street address listed, but Ross didn't care about that. As long as they had a working telephone.

"Yep. Be out direc'ly," said the man.

"How soon?"

"Well. Soon's my hepper's back from over to the yonder. Should be direc'ly."

Ross gave him the address. "Know where ya'll are. Jest past Norwood's place upar offa 184. Recken I'll be takin' Hickory Nut Gap Road to get thar. What with the 'strukshun up to the old folks' home 'n all."

Ross thanked the man. Then he tried to reach Barbara again.

She picked up on the sixth ring, sounding breathless. "We just came in the door, Ross. Tell me, how's Michael?" she said.

"He's doing great, Barb. It looks like the treatment is a success. At least, so far."

Ross summarized Michael's treatment – leaving out the power loss, the flat tire, and fact that both he and Michael nearly froze to death.

"Thank God," Barbara repeated. "I can't tell you how worried I've been. I've tried to keep busy and let you take over. And Emilie. How's Emilie, Ross? she asked. "Did she have any trouble on the way up?" Ross assured Barbara that Emilie was fine. Very fine, in fact.

"Let me sit down a minute, Ross," Barbara said. Ross heard packages crinkling in the background. Then he heard Karen's voice, asking Barbara a question. Ross' heart leaped at the sound of the child.

"Yes, honey," said Barbara's muffled reply. "His bottle's in the diaper bag there on the counter." Then, "Sorry, Ross."

"You've got yourself quite a heavy load there, haven't you Barb?"

"I love it, Ross. I really do. Karen is such a lovely child. So grown up. Seems like she's nine, going on forty." Ross nodded, chuckled.

"Ross, maybe this isn't the time to tell Michael, but I'd picked up the mail just before you called. There's a notice from Mr. and Mrs. Douglas saying that Kevin had gone into respiratory crisis on New Year's Day."

"Oh, no."

"When they couldn't reach you, they took him to the emergency room. They admitted him to the CF floor." She stopped.

"Who was the doctor on duty for — "

"Dr. Fossari."

"Oh my God."

"The letter says that Respiratory Therapy gave him a treatment in the ER, and his breathing sounded good. The therapist assured them Kevin'd be okay for the night, and told his parents to go home. Oh, God, Ross. Kevin died that night. Apparently, in his sleep. His body has already been cremated, and the service was just for the immediate family.

Ross gripped the telephone receiver. "Barb, I'm so sorry that you're there by yourself to get that news."

"I'm okay, Ross. Really. I've got Karen. And Marilyn."

"Marilyn?" Ross knew he'd heard the name from Parkwest, but couldn't place her.

"Marilyn Pelletier. Seven-to-three nurse. Tall. Dark-blond hair. Wears it tied up under her cap. She was Tracy's nurse." Barbara's voice cracked. "Alyce's, too."

"I remember now. Something of an activist. Always taking the kids' side on an issue." He laughed.

"That's her. And what's so bad about taking the kids' side anyway? Besides, Dr. Manchester, nobody's got more notoriety as a troublemaker than you. That's probably why you recognize it in her." Barbara sounded protective of her new friend. "Plus, Marilyn's a lot prettier than you, if you don't mind my being so blunt. Oh, and wait'll you hear what we've got planned."

"Uh oh," said Ross.

"But you've got to wait until you get back to hear what we're doing."

"Sounds serious."

"It is," said Barbara. "And, not to change the subject, but when are the three of you going to leave the mountains, anyway?" Karen tapped Barbara's arm just as Jeff began to wail loudly.

"What?" she said into the phone. "Can't hear you, Ross. What did you say?"

"Tomorrow. Early as possible. Assuming everything goes well tonight." If we get the tire fixed and the electrical problem solved, he thought.

"Okay, Ross, here's Karen. Be sure to call on the drive home, okay?"

Then Karen was chattering before the receiver was up to her mouth. For ten minutes, she rambled about her and Tracy and Barbara and Marilyn doing sign language, and it was really fun, and now she, Karen, was teaching Tracy and they were both going to teach kids to talk with their hands. Some of what she said made sense. Most of it didn't.

"I can't wait for you to tell me more about it, princess." Ross said. "Uncle Mike and Emilie send kisses through the phone."

Just before Ross hung up, Karen said, "Bye, daddy. I love you."

"I love you too, honey." And he meant it.

58

Emilie stared out the window over the sink.   She watched as two men from the New River Light and Power Corporation stood, knee deep in snow, repairing the wires attached to the electrical pole behind the house.

Outside everything looks so harmless, she thought. Peaceful, really. And pure. Like the gentle hand of a mother as she comforts her child. So different from before.

"What?" Michael said from the sofa. He had fallen asleep right after Ross left, and Emilie had tried to be quiet. Now he was propped up on his elbow when she turned to look at him.

"Well, hello there," she smiled. At an easy pace, she walked over to the far side of the couch and tugged the braided cord to open the thick drapes. The late morning sun filled the room with the glare reflecting off the snow. Then Emilie closed the lace curtains, filtering the bright light.

"You were talking to yourself," Michael said. He swung around on the couch and sat with his bare feet on the floor. A bath would be good about now, he thought, as his fingers pulled forward on his chin, bristles dark and uncomfortable on the beard he ordinarily kept tidy and trim.

Emilie stood at the front windows looking through the thin curtains. "It's so beautiful here, Mike," she said. Life is so fragile, she thought. Like this glass. Transparent and delicate. Just waiting for elements stronger than itself to attack and mar its very life. Like yesterday's snow-tears falling along the outside of the window, each one starting out as a perfect feathery flake, then sliding ever downward, warming itself into a dirty debased drop of liquid at the bottom, leaving a blemish in its path. Snowflake gone. As if it never existed. "I think I'd like to live here someday," she whispered.

"What?" said Michael. "There you go again."

"Sorry. I said this place is beautiful."

Emilie's thoughts remained wordless, slipping from her grasp until their musings tumbled about her, and then disappeared.

"Are you hungry?" she said, as she began to fold the bedclothes that lay in a heap at the end of the couch.

"Famished, as usual," Michael said rubbing his face. "But what I'd really like," he said looking up, "is a soak in the tub." Just then, a series of rapid burps came from the bathroom sink. Then stopped.

Michael and Emilie looked at each other. "It's on," he said. "I made it come on."

There was a tiny explosion of air striking against the inside of the pipes between the bathroom and kitchen. Soon they heard a rush of water from the bathroom.

"Yahoo!" said Michael.

"So be it," Emilie said. Then she went to turn off the flow.

As soon as the water had heated sufficiently, Michael moved into the bathroom to shower. Emilie closed up the couch and carried the linens back into the bedroom.

" . . . offer you some coffee?" It was Ross' voice that Emilie heard coming through the open front door. Emilie's pulse quickened.

"Thanks, no," a man's voice said. Then Emilie heard the stamping of snow boots.

"Thanks, again, guys. Appreciate your help," said Ross. The front door slammed, and Emilie walked to the end of the hall near the living room. She stood, mute, and watched Ross remove his gloves and heavy jacket.

Then, without looking up, Ross took quick strides toward Emilie, and scooped her into his arms.

"Oh!" she said, startled.

"That'll teach you to stare at disrobing men," he said into her hair. His lips felt cold on Emilie's ear.

Then Ross stepped back and held her shoulders at arm's length. "You're beautiful, mountain lady." He touched the side of her neck with his thumb. "Rumpled, but beautiful." Strands of hair had fallen in Emilie's face since she'd tied it up earlier. She blushed but remained silent.

Ross heard the shower noises from behind the bathroom wall. "He doing okay?" he asked.

"I wish I felt that good."

"Hey why don't you get comfortable on the couch?" Ross said, remembering his trip into town. "I brought us something to eat. Takeout." Gently, he pushed her into the living room. "There were no fast food drive thru's, but I found Lecka's Food Market and picked up some cold cuts and potato salad."

"I thought you said takeout."

"I did. I took it out of Lecka's."

Emilie shook her head, and sat down on the couch.

"Oh, and wait," Ross said. Emilie watched him pick up his jacket and grope inside one of the pockets. Then the other. Standing in his stocking feet, he looks so vulnerable and young, she thought. A very tall little boy.

"Ah, there it is," Ross said, returning to the living room. "Here." He placed a flat box on top of the low coffee table in front of Emilie's knees. "Open it now. While the patient is AWOL, and we're alone."

"The patient will be returning to duty momentarily, Doctor," she said, picking up the package. She scrutinized the box, turning it one way and then the other. She rattled it next to her ear, then traced the top of the gold bow with her fingertip. "What is it?"

"You'll have to open it to find out, silly. Cause I'm not telling." He pulled the hassock closer to her, sat down, and watched the precision of her movements. "I saw this little place on Main Street with leftover Christmas lights blinking at me. What could I do? No one was in there but the owner. Nice lady. She'd just opened the place a while back. She calls it the Shamrock Shop, and she promised me that you'd look great in it?" He flipped a finger in the direction of the box.

"Now how would she know that?"

"I told her you were Irish. Dark hair, gray-blue eyes."

Emilie grinned. She glided the ribbon off the side of the box, and then with great care, took the wrappings away and laid them on the table. She removed the lid and placed it upside down on top of the wrappings. Then in slow, delicate moves, she parted the white tissue paper, and pulled a long scarf from the box. The smooth cloth felt exquisite in her hands, its aqua and lavender pattern woven into fine strands of silk. "It's beautiful, Ross. Thank you so much." Emilie hummed.

"Do you like it?"

"I love it. I absolutely love it." She held the scarf in two hands and let it dip under her chin. "I hope the lady was right about the color. What do you think?" she said, posing.

Ross nodded. Grinned.

Then Emilie folded the scarf, and laid it inside the box. "Why, Ross?" she said.

For a moment he stared at her. The passion that had grown inside him over the last twenty-four hours pushed hard to be free. "Why?" Then he threw his head back, a laugh bursting from deep in his throat. A gift so scrawny and witless. A thing. A token. A symbol. A joke, really. After she'd given so much.

Ross looked at Emilie and they locked eyes. He reached across the table, a movement too graceful for his size. Then he took both of her hands in his. Her hands, her fingers, they felt fragile, yet strong. Just like the woman herself.

Why? indeed, he thought. A thousand reasons formed in his brain. Sentences that had no beginnings. Like in the English class before he dropped out of school. The teacher had asked him to diagram a sentence on the board in front of the group. Twenty-six kids. Watching him trip to the front of the room and pick up the chalk. Fifty-two eyes boring holes into his back. At the time, the only part of the sentence he could remember how to diagram was the prepositional phrase at the end: *under the tree.* So he had done the easy part first. He'd stared at the diagrammatical lines. Stick people with too many limbs. He completely forgot how to diagram the beginning of the sentence. *I'm a dope*, he had thought when the teacher told him to sit down, and a girl wearing a plaid skirt and saddle oxfords sauntered up to the board and passed by him in the aisle between the desks. *Dope, dope, dope. You lost the beginning of the sentence. The start. The origin. The first. And now you have nothing left but the prepositional phrase at the end. Just three words is all you've got. Three dumb words. Three little words. I love you.*

"Why did you come here, Emilie?" was all that he said.

Emilie held her silence for a moment. Just as she opened her mouth to speak, Michael appeared in the hallway, head down as he rubbed a towel in circles around his wet hair. "I found this nice robe on the back of the door," he said, lifting his face and talking through the parted terrycloth.

Both Emilie and Ross stood at the same time.

"You look great," Ross said, approaching Michael. He tugged at the fabric, brown flannel bunched around

Michael's waist. "Now all you need is an extra fifty pounds, and you'll have it made."

Michael draped the towel around his neck, swimmer style. He took a comb from the pocket of the robe and ran it through his hair.

"I can't believe how good I feel, Ross. No rasping. No coughing. Just like a real person. But I'm so hungry. What gives with that?"

"Your body is beginning to function normally now, Mike. And it knows there's a lot of work to be done to put you in optimum health. So it's trying to compensate for the lack of calories. Your body knows what it needs to build it up to par for the tip-top pre-middle-aged man that you're becoming."

"Hey, wait a minute. What'd'ya mean pre-middle aged?"

"Once you've reached your ideal weight, your appetite will level off. Or let's hope so, anyway. And then you'll only be hungry four or five times a day."

"Sounds good to this pre-middle aged guy," Michael said.

"Speaking of food," Emilie said. "I'll go to the car and bring in the food you, uh, mentioned. Some time ago, Dr. Manchester." Emilie went to the door, stopped, and spoke over her shoulder. "Ross, why don't you go ahead and get cleaned up? Then you'll feel as good as Michael. I'll prepare the meal."

"Good idea." Ross nodded once, then started for the bathroom. "By the way, Em. What do you think of this sprouting beard? I hear that real mountain men all have them. Supposed to be manly."

Emilie stood at the open door, hand on the knob. She felt a cold rush of outside air sweep over her face. "I like it," she said.

59

Exactly what do you think you're doing?

I'm thinking.

Thinking?

Yes.

Well, cut it out, will you? That's how the trouble always starts.

Only in the past, S.F. Only in the past. Maybe this time it'll be different.

It won't be different. Never. Stop being so naïve.

I'm not naïve.

Yes, you are. Look, you promised yourself you'd conform. That's the only way to cope. Remember?

I didn't say I'd conform. I said I would pretend to conform. Big difference.

Well. Whatever. It just won't work the other way.

Why not? It works for other people.

You're not other people. Somewhere along the line, something is gonna go wrong. Slap you in the face. Or stab you in the back.

It's foolproof this time.

You always say that. At first it looks foolproof. Always does. Never is. Always screws you up.

I know.

Then forget it.

I can't.

You can.

Get out of my head, S.F. And get off my back.

Okay, mugwump. But don't say I didn't warn you.

Scram.

Marilyn stared straight ahead at the fog, so thick over the Gulf this morning that the line separating the sea and the sky were indistinct. She was dressed in wrinkled jeans and a sweat jacket zipped up to her chin. Her feet were bare, red painted toes buried in cold sand. Long hair, the color of dark honey, hung loose down her back. A film of mist enveloped her, forming a wet layer on her hair and her clothes.

It was empty on the beach now, just the way she liked it. The tourists were still asleep in their cardboard rooms in the motels that lined the beach. But once the morning chill vanished, and the sun burned a hole in the fog, barelegged parents from the north would follow happy kids to the shoreline, and plop themselves on a thin blanket they snitched from the hotel room, and sit rigid while their frail flesh turn into fuchsia pain.

The gray blur of a seagull screeched in the air directly in front of Marilyn. Then it plunged into the water like an arrow, emerged in a path parallel to the water, flapped twice, and then disappeared into the fog.

Marilyn had been writing in her journal for some time. Writing was the one constant in her life. Articles, short stories, kids' books, poetry, daily entries into her diary, humor, non-fiction, dialogue. Didn't matter much, as long as she wrote. She kept files in boxes marked *Potential Articles, Interesting Names, Crimes and Accidents, and Miscellaneous Mishmash.* Sometimes a manuscript sold. Sometimes she even got paid. Her article on the nursing shortage would be published in RN Magazine this summer. They had promised a check when the edition came out. She was glad of that. It had taken her over a year to research and write that one.

This morning, Marilyn's writing consisted of the first six pages in her *Journal of Progress* that she and Barbara were developing to teach deaf children to sign. It was when she stopped to stretch her fingers that the battle in her head had begun. Happened a lot lately. So often, in fact, that Marilyn gave her devil's advocate a name. Sang-Froid. Or S.F. for short. Sometimes S.F.

was right. He usually came around when a failure occurred in Marilyn's life. Then S.F. was kind to her, licking her wounds with a soft tongue, caring that she hurt. She cried out to him in the night during those times, and when she'd shout out *Why?*, he'd tell her that it's because she's too soft. A vulnerable lady whose trust in the human race was devouring her, gnawing at her soft parts. During those times, Marilyn let herself give in to the luxury of defeat. She agreed with S.F. and cried out her pain until the whimpering stopped, and some of her strength would come back. Along with S.F.'s cynicism.

Then she'd coast for a while, assuring herself that she'd never fall into the trap again. And her Sang-Froid would go away. She didn't need him anymore. Until it happened again.

Marilyn's mind wandered a bit now. To the first time S.F. had come to her aid. It was after the divorce. When Melissa was born six weeks premature, and Daniel hadn't even known she was pregnant. Or cared. From her hospital room, she had called her parents who lived in North Fort Myers at the time.

Mom, they say my baby has hyaline membrane disease. She might not live, Mom. Please come.

After the weekend, dear, we're doing summer inventory at the store now, and . . .

But Mom, please. I need you now. I can't watch my baby die all alone.

And her mother promised to come in a few days. Which she did. Except by then the infant was dead and Marilyn didn't care anymore if her mother came or not.

The afternoon of the funeral, when a few people had come and then gone back to their lives, Marilyn sat in the big chair in the living room of her apartment. She held onto a square ceramic container that was made from a mold that looked like a baby's alphabet block. There'd been tea roses in it, and baby's breath, their delicate stems wrapped in thin wires to hold them upright. And a sprig of leaves the color of pea soup. All of this was poked into a rubbery sponge base that stayed inside of the block. A cottony numbness filled her head that day – from the Librium they gave her – as she rotated the ceramic alphabet block with her fingers. The slick exterior felt cool on her flesh, as she sat in the big chair in her apartment and spoke to the thing, reading the letters painted on the outside.

A, B, C, D. A, B, C, D. A child's toy.

Oh, but a child couldn't play with this block. Even if the flowers were gone. Because if a child played with this block, it would break into a thousand pieces, pointed and sharp.

And the child would get hurt.

Her child wouldn't, though. Not anymore.

A, B, C, D. Not a real hurt anyway. A, B, C, D.

All true sentences have a subject and a verb. At least a verb, anyway, but in that case, the subject is inferred. There are other things that sentences can have, too, like participles and gerunds, but then it gets complicated and errors are made. Stick to the simple statements.

A, B, C, D. A Baby Can Die.

Neat. Tidy. Follow the rules. Keep your nose clean.

Whose rules?

Theirs.

Oh. What about mine? Don't I get to make any rules, too?

No.

Oh.

Her Sang-Froid. He had kept her from having a nervous breakdown. He had given her guidelines to follow so she would be able to cope.

Like: *Be careful what you say to people.*

And: *Watch your back.*

And: *Don't give your soul away, or you won't have anything left for yourself.*

See what I mean?

And she had to agree.

223

So, for the next three months, after Marilyn had thrown the dead flowers in the trash and wrapped the ceramic alphabet block in tissue paper and placed it in a corner of her closet shelf far away from the light where she couldn't see it anymore, she held true to the rules. Sang-Froid's rules.

Then gradually, as her outer zombie shell crumbled and fell away, one tiny chip at a time, Marilyn forgot about the rules again. She knew it was happening. But each time she tried to go back to following the rules, something, someone – a child on the unit, a teary-eyed parent, the new inservice director they just hired who was as nice as she could be, an injured bird on the sidewalk – Marilyn would feel a tug at her core, and she allowed her wall of protection to drop once again.

It felt better that way.

But that's when S.F. came back with his warning. Same pattern every time. She'd scoff and joke at his warning.

"Don't worry," she'd laugh. "I'm okay now. Strong. Don't need this isolation anymore. I want to truly live. Help me, S.F., to share my life with others."

You're a mugwump, he'd say.

And Sang-Froid's pelting would start again, in earnest, every time she hit on a new and creative – and risky – idea.

It won't work.

It will work.

I'm telling you it's not gonna work. You'll see.

And again, S.F. was right. Like last time when the hospital census was low and the corporate guys complained, Marilyn asked for a meeting with head of public relations to discuss an idea that she had.

"A Saturday afternoon party for kids who are scheduled for surgery. To help orient them on what to expect. So they won't be so scared when they get here," she had said on the in-house hospital phone that day. "Introduce the kids to the nurses who'd be caring for them. Balloons, ice cream, games. Give them a fun time so they see the hospital as a place that is friendly and welcoming."

The PR guy had chuckled through the phone in an encouraging sort of way.

"Let's meet tomorrow and talk about it," he'd said.

The next day, when Marilyn entered the PR guy's office, there sat Fossari, a scowl on his face. Marilyn had stood, frozen, in front of Fossari, babbling incoherently for two horrible minutes. And when she was done, Fossari had smiled.

"Miss Pelletier," he had said. "You are a good nurse. And I know you want to continue being a good nurse. And I know you want to remain here at Parkwest. So, you must learn that this is a hospital. Not a kindergarten. And hospitals have certain rules and regulations that must be met." Then Fossari rose, walked to the door, and turned. "Good day," he said, and left her standing there with egg on her face and dripping down her heart.

On the very first day of school vacation that summer, Parkwest Children's Hospital sponsored a hoopla orientation program for kids who were scheduled for routine admission. Also invited were those children whose rich parents had no intention of sending their kids to the hospital, but they dressed them in ruffles and black-patent Mary Janes and came anyway, just in case, because you never know about these things.

Hundreds of families showed up for cake and cookies and giveaway prizes for moms, presented at the rostrum to loud applause and flashbulbs. And milling around with signed invitations tucked in their pockets was the entire membership of the Pinellas County legislative delegation, their campaign managers and political assistants, and anchormen from the media waving mics into hospital execs' faces, while newbie reporters scratched on their wide-lined notepads, with no one paying attention to any of the kids.

Then, when Channel 44 and the St. Petersburg Independent sponsored a Name-the-Event contest, the winning kid and her parents wore gold paper crowns and sat right up front on Parkwest Hospital's float in the Festival of States parade, and every Saturday afternoon after that, like clockwork, the hospital hosted their *Kids Orient Express Party*.

The following year, the hospital made a separate room for birthday parties. To celebrate – just like the roller rinks did – at a reasonable fee per child, plus a hat for the birthday kid, if you wanted it, with an extra cost for pizza, and a face-painting clown you could hire. By the hour, of course.

Now, alone on the beach, Marilyn fought with her conscience one more time. Would Pal Sign work? Or was she headed for more emotional disaster.

Then, right in the middle of the page where she left off writing her journal, Marilyn drew a vertical line in the middle with her pen, all the way to the bottom. She wrote the word *Disadvantages* above the left column, and *Advantages* above the right. She listed in the left-hand side, all the potential hazards of starting a non-profit organization to teach kids sign language. *Too costly. Threat to local service groups. Might get fired.* There were more, but these were the big three.

When she started scribbling in the right-hand column, *Advantages*, she ran out of space on that page, but kept right on going, until she filled up three more pages.

Marilyn looked back over her lists, studying them. Then she hammered the point of her pen once on the paper to make a period that finalized her plan, and slammed the book shut.

"Onward and upward," she said, and stood up in the sand.

Marilyn dusted loose grains from her bottom, numb now, and grinned at two joggers, a man and a woman, who waved back at her as they passed, their feet splashing in the water in unison, gracefully galloping up the beach.

Later that afternoon, Marilyn typed a letter to the Personnel Director at Parkwest requesting her hours of employment be changed from her current 7 a.m. to 3 p.m. shift, to the evening 3-to-11 shift. Marilyn knew the hospital had trouble filling positions for the evening shift, because experienced nurses wanted their nights free. Now she needed the daytime hours to promote her new venture.

Marilyn addressed an envelope. Then she folded the letter, inserted it into the envelope, and licked the flap. Next, she rolled a blank sheet of paper into her typewriter.

She typed:

For Immediate Release

Free Pal-Signing Class for Deaf Children Offered at Local Church

Later, she would take the announcement to the church to photocopy with their Fossil Park Church of St. John the Divine logo in gold and brown ink scrolled across the top. Then she'd mail the announcement to the local media.

60

"You're damn right I'm upset." Michael slid onto the driver's seat of the Buick. He reached down to the adjustment handle near the floor and pulled the seat forward. Then he set the steering wheel, clicking it in place. He slammed the driver door shut with a ruthless tug, then started the engine – revving it long and hard – and spewing black smoke from the tailpipe.

Emilie rode in the front seat with Michael. Ross settled in the back seat of the car. He felt remorseful now, wondering if he'd waited too long to tell Michael about Kevin's death. Or if he'd told him too soon. Michael had just been through an ordeal, and Ross didn't want Michael's progress to backslide. But Ross knew that Michael needed to hear the news from him, and not when he stepped through his front door in a happy trance, and Barbara hit him with the news that she thought he would know by then.

It was on the drive back to Florida that Ross told Michael about Kevin. They had stopped for a quick lunch and were sitting in Big Boy's at an exit just off the Interstate.

At first, Michael didn't respond. They'd had the restaurant to themselves, except for two couples at the far end of the counter up front. The three of them finished their meal in heavy silence. Then Ross paid the tab and they'd stepped out into the bright hazy parking lot. That's when Michael snapped at his friend, and Ross wished it were his turn to drive the next lap. But he kept quiet and let Michael rant.

Emily was positioned at a three-quarter turn, one arm across the seatback. Ross leaned forward from the rear. He touched Emilie's fingers lightly. Then he reached over and laid his hand on Michael's shoulder without saying a word.

When Michael spoke next, he sounded remote, like his voicebox was encased in a small plastic refrigerator bowl covered in Saran Wrap, with the edges overlapped all the way around the top of the dish to keep the resonance airtight, and the only thing you could hear were phonemes of words that bounced around inside. "This remedy," Michael said. "This torpid therapy you treated me with, Ross. Are you sure it has taken care of my disease? For good?"

Ross hesitated. Where was Michael going with this? "Michael, you'll always have cystic fibrosis," he said in a gentle voice. "There's no cure for it. It's in the genes. And you'll need to undergo a series of formal laboratory tests and X-rays at the hospital when we get back. To make absolutely sure that your blood levels are within the normal range and your lungs are as clear as I think. To start with, our medical equipment was mediocre at best. But, unless I've lost my ability to reason – and I don't think I have – what I believe we're going to find is that all these tests will just prove your new good health. I also believe that with a high-calorie and well-balanced diet to keep your insulin and enzymes on keel, that you can remain symptom-free for an indefinite period of time. Maybe you'll have the life expectancy of any other man your age." Ross sat into his seat, watching the back of Michael's head nod slowly over and over again. "We'll be facing a lot of ifs, Mike. Things we haven't even thought of yet."

"Like what?" said Michael.

"Right now, I can't answer that. I'd like to think that I've covered everything. I know I gave it my best. But I'd be a fool to believe that's a given. So, we'll just have to watch you closely and see."

Again, Michael nodded. "You think that under ideal circumstances – I mean without all the secrecy, and be assisted with unlimited staff and equipment – that it could be duplicated?"

"It?" said Ross. "You mean your torpid therapy?"

"Yes."

"I do. I believe it could be repeated on you without any ill effects, yes. But then, it may not be necessary if we — "

Michael punched the air in front of him. "No! That's not what I mean, Ross." He slapped the steering wheel. "What I mean is, could it, the torpid therapy, be duplicated on someone else? I mean, now that you know more of what to expect."

"Possibly."

"If that other person was young and strong, say? And worked out and didn't have major physiological changes in the body from the disease to begin with?"

"It's likely, yes." Ross wrinkled his brow.

Michael didn't speak for several minutes. Then, "Do you think Kevin really died in his sleep, Ross?"

"Oh," said Ross. "I couldn't say, Mike. I wasn't there," he said in a soft voice.

"Ross, this is not easy. Please don't bullshit me." His tone was gentle and pleading in spite of his words. "Did Kevin die in his sleep?"

"I can only say that it doesn't seem likely to me." Ross was uncomfortable. He wanted to be honest – with both Michael and himself. "I think that Kevin's lungs had filled up with mucus after the usual critical time period when complications – if any – take place. I don't know why there was a delay before his condition deteriorated. But apparently it was similar to your post-lavage reaction. Every time Kevin was admitted to Children's, they expected him to die. He finally did."

"What would you have done different, Ross. What would you have done if you'd been there?"

"Well, naturally, I'd've examined him first. But I definitely would have opened an airway for him to breathe. First thing. Immediately. And then I would have done an emergency lavage." Ross felt Emilie's hand touch his from across the front seat.

"One more question, Ross. Then I'll shut up." Michael started speaking in slow, deliberate words, one hand poking the air with each syllable. "If I had agreed to the therapy there in Banner Elk sooner – like two weeks ago, for instance. And if Kevin had come with me and had the same thing done, would he be alive today?"

"Come on, Michael," Ross leaned forward. "I see what you're doing, man. Stop blaming yourself. I don't know whether I would have even agreed to that. Or if Kevin would have either."

"He would have, Ross."

"You don't know that, Mike."

"Yes, Ross. Yes, I do know that."

"What do you mean? How could you possible know?"

"I asked him."

"Oh, God."

Two miles later, without any warning, Michael pulled into a rest stop and parked close to the sidewalk leading to the Men's Room. "I have to go to the bathroom," Michael's voice was barely audible. When he left the car, Emilie turned and touched Ross' face.

"Go to him, Ross," she whispered.

Ross entered the building and saw Michael's feet under one of the stall doors, shoes facing sidewards. Ross tugged the door handle. When it opened, he saw Michael sitting sidewards on the commode, fully clothed, his forehead pushed against the dirty partition. Michael remained still when Ross entered the stall. Ross bent over and put an arm across Michael's upper back. For a long time, neither of the men spoke. Then Ross felt Michael's body heave as he took in great gulps of air and let out his sobs.

When Michael was still, Ross whispered. "Kevin is gone, Michael. And that is a tragedy in itself. But you, Michael. You're alive. And you have a long, tough road ahead of you. A little deaf girl back home is waiting for you to find justice for her. Nobody, Michael. Nobody else in this whole ruthless world can do that for her. Not Kevin, not me, not another lawyer. Nobody. Just you, Mike." Ross paused, gathering strength to continue. He inhaled and let it out slow. "I've done my job for you, Mike. Now you go do yours for that little girl."

Ross straightened and stepped out of the booth. He walked to the row of sinks, removed a folded white handkerchief from his back pocket and drenched it with water. Then he wrung it out and returned to Michael.

"Here, Mike. Wash your face. I'll go get some Pepsi's from the machine, and meet you at the car."

Michael slept the rest of the way home.

61

Marilyn leaned out the window of her car looking for the speaker and microphone grating.

"Two singles, no cheese, no onion. Two Frosties and one large fry," All she got was a face full of static from the colorful cartoon kid with freckles and red pigtails.

"That'll be $4.23. Drive up to the window, please."

On the front seat next to Marilyn, Tracy Thomas sat perched with her fingertips resting on the dashboard radio speaker by the glove box. She slid her fingers back and forth, face contorted in concentration, as Neil Diamond blasted out *Brother Love's Traveling Salvation Show*. The car inched up the line as Marilyn watched Tracy. She picked up their food order and placed it on the seat beside her, then drove around the corner of the Wendy's lot and parked facing the two-story nursing home on the property next door. There was a giant canvas sign swinging from four ropes attached to the outside of the second floor windows. *Breese Manor, Where Love is Ageless* it said in bright navy letters.

Marilyn adjusted the car's position in the parking space and turned off the engine, silencing the radio's music. Tracy's head jarred, as if she'd been struck, and she spun around in her seat. Her face was crimped in distress. Marilyn was busy digging into the paper bag and removing items. She felt Tracy slapping on her forearm. Immediately Marilyn grabbed a French fry and looked up.

"Here, sweetie, take this. I'm just setting up our foo — What, Tracy? What is it, baby?"

Tracy began to hit the dashboard with her fingers. Marilyn saw tears welling up in the child's eyes.

"Oh, no, baby," said Marilyn. She bent across the food between them and stroked the side of Tracy's face. Then Marilyn finger signed *P - I - A - N - O*, and made the question-mark sign. Tracy's arm flew up, elbow bent. She turned her palm toward Marilyn, made a fist up and forward, for the yes sign, and began pumping her wrist in rhythm with rapid head nods.

"Good," Marilyn mouthed. She placed the fingers of her right hand against her lips, then moved them down, placing the back of her fingers into her left palm, both hands facing upward. "That's super, Tracy." Marilyn's face stretched into a wide grin, as she wrapped Tracy inside her arms.

For the next twenty minutes, as Marilyn and Tracy munched on burgers and fries, the car radio blasted with music and talking sounds. Tracy ate with one hand flat against the dashboard, feeling vibrations run up her arm.

Soon Marilyn crumpled the burger papers and stuffed them into the food sack. Then she relaxed in her seat. The afternoon was warm for January, and with the windows rolled up, the inside of the car felt cozy. She closed her eyes and let the pulsing music rebound against her ears. Tracy was so full of sparkle and optimism, she thought. This child's brilliance goes beyond her gift for music.

Marilyn settled back on the seat, and in less than a tenth of a millisecond, within her thinking machine, waves of electrochemical proteins attached to vesicles containing neurotransmitters, dumping their contents into the synaptic cleft inside her brain, and then reabsorbing them, so Marilyn could hold and treasure the long-ago picture of Tracy sitting at the piano in the hospital library playing exquisite music, and then put that image beside the one of Tracy now, struggling to learn sign language. Those thoughts were the endothermic weapons Marilyn needed to continue creating ideas and plans that would impact Tracy's future. And other deaf kids' futures, as well.

Marilyn opened her eyes and sat up in her seat, ready to back up the car and leave. She stopped to watch Tracy. The child continued to tap imaginary keys on the dashboard, but her eyes were staring through the front windshield, fixed on something across the lot at the nursing home. When Marilyn followed Tracy's gaze, she saw two women arguing. One was large, dressed in a white uniform and cap, towering over a wheelchair occupied by a patient whose back curved at an angle that made it difficult for her to look up. The patient was waving tiny thin arms above her head as she spoke. Marilyn rolled down the driver side window, but she couldn't make out what was said. Then Marilyn heard the large woman yell a one syllable word, pointing her finger in the patient's face, and saw her move behind the patient, and jerk the wheelchair around. As she was rolled along the sidewalk, the patient in the wheelchair dropped her head into her hands, and they both disappeared around the back of the building.

Marilyn's lunch turned into a gastric knot. Then she remembered the time during her first semester in nursing school, when she'd worked part-time as a nurse's aide on the midnight shift at Breese Manor to pay for her books. She knew their routine, and the scene she just witnessed was an everyday happening that they ordinarily tried to keep inside the walls.

At first, Marilyn mostly helped feed patients and get them ready for bed. Once in a while she'd come in early and on weekends to do volunteer work. She had loved geriatric nursing, and even thought she'd make it her specialty once she graduated. Her idea then was to replace choice employees with new and kinder recruits.

Then the summer after she first started nursing school, she married Daniel, and her life was complete. They would live happily ever after – Danny, the handsome prince, who would take care of her for life.

And she, the fair maiden, future mother of three, two girls and a boy, all scrubbed clean and shining when their daddy came home from work at the end of the day.

It hadn't worked out that way. None of it.

By the time Marilyn found out about the affair, Danny's mistress was already six months pregnant. By November, one month before graduating from nursing school, Marilyn left Danny, rented an apartment on Pelican Island Beach, and took a full-time nurse's aide position at Breese Manor. It wasn't long after she lost the baby, she passed nursing boards with top grades, and once her Florida license arrived, she moved up to R.N. supervisor. Then the administrator offered Marilyn the Inservice Director's position.

"You're a born teacher," the administrator had said. "And the staff looks up to you."

Marilyn almost took the job, but the employment application she'd filed with Parkwest Pediatric Hospital, finally came through. The letter was personally signed by Dr. Louis Cocuzzo, and welcomed her to the pulmonary floor, 7 a.m. to 3 p.m., starting the following week. The pay was lousy and the pressure exceeded the nursing home's, but Marilyn's first love was children, and she looked forward to going to work.

Then Cocuzzo died.

When the city fathers, the newspapers, and the hospital confusion settled, things returned to normal. That's when Vincent Fossari starting throwing his weight, and Marilyn avoided him whenever she could. And since the time Fossari took her kids' orientation idea as his own, Marilyn shared just one more idea. As she'd told Sang-Froid, this time it was different, simple, and wouldn't cost the hospital a cent. And Cindy, the new Inservice Coordinator, was soft-spoken and seemed kind.

"With all the empty rooms on our pediatric unit, we could convert one into a classroom and library," she told Cindy. "We could tutor the kids with long-term hospital stays whose grades suffer from missing school," she said. "We could recruit high school students, as well as volunteer teachers from the local schools, and . . ."

"Great idea, Marilyn," interrupted Cindy. "Really great. I'll make a note, and get back with you." They shook hands and that was that.

A few weeks later, when the hospital's maintenance crew started hammering shelves onto the walls of a room down the hall, and then dragging in school desks and books, Marilyn was delighted. She ran all the way down three flights of stairs and stood breathless at Cindy's desk. "Wow, I can't wait to see the new library and classroom when it's done," she said.

Cindy raised her head and spoke in a near whisper. "Yes, we're very proud of the hospital's new addition."

"And thanks, Cindy," Marilyn said, "for listening to my idea. I've worked here a long time, and you're the first one to . . ."

"Your idea? I don't know what you're talking about, Marilyn. The ribbon-cutting ceremony will be held in three months. Like all the rest of the staff, you'll receive an invitation in the mail."

Sang-Froid gloated.

Now, Marilyn felt Tracy tap her on the thigh. She was pointing to the radio, turning dials with one hand, and feeling vibrations with the other, happily bouncing her head in exact time with the music. Then Tracy clicked the radio off, and brought her right hand to her face. With her fingers and thumb together, she touched her cheek at the side of her mouth. She moved her hand toward her ear, then touched her cheek again. "Ohm," she said.

"Yes, sweetheart. Let's go home."

62

Vincent Fossari paced back and forth from the living room to the sunroom and then circled back, making the loop over and over again.

He was livid. The tissue of his left hand throbbed trying its best to heal. But at that moment, Vincent Fossari wasn't thinking about healing. Or pain. Or how the fist-pounding strikes against his palm were turning the delicate tissue savage and raw with each blow. Nor did he suspect that the rage within him was creating changes in his cardiovascular system, sending his blood pressure to the extreme limits of safety. All Vincent Fossari knew at that moment was a screaming roar in his head, and the push, push of his anger to break out and kill. They should be dead. Frozen. Natural causes. An act of God.

But Fossari had seen Ross Manchester, not two hours ago, driving down 4th Street North. Him and that brat. Fossari wasn't sure at first, so he drove around the block, turned on 71st Avenue North, and circled the short street behind the parking lot of the Fossil Park Church of St. John the fucking Divine. By then, the beat-up Buick was parked in the sun, showing off its rust and a brand new tire. And it was Manchester himself, all right, who'd entered the church on the heels of his kid.

Now, Fossari pushed through the back door of his house, through the sunroom, and headed outside. Walking ankle deep across the manicured lawn, Fossari removed a key ring from his trouser pocket, and stormed past the seawall, onto a wooden pier projecting forty feet out. At the end of the dock, his '76 Cruise

Craft outboard hung suspended under a high shed. Fossari threw the keys onto the deck of the boat. Then he unfastened the latch to release the crank handle and turned it. Grinding cables lowered the boat until it smacked loudly on the surface of the water. He stepped onto the boat and unhitched the lines from cleats on the pier. Then he started the engine and took off into Boca Ciega Bay, leaving a heavy wake in his path.

Fossari only slowed when he passed through the narrow inlets between Pass-a-Grille Beach and Pine Key on his way to the open Gulf waters, where he broke away, pushing the water aside at a speed of more than 48 knots.

Farther south, Fossari circled a tiny island and eased the boat onto the beach. Stepping off the boat, Fossari's face was riddled with dried salt-water, and his hair was plastered back from his face, exposing the tips of his blackened ears.

If a stranger had met up with Fossari as he splashed through the shoreline, they would wonder why he wore Gucci shoes and a three-piece suit to walk on the beach in water up to his ankles, especially on a cool winter evening on a desolate island.

By the time Fossari headed back, the sliver of a first-quarter moon had already descended to just above the water line. When he tied the lines back at his dock, and the sun was forming thin slices of yellow and brown across the sky, Fossari's dull mind still had no plan.

Back inside the house, he dropped his stiff clothes onto the floor of his bedroom. He showered, dressed, and combed his thick hair over the top of his ears. Then he left for the hospital.

63

Marilyn sat in the dim light of the nurses' station. She had just returned from checking the rooms on both halls, shining her flashlight with care on each of the kids' beds.

It was her third day working the evening shift, and tonight the census was low. She was still surprised – and delighted – at the light workload compared to day shift. After the first few hours on duty, the administrative staff went home. Along with the therapists, clerical workers, dietary employees, X-ray techs, and the retired women in their pink-striped costumes. And the doctors. Thank God, the doctors departed, including the ER docs-in-a-box whose beepers could buzz anytime, intruding on their night at the opera or ballet, when they'd scurry noiseless into the theatre lobby, telephone the student resident of choice, and then slither back to the balcony seat beside their woman who was dressed to kill.

At this time of night, there were no dietary carts rattling in the halls, or housekeepers barging into the nursery waking babies connected to oxygen tubes and I.V. lines. No lab report deadlines, or phoning a doctors' receptionist and beg they ask their boss to please call back.

Best of all, there were no loud vacuum noises to mask the alarm of call lights from kids needing help, or sidestepping cords snaking up and down the hall. Like the time on day shift when a toddler squirmed in her arms. Both she and the baby nearly tumbled when an electric cable wrapped around Marilyn's foot as the housekeeper sucked up debris from the floor. Luckily, the cord pulled out of the wall socket and Marilyn managed to hold both herself and the toddler balanced upright, while the housekeeper tsk-tsked, as if the whole thing were all Marilyn's fault.

During this three-to-eleven shift, a calm washed over the unit after the lights-out curfew at 9 p.m. All that was left was PRN meds and final Nurses' Notes in the charts.

Again, Marilyn left the nurses' station and tiptoed up the hall, flashlight in hand. One more check on the kids who'd been burned in the tent fire.

She stepped just inside the room, pointing her light at the floor. It broke her heart watching the children sleep, their chubby faces the only parts of their bodies that hadn't been mutilated by the flames. Now, three months later, 3-year-old Billy and his 5-year-old sister Mandy were still experiencing agonizing pain. To make matters worse, they still had a series of skin grafts and exfoliations to endure in the coming weeks. The kids had taken their final dose of meds on Marilyn's last rounds, and now, mercifully, they slept.

Marilyn stood in the doorway another five minutes, just to be sure, and then she padded back to her desk and finished her charting.

Then it was time for her break. She took a carton of skim milk from the refrigerator in the med room and returned to the nurses' station. She opened a deep file drawer, and dug around in her purse, then removed a drawing pad and laid it on the desk.

She stared at the spiraled wires along the top of the tablet, clicking the pen against her teeth.

She started writing, scratching through a word here, a line there. She stopped and reviewed the poem.

Old Herman's a clown who forgot
Whatever there was and was not.
His problems soon went
With a string that he bent
'Round his finger and tied in a knot.

Silly, she thought. But not too bad. Just what kids need. Herman was the tenth in a series of nonsense poems about clowns that Marilyn had created in the past two days. She was anxious to test them on Karen and Tracy at the next sign class at the church. She planned to put together a picture book for beginning sign students that was both educational and fun. The text, to be called *Concerning Clowns: A Simple Sign Book for Kids*, would include comical poems about clowns, using basic words for young readers, along with the pictures of the signing symbols to accompany the words. If it worked out well, other, progressively higher levels of reading and signing could be introduced into Pal Sign Picture Books, each one with a different theme. *Especially Elves. Favorite Fairies. Primarily Puppets. Wonderful Witches.* The list was endless. And with Tracy and Karen to help her think like a child – which really she had no trouble with on her own anyway – Marilyn hoped the books would stimulate interest in signing by the kids who joined her classes.

Marilyn's nursing pen skated over the pages below the poem she had just written about Herman, the forgetful guy. With short, back and forth strokes and zigzag lines, she sketched a picture of a hand, one huge finger pointing to the top of the page, a perfect loop laced around his outstretched digit. Then she drew his head to be disproportionately smaller than the hand. Next a Swiss-style hat. What about a feather, broad and flowy, atop the hat? Finally, Marilyn added a full and up-swept mustache under Herman's tilted nose. The reader's viewpoint of the clown was from

242

underneath. Marilyn moved the sketch pad to study the effect from farther away. "That'll work," she said out loud to herself.

As she finished the routine chores on the unit, Marilyn's new idea rolled around in her head. This'll be fun, she thought. But, of course, Sang-Froid'll be there with advice on the pitfalls ahead. Trouble looms, he will say, and give specific examples. Like the disapproval, disparagement, and denigration bound to get thrown at her from others. You're not a real teacher, they'd say, and so had no business pretending to be one. Act like an adult, for God's sake. You're a nurse, set an example for the kids. Not act like them. And, anyway, what expertise did she have to teach kids to sign? Come to think of it, S.F., I don't know myself.

Marilyn was sure that in the weeks and months to come, she'd be defending these censures, and more. Some she hadn't even begun to imagine. She'd been through it enough. But it was Karen who had prodded her when she doubted herself. They had just left the church the day they'd met Mary and Gert and were walking to the car. Marilyn made an offhand comment to Barbara, something about her lack of teaching credentials, and what if the Pal Sign program fell flat. Karen had stopped in her tracks.

"Marilyn, don't say that," Karen harrumphed. "Look at what Anne Sullivan did, and she didn't finish sixth grade. You said so yourself. She wasn't a real teacher, but she taught Helen Keller a whole bunch of things. Besides, you're already teaching kids sign language. Lookit me and lookit Tracy. See what I mean? And anyway, we won't know if we don't try."

Karen, the prophet. She was right, of course, and next time Marilyn heard from S.F., she'd let Karen represent her in an argument with him.

A soft buzzer interrupted Marilyn's thoughts as she cleared off her desk and prepared her notes for report to the on-coming shift. Checking the nurse-call board, she saw that room 412 was lit up. Bryan DeKalb, the 6-year-old who came in yesterday with herpetic gingivostomatitis, his tiny baby teeth nearly hidden beneath red and swollen gums. She pressed the lighted button. "Hi Bryan," she whispered into the microphone on her desk. Because of the low patient census, the child was in a room by himself, and Marilyn thought he may need some company before he went back to sleep.

Bryan's voice came through the desk speaker. "I have to go to the bathroom," he said in a shaky voice. "And my hand hurts. The needle is sticking me."

"Hang on, Tiger," Marilyn said. "Be right there."

One of the aides popped her head out the door of the kitchenette behind the nurses' station. "Need any help, Marilyn?" she said.

"Nah, should be okay. Thanks anyway, Trish." As an afterthought, Marilyn grabbed her sketchpad and tucked it under her arm.

Marilyn adjusted Bryan's I.V. on the pole. The line was open and running, drip rate good, and the needle in his hand looked good. She adjusted it anyway, to make him feel better. She aimed her flashlight at his mouth. "Open," she said. "I won't touch." She nodded. "Looks better, Tiger. You'll have this thing whupped before you know it." Then she steadied his back, helped him swing his legs over the edge of the bed, and walked him and his I.V. pole to the bathroom.

"You really did have to go, didn't you, Bryan?" she said, supporting her back against the doorframe and looking away to give him privacy.

"That's what I said before." Bryan pushed the I.V. pole on its wheels toward Marilyn.

"Whoops, don't forget to flush. And . . ." she said. Then she bit her tongue, wondering if she was supposed to measure his output. No, wait a minute, Bryan's chart had new orders to DC his I&O. Since there was nothing in the orders to remove the needle, she assumed the doctor planned to take it out himself in the morning.

"And wash your hands," she said, steering Bryan towards the sink. "Don't want to sleep with pee-pee germs in the bed, do ya?"

Bryan looked up at her, insulted, and Marilyn felt foolish. It was so hard to know exactly when a child's perception of life changed from spirited to sober. Some kids were born serious. Others, like herself, God forbid, held onto their kid-hood, saving precious fragments in the pockets of their grown-up attire to keep them warm and safe when things got rough.

Ho boy! Wouldn't S.F. have fun with that one?

With Bryan tucked into bed, the mattress raised to the angle he liked best, Marilyn offered him ice chips from the pitcher to sooth his sore mouth. He shook his head. Marilyn sat propped against the windowsill and chatted with Bryan about school. Then she told him about the poems she was writing for kids who were deaf, and asked him if he'd like to see them.

"Sure," he said in a flat tone, sounding like a teller at the Barnett Bank, who she'd just asked to change a ten.

Marilyn read the first three poems with as much zeal as she could muster, her voice in a forced whisper to keep it inside the room. Then she held up the clown illustrations that went with the poems. Herman and his hand. Amanda with the blue snake in her shoe. Then Arthur with his tune upside down. Marilyn pointed to a musical note tumbling upward from a huge saxophone, a balloon tied to the neck.

Bryan nodded. "Balloon's crooked," he said.

"So it is," said Marilyn, laughing inside. "So it is."

By the time Marilyn finished the next two poems, Bryan was asleep. Or pretended to be. Oh well. You can't win 'em all. And besides maybe the books'll be popular because they put kids to sleep. She closed her drawing pad and reached out and pushed a soft wisp of auburn hair away from Bryan's closed eyes. Then she bent and lightly kissed him on the forehead.

"Good-night, angel," she said.

Bryan stirred. "Night," he said, and rolled to his side.

Just as she returned to the desk, the night nurse stepped from the elevator giving Marilyn a yawning hello.

64

Karen hung from the back of her knees on the slant board. Her father was beating on her chest with a cupped palm in short, quick whacks.

"So, you like the idea, then?" he said. "I thought you would. Okay, cough. Now roll over. We'll do the left side next." Karen rotated on the board and raised her arms over her head. Ross continued to talk as he pounded on her ribs with a cupped hand. "I've watched you and Emilie," he said, and you two get along like peas in a pod." Ross nodded to himself. "Now I wonder why we hadn't thought of it sooner."

Karen flung her arms down, and pushed herself up on the slant board. Then she jumped to the floor. Ross leveled the surface and lifted her to a seated position. Then he sat beside her, folding his long arms across his chest. Karen coughed three times, inhaled deeply, and then blew it out with drama. It was her signal to her stepfather that she had had enough for the day. That her lungs were now clear.

"Okay, baby. Talk to me. What should I do?" said Ross.

Karen knew the old familiar pattern by now. Whenever her father wanted to talk with her without her usual vocal intrusions, he'd speak to her during the postural drainage treatments. She could hear him through the dull echo of his palm bashing her chest, but it was impossible for her to reply. The loosening mucus, passing into her throat triggered the cough reflex, moving the material down her esophagus and into her stomach as she swallowed. So, for the past fifteen minutes, Karen had been listening to her dad talk about

247

Emilie. He told her about Emilie's arrival at the cabin, and the important part she had played in rescuing him and Michael. As Karen listened to his story, what she heard was a fairy tale about a beautiful princess and a handsome king. Her father was too old to be a prince.

He told her about his drive into town and the scarf he'd bought Emilie. That was the only time Karen had interrupted his story during today's back-clapping routine. She had stretched her arms up in midair. "Wait," she said, waving her hands and grabbing his wrists. "Why did you buy Emilie a present?" Then she abruptly let go and waited.

"Well, why do you think? I bought it because I like her." He always answered his own questions when she couldn't speak. He reminded Karen of her dentist – his hands deep inside her mouth, probing at her teeth. *So. What grade are you in this year?* Or, *Tell me when you feel what I'm doing.* By the time you got your mouth to move around the dentist's fingers, the ordeal was over.

Ross stared at the floor for a very long time. But Karen didn't mind. Postural drainage treatments always made her tired. And it was nice he took a think-break. You'd'of thought she'd get used to the treatments. That she'd toughen up. But she never did. Her stomach muscles and the ones between her ribs always felt sore when they were done. Sometimes she'd sleep afterwards. Well, at least it's just once a day for her. Not like most kids with cystic fibrosis, who have to go get postural drainage five times a day. Like Alyce did.

"What did you say, Daddy?" Her mind must have wandered. She slid her bottom off the table and reached for Ross' hand. "Come on," she said. "Let's get something to eat. I'll fix us tuna with pickles. And we can talk more about Emilie."

They took their sandwiches out onto the deck by the pool. Sitting down, Ross moved a lawn chair to the front of him and propped up his feet, one ankle crossed over the other. He wore rubber thong sandals. Karen rested her elbows on the table and wolfed down the potato chips. The salt tasted good as she licked at her fingers.

Ross watched Karen through his dark glasses. The umbrella was tilted to the side, and the warm sun felt good on his face. The tuna aroma reminded him of a cabin meal with Emilie. Ross laced his fingers behind his head and raised his chin, speaking to the sky. "I don't even know her favorite food." He blinked. "Do you?" he said.

Karen lifted her insulated mug and took a swig, shaking her head. "Uh uh," she said from deep in her throat, and iced tea spilled down her chin. She set the cup back on the table and rubbed a paper napkin across her face, then dabbed at her wet lap. "Why don't we ask her," she said, standing up. "Let's you and me guess what it is. Then we'll ask her, and we'll see who's right. Okay?"

Ross smiled and reached for Karen's hand. "Okay," he said, pulling her close to his chair. "You first. What do you think is Emilie's favorite food?"

Karen squinted and bit her bottom lip. "Broccoli soup," she said. "I think Emilie likes broccoli soup the best. Or maybe yams."

"Only one guess."

"Well, okay, then . . . broccoli soup. What's your guess?"

"Hmmm," Ross said. He rubbed his chin, remembering what Emilie had said about his beard being manly. "Emilie's a pretty sophisticated lady, you know." Karen nodded. "She's got a good background. Classy genes. Wouldn't you agree?" Nod. "Then my guess is that she likes steak the best. Medium rare."

"Oh, daddy, no. She wouldn't eat a cow. Bet me. Okay, let's see who's the rightest. I'll get the phone and we'll call her." She ran across the deck and slid a broad glass door to the side, unplugged the telephone line from the jack just inside the family room. Then she returned and plugged in the phone on the outside wall near the table. "I'll dial. You ask. Okay?"

* * *

Emilie held the hair dryer up to her head, and didn't hear the ringing at first. Then she flipped the off button, paused, and scurried into the bedroom.

"Hello?" she said, sitting on the side of the bed and fluffing her damp hair.

Without introduction, Emilie heard the familiar deep and slightly-Virginia twang. "If two people had a heavy bet on a question that only you could answer, would that make you nervous?" Ross' voice said.

Emilie's heart lurched and her fingers went stiff on her scalp.

"What?" She inhaled.

"Well, young lady," I'm calling from radio station WOIX, where goofy mountain folks listen in from far to the yonder of Boone, Blowing Rock, Beech Mountain, and beyond." Emilie heard a little girl's giggle. "And since you were able to answer your telephone on the 11th ring, you, my dear listener, have just won a free dinner of your choice, to be accompanied by today's D.J. – me – and the cutest munchkin this side of Oz. And all you have to do, dear listener, is to identify to me, right now, no cheating, the food preference you find to be the most palatable."

"You are cra-zy," Emilie laughed.

"Okay, now, the clock is ticking. What is your favorite food?" Ross stopped, his question hung in silence. Then, "Tick, tick, tick . . ." he said.

Emilie felt as if she'd just run the eight-minute mile. She knew what it felt like, because she jogged every other day after work. Now her chest pumped against the towel wrapped around her middle and tucked in a knot over her breasts. She felt the phone's receiver slide in her hand as she pressed it against her ear. She didn't quite know what to say.

"Buzzzz, I'm so sorry, ma'am, but your ten seconds are up," she heard Ross say. Didn't he ever stop? "So for the booby prize, ma'am, I'm afraid that you have no other choice but to concede to the D.J. and the munchkin, and be dragged to dinner, anyway."

"Yeah!" Karen's voice sounded closer.

"Now, Miss Contestant, when can we pick you up? 7:30? Eight o'clock?"

"Doctor Manchester, are you asking me for a date?" She sounded confident. Good show, she thought.

"Yes, ma'am, I am."

"Tonight?"

"Uh huh."

"I can't, Ross." Damn.

"Oh." Shit.

"Wait." Emilie said, hearing the disappointment in Ross' voice. "I promised to meet with Michael at his apartment tonight. Mike and I have been working together on several social issues. The research on Tracy's hospitalization is turning up some odd data, Ross. Michael thinks there may be something useful I can add to her case." Emilie didn't want to say too much just yet. Michael had asked her to keep things confidential. He wanted to take Tracy's case to trial shortly, and the way the soon-to-be defendant was targeting Ross, Michael didn't want any unintended leaks.

"I'm free tomorrow," Emilie said. Did that sound too eager?

Emilie heard Ross' voice muffling, "Karen, want to go tomorrow?" Then, "Reporting from Oz, the Lollipop kid has a mild case of Munchkin slump. Oh, but wait, head-bobbings tell me recovery is imminent. Soon she'll be skipping up the yellow brick road."

"I'm sorry, Ross. Tell Karen it's for Tracy."

"No problem, my dear. That's what we get for being so impetuous."

251

Emilie thought about that. "No, Ross," she said. "It's called spontaneity. Abraham Maslow says so. And if you don't believe me, I'll bring my *Advanced Sociology for Social Workers* text on our date."

"Hope you're right, 'cause I don't want to be teaching my munchkin bad habits, you know."

"Hey," said Emilie. "You still don't know my favorite food. What do you think it is?" When he told her about their guesses, she laughed a rich, throaty sound into the phone. "I don't eat meat, Ross. For lots of reasons. In fact, the only high protein food I do eat is wild salmon," she said. "Except for the tuna sandwiches I was forced to eat for cabin survival.

"Wild salmon? As opposed to?"

"Ross, most people don't realize that there are two types of salmon. There's factory farmed, and there's those that are raised under natural conditions. It's the wild salmon that are grown naturally. Those are all I'll eat."

"I didn't realize."

"Please, Ross, don't get me started. I try to keep my soapbox tucked away. But it's portable, and unfolds in an instant."

"Emilie, if this is important to you, I want to hear it," he said.

"Okay, you were warned. Well, for one thing, there's the save-the-dolphins issue. When fishermen cast driftnets into the ocean, they create death walls for dolphins, whales, and porpoises who get trapped in the nets. They can't surface anymore to breathe, and every year, hundreds of thousands of these cetaceans die a slow painful death this way. Then there's the issue of salmon farming, which can be more like the agrarian type. The concentrated animal feeding operations, or CAFOs."

"CAFOs?"

"You've heard of factory farms, I know, Ross. That's where the meat industry raises farm animals in close confinement. Operates like a factory. High-density stock in small spaces. Disease is rampant. Chickens, cows, pigs. They even clip chicken's beaks way up high with no anesthesia, to keep them from pecking each other. The whole idea of the tight-quarters assembly line is to produce the highest output at the lowest cost. It's capitalism at the expense of living creatures who are powerless against the system. But the pain and suffering to the animals is immeasurable. And so is the social stress caused to them when the factory farmers take away the animal's natural maternal nesting behaviors, separate the moms from their babies. There's the extreme mental torture from overcrowding, restricted movement, and then watching their cage-mates killed before their eyes."

"I thought this treatment was only done in the medical field. Scientific experiments," said Ross.

"Well, partly it is, Ross. Especially experiments to give farm animals antibiotics and hormones. To see how quickly they get fat. And to try to keep some of the disease at bay. But then when the animals are killed, they're loaded with chemicals. And people eat them."

"Hmmm, I see what you mean."

"I could go on and on, Ross. But it's too upsetting. I just wish there were some way to tell people about the inhumane mass production of animals and fish for factory farming, and the grotesque practices that are legally okay. They're not okay. But I work for the government and I don't want to lose my jo . . ."

"Maybe there is." Ross said. His head was spinning. "This may sound crazy, but I have an idea. Let's talk about it tomorrow. Over a wild salmon dinner."

"Sure, Ross. Okay. Where?"

"I know just the place. A little restaurant on Madeira Beach. Sculley's Boardwalk."

"It's a date," Emilie said.

65

Looming. Distorted, as if looking through a fog. A huge crystal sphere, fragile and thin, suspended over Michael's head, distinctless as the separate but blurred colors of a rainbow, and when it came close, he reached out his hands, face tilted upward, only to see the image explode, scattering itself in a prickly mist on the skin of his face, and blinding his vision in an acid mockery. That's how Tracy's case seemed to Michael.

As he and Emilie pored over the papers spread on the table in Michael's dining room, he searched for the elusive fact pattern he knew had to be there. If he could only find the missing link. There was a girl out there who had the answers. But where was she? And, for that matter, *who* was she? Right now, the girl was a ghost who stood before the mirror and reflected no image. Looming.

But it was all he had.

Irene and Wayne Thomas had pushed for immediate action, and just yesterday, Michael's initial motion was set on the court calendar. He expected to hear from Fossari's attorney by early next week, and wondered who he'd be up against when the case went to trial.

Now, he ruffled through papers on the table. "Where's Karen's file?" he asked.

Emilie pointed a lacquered fingernail toward the corner of the table near Michael's elbow. "Over there," she said.

"Thanks, Em," said Michael. "With so much data, it's a wonder we can find anything at all in this mess."

Why did Michael keep taking material from Karen's files? Emilie thought. They were two separate actions. Tracy's personal injury lawsuit was one. And filing formal adoption papers and hunting for Karen's parents was the other.

They had been at it for hours. Barbara had helped for a while, but at 10:30, when Jeff cried out from the nursery, Barbara had excused herself and taken her novel into the bedroom to read while she nursed him. Now, at midnight, Emilie's brain was addled. And she wondered if Michael's could be, too, what with him mixing up the two different case files.

She picked up the two empty coffee mugs and carried them into the kitchen, then returned to the table, and stared at the papers in front of her, not seeing them. Her nostrils flared as she suppressed a yawn. Then she remembered her dinner date for tomorrow, and her mind leaped to the contents of her closet. One by one, Emilie mentally went through the racks. Something red. Good color. Maybe the white linen dress. Red jacket. In her mind, she dressed in the outfit, pushing the jacket sleeves high up her forearms. Turned up the collar. Madeira Beach might be a little warm and muggy, but if I . . .

"Damn!" Michael threw his pen down, hard, on top of the table. "Where the hell is she?" he said, scrubbing his face with flat hands.

Emilie jumped. "Who?"

Michael slid his chair back from the table and placed the outside of one ankle on top of the other knee. He picked up a stack of papers that had been stapled in the corner, and slapped at them with the back of his hand. "The woman who will rescue Tracy." He threw the papers back onto the table. "I don't see how we can win this case without her. And, if I'm wrong about her, then I'm chasing my tail around in circles anyway."

Emilie reached over and tapped Michael on the shoulder. "Excuse me, counselor," she said. He looked

255

up and through her as if she wasn't there. She waved her palm back and forth in the air. "Hello, hello. Remember me?"

Michael joggled his head. "Sorry, Em. I get so wrapped up in this. Forget where I am. There's so much preparation to do for even the simplest case. But this one is not only top priority for all of us, but it's such a slippery booger."

"I know," Emilie said, "But who is the girl you keep referring to? The woman? And how can I help?"

"Oh, Em, I don't know. That's just it." Michael squeezed at his temples with the fingers of one hand. "I don't even know what her name is."

"Where does she live?"

Michael shrugged. Snorted. "Terrific, huh? No name, no address. For all I know, there may not be any such girl at all."

"Michael, you're basing your thoughts on something. You wouldn't just dream up nameless people to come walking out of nowhere and solve mysteries for you. I've seen you in action, Michael. You don't operate like that. What is on your mind?"

"Who knows? Maybe it's just that I want to win this case so badly that I'm fantasizing. Or maybe when I was out cold up there in Banner Elk, my brain cells actually froze. And stayed that way."

"No Michael. The fact is that you look better than ever. And your alertness astounds me. Here I am, falling asleep on the job, and you – you've been working non-stop on these papers since . . .when?"

"Six o'clock."

"This morning?" Michael nodded. "Good grief, Mike. Maybe we should all have an annual hibernation day. Make it available for everyone. Like a yearly checkup or something."

"I wouldn't recommend it." Michael started gathering papers and making short stacks on top of the table.

Emilie slipped on her shoes and stood up. She arched her back, stretching her arms overhead. "I'll be gone for most of the day tomorrow, Michael," she looked at her watch. "Or rather today, Sunday. But if you want me, leave a message on my phone recorder, and I'll call you as soon as I return."

Michael murmured an acknowledgement.

"And Michael."

He looked at her.

"Take it easy, okay? It's Sunday. Spend some quality time with Barbara and Jeff. Slow down a little. Besides, Ross said that you're not quite home free, remember? Please don't push your health. Fossari's not going anywhere. He'll keep marching along until you catch up with him."

Michael walked Emilie to the door. His small frame looking weary but beginning to fill out with health. He turned the knob and pulled the door inward. "It's not Fossari's marching feet that I'm concerned about," he said. "It's the soundless orchestra in Tracy's ears that's pushing me."

Emilie smiled. "Graphic," she said.

They hugged and Michael closed the door.

66

"I know! I know! Pick me! Oh, pick me!" A small hand waved high in the air, just beneath Marilyn's nose, chubby fingers outstretched and waving, held in place at the elbow by the opposite hand balanced on the top of a little girl's head.

Marilyn pointed, then heard groans from two other children who had raised their hands.

Marilyn grinned. "Sorry guys, you'll get a turn. I promise." Then, "Okay, Stephanie," she said reading the sticky Hello-My-Name-Is tag curling off the little girl's T-shirt. "What sentence would you like to sign?"

Marilyn stepped to the blackboard, and held the chalk poised in the air. "Nice and loud, Stephanie."

There were two lists on the board. One side was for words that appeared in the sign language book, the *Are-In* list. On the other side, Marilyn had been writing words not found in the book, calling it the *Are-Not-In* list. From the *Are-Not-In* list, she planned to create her own Pal Sign finger-spelling glossary for kids.

"Chocolate toothpaste is better than regular brands," said Stephanie, followed by a chorus of laughter.

"Stupid girl!" said a boy sitting in the back of the room who'd been happily waving his hand moments ago.

Marilyn ignored the boy's comment, and began writing Stephanie's sentence on the board, just above the two columns. Then, holding the book open on the top of the folding table, Marilyn flipped to the index of the book. C. Ch. Chain. Check (Up). China. There. Chocolate: sentence 12, page 102. Quickly, Marilyn wrote the word chocolate in the left column.

The children cheered.

Marilyn felt comfortable in this room. Its warmth and acceptance was like an old friend she hadn't seen in a long, long time. She felt one with the group. The children were so eager to participate, to build with their minds, to create. They were her kind of people. As she leaned over the opened pages, Marilyn practiced the signing symbol for chocolate several times. She made a loose C handshape, with her right thumb resting on the back of her left hand, palm forward. Then she made two circles with her right hand.

Things had been moving fast. Especially the past two weeks. When the announcement came out in the church bulletin about the Pal Sign classes, Marilyn had received calls from four parents whose children were deaf. Two moms called saying they heard about the class from a friend. Then Emilie called from the Department of Social Services, to register a 4-year-old deaf child from one of the foster homes. Marilyn realized that her first problem was staring straight at her. Applicants were coming only from those who were deaf. To keep the integrity of her learning concept of matching up a deaf child with a hearing child, Marilyn now had to attract children who could hear.

On a whim, Marilyn called the teacher in Karen's gifted program, Ed Kohler, and ten minutes into the conversation, he invited Marilyn to come and speak to his class.

"We're between projects right now," Kohler said, "and you may have a topic the kids can sink their teeth into. "But remember," he warned, "these kids are different than those you find in the average classroom. They are animated and full of energy. Psychic energy." Marilyn thought of Tracy and Karen, who both fit the description. "Don't get me wrong, they're wonderful and I love them all. But if you're of the shy type at all, they'll topple you with their intellectual acrobatics."

Well, the man hadn't been wrong. Throughout her talk at Pasadena Elementary, Ed Kohler stood at the far back wall of the classroom, and each time the children buffaloed her, Kohler grinned and held up a blue-line sheet of paper on which he had written *I TRIED TO WARN YOU* in large crayoned letters.

When the bell rang, Marilyn felt like a limp cloth. But she knew she had found what she wanted. Now, she and Mr. Kohler were perched side by side on a long sturdy table, legs swinging as they talked. Karen sat in her school desk nearby, one forearm propped on a bright red book bag, eyes darting back and forth across a library book she held open with her fist.

"Well, I've got to admit, young lady, you did all right for yourself," Kohler was saying. "Ever work with kids before?"

"Not in this capacity," she said, "but it feels right somehow." Then she explained her job as pediatric nurse at Parkview Hospital. "But these kids are different," she smiled. "Just like you said." Marilyn stared into the middle space, trying to identify – and explain – what she sensed was so distinct in working with gifted children. "It's like being hungry for a long time," she said. "You don't know that you're hungry, exactly. You just know that something is not right in your gut. Every once in a while you reach for a cookie or a slice of bread, and you get smacked. So you retreat, and try it again later when you've forgotten about the pain in your hand. Then it happens again. But you never give up, because your memory of what happened before dims, and all you remember are the good parts."

Marilyn sensed Kohler studying her face. Should she trust him? Had she already said too much?

Pull in your soul, Marilyn. Now. Sang-Froid was trying like heck to get through, but her words flowed as a river after a storm, covering and drowning out any outside sound.

"And then one day, a table covered with food stands before you, and the dishes are smiling, and no slaps lay waiting as you reach out and pluck a grape, cold and glisteny and bursting with juice. The funny part of it is . . ." Marilyn smiled to herself and looked directly into Kohler's crystal blue eyes, doorways, open and friendly, to the mind behind them, " . . .that it's not really nourishment for your belly at all. The grape turns into an expectation, a hope that saturates your brain with delicious satisfaction. It makes you reach again and again, each time building the dream."

Suddenly Marilyn stopped. Fear prickled her mind for an instant, and then vanished. She blinked. Ed Kohler was touching her shoulder.

"You think I'm crazy," she said. "I'm sorry."

Kohler twisted his head very slowly, side to side, then his huge square face lit up, and his smile showed a row of white teeth beneath his coppery silver mustache. Marilyn saw that one front tooth overlapped the other. Then he spoke.

"Genius," he said in a velvety voice, "is the capacity to see ten things, where an ordinary man sees only one. And where the man of talent sees two or three, plus the ability to register that multiple perception in the material of his art. Ezra Pound said that. But, my dear, it is I who says that you are the one who sees the ten. And you have been hurt. I saw it as you spoke. And now here is my pittance. It's not much. Because, you see, although I am a teacher of the gifted, I, myself am not a gifted teacher. I am an ordinary man. And I give you my trust."

Not ordinary, thought Marilyn. But she only listened and watched. Then his expression changed.

"Well, now," he said, straightening his back and shifting his position so that one foot sat firm on the floor. He picked up the manual that Marilyn had been using in her talk to the kids. He poked it in the air.

"This is an excellent resource book, as you have already figured. But I have many, many more you can use."

Marilyn wrinkled her brow.

"Yes," he said. Then he straightened and wriggled a wallet from out of his back pocket. Marilyn heard the ripping of Velcro.

"This is a picture of my wife," he said. Marilyn saw a woman about forty, pretty face staring out of the photograph. "She died two years ago," he said. His movements were rapid as he replaced the wallet. As if he must get it out of sight. "We never had any children," he said. "And when Susan was 34, she was diagnosed with Alzheimer's disease, an illness that destroys personality and intelligence." Marilyn had studied the newly discovered condition at a continuing education workshop two years ago. "It's unusual for young adults to get this form of dementia," Kohler continued. "Nevertheless, Susan deteriorated almost in front of my eyes. And when she died – a vegetable – it was a blessing."

Marilyn opened her mouth, and Kohler held up his hand. "No, don't say anything. I usually can't talk about it like this. Please, let me go on.

"You might say that Susan never was very lucky. We had started to date in high school. You know, the old football-jock-meets-majorette syndrome. We had decided not to get married until we both had our college degrees. Well, during the summer before Susan's sophomore year at the University of Houston, we went scuba diving, and Susan went down too deep in the water. When she came up, she was screaming in pain. Both of her eardrums had burst." Marilyn inhaled in a gasp through her nose. "There were several operations, but they never did any good. When I went back to school in the fall, I had switched my major to special education and took courses in teaching the deaf. Susan dropped out of college then, and we got married. I learned more from her than I ever did from the books, and she helped me with my homework, studying right along as if she were taking the classes, too.

"When I graduated, I got a job at a state institution. Teaching the deaf. I did okay for several years. Then when Susan got sick, I just quit one day. Stayed home with her for six months – until she had to be admitted to a rest home. God, that was awful." Now it was Marilyn's turn to reach out and touch him. He didn't seem to notice.

"I've been with the school system since then. It was easy getting back. But I don't like it that the law categorizes gifted children in the same lump as all exceptional children. Gifted, deaf, mentally retarded, et cetera. They're all very precious, and have their own special needs. Very real, very defined sets of needs that differ from each of the others within the exceptional children category. For fairness to each child, we need to recognize their specific and individual requirements. Get rid of the lump stereotyping.

"And now . . . " he said, throwing both hands in the air, and then slapping them down on top of his knees, " . . . here I am." He smiled at Marilyn. "And here you are."

Marilyn studied Ed Kohler's face. "Thank you for sharing your story with me," she said. Then she paused. "You said you quit working with deaf people. And it seems obvious to me that you love the challenge of working with gifted children. I guess what I'm wondering is: which do you like the most?"

"Both."

"Oh."

"That's probably why I jumped at the chance to have you come here when you phoned. Why I'm so interested in what you're doing. I see possibilities for me to help you. But I'm not yet clear on exactly what you want to do." His eyes flashed to a large round clock on the wall. "School's out," he said. "Are you in a hurry? I'll buy you a milkshake or something, and we can talk."

"Yes!" said Karen, looking up from her book.

"Oh, my God," Marilyn jumped, remembering her schedule. "I was so wrapped up in what we were talking about, I forgot I have to work today." She was already late. Report would've been over five minutes ago. In an instant, she made a decision.

"Where's the nearest phone?" she said.

"My office. Across the hall." He pointed. "I'll stay here and close up the room."

Marilyn returned from his office. "All taken care of," she said. "That's the first time in a year that I've called in sick. Patient load is small, and they can call in a float from another unit."

Their conversation at Arby's started out discussing the two classes that Marilyn conducted at the church.

"Really, though, I'm not qualified to do this," Marilyn defended, "But I see it as a need locally, and, well, I just think someone needs to do it. Dumbo, or not." She laughed nervously.

"Nonsense. You can learn what you need to," said Kohler. "I'll teach you if you want. The important thing is that what I see in you is something that no one – no matter how much training they get – will ever have if they don't have it to begin with. Moxie. Guts. And the brilliant mind to see it through."

Marilyn blushed. "Thanks, Mr. Kohler. I wish you were right."

"I am. And, by the way, it's Ed. Now, tell me more about your style of teaching and about the hearing-impaired children working on a one-to-one basis with children who can hear normally. It's a concept I haven't heard of before."

"Neither have I," she said. "Actually, I made it up. It just popped into my head. It's a figment of my imagination, you might say." She told him about her experience with Tracy Thomas at the hospital, and the other deaf kids on the unit who she'd taken care of. "I guess it just sort of evolved. No bright lights or sudden flashes of greatness."

"Tell Mr. Kohler about the clown poems, Marilyn," Karen blurted through a mouthful of French fries. "Mr. Kohler, can I call you Ed, too? Or is that just for grownups?"

"Only if you can remember to switch back to Mr. Kohler when we're in school. Can you do that?" he said.

"Okay." Then, as if the subjects were one and the same, "Well, she's made up a whole bunch of poems about clowns and the funny stuff they do. And they rhyme and everything. Show him, Marilyn. He won't laugh. I mean, he will laugh at the poems, but he won't laugh at you or anything." Karen looked at Kohler. "You won't, will you, Ed?"

"Maybe I will. And maybe I won't," he said.

Marilyn handed him her sketchbook. He began leafing through it, chuckling as he moved from one page to the next, reading in silence. "I love them," he said. "What other little gems have you not told me about yet?"

Marilyn removed a sheaf of papers that she'd rolled up to fit in her purse. "Just this," she said. It looked like a report, with the title typed in the center of the cover.

Pal Signing for Children:
A Concept of Growth and Enrichment
For Both Hearing and Non-Hearing Children
by Marilyn Pelletier, R.N.

The manual was typed, double spaced, with *Project Rationale* heading the first page, then *Long and Short Term Goals, Objectives for the Student, Description of Methodology, Evaluation Techniques to Measuring Effectiveness of the Program,* and on the last page, *Summary and Suggestions for Using the Program Elsewhere.*

"I am impressed," Kohler said. Such flexibility, he thought. She could shift from playful pup one minute, to a serious scholar the next. He liked that. "Can we make a copy of this so I can read the whole thing?"

"Sure," said Marilyn. "It's really just a rough draft for myself, so I can follow some guidelines. I expect the process to change many times as we actually implement the program over a period of time. It would be great if you'd read it. Wow. In fact, you can write any comments, ideas, corrections, additions, or deletions. Scribble all over it if you want. I'm flattered you'll even read it."

Kohler's eyes were still scanning the document. "What do you mean, here?" He pointed to a paragraph on the fifth page, "Where you explain the term Pal-Signing?"

"That's just a term I coined. To my knowledge, there is no other combination of words like that being used by other kids' programs. It just means a buddy system where two kids, one deaf and one hearing, work together as pals. They're a team that support each other, give answers when the other is unsure. The idea is to build a sense of trust between the two children. Rather than forcing a deaf child to learn communication as we who can hear know it. Pal-Signing encourages both children to develop empathy for the other, and if any burden of learning is present at all, it would be weighted toward the hearing child, who can more easily tolerate it."

"Why do you say that? That the hearing child can more easily tolerate a learning burden?"

"Well, it would seem that there are broader avenues for the hearing person to enter the world of the deaf at will once they begin to recognize and understand the deaf child's perspective, and develop a sense of compassion and deep appreciation for what it must be like in specific situations if they were deaf. I think it's impractical, if not impossible for the deaf child to enter the world of the hearing. Especially if the child has been deaf since birth and has never heard speech or other sounds. That's why I think that lip-reading can be so frustrating sometimes, and doesn't work for congenital deafness."

Kohler tweaked his head backward, blinked. "I thought you said you didn't know much about this."

"I don't. I read a lot," Marilyn grinned. "I know I've got a long way to go with this. There's so much to learn. So, at this point, I may be drawing conclusions that are way off. But I believe in what I'm doing. And if I'm wrong, well, okay. I'll try something else until I get it right."

"It seems to me that the potential here, if it works, could open doors of trust and communication for these kids that'll reinforce a lifetime of free-flow expression," Ed said. "Not only in the art of signing, but also by enhancing other creative expressions for the children as well. Such as writing, painting, touch music, et cetera, depending on the interest and talent of the individual child."

Karen's eyes bulged. "Music?" she squealed. "Tracy? You think she can learn music?"

"I don't know, Karen." Ed closed the document and patted Karen's hand. "But I think we're about to find out."

67

Partly cloudy. Scattered thunderstorms expected later this evening. Lows in the upper 60s near the coast and in the lower 50s inland. East winds around 10 miles per hour. Chance of rain 30 percent.

Ross depressed the Off button on the car radio. "A little iffy, but not too bad," he said. The sky had been threatening when he and Karen picked up Emilie, but as they crossed over the Treasure Island Causeway lightning had moved farther north, brightening the clouds just enough to see them roll past, exposing the bottom sliver of a full moon. Ross tapped the Buick's blinker to the right and turned onto Gulf Boulevard. By the time they'd crossed over the bridge, rounded the short winding streets of John's Pass Village, and into the parking lot at Sculley's Boardwalk Restaurant, the entire moon was reflecting on the inlet waters.

They strolled past the Block & Tackle Tavern, and entered the main restaurant, pushing through weathered wood doors with eye-level life preservers circling glass portholes. Inside, they selected the last vacant booth at the corner of the wide picture window that gave them a view of the deck and bright moon beyond.

Both Emilie and Ross ordered the house salad with wild salmon, and Karen chose fantail shrimp with fries and Island potato salad.

"So, Karen. How did the kids in your gifted class like Marilyn telling them about sign language?" Ross said. Then he turned to Emilie. "She's been itching to talk about the meeting all afternoon. But I asked her to wait and tell you and me together. I suspect it relates a bit to the idea I mentioned on the phone yesterday. When you were talking about inhumane treatment of animals."

"Yeah," said Karen. "That makes this a sort-of celebration date." Karen giggled. "And we can all make a wish when we eat our dessert."

"You got it. Now shoot," said Ross.

Karen explained that Marilyn asked the kids to make up silly sentences. To look up the words in the sign book. Or to see if they weren't in it. Then she showed how to sign the word. "Like me and Tracy do," she said.

Karen wrinkled her brow. "Then, when Marilyn picked Stephanie to make up a sentence, Rodney called Stephanie a stupid girl."

"What was Stephanie's sentence?" said Emilie.

"She said, 'Chocolate toothpaste is better than regular brands.' I thought it was funny." Karen said.

"I'm curious," said Ross. "Did you find chocolate in the sign language dictionary?"

"Yep.   Here, watch."   Karen signed the C handshape, and made two circles over the back of her left hand.

"Pretty good," Ross said. Emilie tapped her hands in a dainty applause.

"Then, after the bell rang, Marilyn and Mr. Kohler sat on the back table and talked for a really long time. I read and almost fell asleep. Then we went to Arby's."

"Did Marilyn tell Mr. Kohler about the Pal Sign program?" Emilie asked.

"She sure did. She told him she needed kids who hear okay, so they could buddy up with kids who were deaf. Like me and Tracy. That's why Marilyn came to our class in the first place."

"That is such a great idea," Ross said. "It seems that Marilyn has a whole head full of ideas. She's amazing."

"Yeah. Mr. Kohler called her a genius," Karen said.

"It sounds like Mr. Kohler is a very smart man," Emilie said.

"Yeah, well. He's always telling that boring story that he's a teacher of the gifted, not a gifted teacher. But, you know what? I think he's gifted, too. Else, how would he know what we're thinking all the time? And, besides, he said I could call him Ed as long as we're not in school. Then I have to call him Mr. Kohler. So the other kids won't know he's my friend."

"What else did Ed . . . Mr. Kohler say?" Ross asked.

"Let's see. Oh, he showed us a picture of the lady he used to be married to. But she died. He said she had hymers disease and it made her die."

"Hymers?" Emilie said. "I never heard of it."

"In her brain," Karen said.

"Do you mean Alzheimer's?" Emilie said.

Karen nodded. "Um. Maybe. Yeah, I think so."

"That's the new condition they just discovered." Emilie said. "Or rather, they just put a name to it. Different from most dementias. I believe they're starting an association soon to investigate it further and to support families and loved ones."

"Mmmm," Ross whispered. "And Ed Kohler's wife died from something like that?

"Yeah. He used to be on the football team in school. He said she was a majorette. I had to stop looking at him right then, though, because he looked really sad. But that's not all. He said she was deaf."

"What?" Ross said.

"Yeah, Mr. Kohler's wife was deaf."

The waiter approached and Ross discretely ordered key lime pie for all three of them.

Emilie reached for Karen's hand. "He said that? Mr. Kohler said his wife had been deaf?"

Karen watched the waiter head towards the kitchen. "Mr. Kohler said that she went swimming and she went too far down. It broke her eardrums." She placed her fingers over her ears. "He said it really hurt, and then she couldn't hear anymore."

"That explains why he invited Marilyn to come talk to the kids about her Pal Sign program," Ross said, nodding. "Wow."

"Then we showed Ed Marilyn's clown drawings and stuff," Karen said. "That part was more fun."

"What did he think?" Emilie asked. "Of Marilyn's clowns? Did he like them?"

"I think so. At first I didn't think he would, 'cause they're for kids. But he laughed when he saw them. But he was more interested in the Pal Sign booklet she had. It looked like a teacher's manual to me. Except she made it up. Mr. Kohler took it to a print shop and got a copy of it."

"I didn't know about that," said Ross.

"Me either," Emilie said. "But it sounds like she's done her homework. We'll have to ask her about it." Emilie took a bite of her pie. "Okay, Dr. Manchester. Your turn. What were you referring to on the phone yesterday to turn humans into humanes?"

"Actually, it's simple," Ross said, smiling at Emilie. "No mystery. I'm thinking that with all the brainpower of the women in our group – well, now there's Mr. Kohler, too. I'm thinking, why don't we write a kids' Pal Sign book about how to treat animals. Include farm animals, wild animals, fish, whatever. Keep it broad. Cows, pigs, chickens, marmots, monkeys, salmon. Explain the difference in how animals live and behave. And that people need to respect their natural habits and environments. Now that Mr. Kohler's shown an interest, we could suggest he make it a project for the gifted kids in his class."

"Wow, oh, Daddy. Wait'll I tell Tracy."

Emilie smiled, "I like it."

Outside the restaurant, they found a slatted bench overlooking the bay and the west tip of Eleanor Island. As Ross and Emilie sat, Karen ran the length of the boardwalk. The only sounds were the voices of far off diners on the restaurant deck. In the moonlight, a small Hobie Cat glided through the water.

For a long time, Ross and Emilie sat in comfortable silence. They had been through so much together. Strangers who shared a lifetime of experiences.

Then Ross tilted Emilie's chin and kissed her lightly on the lips. "Don't say anything," he whispered close to her face. "But I want to marry you."

68

"I move to adjourn."

"I second the motion."

"All in favor . . ."

Everyone in the room said aye in one voice. A few nodded.

"This meeting is adjourned."

Barbara looked at her wrist and wrote down the time. The group was gathered at Ross' house, and they had accomplished a great deal at the first organizational meeting to establish Marilyn's idea into a legal corporation. Temporary officers for the new Pal-Sign, Inc. included Marilyn as temporary chair, and Barbara as temporary secretary/treasurer. Michael had agreed to file for a state charter and to begin application as a tax-exempt federal 501(c)(3) nonprofit agency. Those present formed a committee to draw up a constitution and by-laws, and to become the representative board of directors until the legalities were in place.

"Well, we're off and running," Ross said, pouring a drink into Michael's paper cup from the pitcher of punch. Karen and Emilie had insisted that Ross do the hosting for the occasion, and now he stood at the end of the long counter that separated the kitchen from the family room. Michael stepped aside, as Ed Kohler held an empty cup for Ross to fill. "Ed," Ross said. "It's a pleasure that you're joining the group. Karen has bragged about you so much, I started to worry about her luring you off to some faraway place with questionable intentions."

Ed laughed from inside his belly. The man was both muscular and tall, and his dark olive skin set off clear blue eyes and coarse silver hair. Each morning, no matter what goop he tried, the mane fell on his face in copious waves with a will of its own. The only hint of his boyhood nickname was sprinkled throughout his mustache. *Red Ed is what we said,* was the chant he'd heard over and over as a child. Susan had been the last person to call him that. And now, at 43, Ed Kohler looked regal in a scholarly way. His casual attire and generous smile gave an onlooker the feeling of authenticity and warmth when he spoke.

"You've got quite a girl there," he said, pumping Ross' hand. "A good reason to be proud." Then Ed took his drink and glanced around the room. "I am just delighted to be part of this new venture," he said. "From what I've seen, Marilyn has chosen her colleagues well."

Michael, who had been listening, poked the air with his cup. "When we talked before the meeting, Ed, you said you had just recently met Marilyn. What's the connection?"

Ed explained that Marilyn had called to see if he knew of any hearing children who might be interested in joining her sign language class, and he'd invited her to speak to his gifted students. "I have to be honest, I was bowled over by the way she and the kids took to each other," he said. "It was as if she'd been in that room with those students right along with me all year." He shook his head. "I know she works with children at the hospital. But so do a lot of people. And frankly, most of them aren't worth a tinker's damn if you ask me." Ed saw Michael and Ross exchange a private smile with their eyes. "As far as I'm concerned, Marilyn is one young lady who has got her act together. She knows what she wants, and is determined to get it. I respect that in anyone. But with Marilyn, it goes further. She's not motivated for her own self-interest. Well, except for the challenge to herself. And I honestly think she can pull this thing off. And help a helluva lot of kids doing it."

"Amen," Michael said. "And she's got a strong base of support here with this group. In addition to Marilyn bringing her pediatric nursing experience into it, and with Ross as a physician who specializes in children, there's Emilie. Her social work expertise is phenomenal. And my wife, Barbara is a knockout when it comes to organizing and handling paperwork." Michael looked up at Ed. "And now with you in the group, Ed, your background with both deaf and gifted kids will certainly round us out."

"Oh, ho, don't forget that little tyke over there." Ed pointed to Tracy, who had just climbed up on the stool in front of Ross' piano. "With Karen as her Sign Pal – and her own animated brilliance – she's on her way to achieving great excellence. No matter which direction she eventually goes." Ed watched Tracy finger piano keys. "How're her parents adapting to Tracy's new way of life? I see they're not here tonight." He looked from Michael to Ross.

"The Thomas' are the official babysitters for this gang," he said. "They agreed to watch our son Jeff. To free up Barbara and me."

Ed frowned briefly and stared at Tracy a moment longer. "Seems odd," he said.

"What?" Ross' eyes moved from Ed to Tracy, then back to Ed.

Ed hesitated. "I can't put my finger on it. Maybe it's just me. But it seems that Tracy's parents would want very much to be in on all of this." He moved his open palm in an arc through the air.

Michael's mouth formed a lopsided grin. "Pretty perceptive fellow we've got here, Ross," he said. "Truth is, Ed, that some of us are a little worried about Irene. Tracy's mother. I'm afraid she's taking it pretty hard. In a way, it's understandable. She'd had such high hopes for Tracy's musical future. But Wayne says

Irene's refusing to leave the house even for the simplest errands. Won't see her friends anymore, either. Wayne, Tracy's dad, is struggling to make things easier for Irene. But the guy's distraught, too. As any father would be. And now, having to worry about his wife. He's afraid she'll have a nervous breakdown if she keeps going on like she is."

Ross nodded. "I talked with Wayne myself the other day," he said. "Told me the only time Irene seems to come out of her shell at all is when you or Barb bring Jeff over. I'm no psychiatrist, but I'd be damned worried, too, if she were my wife."

Ed turned toward the piano. "Mind introducing me to Tracy?" he said. Then, catching Marilyn's eye, he crooked his finger for her to follow.

Ed moved to the side of the piano at a distance meant to be comfortable to Tracy. When she looked up, Ed smiled but made no move to interrupt her. Tracy grinned as her fingers kept moving across the piano an inch above the keys.

In a slow, fluid movement, Ed stooped at Tracy's side, one leg kneeling on the carpet and the other one a resting place for his forearm. He was eye level with Tracy now, and when she turned her body on the stool to face him, Ed made simple signing gestures telling Tracy he wanted to hear her play the piano.

Tracy's face lit up. She looked up at Michael, then Ross, who were standing behind Ed. Ross nodded. Then Tracy slid across the piano bench and patted the seat next to her. When Ed sat down, Tracy gently thumped her chest twice, with the thumb side of a fist. The sign for self. Then she fingerspelled p-l-a-y p-i-a-n-o, and squiggled a half moon in the air, and poked it underneath with her index finger. "Tray-cee play pee-an-oh?" she said.

While nodding his head, Ed held up a fist, palm forward, then raised and lowered his wrist in an up and down motion. Tracy did the same.

Then Tracy hit the first note. The room hushed as every head turned. Tracy started off timidly, hitting keys with her right hand, while pressing the palm of her left hand against the vibrations she felt coming from the front of the cabinet. She banged at varying volumes, testing the strength of the resonance. Then she laid both hands on the keyboard, and began to play. Some of the notes were a bit off, but the tune was recognizable.

Ed began to sing and sign as Tracy played *It's a Small World*. Karen moved to Ed's side, and started singing along. Then, one by one, the others in the room added their voice as Tracy played.

It's a world of laughter, A world of tears.
It's a world of hopes, And a world of fears.
There's so much that we share,
That it's time we're aware,
It's a small world after all.

At the end of the song, the audience gathered around the piano to applaud and whoop. Then Emilie whispered in Ross' ear, and they agreed not to go ahead with the plan to announce their engagement just yet.

And, at the very next board meeting, when Ed Kohler moved to adopt *It's a Small World* as the Pal Sign, Inc.'s official theme song, and seconded by Barbara, the vote would be unanimous.

69

It wasn't easy. She knew it wouldn't be. But once Marilyn turned in her resignation at the hospital, her mood lifted and she felt light and carefree. Sure, there were risks involved. Like loss of benefits. And the security of a day-to-day job. A regular job. Routines. Coffee breaks and dinner times, when someone else told you when you should be hungry.

Could she really see herself as her own boss now? Her own self-disciplinarian? Could she stand the unpredicted ups and downs? Could she take a whole different kind of pressure?

Marilyn had thought long and hard about being on her own versus the stability of working for someone else – along with the frustrations and indignities that went with conforming to something she didn't believe in. Of letting someone else own her so they could put their name on her paycheck. But was that really security? Or was true security built inside a person? Must be, she thought, because she felt secure taking on a leadership role that was never available to her as a follower at the hospital because she was always bucking the system. Freedom of choice felt good to her.

So, when Wayne Thomas called Marilyn a few days after the Pal Sign board meeting and asked her to tutor Tracy on a full-time basis, she decided on the spot. It was to be the first contractual agreement for Pal Sign, and even after tallying the cost to operate as a business, Marilyn's income would still be greater than her salary as a nurse. At the organizational meeting, the motion had been made that those persons who were interested and able, were to make a monthly donation to the corporation to cover expenses until the operation was on its feet. To Marilyn's surprise, everyone present had contributed, and under Barbara's careful hand, as the newly-appointed treasurer protem, a ledger accounting was made, as well as plans for opening a bank account. Ed Kohler offered to help Marilyn run the weekly sign classes at the church, and suggested that Marilyn assist him with the gifted students in his class.

Marilyn felt that her whole life was beginning to follow a well-directed plan, over which she had complete control. The spontaneity of her decisions only added to the pleasure of the plan's creativity.

Tracy went everywhere with Marilyn, now. And they made use of simple, everyday experiences to learn informal lessons in sign for both of them. A trip to the office supply store to pick up a typewriter ribbon. The inner workings of the print shop where business cards and letterhead were ordered. Everything they did together became an education for both of them. Tracy was a rapid learner, and soon the conversations between them expanded to include Ed Kohler. Marilyn knew that one day she would have to find time to learn the basics of music, so that she and Tracy could practice piano together, and she'd have some clue what was going on.

Two weeks after Marilyn quit her job, Michael called with news that they were granted a state charter and the issuance of a corporate number. Another meeting was set for the following evening. At Ross' request, the group would gather at the Wine Cellar on North Redington Beach.

70

A light rain had fallen all day, dropping the evening temperatures into the low fifties, as Marilyn drove north on Gulf Boulevard. The radio played rock music and the windshield wipers clicked in staccato splashes in front of Marilyn's face. Leaning forward, nose across the steering wheel, she felt annoyed with herself for starting out so late. And now she could hardly see the road.

She'd been to the Wine Cellar restaurant once before, a long time ago, and she couldn't remember the exact location. She shot her eyes to the dash clock and realized she'd been on the road over 45 minutes, and decided she'd missed the turn. When she saw the Park Boulevard cut off, she knew she was too far north. She approached a darkened Shell Station, and swerved into the empty parking lot, made a U-turn and headed back on Gulf Boulevard. The sudden turn made Tracy look up from the radio's speaker, where she held her hands.

"Sorry, sweetie," Marilyn said, keeping her eyes on the road as she reached out to touch Tracy's leg. "I just don't want us to be late."

Then she saw lights surrounding the maroon and beige marquee sign, *The Wine Cellar Restaurant and Cocktail Lounge.* She put on her signal light and pulled into the lot. Just as she drove past the covered entryway, she saw Ed step forward, waving to her, holding an umbrella. She stopped the car and rolled down the window.

"They usually have valet parking," he said, "But I don't see anyone tonight." He looks so handsome, Marilyn thought. The damp breeze had whorled his hair into ringlets across his forehead, and there were drops on his eyelashes and cheeks. "Here," he said, reaching for the door handle. "Let me park this for you. You and Tracy go on in and get warm. I've got a place saved for you at the table."

Marilyn stepped out of the car, then shifted around and leaned back in to help Tracy slide across the seat to exit from the driver's side. Marilyn was aware of two sensations at the same time. The icy wind that punished the inside of her thighs, and the gentle pressure of Ed's hand on the curve of her back as she reached for Tracy. Ed took the child in his arms and held the umbrella over Marilyn's head, as they walked through the rain to the front door of the restaurant. Then Ed jogged back to the car.

In the dimly-lit lobby, Marilyn was drawn to the stained glass windows, red brick, and oval plaques along the walls. Through a long hallway, she saw the main dining room, with its paved walkway separating rich maroon carpeting. Wine glasses, stemmed flowers, and flickering candles adorned bright white tablecloths. Tracy spotted a wishing well display in the center of the lobby and ran to touch it, signing *What is it?* to Marilyn.

By the time she saw Ed enter, Marilyn was seated in the dining section designated as Sign Pal's private area, and the waiter was filling her goblet with wine. Ed sat one seat from Marilyn, with Tracy in between. Marilyn briefly closed her eyes and listened to the hum of her friends' voices around her, aware that her own mood had rearranged itself, and a pleasurable warmth diffused through her entire core. When she opened her eyes she saw Ed easily signing with Tracy about menu choices, and Marilyn relaxed on the high back of her chair and watched.

It was a brief meeting that followed the meal, and when the proposed draft of the by-laws and constitution were distributed and the officers formally installed, the meeting was finished.

Then Ross stood and clanked a spoon against an empty carafe. "This meeting may be adjourned," he said. "But it is not finished." Everyone at the table looked up.

"I'd like to have your attention, please," he began. "It has been no accident that the environs of this lovely place of fine sustenance should be the preference of our meeting place tonight." He grinned and looked at the faces around the table. "First, I wish to inform you all that I have arranged to pick up the tab for tonight's meal."

Ross held his palm out in front of him in a mock gesture of argument with Michael. "No, no, no, do not wrangle with my decision, counselor." Michael blinked, and the others grinned.

"This whole evening has been prepared with much effort and care," Ross continued. "Of supreme importance is the absence of a piano in this room, so that I alone may prevail upon your attentive minds, so that the full extent of my message can be accepted with full understanding and worth."

Emilie tugged on Ross' sleeve. He looked down at her and bent his ear to her lips. Then he straightened.

"Scuse me, folks," Ross said and sat down in his seat, rotating his hands in front of his shoulders, indicating his bewilderment.

Emilie stood. "What Dr. Manchester, the silver-tongued – and rambling – gentleman is trying to tell you is that he and Karen and I are getting married. Tomorrow." There. "It will be a private affair in the tiny alcove of the Pinellas County Courthouse, with just the three of us. We wanted you all to be the first to know." Emilie sat down.

"She's absolutely right," Ross slurred, lifting his wine glass high in the air.

Amidst cheers, Michael stood. "I propose a toast. And since to miss out on Ross and Emilie's wedding would be to . . ."

"And mine," Karen chirped.

"Excuse me, young lady. Please accept my apologies. And since to miss out on Ross and Emilie and Karen's wedding would be to cheat us from attending such an affair, I so move that each person here invite no less than ten of their closest friends and neighbors to a gala wedding reception tomorrow night at the home of . . ." Michael looked around him. "Who among us – other than the prospective bride and groom here – has a residence that will accommodate ` a crowd of that expanse?"

Ed Kohler's finger went up. "My place'll hold seventy," he said. "Well, actually you could fit about a hundred and twenty very thin people if you tired, but they'd have to exhale a lot."

"Good." Michael said. "Now, then, if everyone brings food, and Barbara orders a cake, we're in."

"Bravo!" said Ross. "But this isn't really necessary folks, and if . . ."

"Shush up, man," Michael said. He looked at the others. "The guy's afraid we'll dominate his wedding night. Well, never you mind, Ross. You and Em can leave the party any time you wish." Several people applauded, and then Michael asked, "Any other comments or suggestions?"

It was Ed's turn to stand. "It seems to me that the reason all of us have come together as a unified group, is because of the children. And I would just like to submit that we call up the parents of the kids who have shown any interest at all in the Pal Sign program, and invite them to the party, too. What I'm saying is that we have children there. Lots of children."

Immediately, three heads nodded, and the others murmured affirmative replies. When Karen clapped her hands together, and Tracy looked confused, Marilyn's fingers made a twisting Y sign, indicating party. Tracy repeated the sign. "Par-tee," she said, and then she clapped, too.

From his position, Ed watched. Then he picked up his wine glass and moved it in a circle over the table. "Another toast," he said. "To the children." Glasses rose high in the air. "What a beautiful noise that will be," said Ed.

71

Hostility.

He could have been any ordinary man sitting there, resting his feet after a demanding day at work, pleasant pot-roast smells filling his nostrils as his wife hands him a Budweiser.

He wasn't, though.

This man who sat with his legs extended on the ottoman, his third bourbon on the rocks balanced above his thigh in a clenched fist, was unordinary in every way.

Deep within the core of Vincent Fossari's belly, an impassioned seedling that had long ago been planted in madness and hate, now sprouted upward and outward inside his being, filling the interstitial spaces of his body with germinating malice. Rather than narcotize his anger, the fermented mash in his glass served to heighten his mentalism.

Fossari, freely aware of his needs, watched from his chair as a flock of pelicans skimmed the water. He inspected the scene as the huge birds gathered on the pilings near his dock. Unmindfully, his hand went up and touched the deadened tip of his right ear. Through the window, he regarded one pelican with special interest as it flew gracefully over the riffle of high tide, a pocketknife of angles, opening and closing appendages in the air, then plunging beneath the surface of the water and rising again, wingspread, with a captured meal wiggling at the tip of its beak, then gone in a shadow just above the surf.

There were five of them, and as he watched, Vincent Fossari realized that one of the pelicans stayed on its perch, huddled and tight. Occasionally, the bird stretched to accept fish offerings from one of the others. Charity. Sacrifice. Naked friendship.

Fossari thrilled at the thought of the injured bird. He raised the tumbler in his hand and drained the liquid. Then he walked to the window and stood, his hands deep in his pockets, eyes focused on the brown and gray creatures cutting through the distance between him and the sunset.

After some time, Fossari stepped from the house and approached the edge of the water, where waves sloshed at the base of the seawall beneath his feet. All of the birds, save one, flew to the far end of the pier, landing, one by one, on separate wooden posts that projected from the water. They watched the man watching them.

The last bird hunched closer into itself, hairfeathers separating in the breeze in odd directions, some up, some down on his head and on his body. An orange eyeball jerked, anxious, in the tiny skull, preparing for flight in a body wrapped in a fisherman's line, winding around the spaces of its webbed toes and knotted in circles about its neck. A hook, rusty and bent, protruded from the side of the pelican's bill, and a loop of the line held fast to the barnacles on the piling. In the struggle to free itself, the bird squirmed within the confines of the filament that trapped it. A voiceless trembling bounced inside its throat.

Delight welled up in Fossari's gut, fanning his furor to a peak of excitement that he could hardly contain. Nor did he want to.

Fossari walked the length of the pier to the portico over his boat. He raised the seat of the long storage bench along one side of the shelter, and removed a large fishnet. Then he dropped the board down with a thud, and headed toward the bird. If his next-door neighbor, Ester Hardaway, were home today, she would have approved of the doctor's seeming rescue of the captive creature on the piling.

Once he had the net secured around the bird's body, Fossari tugged on the line that was caught in the barnacles. It stretched and then snapped, upsetting Fossari's balance. He caught himself with his knee hitting the sharp wood deck and snagging the fabric of his trousers. A pain shot up his thigh and he cursed loudly.

Fossari carried the bird to the lawn just inside the concrete wall. He untangled the line, and then coiled it tightly around the pelican's bill, fastening the end length to its neck. The terrified bird's beady eyes swiveled in their sockets. It was completely helpless now as Fossari carried the heavy weight of its body back toward the boat.

Hidden from view by the overhang of the boathouse at the far boundary of the dock, Fossari stepped close to the surface of the water where three wide steps made of wood went down between the pilings. He crouched over and placed the bird in the water. Fourteen pounds of feather and bones barely moved as the trammel was pushed under the water. Fossari felt, rather than heard, the muffled shrill as he lowered the bird, stopping with its neck at water level. Above him a group of pelicans hovered, screeching at the man, waiting for a chance to save their kin. Fossari looked up and grinned, dipping his victim under the water. Then he counted twenty-three seconds.

When Fossari lifted the net above the water, the bird felt heavier, but its eyes begged to be set free.

Again, Fossari lowered the net, pulled it up. Lowered the net, pulled it up. When he was satisfied that the bird was dead, Fossari hauled the corpse to the bench seat on the upper level of the dock and took the net from around it. Then he untied the line and tossed it into the water. From the front pocket of his drenched pants, Fossari held a folding knife and extended the blade. As the bird lay prone with its wings stretched five and a half feet from tip to tip, Fossari sliced through the dripping feather coverage of his chest. Its wishbone will bring me luck, he thought, as he inserted the razor sharp point deep into the pelican's clavicle.

With closed eyes, and the blade still in place, Fossari raised his head upward toward the rafters of the boathouse ceiling.

"I shall be found innocent," he said aloud. "Not only shall I be found innocent, but I shall have Manchester's fucking license when the matter is brought before the State Board of Medical Advisors."

Fossari lowered his head and jammed the knife's edge down along the bird's sternum, slicing into the thin-walled air pouches and then into its lung. Dark fluid spurted onto Fossari's hands and arms, and when he held up his palms to examine the mess, he suddenly felt nauseated and stepped back from the bird.

With his stomach lurching in spastic contractions, Fossari inhaled deeply trying to fill his chest with salty air. Then he turned and kicked the pelican's corpse, spattering blood on his shoe and sending the bird into a heap on the deck. Fossari kicked again, and this time the pelican hurled over the edge of the dock. It floated on the surface for three seconds, then bubbled down to the sandy floor seven feet below.

The heels of Fossari's shoes knocked against the pier as he lumbered along the dock toward the house. But he didn't hear the sound of his feet. Nor did he see four grieving pelicans circling low in the sky in the space just beyond the boathouse.

72

Two Months Later

"All rise," roared the bailiff. "The court is now in session. The Honorable James Pfaff presiding." An inert court reporter pressed keys on a soundless machine.

For Michael, it seemed that he had been plummeted headlong into a racecar that was moving too fast for him to control. And now, he studied the jurors, their eyes on the judge, faces barren. He wished he had had more time to prepare. Instead, he was about to present his opening statement in the case of Thomas versus Fossari. And seated beside him at the plaintiff's table, Wayne Thomas put his belief in this trial.

Spectators and participants settled into their seats, and the judge instructed the jury on what they'd expect in the days to come. The judge turned to Michael, and nodded once.

"You may proceed, Mr. Sutherland."

"Thank you, Your Honor." Michael stood. He took four steps toward the jury box. Not too close. Not yet. In a soft voice, Michael greeted the jurors and slid through the legal amenities. Then, "Ladies and gentlemen of the jury, during the course of this trial you will hear a great deal of evidence and information from both the plaintiff and the defense. You will hear that information along with almost everyone else who is sitting here in this courtroom. There is only one person in this room who will not hear any of the goings-on in the course of this trial. Not one sound of it. No matter how hard she tries to listen." Michael's eyes moved past the jurors to the back of the room. "That person is a little girl who sits in this courtroom reading her books. Her name is Tracy Thomas. She is six years old. A little over a year ago, Tracy Thomas was a gifted and promising pianist. Now she is profoundly deaf."

Michael had polished his opening statement during the last few weeks and had it memorized. But as he walked into the courtroom this morning, he switched tactics.

"During this trial, you will learn about what happened to 5-year-old Tracy Thomas after she entered Parkwest Children's Hospital to have a simple tonsillectomy. Parkwest enjoys the reputation of being staffed by the finest doctors in the country. Nevertheless, a series of errors in judgment by one of those doctors occurred. Errors that caused a child's life to be put in jeopardy. Errors that then caused Tracy to become deaf."

Michael waited for an objection from the defense table. When there was none, he continued. "A tonsillectomy, ladies and gentlemen. A common surgical procedure to remove Tracy's tonsils to avoid an occasional sore throat. And the results of the care that Tracy received after her tonsillectomy is at issue in this trial."

Then speeding his pace, "During the course of this trial, we will prove that because of errors in judgment by the defendant, Dr. Vincent Fossari, recovery for Tracy did not take place. She failed to improve in the predictable manner after she was put in Dr. Fossari's care."

Vincent Fossari sat unmoving at the defense table between his two lawyers, Royce Holding and Steven Elliott. On his lap, Fossari's palms secreted sweat and salt, and dampened the scar in the center of his left hand.

"This trial will show that Tracy's injury, her pain and suffering while in the hospital, and the torment she

290

will continue to suffer for the rest of her life, was due, ladies and gentlemen, entirely due to the defendant's negligence." Michael pressed a fist against his mouth, clearing his throat. Somewhere in the trained reflexes of his mind, Michael waited for the coughing spasm that never came.

"You and I will hear from witnesses, that what was done to Tracy was both negligent and injurious. And it was done with proximate cause." Michael saw the head juror shift in his seat, tugging at creases in his slacks.

In the back of the room, Ross and Emilie Manchester sat beside Barbara. Karen and Tracy were situated between Marilyn and Ed. They were all looking at Michael.

"As a result of improper judgment by her doctor, Vincent Fossari, Tracy Thomas almost died. But that wasn't enough. When Tracy overcame her infectious coma, she was given drugs in improper amounts for a period of time to cause the nerves in her ears to stop functioning."

At the defense table, Royce Holding leaned in and pointed to a legal pad in front of Steven Elliott, and Elliott wrote a note on it.

Michael continued, "Will Tracy Thomas finish her studies in piano? No. Will she become the fine pianist that she and her family had dreamed of? Again, the answer is no. Tracy Thomas will never know a normal life again. Because Tracy Thomas will be deaf for the rest of her life!" Michael's voice had risen steadily, and the last sentence was almost a shout.

"Objection, Your Honor." Steven Elliott stood in front of his chair. "Mr. Sutherland is arguing his case, rather than giving an opening statement." All eyes in the courtroom shifted toward the defense table.

Judge Pfaff, who had been listening to Michael's oration, blinked behind horn-rimmed glasses. Frowning, he realized that Michael's storytelling had taken him in. "Objection noted, Mr. Elliott," he said.

"Mr. Sutherland, this is just your opening statement. Please keep your remarks within a brief outline of what your case will present."

"Yes, Your Honor." Michael said with a nod to the judge.

Elliot grinned as he sat down.

Michael waited for Fossari to complete his whispered comment to Elliott before turning to the jury. "Ladies and gentlemen, this is not a criminal case. There is no charge to anyone for deliberately doing harm to the plaintiff. However, what we intend to do is to show that the harm, the injury to Tracy, took place because of a continuous sequence of events, that could have been interrupted by Dr. Fossari. Events that produced near death and actual hearing loss in a five-year-old girl who had no choice in the matter." Michael saw hushed conversation at the defense table. He decided to change his approach.

"Remember, these are not criminal charges against Dr. Fossari. This is a civil case, and as we attempt to go inside the hospital walls and reconstruct exactly what happened during the time of Tracy's confinement, it may sometimes appear complicated. The truth is simple, however. And the truth of Vincent Fossari's guilt will soon become evident to you."

"Thank you for your attention." Michael walked to the plaintiff's table and sat down.

Not one juror moved. Or blinked. Or showed any life in their eyes. Flat affect, Emilie would have called it. No indication they cared one way or the other. Not the lanky man who, just before he sat down, had removed a faded green cap with the John Deere logo across the front, exposing his own lid of pure white scalp and dreary gray hair. Nor the girl whose tattoo peeked from under her collar, a snake spiraling up to her ear. Not even the bespectacled woman with blue-tinted curls done up in a new style since Michael saw her last week, who'd been the last juror selected, after the defense almost discarded her because she said she was the proud grandmother of four, but then added they were all boys, three of them fathers themselves, and no, she had no recollection of anyone she knew who was deaf or disabled. The defense had let her stay.

Judge Pfaff stifled a yawn and looked at his watch. "It's past noontime, ladies and gentlemen. The court will recess for lunch and reconvene at one-thirty." He struck the bench with his gavel.

Ed and Marilyn took the girls to a fast-food drive thru for lunch and ate at a nearby park, so Tracy and Karen could expend their pent up energy. In the tiny restaurant across the street from the courthouse, Ross, Emilie, and Barbara spoke in whispers, as Michael and Wayne talked about strategy and made notes on a legal pad.

On the walk back to the county building, they stopped at the corner waiting for the light to change.

"You know, Mike," Barbara said, taking his arm. "Your remarks to the jury were very good. But I didn't realize you were going to take that approach with your opening statements."

"Neither did I," Michael said. "I cringe to think how I came across."

They stepped off the curb.

"What do you think of the jury so far?" Barbara said.

As they started across the street, a car made a right turn into their pathway, and the group stopped. "Hard to tell, Barb. What I'm wondering is if the noon recess is in our favor or not. I want to make a few points early on. But if we don't get started with witnesses, the timing'll be off. I don't want the defense to leave the jury with a long time to ponder Fossari's credentials. With the background the defense is bound to present, the jury will think he's God. I have to overcome that image somehow, without making it look like an attack. Just wish we hadn't started so late this morning."

293

"If you ask me," Ross said, walking behind Michael and Barbara. "I'd say that the recess was in your favor. I know I'm not a legal expert, but then neither are any of the people sitting in that jury box. I watched those people, Mike. They're plain as rain. Maybe one or two hard-nosed ones, but they're the minority. The farmer, maybe."

They were nearing the courthouse steps. Holding Ross' hand, Emilie stopped. "With the material you have on Fossari, Mike, I can't help but think that the jury will see what he's done," she said. "Most of them, anyway."

"Most won't do it, Em," Michael said. The four of them trudged up the courthouse steps. "We need all of the jurors on our side."

73

Steven Elliott flipped through his newly written notes. Missing lunch during recess was time well spent. Sutherland had let the plaintiff's strategy out of the bag so soon into the trial. Big mistake, Elliott thought, but one that gave the defense a slight advantage. And he hadn't even approached the jurors yet.

He had been with the firm for almost ten years. That, and the width of his shoulders, gave him a look of confidence and power that belied his sun-bleached hair, which he slicked away from his face. With a big check from his clients, most of his cases were settled out of court. Or won.

Now, with the court back in session, Elliott tucked a small spiral notebook into the breast pocket of his suit coat. As he rose from his seat, he buttoned his jacket, and then pushed his chair back under the table. Standing beside Fossari, he placed his hand on the doctor's shoulder, and dipped his chin a quarter-inch, addressing the judge.

"May it please the court?"

"You may proceed, counselor," Judge Pfaff responded.

Elliott turned toward Michael, politely acknowledged him with a nod, and then moved to the well of the courtroom. When he reached his preferred speaking position at a spot just back from the rail, and dead center of the jury box, Elliott paused for a moment and made eye contact with each of the jurors.

"Good afternoon, ladies and gentlemen of the jury," he said through a perfect smile. Let me begin by saying that the defense agrees with everything that the plaintiff said this morning . . ."

What? thought Michael.

" . . . except for the fact that my client, Dr. Vincent Fossari, did what any reasonable doctor would have done under the same set of circumstances. And, in fact, that he went further to save the child after she suffered from an extremely dangerous manifestation of her surgery. And the defendant, Dr. Fossari, managed to pull her through in an otherwise fine state of physical health." Several of the jurors turned to the back of the room, where they saw Tracy's cherubic face poke forward between Marilyn and Karen.

Steven Elliott continued, denying any wrongdoing on the part of the defendant, and that defense intended to prove to the court that Vincent Fossari, M.D., is, in fact, a hero and deserving of acclaim for his acts in saving the child's life, and that he is a victim, enduring humiliation and professional embarrassment with this frivolous and degrading trial in which the good doctor is subjected to defending his actions, which were within, and above, the high standards of medical practice that he had always lived by.

Elliott's voice rose and dipped, and once during his remarks, he weighted his comments with a sprinkling of puzzlement and anger.

"Counsel for the plaintiff would have us believe that the defendant has deliberately caused harm to a child," Elliott said. Michael started to raise an objection, but wanted to see where this was headed. "But the truth is that Vincent Fossari is not only innocent of any wrongdoing – and we shall prove that to you during this trial – but he is also a man of fine character in the medical community in many ways. A community that respected his father as a fine surgeon, and who has taken very seriously the responsibilities that come with the practice of medicine. Dr. Fossari's reputation is untainted, and you shall hear this attested to by expert witnesses throughout this trial."

Elliott paused a brief moment, chin in hand, eyes to the floor.

"As many of you are parents, so am I the father of two children. Girls. And I can understand and sympathize with the plaintiffs. It is most unfortunate that this situation has occurred. But I ask you to please consider the possibility that the child who was a patient of my client, is she now being victimized by her own parents, possibly to receive monetary value for . . ."

Michael jumped to his feet. "Objection," he spat. Irrelevant and inflammatory, and a whole bunch of other unethical reasons, he thought. But he sat back down, knowing his objection would be justified without explanation. He didn't want to look to the jurors like the villain who blocked the defense attorney's freedom of speech. Or some other such censure that the jurors might think he was causing Mr. Muscle Beach lawyer to bear.

"Sustained."

"Sorry, Your Honor, I can't help but be taken in by the nature of this case," said Elliott.

Bullshit.

The judge waved a hand to Elliott, indicating he go on without the nonsense.

Elliott became thoughtful, rubbing his chin as he strolled to the railing in front of the jurors. Pity the poor chastised boy. "There are several elements here that are undisputed," he said. "First, it is true – as the plaintiff's counsel indicated – that the child cannot hear the same as you and I. There have been tests to show that. That is not denied.

"It is also true that the girl may have been a musician one day. Who really knows? She may well not have. However, we will go along with these statements that Mr. Sutherland has made. Undisputed." Elliott moved closer to the jury box and leaned his palms on the front railing, arms outstretched. He lowered his voice. A good friend telling a secret. "However, these concerns are not the issue here today, are they? The issue – and the only concern of this case – is: Is my client at fault for making errors that were within his jurisdiction to control? And the answer to that question, good people, is emphatically no."

Elliott stepped back and slid one hand underneath the front tail of his jacket, and pushed his fist into the pocket of his trousers. The other arm swung toward Michael.

"On the contrary to what the opposing counsel has said in his statements this morning, the defense will prove to you that in spite of a life-threatening situation, which took place with my client's patient, Dr. Vincent Fossari performed an act of courage and skill when he saved that little girl's life. And his decisions were all within the high standards of excellence, of performance, and of judgment, and would most likely have been the same decisions as those carried out by any other competent medical professional."

Elliott ambled to the defense table and stood beside Fossari, hand once again, on Fossari's shoulder. He smiled at the jury, nodded. "Thank you," he said, and sat down.

Michael saw Vincent Fossari lean toward Royce Holding, hand over his mouth. Michael stood.

"Your Honor, without further ado, I call Dr. Vincent Fossari, the defendant, as my first witness."

Fossari froze, his hand still at Holding's ear, then he turned, wide-eyed and stared at Michael.

Holding wrote on a legal pad and slid it across the table to Elliott. Fossari looked from one attorney to the other. Holding's nod was almost imperceptible, and Fossari tugged at his lapels as he pushed the chair back and stood.

Approaching the witness stand, Fossari placed a meaty hand on the Bible and took the oath. Then he stepped onto the platform, swung the mahogany gate, and perched on the chair with his fists gripping the rail. Judge Pfaff leaned over the side of his roost, stretched his neck toward Fossari. "Dr. Fossari, you may want to sit back and relax," he whispered. Then winked at the witness.

Fossari's fingers went to his temple and nervously poked at his hair. "Yes. Yes, of course," he said and placed his back against the wood.

From his position among the spectators, Ross Manchester watched Fossari's hand movement. In that brief moment, Ross glimpsed the raw scar tissue in the center of Fossari's palm. He also saw the deformed ear cartilage on that side of Fossari's head as the hair was pushed aside. A shock went through Ross' body then, as his mind darted to a place almost a thousand miles away. A place where snowstorms are common. Where people can die without electricity. And where a temperature drop can cause frostbite on the tips of a person's ears.

"Please tell the court, Dr. Fossari, was Tracy Thomas ever a patient of yours?" Michael said.

"Yes. She was."

"And how did Tracy become your patient?"

"I beg your pardon?" Fossari glanced over to the two defense lawyers, but neither man saw Fossari's eyes. Royce Holding was intently watching Michael, and Steven Elliott was scribbling on his large yellow pad.

"I'm sorry, Doctor. I will rephrase the question." Michael looked at the witness and spoke at a very slow pace. "Please tell the court the events that led up to the time when you first accepted Tracy Thomas as your patient."

Vincent Fossari spoke in a low monotone. He responded to Michael's query by telling of the operation performed by his colleague, John Burton, M.D., and of his acceptance of Burton's patient after Burton left for a conference in Los Angeles.

"At that time, you became Tracy's physician. Is that correct?"

"Yes. That is correct," Fossari said in a near whisper.

To establish a basic background and try to put Fossari off guard, Michael asked several simple questions, speaking in short, clipped inquiries, while Fossari responded in a slow, almost lethargic tone. Twice the judge asked Fossari to speak louder so the court reporter could hear.

It was a ping-pong warm-up, before the real competition began.

Michael cleared his throat. "Now, Dr. Fossari, tell us about Tracy's general health before her hospitalization. Was she a sickly child, or did she appear to be in robust health? Except for a chronic sore throat, of course." Michael said.

"Objection, Your Honor," Steven Elliott said without standing. "My client did not know the patient prior to her hospitalization. He should not be expected to answer that question."

"You are correct, Mr. Elliott," said the judge. Then he faced Michael. "The objection is sustained, counselor. Please direct only those questions to this witness that he is prepared to answer."

"Yes, Your Honor, I apologize." But a seed had been planted, Michael hoped. A kernel of doubt in the jury's mind. That Tracy was unmarred, unmaimed before she was placed under Fossari's care.

By the time court broke for the day, Michael felt that he was beginning to scratch the surface of information that he wanted to bring out. He had just begun to broach the subject of Tracy's initial hearing loss when the judge called an end to the session. To Michael there was nothing yet, so far as he could tell, that had put more weight in favor of one side or the other. And the defense hadn't even started.

74

Michael arrived at the courthouse early the next morning, eager to resume questioning Fossari. Alone and lost in thought, he didn't notice the cold March wind cut across his face as he walked up the steps to the courthouse. Nor was he aware that he struggled with the heavy door to the men's room on the first floor.

Most of the night Michael had spent preparing his lead-in statements for today's questioning. It would set the stage for a broad picture of Vincent Fossari. Then maybe during his weekend trip, he could unravel the rest of the details that were still stuck like prongs in his craw. Inside his overcoat pocket was an airline ticket to Long Island. Barbara, Emilie, and Ross had been puzzled when Michael told them what he planned to do. But they agreed to car pool to the courthouse this morning, so Michael could travel alone, then leave for the airport after today's recess.

How could he tell them his hunch might be the evidence he needed to win the case? He wasn't even sure himself. And even if it was what he needed, Michael didn't know if he could convince the girl to come to Florida to testify. But he had to take that chance. He had tracked her down this far, and would confront her on Saturday. He had to know the truth. She'd have nothing to gain by getting on the witness stand, but a whole lot to lose. And she had lost so much already. For all Michael knew, she might be running away again right now. But he didn't have time left to keep chasing. He had decided to find out the answer tomorrow. Whether or not he liked that answer couldn't concern him at the moment.

As the trial resumed, Michael inhaled a silent breath and approached the witness stand, trying not to think about the disgust he felt for the man in front of him.

"Dr. Fossari," he began, "when the court recessed yesterday afternoon, you had said that Marilyn Pelletier, the nurse from Parkwest Pediatric Hospital, called you at your office and told you that Tracy's condition was deteriorating. Is that correct?"

"Yes." Fossari looked more confident than he did when the court dismissed him yesterday. No doubt that last night had been spent in briefings and role-playing for his attorneys, covering well-chosen hypothetical questions and the best answers to strengthen the defense.

"And what did you tell Ms. Pelletier that day when she spoke to you about Tracy?"

Fossari coughed. "I said that I had patients in my office right then. I have a responsibility to all of my patients, Mr. Sutherland. I had already given my time to the hospital and to the child in question the previous day." Fossari twisted his head and spoke to the jury. "I spend twelve hours at the hospital on most days," he told them. "I cannot go running back and forth every few hours because the nurses don't watch my patients."

From her seat in the back, Marilyn's grip tightened on Karen's hand.

"I understand, Doctor," Michael lied. "Now, Dr. Fossari, please tell the court. Did Ms. Pelletier say that Tracy was having difficulty hearing at that time?"

"She implied that."

"She implied that." Michael repeated. "Did Ms. Pelletier also offer to see that the laboratory work was done and to schedule Tracy for audiology testing?"

"I don't remember."

"You don't remember?" Michael emphasized *remember.*

"No. That conversation is vague in my memory."

"All right, Dr. Fossari. When Ms. Pelletier called you, had Tracy been receiving any medication for her . . ."

"Objection!" Royce Holding spoke for the first time. His voice was smooth and deep. "Mr. Sutherland is leading the witness, Your Honor." In his late fifties, Holding was a tall, large-boned man, whose dark hair and silver temples had been trimmed salon perfect. His face was clear and unwrinkled. As chief counsel for the largest empire in the tri-city area, Holding's malpractice expertise made him a sought-after attorney. Although his professional ethics were often polemic, he was respected – and feared – for his record of wins.

Judge Pfaff nodded. "Thank you, Mr. Holding. Objection is sustained." To Michael, the judge said, "Mr. Sutherland, please rephrase your last question."

"Of course, Your Honor." Michael was surprised at the judge's action. He felt that he had not at all been leading in his interrogation. But he mentally shrugged it off.

To redirect his thoughts, Michael walked to the plaintiff's table, and picked up an index card with his outline from the night before. It gave him time to think.

"Dr. Fossari, what was the drug Tracy had been receiving to treat her infection?"

"Garamycin," Fossari said, overtly pleased with both the judge and himself.

"And what was the dosage you ordered for her to take?"

"I ordered 60 milligrams of the antibiotic." Then he added, "To be given I.V."

"And how often did Tracy receive the medication in that dose – 60 milligrams?"

"Every four hours."

"Dr. Fossari, from the time of the first administration of Garamycin, how long did Tracy receive it until it was discontinued? How many days had passed?"

"Until I took her off it on Tuesday, the ninth." Fossari looked annoyed. "It's all there in the record."

"That was after Marilyn Pelletier called you the second time?"

"Yes."

"And how many days was that?" Michael was determined to get Fossari to answer his question, before an objection was raised.

"About 18 or 19, I believe."

"Thank you Doctor. Now if you will indulge me and the court for what may seem to you as my limited knowledge of medicine," Michael's eyes flitted toward the jury box, and saw two heads bob slightly, "please explain what action the drug Garamycin has on the body."

"Garamycin is an antibiotic, Mr. Sutherland."

"And an antibiotic fights infection, does it not?"

"It does."

"What type of infection is Garamycin usually effective against?"

"There are many, Mr. Sutherland. Shall I quote the P.D.R. for the court?" Fossari clipped, sure of an unseen trap.

"I'm sorry, Dr. Fossari," Michael said calmly as he stepped closer to the witness stand. "An example will be fine."

"Garamycin is the trade name for gentamicin sulfate. It is an aminoglycoside, which is effective in combating serious infections caused by Proteus, Staphylococcus aureus, Pseudomonas aeruginosa, and Escherichia coli – that which is found in human feces." Michael heard someone in the front row giggle uneasily. "Aminoglycosides are bacterial antibiotics with broad-spectrum properties. Generally speaking, they are used to fight life-threatening infections." Fossari ended with an expression that said to Michael: *There's an answer for you, you bastard. Let's see what you do with that one.*

"And you felt that Tracy had a life-threatening infection, did you not, Dr. Fossari? Michael said, ignoring Fossari's glare.

"I did."

"What was the infection that you were trying to fight, Doctor?"

Rising halfway out of his chair, Steven Elliott balanced his broad body on the palms of his hands and leaned forward on the table. "Objection, Your Honor," he said in a tone often heard inside a third-grade classroom.

The judge looked stunned. He had been following the questioning with interest. "On what grounds, Mr. Elliott?"

Steven Elliott slid his chair back, and stood up. "Mr. Sutherland is going around in circles with this line of questioning. He is badgering the witness, Your Honor," he said.

"I see no badgering, Mr. Elliott," said the judge. "Objection overruled. Go on, Mr. Sutherland."

Touché, thought Michael, but he couldn't help wondering what the judge would have said if the objection had come from Royce Holding.

"If it pleases the court, Your Honor, I would like to have the stenographer read back my last question," Michael said.

"Of course." Judge Pfaff leaned slightly forward, his bulk resting on his forearms as he spoke to the woman near the bench. "Miss Anderson, please read Mr. Sutherland's last question."

A small, dark-haired woman in her early thirties reached for the paper tape on the stand between her knees. She said, "Mr. Sutherland said, 'what was the infection that you were trying to fight, Doctor?' " Then the reporter quickly folded her notes back into the tray and re-positioned her manicured fingers on the keyboard.

Michael looked at Fossari. "Doctor?" he said.

Vincent Fossari, unaccustomed to justifying his actions, appeared flustered. He adjusted his tie. "Tracy had Pseudomonas aeruginosa," he said.

"How did you know that, Dr. Fossari? Was her throat cultured?"

"No."

"Then how did you know Tracy had Pseudomonas?"

"Although taking a throat culture is the usual procedure with Pseudomonas, we, I, felt sure that the child had a gram-negative micro-organism that would respond best to Garamycin."

"How could you be sure, Doctor? Without a culture?"

Vincent Fossari riveted a brief gaze at Michael and then rested his elbows on his knees, looking at his hands as they hung between his legs. "Because the child in the bed next to Tracy had a lung infection that was already cultured for Pseudomonas."

Michael leaped on it. "The child in the next bed?"

"Yes."

"Was the child in the next bed recovering from surgery, too?

"No."

"Without revealing the name of the child in the next bed, what was the diagnosis of that child?"

"She had cystic fibrosis."

"She was not post-op?"

"No."

"What unit of the hospital were the two children on, Dr. Fossari?"

Fossari looked over at the defense table. Royce Holding and Steven Elliott were heavily into deep whispers and taking notes.

"Answer the question, Dr. Fossari," said the judge.

"Fossari's head jerked toward the judge, then back again. "They were on the medical unit."

"Is it usual procedure, Doctor, for a non-infected surgical patient to be admitted to the medical floor after they awake from their surgery?"

"No."

"Then why was Tracy Thomas admitted to the medical floor and put in a room with a child who had been cultured and was known to have a serious infection?" Michael asked.

"We usually try to keep surgical patients separate from medical patients, Mr. Sutherland. The fourth floor is the surgical unit and the third floor is the medical unit. A portion of the fourth floor has been closed for some time."

Michael nodded, and toyed with the pen in his coat pocket. He's trying to confuse the jury, Michael thought. The bastard. Aloud he said, "I'm not sure I understand you, Dr. Fossari. You said you usually try to keep surgical patients separate from medical patients. They are not even kept on the same floor in most instances. Is this to prevent infections from developing with surgical patients?"

"In part, yes. There are other reasons as well."

"Like what?"

"Like staffing, for instance."

He's not getting away with that one, thought Michael. "And yet Tracy Thomas was not only put on the same floor as the medical patients – some with serious illnesses – but she was also put in the same room as a child who was a known carrier of a serious infection. An infection so lethal that soon after Tracy was admitted to the room with her, the other child died from that very infection."

A rush of spectator voices hummed briefly, then stopped.

"Did she not, Dr. Fossari?"

Fossari was silent.

Michael proceeded. "The infection that was carried by the other child eventually spread and contaminated

Tracy, infecting the open wounds of her throat. Did it not Doctor?" Michael tried with all his might to keep his emotions intact. But his words poured out. "And, in fact, nearly killed little Tracy Thomas."

Steven Elliott bolted from his chair and ran his hands over his hair. "I object, Your Honor. The attorney for the plaintiff is clearly harassing the witness." He remained standing.

"Objection sustained, Mr. Elliott. Though I hardly think the witness is being harassed." Judge Pfaff addressed Michael. "Please rephrase your question, Mr. Sutherland."

Elliott sat down, flesh on the front of his neck mottled in shades of lavender above his starched collar and tie.

Michael was happy to rephrase the question. He had made his point. And repeating it helped it sink in to the jurors' minds even more. "Yes, Your Honor. Dr. Fossari, did you admit Tracy Thomas to the same room as a child who was known to have had a serious lung infection? And then the other child died of that infection?"

Vincent Fossari looked at Royce Holding. When the attorney didn't move, Fossari nodded once.

"Let it be noted on the record that Dr. Fossari has answered in the affirmative," said the judge. Then he added, "It's almost noontime, Mr. Sutherland. How much longer do you plan to question Dr. Fossari?"

"I have just a few more questions, Your Honor." Michael wanted the jury to take Vincent Fossari's statements with them to digest with their lunch. If the doctor's ability as a physician were to be questioned, the jury needed to get used to the thought. Now, before Royce Holding started on the witness. "Dr. Fossari," Michael said, "How much does Tracy Thomas weigh?"

Verbal chaos could be heard from several sections of the room. The judge, feeling discomfort in his belly, and eager to relieve his bulging bladder, was not in the mood for delays. He pounded his gavel twice. "Quiet, please," he said to the audience in general. Then he looked at Michael. "Mr. Sutherland, I hope this line of questioning will prove relevant soon. We are already beyond our lunch break."

Michael knew he risked offending the hungry beast, and had often seen relationships crumble between judge and lawyer, causing prejudice throughout an entire trial. But Michael wanted to finish his questions. His mind raced. "Thank you for your patience, Your Honor. I assure you that I will finish in a moment."

"All right then, Mr. Sutherland. You may continue for a brief period."

Vincent Fossari had been watching the discourse. Now he sat rigid in the chair.

"Again, Dr. Fossari. How much did Tracy weigh when she was admitted to your service as a post-op patient at Parkwest Children's Hospital's medical unit?" That was specific enough.

"I don't remember how much she weighed, Mr. Sutherland." Then abruptly, Fossari spat out. "The child is large for her age. That's all I remember." His hand flipped in the air as if to dismiss the subject.

"What is the average weight of a five-year-old-girl, Dr. Fossari? Twenty-five pounds? Fifty pounds?"

The color in Fossari's face deepened. "About forty pounds. I do not usually deal with *average* children, Mr. Sutherland. I deal with sick children." Fossari's nostrils flared.

"Deal with, Dr. Fossari? You deal with children?" Then before Elliott could object, Michael said. "Scratch that question."

Michael moved a step closer to Fossari. "So then, the average, healthy child of five years should weigh approximately forty pounds. And since Tracy was a little healthier, er, larger than normal . . . " It was another risk, but Michael chanced it. " . . . would you

310

say that forty-four pounds would be about right for Tracy, Dr. Fossari?"

"Could've been."

The bastard didn't give an inch. Fossari knew well that Tracy's weight was recorded on the hospital admittance sheet as exactly forty-three and a half pounds. "Okay, then. We'll agree that Tracy weighed forty-four pounds." It wasn't a question. "And the usual dosage for Garamycin is what, Doctor?"

Fossari looked at the ceiling. His voice sounded strained. "Usual dosage is between two and two point five milligrams per kilogram of body weight."

"Over what period of time?"

"Eight hours."

Michael moved to the defense table and opened a large book. It was the same one that Marilyn had used to brace Alyce's back when she began CPR. "Your Honor, with your permission, I would like to read from the *Physician's Desk Reference* – the publication on drugs that is used by most doctors."

The judge sighed. "Go ahead, Mr. Sutherland."

" 'Gentamicin sulfate, which may go by the trade name of Garamycin, is to be administered to children with normal renal function in the following manner: two to two point five milligrams per kilogram of body weight, I.M. – intramuscularly.' " Michael stopped, looked up at Fossari for a moment. " ' – or I.V. infusion, every eight hours.' Exactly as you said, Doctor."

Fossari didn't move.

Michael continued. "It also says that this potent drug should be used cautiously and only after the patient's baseline weight has been established. It says that the usual duration for this medication is between seven to ten days, during which time the patient's hearing should be evaluated on a regular basis. It says that this is necessary because the drug is known to have a deleterious effect on hearing."

311

Michael slammed the book shut, and picked up a small sheet of pink paper with blue handwriting. "Your Honor, may I approach the witness?"

"Go ahead, Mr. Sutherland."

"Dr. Fossari, will you examine this prescription order and tell the court whose signature is on it?"

Fossari didn't make a move toward the paper, but only flicked his eyes over the face of the sheet. Then he nodded without speaking.

"I'm sorry, Dr. Fossari, I didn't hear you," Michael said.

"Mine."

"Then you ordered this medication as indicated on this form, in the dosage, route, and time indicated. It was your doctor's orders?"

"Yes."

"Thank you, Doctor." Michael walked over to the judge then. "Your Honor, I would like to enter as evidence in this case this drug order taken from Tracy Thomas' chart. This is an order for the medication Garamycin." Placing the document in front of the judge, Michael said, "This prescription for Garamycin was ordered from the Parkwest Pediatric Hospital Pharmacy on September 19th."

The judge perused the paper and then looked at Michael. "The court accepts the prescription order as evidence in this case, Mr. Sutherland," he said. The judge mumbled something to the stenographer about marking the evidence.

With slow, exaggerated movements, Michael walked toward the jury box. He slid the paper through the air in front of the jurors.

"This order for Garamycin clearly states that the dosage to be given to Tracy Thomas, and, in fact, was administered to the child who was then in a coma from the infection that she contracted because she was placed on the wrong unit, was in the amount of sixty milligrams. Not forty milligrams as advised by the medical journal. It was given to her, through her veins every four hours, not every eight hours. And it was given from September nineteenth until October tenth. Over 21 days. For more than 21 days – twice the maximum number of days that were explicitly stated in the physician's drug book – Tracy's body sucked up a dangerous drug that was, day by day, destroying her hearing. And it wasn't until the nurse on duty called the dilemma to the attention of Dr. Fossari. Twice. That this medication was stopped. By then Tracy Thomas was deaf."

Michael turned quickly toward Vincent Fossari and then back to the jury. "It was the *nurse* who discovered the error. After she returned from several days off," he said. "Not the doctor. And then it was too late for Tracy." His voice slowed. "Tracy Thomas not only received a powerful drug in an amount too great for her tiny body's size, but she also continued to receive the toxic chemicals into her veins, day after day, until Tracy Thomas, the little girl who was a brilliant pianist, became deaf. Profoundly deaf."

Amidst the bustling voices in the courtroom, Michael said, "I have no more questions at this time, Your Honor," and he walked to the plaintiff's table to join Wayne Thomas, who was holding his face in his hands.

The court broke for lunch until two o'clock.

75

"My daughter is dead. She killed herself six years ago."

The words reverberated inside Michael's skull, as he drove home from Tampa International Airport early Monday morning. He had left an airline ticket with the girl's mother, even though the woman told Michael that she was not interested in helping him out.

And now, as Michael sat in the courtroom watching the spectators file in, his spirits were low. He saw Ross, Emilie and Karen wave to him when they passed through the courtroom doors. They took seats next to Barbara. Ed Kohler came in next, and after looking around, stood by the back wall. Within a few minutes, Marilyn appeared, holding onto Tracy's hand. Marilyn's other arm enfolded a large book, and Michael saw part of a familiar cartoon figure. Herman, the mustached clown wearing a Swiss-style hat, one stringed finger pointing to the top of the page. Then, as the double doors to the corridor opened and several people moved into the room, Michael saw Wayne Thomas in the hallway smoking a cigarette. Then a clear voice rang out.

"All rise."

As Michael expected, Royce Holding and Steven Elliott took turns questioning Vincent Fossari, creating images that not only gave their client credibility as a competent and reliable physician, but also expounded on the merits of the hospital. Throughout the well-rehearsed dialogue between Fossari and his attorneys, Michael's weariness grew. Occasionally, he scanned the back of the room to see who'd come in or gone out. His mind wandered and his head ached. He wondered if his all-night flight and current fatigue would impair his alertness and hurt the case.

Then he became aware of a new line of questioning at the witness stand. It baffled him at first. Then it occurred that it might be something useful. A threshold for new information that might otherwise be tossed out as irrelevant. Too bad, thought Michael. Too bad he didn't have a decent witness to help strengthen this case.

Steven Elliott was asking, "Tell the court, Dr. Fossari, have you ever performed an act as a physician that resulted in an accusation of poor judgment?"

"Absolutely not," said Fossari.

"I apologize, Doctor, for even bringing it up. But it is important that we establish your performance in the medical profession as flawless, a fact that will also be reinforced by others. Experts in the field."

"No problem," said Fossari, and for the first time during the trial, he looked to Michael as if he were the powerful doctor back in control.

"Then let me repeat this for the court, so that it is perfectly clear: To your knowledge, to your memory, Dr. Fossari, your performance record has never been questioned with a malpractice suit?"

"No. Never."

"When were you first issued a license to practice medicine, Doctor?"

"In 1968. Thirteen years ago."

"And your medical license is clear and active?"

"Yes."

"Have you ever had disciplinary action against your license? From Florida or New York, where you were previously licensed?"

"No."

"Have you ever caused injury or pain to one of your patients that would cause them to suffer?"

"No."

315

Holding and Elliott rarely introduced this type of strategy. It could be risky. But Michael knew they wanted the jury to believe that Fossari's medical reputation was impeccable, error-free, and above board.

In his mind, Michael shuffled through the information he had been collecting for over a year. Much of it tucked away in the two boxes at his feet. As Steven Elliott continued to interrogate Fossari, his words were so carefully chosen that Michael was hard-pressed to disrupt the discourse with an objection. On the one occasion that he did – on grounds of improper evidence – it was overruled by the judge because of relevancy of the defendant's workplace. At least it was on the record in case he needed it later for an appeal. He certainly needed something. With the exception of a slight upsweep of media interest, the case was moving in a straight and routine line. Straight toward a victory for the defense. Even the St. Petersburg Independent, the only paper to cover the trial, had focused their weekend story on the plight of a poor deaf girl. Dr. Fossari's zero newsworthiness kept his name out of the news so far.

Steven Elliott finished questioning Fossari, and Michael did not cross-examine. Other than Marilyn, the one witness Michael needed to put on the stand, was dead. And now all he could do was try to pick up the pieces, look for ways to buy extra time, and to grapple with the defendant's expert witnesses who praised Fossari's character and status in the medical community. Buying time was the only reason Michael agreed to the defense's request to put one of their expert witnesses on the stand out of order, if it pleased the court, so the surgeon could return to his operating schedule immediately.

Elliott had just sworn in Dr. Elwood Phillips, a noted neonatologist and pediatric pulmonologist with Tampa General Hospital, who said he had known the defendant, Dr. Vincent Fossari for eleven years. In addition to his private practice in Temple Terrace, Dr. Phillips had served for eight years as expert witness in malpractice cases both for the defense and for the plaintiff.   Elliott emphasized the word *and*, looking directly at Michael.   He went on to elicit lengthy credentials.   " . . .and finally, Dr. Phillips, are you an active member of the Professional Standards Review Committee that works closely with the Florida Legislature to monitor health care cost containment and standards of professional medical care around the state; and which, does it not, make recommendations on a federal level?"

Dr. Phillips agreed, that yes, he did, and they did. All of those things.

For a lengthy time, Elliott questioned Phillips, receiving from his mouth glowing accolades on Vincent Fossari's sainthood.   In his final remarks, Dr. Phillips assured the court that in his professional opinion, the defendant did not, would not, in any way, carry out his duties as a practitioner of medicine, which could be interpreted as anything less than exemplary, nor that which any other highly respected physician would have done under similar circumstances.   Then Elliott was finished.

"Your witness, Mr. Sutherland."

"I have no questions for this witness," Michael said from a half stand at the plaintiff's table.

Having performed his civic duty to protect the medical profession from the likes of patients such as Tracy Thomas who are causing the skyrocketing trend in malpractice litigation, insurance liability, and costs to health care professionals, Dr. Phillips stepped down from the witness box, tipped his head slightly as he passed in front of the jurors, and then continued to walk the straight line to the double doors and out of the courtroom.

During lunch break, Michael remained at the plaintiff's table, surrounded by a room full of empty chairs. He still had a few strategical options he could attempt that might strengthen Tracy's case. Or at least slow the speed of its nose-dive. One direction he could go would be to expose the statistical research from a nationwide study that had recently been completed by the American Cystic Fibrosis Congress, which detailed the morbidity and mortality rates of 126 CF clinics around the United States. The report, which is not made public, showed that the cystic fibrosis clinic at Parkwest Children's Hospital currently rated at the bottom. Among the three worst in America. In fact, the chances of death occurring to a cystic fibrosis patient while under the care of Vincent Fossari, was twelve times greater than at any other clinic except two. But if the situation was that the child with CF had been transferred to Fossari from another hospital – versus when the child transferred from Fossari early on – Fossari beat those two clinics in the statistics, and went to the bottom of the list.

But that was below-the-belt tactics, reasoned Michael. The judge might even call a mistrial, despite the fact that Elliott had opened the squeaky door to Fossari's medical performance. And even though Fossari's batting average would be exposed, there were too many bags of worms that might open with that one. Especially if he brought in the CF Congress' report on Fossari's dirty laundry.

Michael had two other expert witnesses standing by. A physician and an infection-control specialist. He had wanted to put on the stand both Dr. Burton and the hospital pharmacist who disagreed with Fossari's medication order for Garamycin. But oddly, both men had both gone on vacation abroad, and wouldn't be back for a month.

Another approach that Michael considered was to put Tracy herself on the stand. But he was not comfortable with that, either. The jury already knew that Tracy was deaf. No one had denied that. They had seen the child, robust and active for several days now, sitting beside Marilyn in the courtroom, gaily-colored attire, clearly content in her silent world. Then for the jury to watch her squirm as a public display toy, trying and failing to sign even the simplest legal questions, would debase the child's dignity. No. He would have to come up with something better.

Soon.

76

When the court reconvened, Michael called Marilyn Pelletier as his next witness. Following her introduction to the court, Michael led the line of questioning to the time that Marilyn met Tracy.

"Please tell the court, Ms. Pelletier, when did you first see Tracy Thomas?"

Michael had talked with Marilyn several times prior to the trial about how he would interrogate her on the stand. *Just tell the truth, and answer the questions as briefly as you can*, he'd told her over and over again. She had no problem with the telling the truth part of it. But in spite of all Michael's tutoring during their mock trial practice, now that she was here, Marilyn was finding it difficult to stop with a simple answer to the questions. She wanted to blurt out to everyone in the courtroom about Fossari's evil ways, and she wanted to do it in one long-winded story. About the interactions at the hospital between Fossari and her. Fossari and the other nurses. Fossari and parents. But mostly, Marilyn wanted to talk about Fossari's attitude toward sick kids who were under his care. The way she had seen him treat them. She knew the jury – and the judge, too, for that matter – would be interested to hear some of the stories about this man who was on trial.

Marilyn glanced at Fossari sitting there at the defense table. Arrogant. Immoral. Powerful.

"It was on the day Tracy was admitted to my unit at the hospital," she said.

"And what floor was that, Ms. Pelletier?"

"The medical floor."

"The medical floor," repeated Michael. "And how does the medical unit, or floor, how does it differ from any of the other units at the hospital."

"On the medical unit we admit patients who have a medical diagnosis," Marilyn said.

"Such as?"

"Well, the children who are admitted have chronic illnesses. Such as leukemia, sickle cell anemia, juvenile diabetes, cystic fibrosis. That kind of thing." She paused. "There were also children with kidney and bladder conditions, pneumonia, or bronchitis. Even failure to thrive cases, when babies become malnourished and emaciated," she said.

"Anything else?"

"Well, yes. There are hundreds of different diagnoses that we saw in say, a year's time. But they are usually of the chronic or acute type most of the time.

"Usually, Ms. Pelletier?"

"Yes." It was getting tougher and tougher for her to stick to the script.

"Could you explain to the court in more specifics what you mean by usually, Ms. Pelletier?"

Out of the corner of his eye, Michael saw Royce Holding tip his head toward his legal colleague. Steven Elliott stood. "Really, Your Honor," he said. "I object to the tedious manner in which Mr. Sutherland is questioning this witness." He remained on his feet until the judge addressed Michael.

"Is this heading anywhere, Counselor?"

"Yes, it is Your Honor," Michael said. "I intend to make an important point momentarily."

"Objection overruled. Proceed as you were, Mr. Sutherland."

"Thank you, Your Honor. Now, Ms. Pelletier." Michael rubbed his chin, feigning a memory lag. "You were going to tell us what you meant when you said that the conditions of the patients, the children, who were admitted to your medical floor, were usually diagnosed as needing medical care."

"That's right. In nursing school, one of the first things we learned was that it is important to separate certain patients from other patients, whether those patients were children or adults. But it is especially true with children, because of their differential body volume to body surface ratio."

Michael blinked. That was new.

"And most of the time the selection of a pediatric patient for the medical unit is done by designating units or floors as to which patients will be accepted. Patients who are classified as medical or surgical, and then placing them in the unit where they will receive the best care. There are other categories as well," she added. "Psychiatric, geriatric, et cetera. But at Parkwest, that was not of concern. Just treating children."

"I see." Michael walked away from Marilyn and turned his head. His intention was to steal a look at the jurors, but his eyes never got that far. Because just then the double doors at the back of the courtroom opened, and there stood a woman he recognized. A woman who had made use of the airplane ticket he gave her for a flight from Farmingdale, Long Island, New York, and was now approaching an empty aisle seat in the fourth row of spectators. Michael suddenly felt heart palpations in his chest. He forced his mind back to Marilyn.

"What was so unusual about the day Tracy was admitted to your unit?" he said, and continued to interrogate Marilyn to bring out the facts they had discussed earlier this morning. She told of Dr. Burton's order to have Tracy moved to the surgical floor, of her, Marilyn, questioning Dr. Fossari about a post-op child being admitted to the medical floor, and of Fossari's insistence to keep Tracy there. Marilyn told of Tracy's infection that was similar to the child in the next bed, and the medication that had been given to Tracy after she'd been sent to the Intensive Care Unit.

Marilyn commented that one of the I.C.U. nurses had told her about the pharmacist's hesitation to fill the large order for Garamycin, but her dialogue was cut-off mid-sentence.

"Hearsay," Elliott snapped, and the judge ordered that part of the testimony to be scratched from the record. From the witness box, it took Marilyn's entire store of self-discipline to suppress the urge to make a wild jump over the rail, attack the lawyer, and pull every strand of bleached blond hair out of his gorgeous skull.

"Your witness," Michael said at last, and visually confirmed that his next witness was still in the courtroom.

"Mr. Elliott," said Judge Pfaff, "You may question the witness."

But it was not Steven Elliott who spoke next. "Good afternoon, Miss Pelletier," Royce Holding said, still sitting at the defense table. "I have only one question to ask you."

Good, Marilyn thought. *Please, dear God, make this be over quick.*

Deep in the Pinellas county archives, documents showed that the remodeling architects and lighting experts who'd been hired by the county commissioners had done a superb job to assure vivid and equal illumination on all physical matter viewed by taxpayers and taxspenders who entered the courthouse. But when Royce Holding stood up behind his client that day, and beamed his radar at Marilyn, the lawyer's cavernous umbrage deployed him into a self-propelled Howitzer that obstructed everything else from view.

"Miss Pelletier, we have just heard you testify. In your own words. In your own opinion. Which you so graciously gave. And your opinion of the circumstances surrounding the admittance and care of the patient in question."

What? thought Marilyn.

"And it occurs to me that you, Miss Pelletier are only a nurse." He paused, then took several long strides, stopping directly in front of Marilyn. "A nurse."

Marilyn's heart began to race, and her lips stuck together. She inhaled and exhaled through her nose. With her perceptual field narrowed to twelve inches around her body, she couldn't possibly have noticed Ed Kohler's large frame tense as he watched from the back of the courtroom.

"And being a nurse, Miss Pelletier, please tell the court what qualifications you possess to practice medicine in the State of Florida."

"Objection!" Michael had heard enough.

"Sustained," Judge Pfaff blurted. "Proceed with your question, Mr. Holding."

Royce Holding took possession of Marilyn's mind, and, as if he hadn't heard the interruption between Michael and the judge, he continued. "Tell us, Miss Pelletier, besides this one job that you held at Parkwest – which I might add, a job that you no longer have – tell us, about your experience as a nurse. My question is: Have you, Miss Pelletier, ever worked anywhere else as a registered nurse?"

Panic gripped Marilyn. "No," she said in a whisper.

"I'm sorry, Miss Pelletier, I didn't hear what you said." Holding continued to stare.

"No. Parkwest is the only place. But I had worked there for . . . "

"Thank you, Miss Pelletier. You have been very helpful." Royce Holding tipped his head at the judge and sat down.

When Michael called his next witness from the audience, several heads turned. Outside the courtroom windows, the clouds separated from the sun for the first time that day, and draped a straw-colored glow across the room. A man next to the bank of windows stood and closed the vertical blinds in a motion that swept narrow stripes across the faces of those nearby, and then turned their features to gray. By then the new arrival had approached the judge's bench.

"Do you solemnly swear that the testimony you are about to give is the truth, the whole truth, and nothing but the truth, so help you God?"

"Yes," said the woman. Then she pivoted on delicate shoes, stepped onto the witness box platform, and sat down.

"Good afternoon," Michael said. "Please give us your name."

"Mrs. James Campbell."

"And where do you reside, Mrs. Campbell?"

"At 145 Arlington Lane in Farmingdale, Long Island, New York.

"What is your occupation?"

"I retired from teaching – second grade – last year. I am now a housewife."

"And what is your husband's occupation?"

"He is a minister."

"Thank you," said Michael. His words were articulated with a tenderness that had not been used in the courtroom so far. "Looking around this room, and at the people here, can you tell us, Mrs. Campbell, if you are related to anyone present?"

The woman had already done that some time ago. "Yes," she said.

"To whom, Mrs. Campbell? To whom are you related?"

"I am the grandmother of Karen Reo." Emilie gasped, and several people in the front rows turned their heads. Ross wiped his palms down the tops of his thighs. Karen sat frozen, staring at Mrs. Campbell. *She's so pretty.*

"Now, Mrs. Campbell, if you'll just bear with me a minute – and I know this is terribly difficult for you.

But, although it is a very, very important fact that Karen Reo is your granddaughter, that is not the reason you are testifying in this court today, is it?"

"Objection, Your Honor. Mr. Sutherland is leading the witness."

"Sit down, Mr. Elliott."

Without looking at the judge, Michael said, "I will rephrase my question, anyway, Your Honor. Mrs. Campbell, you are testifying here today for another reason, is that correct?" Michael's words touched the woman's ears like a butterfly flittering softly on a tiny orchid petal.

"Yes," she whispered.

"Now, Mrs. Campbell, is there someone else in this room who you knew even before Karen was born?" The woman nodded, and raised her eyes to Michael. Then she turned her head slowly away.

"Who else in this room do you recognize, Mrs. Campbell, and how do you know that person?"

For a long moment, the woman remained silent, staring at the back of the room in the direction where Karen sat. Michael thought the woman hadn't heard his question. Then, just as he started to repeat what he'd asked, the woman blinked, then cleared her throat. "I recognize two in this room. One of them is Dr. Vincent Fossari, the defendant." She said it in a calm, controlled voice, poised and dignified. And no one saw the grizzly pain she felt crushing through her heart. "My son died because of him," she murmured.

As the six words tumbled softly from Amy Campbell's lips, they arranged themselves into a velvet hammer that arched in the space before her, aimed, and then struck their tocsin. Hard.

Suddenly pandemonium exploded in the room, drowning out the judge's gavel. "Quiet," he said. "Quiet, please."

Amy Paulter Campbell sat stiff and upright in the witness box, tears streaming down her cheeks when Judge Pfaff called a 15-minute recess.

77

"What do you mean, you don't know who she is?" Royce Holding was brandishing his arms through the air. "The woman knows you, Dr. Fossari."

The three men, Holding, Fossari, and Steven Elliott, had holed up in the small conference chamber three doors down from the courtroom.

"Okay, okay," Holding shouted. "So you don't recognize the woman. Campbell. Think. Her face doesn't do anything to you? Think, Fossari. You have got to tie her in to something. Some patient you treated sometime in the past." Then, he added, "God I hope not."

Fossari sat at the large table, the top thick and heavy under the weight of his elbows, fingers pushing against his temples as he stared down at the wood. Holding stood across from Fossari, gripping the back of a dark leather chair. He lowered his voice. "Dr. Fossari, I cannot go out there in that courtroom," he pointed to the wall in quick stabs, "and interrogate that woman, without knowing what her answers are going to be. Damn." He slammed a fist into the back of the chair. "Goddamn that Sutherland. Goddamn punk lawyer. A sickly son of a bitch who looks like he couldn't wipe his fucking ass without help from his mother. And he's got me stymied with a surprise goddamn witness who causes a fucking uproar in the middle of a sure-win case, before I even know what the fuck she's going to say."

Holding walked the length of the table. Then around it, until he was back where he started. "I don't even have the little goddamn time that it takes to check her out. I have to go in there and let her dump shit all over this case." He ran his fingers through his hair and continued to pace. Steven Elliott sat immobile in one of the chairs.

Fossari hadn't moved. His blinkless eyes remained glued to the tabletop. Something inside his head began to grind. Slowly at first, gears propelled by a chain, unoiled and rusty, moving through fine sand crystals, the grit-speed lessened to a sluggish crunch and then finally stopped. When Holding yanked back the chair next to Fossari, and slammed his fist on the table, Fossari barely raised his head.

"Goddamn it, Fossari, say something!" he demanded.

When Fossari didn't reply, Holding shouted, "I'll tell you one thing," his finger poked into Fossari's face. "If you make me look like a fool out there because of something you haven't told me, I guaran-damn-tee that you, brother, and me, are going to have something to settle."

Steven Elliott cringed. He'd seen his partner's wrath before. It went with the man's legal brilliance. "Come on, Royce," he said. "Take it easy. Maybe he doesn't remember the woman. People change. They get married. Dye their hair. Give the guy a break."

"Horse shit!" said Holding.

When recess was over and Michael approached his witness again, the two defense lawyers projected self-assurance and equanimity.

"All right, Mrs. Campbell," Michael was saying. "Just before the recess, you said that you were acquainted with Dr. Vincent Fossari. Is that correct?"

For the previous ten minutes, Amy Campbell had remained alone and protected after Michael shuffled her into a small room just off the side of the courtroom. Then he jotted a quick message and gave it to Barbara. *Stay put. Stay out of sight from the media. And keep*

Karen okay. He knew that whatever happened in the next hour was vital to his case.

"In what capacity did you know Dr. Fossari, Mrs. Campbell?"

"He was the physician for my son."

"When was this?"

"1968."

"And where was it you first met Dr. Fossari, Mrs. Campbell?"

"It was when my son was admitted to Northfield Medical Center. On Long Island."

"Thank you, Mrs. Campbell. We all realize that 1968 was a long time ago. And many things happen over the years. There may be some things that you have forgotten. But to the best of your memory, what were the circumstances surrounding your first meeting with Dr. Fossari?"

In the hush that followed, Michael held his breath and watched as Amy Campbell's mind went back in time.

"I remember it well, Mr. Sutherland," she said. Then she stared into space, eyes unfocused. "We had just celebrated my daughter Janet's thirteenth birthday. We had promised her that we would take her to the Lincoln Center as part of the celebration. And there was a play on Broadway that she wanted to see. The musical *Hair*. Normally, I wouldn't have been so extravagant, but Janet wanted to see the performers sing *Let the Sunshine In*. And with her sensitivity, I wanted to instill at an early age, values that would last her a lifetime. The play questioned societal values. Racial inequality. Poverty. Human suffering. As things turned out, we never did see the show. But Janet got more than her share of human suffering."

Royce Holding and Steven Elliott listened carefully to the woman's discourse, hoping to pick up clues that would trap her later, and turn the story around to favor their client.   But each statement the witness made seemed pointless and vague.

" . . . so when Janet and her younger brother played chase on the pool deck outside the motel, and he slipped, Janet suffered more than her brother.   She felt extremely guilty. She said that since she was the older sister, she should have known better and not chased Joel around the pool. Which of course, none of it was her fault."   Amy Campbell blinked and looked at Michael.

"I'm rambling, Mr. Sutherland. I'm sorry." A thin smile crossed her face and she went on with her story.

But Vincent Fossari didn't hear her anymore. He was still back at the word Joel. The woman had said it in a unique fashion. A one-syllable echo, as if the letter J was stuck in a hole.

Fossari's face blanched as he sat in the middle of the huge courtroom between two columns of men. Not one person saw Vincent Fossari fade as the chair in which he sat reached up and swallowed him.   The vigilance of the people in the courtroom that day was directed at Amy Campbell.

"It was in the emergency room that I met Dr. Fossari. Joel's left arm was fractured in the fall, and Dr. Fossari put a cast on it. Then he suggested that Joel stay in the hospital overnight so the plaster could dry. Well, apparently Dr. Fossari wrapped the cast too snugly, because when . . ."

"Objection!"   Royce Holding was on his feet, startling even the judge. "Your Honor, this witness is drawing medical conclusions with her statements. Conclusions that she is not qualified to make."

The judge looked from Holding to Michael.   He creased his brow and held it a few seconds, then he said, "Mr. Sutherland?"

Michael stretched to his full height. "It seems at this moment that the defense attorney is correct with his objection, Your Honor," he said.   "But I would request that the court allow me a tad of leeway here, and I believe I will show that what Mrs. Campbell has said is not a medical conclusion at all, but rather it is based on what she actually saw for herself." There had not been time for Michael to read through the medical records that Amy Campbell had brought with her from Joel's hospitalization in 1968, but he was sure that what evidence he found in it would back up his remarks. It was worth a try.

"I will permit some degree of latitude here, Mr. Sutherland. But you must be able to produce proof that what the witness is saying is true."

"I intend to, Your Honor. Thank you."

Royce Holding sat down, beads of sweat on his brow.

"Now, Mrs. Campbell, you said that Dr. Fossari had put a cast on your son's arm, and admitted him to the hospital for the night. Then what happened?"

"Well, Joel was all right for a little while. He thought it was a big deal to have a cast on his arm for the other kids in school to sign." Her eyes glazed for an instant and she smiled. "But by the time he got settled in his room, I could see that the cast was bothering him. At first he didn't say much, because he didn't want to make Janet feel any worse than she already did. But then, after my husband took Janet home, I stayed for a little longer. To read to him, make sure he went to sleep. He told me his arm hurt. That he could feel something *bumping inside it* is what he said. To be honest, when I looked at Joel's arm, I couldn't see anything. So I called the nurse and she promised me she would call the doctor immediately."

"The doctor?" Michael's words slipped in among the woman's with an ease that made it sound like they came from her lips.

"Yes. Dr. Fossari," she glanced toward the defense table where Fossari sat like a brick. "It seemed like an awfully long time before he came to see Joel, and then he had the nurse give him something. Some kind of sedative. And Joel went to sleep.

"Then the next morning when I came back to take Joel home, he was hysterical." She removed a tissue from her blazer pocket and dabbed at her nose. "If I had only known then what was happening to Joel. I would never have let him stay for the night. His arm swelled the entire time I was gone." Her voice was more controlled than Michael thought possible as she re-lived the incident.

"By the time Dr. Fossari came in to see Joel that morning, it was too late to save his arm. Or Joel, either. That's when he died. That night."

"I don't understand." Michael said. This was not the same story Amy Campbell had told him when he flew to New York.

"They had to amputate my child's arm, Mr. Sutherland. So they called in the man who was chief of surgery at the hospital to do the operation. It was Dr. Julian Fossari, the defendant's father. But I never saw Joel alive again." She blew her nose. And when she saw the white Styrofoam cup someone had discreetly placed on the railing, she picked it up and swallowed once. Then she looked at the judge. "I apologize," she said.

"It's perfectly all right, Mrs. Campbell. Take all the time you need."

Amy Campbell pulled in her lips and bit down, in an effort to gain control

"Joel wasn't the only one who died that day," she said. The defendant's father, and two other people who worked at the hospital. They were assisting with Joel's operation. They were killed in the explosion, too."

The courtroom spectators had been hunched forward to better hear the witness, and with her last statement, there was a huge unified inhalation from the crowd that sucked molecules of outside air into the room from around the door and the window frames.

333

"An explosion?" asked Michael. This was not at all what he had expected. "There was an explosion in the operating room?"

"I found out later that the anesthesia they had used on Joel was called cyclopropane. It is a highly explosive gas that was used in small doses as a general anesthetic back then. It isn't used anymore." She peeked at Royce Holding. "But I am not a doctor, and I can only tell you what I know."

Michael briefly closed his eyes.

"The way I understand what happened," she continued, "is that during the operation, as the blood vessels in Joel's arm were to be cut, they had to sear those vessels to keep him from hemorrhaging. It's done with a heated tool – a cauterizer, I believe it's called."

A chill went through Michael.

"Apparently, a spark from the cauterizer ignited with the gas fumes, and . . ." Amy Campbell's voice choked up.

When she gained control, and looked at Michael, he said, "Thank you, Mrs. Campbell. I know this has been very difficult for you." He turned toward the plaintiff's table to join Wayne Thomas. Royce Holding shuffled papers at the defense table in preparation to question the witness.

That's when Amy Campbell reached for the railing in front of her chair and very slowly pulled herself up. Like a nightwalker having a dream, she spoke in a monotonal whisper. "My son was killed. My daughter committed suicide because she couldn't live with her brother's death. To me Dr. Fossari killed them both." Then she sat down, and it was as if she had never moved or spoken at all.

At the plaintiff's table, Michael felt like a rag of a man, whose emotions twisted in his gut.

78

It was a blow. No doubt about it. But Royce Holding had recovered from worse. And, he was sure that the judge would recess for the rest of the day after Campbell's emotional outbreak. To calm the jury. And, more importantly, give him time to prepare his interrogation of the woman.

But the judge did no such thing. And Holding knew there was nothing he could say to this witness that would help his case at the moment. Not one member of the jury was capable of hearing the other side today. If there was another side. To question Campbell further would appear as deliberate chafing to inflame her sores. She was a woman every heart in the room went out to. And it was too late to negotiate for a settlement. The plaintiff made that clear a long time ago.

So the only salvation the defense might have would be through a well-equipped summation, presented to the jury tomorrow. A closing statement that would bring out angles they hadn't even thought of yet. And neither had he, for that matter. But Royce Holding had been known to turn a jury to his way of thinking at the end of a case that would have been a sure win for the opponent if he had left those words unsaid.

The summation.

Tomorrow.

"No questions, Your Honor," he said.

The judge looked at his watch and then up at the throng. The people seemed as tired as he felt. Was it his imagination, or was the crowd getting larger?

"This court will recess until nine o'clock tomorrow morning," said the judge slapping the bench with his gavel.

79

Michael saw the television station's news van in the parking lot the next morning when he arrived at the courthouse.

After dropping Amy Campbell at a motel for the night, Michael had gone home and crawled into bed early. Then he awoke before dawn, and with a clear head, he wrote notes for his closing remarks. He knew he would change the statement a number of times before he spoke to the jury, and probably discard the entire dossier in favor of spontaneity anyway, which likely would be determined by the defense's summary. But he was filled with energy to spare this morning, and by the time he left the house, he had six pages of notes.

As agreed, Michael stopped by to pick up Amy Campbell on his drive to the courthouse. Barbara would ride with Ross, Emilie, and Karen.

Sitting beside him during the drive, Amy had been silent. Now he parked behind the courthouse, and cut the engine.

"I'm glad you found me," Amy said to Michael in her typical soft manner. Her hair was more silver than brown, and she wore it in a short style that flattered her delicate features. "So much has happened since you first called me, Michael," she said. "I've done a lot of soul searching and redefining my goals." She looked down at her hands.

"After Joel died, Janet changed from an outgoing, happy child to a moody one. Her early teen years were one tantrum-filled day after another. When she found out she was pregnant, her boyfriend Tom was delighted, and they were married right away. My husband and I

337

both liked the boy, and even though they were so young, we thought that with our support, Janet and Tom would be able to settle down. Have a happy life.

"Michele was a beautiful baby, and we thought that her presence would fill Janet with the love that she needed to recover after the setback of Joel's death."

Amy Campbell looked ahead through the windshield of the car and watched the parking lot spaces fill.

"Then Michele was diagnosed with cystic fibrosis and died one week before her first birthday. Janet was treated for depression with medications and counseling, and that helped some. But she was pregnant again, and had to stop taking the drugs. The night Tom brought Karen to the emergency room and Dr. Manchester saved my granddaughter's life, Janet thought there was no hope for the child. As you know, they left the baby at the hospital and never came back.

"Janet and Tom moved to Massachusetts, and we didn't see or hear from them at all. In fact, it was a long time before I learned where they were and that they had abandoned Karen. When we couldn't reach Janet or Tom, we thought Karen had died of cystic fibrosis just like Michele.

"Then one day Tom called and asked if Janet was with me. He said she had left and he couldn't find her anywhere. He was frantic. A few days later, the highway patrol found her body in an all-night rest stop along the Interstate. She shot herself in one of the stalls." Amy Campbell's voice grew hoarse.

"For a while I thought I would lose my mind. I did crazy things that don't make any sense to me now. And finally, Howard Paulter had had enough. He divorced me. I don't blame him. I was a bitch.

Two years ago, I married Jim. His patience has given me the strength I need to go on. It was Jim who talked me into coming to Florida for the trial. And he would have joined me if I hadn't insisted I do it alone."

She turned in the seat and looked at Michael. "I didn't know what to expect when I got here. Nor did I know what I'd say in front of that jury. Because I hadn't told you the whole story. But you know . . . " Amy Campbell smiled, and Michael saw something in her eyes that wasn't there before. " . . . that emotional purging yesterday was like a catharsis somehow. I needed to tell my story. I feel different now. More confident. And there may be a ray of hope out there after all. No matter how the court decides, I feel that I have done my part to help Tracy Thomas. And Karen, too.

"Jim is driving down tomorrow, and we'll stay here about a week – get to know my grandchild. She looks so much like Janet."

"She's a wonderful child, Mrs. Campbell," Michael said. "I'm sure you'll soon see that for yourself."

"Oh," she said. Then she opened the clasp on her purse and removed a thick envelope. "Karen's father, Tom Reo, asked me to give you these adoption papers you wanted signed. When I told him about your request, he was happy to help. Said he would love to see Karen some day."

Michael took the envelope. "When we get inside, why don't you tell Ross and Emilie Manchester what you just told me?" he said.

Then Michael Sutherland and Amy Campbell emerged from the car and headed across the parking lot to the courthouse.

80

Royce Holding had been summarizing the defense's case for ten minutes. During that time, he brought out the argument that all during the treatment of Tracy Thomas, his client, Dr. Vincent Fossari, had tried to do everything he believed was necessary and possible in the best interest of his patient.

Holding stated that Fossari's years of academic learning and accomplishments, his forbearance and strength of character alone should convince any jury that he was above any wrongdoing.

"Why, this man," he gestured dramatically with his open palm toward Vincent Fossari at the table next to Steven Elliott, "this dedicated man has been so devoted to the cause of saving human lives and alleviating suffering, that he has not even taken time out for a private life. In order to put his patients first, he has never married, sacrificing a family life of his own."

In a singsong monologue that he accentuated with hand-waving and struts, Royce Holding spoke to the members of the jury as if they were of one mind, one body with him – lovers whose secrets they alone shared.

"The plaintiff is asking for money, ladies and gentlemen. Money." He spat out the word as if he had just discovered it to be the diseased wing of a housefly that had lodged between his teeth. "Money will not bring the girl's hearing back." Then, flourishing his arms over his head, "What will it do? What will a monetary reward really do?"

Holding paused and settled the tips of his fingers on top of the jury railing like a lineup of ballerinas. He lowered his voice. "A ruling in favor of the plaintiff will only negate the promising future my client has. A future that would allow him to continue his role as a physician." He nodded, agreeing with himself. "We all know how unfortunate it is that the child is deaf. But to castigate my client now, would only be adding more suffering and pain to an innocent man – a man who should not be punished for doing his job in the best way he knows how."

Holding looked at the jury foreman. "Do we punish the tennis player who loses the match? No, we do not! Do we punish the student who fails a difficult test? No! Do we punish the lawyer who loses a case? Again, I say no! Nor can we expect a physician to win every time he fights to save his patient.

"Alas, the supreme battle for this patient was, in fact, won. We cannot forget that, can we? The dangerous warfare that was fought against her enemy – death – was won. When the child lay dying, it was Vincent Fossari, her physician, who used all the skill he could muster to save her young life. And he did.

"And Tracy lived."

Royce Holding looked at the floor and shook his head slowly. "Vincent Fossari regrets the misfortune of the child's hearing loss more than anyone. And so do the counsel for the defendant. But to haul an innocent man before a court of law, and force him to prove that what he did was right and proper and good, to insist that he justify his motives for saving a girl's life. To turn Dr. Fossari's masterpiece of medical art into a court trial is a slur. A disgrace to our judicial system."

Standing in front of the courtroom, Royce Holding was the image of power. Michael watched him intently, the actor reciting the lines of a play. He's good, Michael thought. Damn good.

"And so, ladies and gentlemen of the jury, you have heard the evidence presented by both sides of this case. And I can see from your faces that you are good people.

You are people who want to do the right thing. And that you will see the truth in this case.

"I'll close by asking you to explore your mind for the facts. Not the emotional outbursts that you have seen here. But the facts. And if there is any doubt whatsoever in your mind as to the greater weight of evidence, then you will decide in favor of my client, the defendant, Dr. Vincent Joseph Fossari. Thank you."

Although the room was packed, there was silence from the spectators and jurors alike as Royce Holding took several long steps to his seat beside Fossari and Elliott.

Michael waited for the judge to speak, before he rose from his chair.

Until that moment, Michael had been apprehensive. Each argument he had accumulated in his neat piles in front of him seemed trivial now, vague when compared to the exhibition he had just heard. In the past, Michael's cases had been won through his attention to detail and facts. He had always appealed to the reason and logic of a jury. Sometimes they listened. On the other hand, a jury that responded to drama and flair could easily be lulled by a serious point if he came across with even a hint of changelessness in his performance to them. He would have to peel off the varnish from Royce Holding's matinee and convince the jury that Tracy Thomas was the victim here, and not her doctor as his counsel would have them believe.

These were the thoughts that crossed Michael's mind in the seconds that it took him to stand up and push his chair back under the table. By the time he approached the jurors, he knew exactly what he wanted to say.

Michael thanked the people of the jury for their attention and their concern during the days of the trial. His words were genuine when he expressed his empathy for the tremendous job that lay ahead of them in deciding the future of the people involved in the case.

He told them that his labor would be over soon, and that the hardest part for them was still to come.

Then he took a breath, and concentrated on the transition to persuasion.

"Patterns," he said. "What I have seen in the behavior of the man on trial here are patterns. Patterns by a medical doctor who should have − at the very minimum, the very least − should have protected his patient from harm. Which would have, if they had been carried out. Ordinary precautionary measures that would have protected that small child, Tracy Thomas, from harm. Again, if they had been carried out. Unfortunately, those measures were never carried out by the defendant, Dr. Vincent Fossari. Never. Not once.

"At first, the patterns weren't clear. Their slipperiness didn't surface at first, because I wasn't sure what the patterns meant. I even thought that maybe they were just questionable coincidences. Until . . . until the defendant himself introduced testimony that allowed me to interrogate his forgotten deeds. Only then did I begin to see that the occurrences, that the patterns in Dr. Fossari's medical-practice behaviors were not questionable coincidences at all. But rather, they were configurations that repeated themselves over and over again. In fact, those behaviors became his standard of practice that he had embroidered into a theme of treatment for his patient caregiving."

Careful, Michael.

"Along with me, ladies and gentlemen, you have learned from the study of this case − from the defendant himself − as well as from others, that several happenings put my client in physical danger. Happenings that, had any one of them been interrupted by the defendant, then my client, little Tracy Thomas would not be deaf today.

"First, Tracy was admitted to the wrong unit of the hospital. Where was the precaution here?

"Then she remained in the same room with a patient known to have a lung infection. Where was the precaution there?

"When Tracy went into a coma from the resulting infection, she was given an unusually high dose of medication over a period of time that was excessively long. This medication was known to cause destruction of the nerves in the brain that causes deafness. And yet Dr. Fossari chose to look the other way. Where was the precaution?

"Then, there were no tests given to monitor Tracy's hearing after she was given the medication. In fact, it was the nurse who discovered that Tracy was deaf. It was the nurse who brought it to Dr. Fossari's attention. Where was his precaution?

"The pattern of undone precautions that should have been carried out, never were. And so Tracy Thomas, the little girl who entered the hospital for a simple operation to remove her tonsils, was subjected to three types of suffering that never should have occurred."

Michael pressed one finger at a time. "Infection, near death, deafness.

"Fortunately, Tracy has recovered from the first two conditions. But I'm afraid that although she experienced the joy of hearing for her first five years of her life, Tracy Thomas will spend the rest of her life – seventy-plus years – profoundly deaf.

"Part of what Mr. Holding has said is true. The money won't bring back Tracy's hearing. But what it will do is several other things. It will pay for the expenses for her to attend the Kendall Demonstration Elementary School for the Deaf in Washington, D. C., where her family will move if they have these finances.

"Tracy will never be able to pursue the musical goals that she would have if she had not entered Parkwest Pediatric Hospital on that fateful day. But when she completes her elementary school education, she will then be able to continue on at the same school campus in Washington, with courses of study for the deaf at the Gallaudet High School and College. Without a monetary award, it is unlikely that she would do so."

Michael felt drained. He had said what he felt to be the best argument in Tracy's behalf.

"Because Tracy's life is not a tennis match or a high school mathematics exam – as counselor for the defense so graphically put it – I would like to ask you, ladies and gentlemen of the jury, to award Tracy Thomas a monetary justice in the largest amount that the law will allow. Anything less won't do."

Michael took one step closer to the jurors, a gentle yet serious smile in his eyes. "And now, we lawyers end our part in this trial, and turn over to you a decision that only you can make. Then as you close and lock the door to deliberate, I'd like to offer you a gift from Mahatma Gandhi for you to think about.

"This great humanitarian said,

"An error does not become truth by reason of multiplied propagation. Nor does truth become error because nobody will see it."

From the short distance in front of the jury box, Michael quietly stroked the eyes of each juror with his own. Then he nodded, mouthed *thank you*, and joined Wayne at the plaintiff's table.

No one spoke as Michael settled into his seat, not even the judge, who seemed to watch with the others, as molecules of sound grew too heavy for the upward-flowing air to keep each syllable suspended. The cloud's morphemic droplets began falling in a gentle mist on the jurors' faces as they tried to grasp the significance of Gandhi's words. Then, a negative charge at the base of the word-cloud attracted itself to a positive charge inside each juror's head. When the difference between these two charges became strong enough, the normal insulating qualities of analogical thinking broke down. One by one, the lightning bolts struck. And the jurors understood.

81

When court reconvened at one o'clock, the judge spoke to the jury. He reminded them of the law and touched on what had taken place in his courtroom over the past several days.

At 1:45, the jury withdrew to deliberate on a verdict. Then the rest of the room emptied.

––––––––––

The waiting was difficult, but some of the sting of anticipation was overshadowed by jubilance when Amy Campbell announced to Ross and Emilie that she'd given Michael the adoption papers signed by Tom Reo, Karen's biological father. They'd walked to an outside café two blocks from the courthouse, and had pushed two metal tables together to regroup and let off steam.

Karen herself took the news in stride. "I knew Michael'd come through," she said, She snapped up Tracy's hand on one side and Amy Campbell's on the other. "Come on, Grandma," she said, pointing to a vacant table at the far end of the sidewalk. "Let's go over there so Tracy and I can show you how we do sign," and the three of them scurried off.

Even Marilyn was surprised by Karen's composure. "These kids are something," she said. "Here we are a bunch of frazzled wrecks, and they hang in there like it's just another day at the beach."

Ed had been low keyed all during the trial. Now he wanted to know, "What is there we can do now, Mike?"

Michael looked around the table at his wife and his friends. His supporters. Then watched Tracy happily showing off her signing skills for Amy Campbell. "We pray," he said. "We pray."

82

For an hour and a half, the group stayed at the sidewalk café drinking iced tea and coffee to pass the time. Every once in a while their conversation lagged as one by one they drifted into their own private thoughts.

Then Wayne Thomas spoke up.

"I'm worried about what a negative decision will do to Irene," he said. "She's not getting any better, and a ruling in Fossari's favor will push her over the edge."

Marilyn leaned forward, fingers wrapped around her cold mug. "Tracy has been her whole life, Wayne," she said. "All Irene tried to do was prevent Tracy from getting sore throats. Then she was traumatized when Tracy went into a coma. I was there, Wayne. I saw how Irene suffered. It was bad. Then Tracy's hearing was gone. And now, the trial. It's more than any mother can take."

Wayne Thomas stared at his hands. "She won't leave the house. And all she does is cry," he said.

"Would you like me to give her a call, Wayne?" Marilyn said. "She and I have a pretty good rapport. Maybe she'll come here and be with all of us. Do her good. Then, no matter what the news turns out to be, she'll be surrounded by people who care. And not hear it alone."

Marilyn saw a shadow cross Michael's face. "It will be good news, Michael," she said. "Oh, God, it's got to be good news."

Ed, who had been following the entire discourse, piped up. "Hey, Mike, the lady's a witch. Marilyn says the verdict is good, the verdict is good." He indicated with both hands that there was no question about it. "Matter settled."

"For now," Michael said.

"Well, what do you think, Wayne?" said Marilyn. "Do I call Irene and invite her to join us? I'll run get her if she says yes." When Wayne hesitated, she said, "Okay, let's vote on it. Since Ed doesn't know Irene, he gets to count votes." She winked at Ed. "All in favor that I call Tracy's mom and ask her to come here for the final session, raise your hand."

Marilyn's and Ross' hands popped into the air. Then Emilie raised hers. And Barbara.

"Four in favor," said Ed.

"All those opposed, say Nay." Marilyn eyed Michael.

"I don't know, Marilyn," he said, shaking his head. "What if we lose? That is possible, you know."

"We won't lose."

"Tell that to the jury," said Michael.

"Okay, I will," Marilyn was tired and getting annoyed with Michael's pessimism. "Look, let's just decide. Do I call her or not?" She looked at Tracy's father. "Wayne?"

"Sure, Marilyn," he said. "It's worth a try. Go ahead. Call her."

Marilyn jumped up and walked into the café. Through the plate glass, the group watched her approach the counter and talk to a clerk. A telephone appeared. Marilyn adjusted herself on a stool and all they could see was her back. They saw her nod twice and hang up the phone. As she emerged from the restaurant, she kept walking. "I'll be right back. Meet you at the courthouse in 45 minutes."

By the time Marilyn returned with Irene, the courtroom was beginning to fill up. Just as they found seats in the same row as Ross and Barbara, the door to the judge's chamber swung open.

"All rise," said the bailiff, and Marilyn reached for Irene's hand.

When the foreman stood and read the jury's decision, Marilyn had been right. Unanimously in favor of the plaintiff. And the jury recommended that Tracy Thomas and her family be compensated to the maximum extent of the law, $650,000.00, plus medical costs. Plus punitive damages of another $400,000.00.

For an instant no one in the courtroom spoke. Then those who'd been rooting for Tracy began to whoop and holler, hug and kiss, handshake and backslap. Barbara ran to Michael and almost knocked him over. Without a word, she held him in her arms, conscious of the joy they both felt.

The courtroom stayed in a mood of gaiety for some minutes, mindless of the judge's final words.

When the dust settled, and Michael approached Royce Holding and Steven Elliott to make a professional courtesy remark, he saw that Fossari was gone. In the clamor that had followed the jury's verdict statement, no one had seen him leave. Except for the media photographer from the St. Petersburg Independent who had the foresight to stand by the door.

83

Fossari stalked out of the courtroom in a fury, hidden and alone in the midst of the exiting crowd. He thrust his car into the busy downtown traffic, tires squealing on pavement, and then sped up the one-way street heading home.

In the kitchen, he poured a 36-ounce tumbler of bourbon, without ice, drank it down in gulps, then threw the glass into the sink. The force sent glittering chips onto the counter and the floor. He rushed into the garage and returned carrying a pressurized tank labeled C_3H_6.

Fossari ambled across the back yard and onto his dock, still lugging the tank. Overhead, darkening clouds joined together in the sky over the water to cover the last traces of sun, and then thicken into steely strips that pushed away more and more daylight. Lightning and loud thunder seemed to draw their anger from the man below, as he stepped onto the deck of his boat.

From her position at the window of the neighboring house, Ester Hardaway held the curtain out of the way so she could see outside. She tsk-tsked as the Cruise Craft pulled away from the dock and sped toward open water amidst heavy lightning and thunder.

"Crazy guy," she mumbled, dropping the curtain. Then she turned and walked into the house, clicked on the living room lamp, and sat on a large sofa in front of her television set. The noise from the TV muffled the explosion far out over the water, so Ester Hardaway didn't bother to get up. The eruption shattered the Cruise Craft into shards of metal and plastic and wood, sending them high into the air, and then settled them down again on the water's surface, to float on the whirling surf, until fragments were found the next day along the backyard seawalls of the expensive homes lining the narrow inlet between Pass-a-Grille Beach and Pine Key.

When the divers searched for Vincent Fossari's body, all they found was a large remnant of his radius bone, still attached to a portion of humerus that was severed just above the elbow. The news reporter quickly photographed Fossari's floating remains in grainy black and white that you could barely make out, but it appeared anyway in the afternoon delivery, page six, column right.

As Ester Hardaway folded her newspaper and stuffed it into the under-sink trash, she shook her head, wondering who her new next-door neighbors would be, and thinking how the newspaper photograph showing the wizened chunk of Vincent Fossari's remains resembled a child-sized plaster cast.

Epilogue

Ross

The year following Michael's hibernation procedure, Ross Manchester was nominated for the 1984 Nobel Prize in Physiology or Medicine for his Torpid Therapy research, which by then, had kept Michael's disease in remission.*

Although Ross and Emilie attended the Karolinska Institutet awards ceremonies in Stockholm, Sweden, the Assembly gave the prize to three researchers from other countries, who tied for the honors with their theories concerning the specificity in development and control of the immune system and the discovery of the principle for production of monoclonal antibodies. But it was close. And Dr. Manchester felt honored to be nominated in the first place, and he said just exactly that every time he spoke at healthcare workshops or a legal body of some sort.

The chairman of the Florida Medical Board gave Ross an official reprimand for the great jeopardy he had put their profession's reputation in, and cautioned Ross not to repeat this violation of medical ethics in the future. Then the man invited Ross to join the medical board. Ross refused. When Ross was tapped to sit on the board of directors for the newly forming Psychologists for the Ethical Treatment of Animals,** he accepted.

Emilie took Ross' kids' book idea on the humane treatment of animals, and ran with it. Under Marilyn's and Ed's guidance – illustrated by Ed's gifted classes –

Emilie wrote a series of four picture books called, *Animals are People, Too! by Auntie Em*, and individually dedicated them to the memory of Alyce Hobbs, Kevin Douglas, Janet and Michele Reo, and Susan Kohler.

Seven months later, Ross wrote another report entitled, *Principles of Humane Experimentation in Biomedical Research: Preserving Animal Health and Welfare*, but when they made it into hardcover print, he refused a book tour because of Emilie's pregnancy. When Karen's wish for a baby sister came true, she got to name Janet Marie Manchester the day she was born on Christmas Eve.

By her fourteenth birthday, Karen had grown gangly and strong, and when she tried out for the cheerleading squad, the coach said she was too tall for the team and gave the slot to a girl named Heather, who was just the right size. So Karen took a modeling job at Foley's Department Store after school, and convinced the manager to hold Pal Sign fundraisers and hand out brochures just inside the front door of the department where they sold baby clothes and toys.

Watching his child strut on the runway, Ross knew a contentment he'd never dreamed possible at the time he saved the life of a 6-week-old infant who had stopped breathing in his emergency room that long-ago October night.

---

*   *As of this writing, there is no cure for cystic fibrosis. For more information on the disease and latest updated statistics and treatments, prognosis, etc., see the following CF-specific websites, as well as additional References and Resources at the end of this book.*

Cystic Fibrosis Foundation; https://www.cff.org/

Psychologists for the Ethical Treatment of Animals was created in 1981, then became Society and Animals Forum. In 2005, it merged with the Institute for Animals and Society, and is now known as the Animals and Society Institute, Inc. It is a federal 501(c)(3) organization, whose mission is to work with social scientists, mental health providers and other animal protection organizations to reduce the suffering, exploitation, and violence against both human and nonhuman animals.

http://www.societyandanimalsforum.org/aboutus.html

Marilyn

Pal Sign, Inc., the organization Marilyn founded in 1980 to teach Tracy Thomas to communicate, and which first met at the Fossil Park Church of St. John the Divine, grew rapidly during its first year of operation.

By January 1983, just six weeks after Marilyn and Ed Kohler were married, Pal Sign had 18 employees to cover their two schools and outreach services. Marilyn's former co-worker from Parkwest Pediatric Hospital, Susan Brittan, R.N., took over the branch office in Tampa whenever Marilyn traveled to consult with the Florida School for the Deaf and Blind in St. Augustine.*

Tracy visited on summer vacations, and when Marilyn saw the value of Tracy's service dog, Pal Sign adopted two Labrador retrievers from Guide Dogs for the Deaf in Orlando.

By the end of the third fiscal year, Pal Sign, Inc. grossed a quarter of a million dollars in contributions, in-kind donations, and fees for services. That was the same year that hundreds of deaf children in central Florida participated in a stage play called *Alyce Thru the Looking Glass*, produced by Karen Manchester.

And Marilyn gave a series of continuing education programs for several of the state nurses associations, entitled *Power-With versus Power-Over: The Sangfroid Paradigm in Healthcare*. Each participant received four contact hours. And her old Sang-Froid retired for good.

---

* See References and Resources at the end of this book.

Michael

Three months after the trial ended, Michael's weight dropped four pounds in one week. He had almost reached his weigh-in goal of 155 pounds. His weight gain since the hibernation treatment had been steady and hale. So when he stepped on the scales that day in the medical office, Ross tensed. Then Michael divulged his new daily routine of bodybuilding and jogging, and Ross told Michael to slow down a tad.

Aside from the occasional melancholy Michael felt at the loss of Kevin, who he thought of whenever he trained, Michael was content. His involvement with Pal Sign, Inc. was almost as satisfying as watching his son grow. And when he helped Barbara deliver their daughter a year later, Michael was ecstatic.

Neither of the children showed signs of cystic fibrosis, giving Michael hope that Barbara wasn't a carrier of the gene, and would likely result in good health for future children. At least the percentages were in their favor. The Sutherlands conceived one more time, and when identical twin boys, Jimmy and Johnny, were born, every pediatric pulmonologist in the country took an interest in the family, especially the father, Michael Sutherland, whose cystic fibrosis symptoms remained absent.*

---

* As of this writing, there is no cure for cystic fibrosis. For more information on the disease and latest updated statistics and treatments, prognosis, and outlook, etc., see the following CF-specific websites, as well as additional References and Resources at the end of this book.

Cystic Fibrosis Foundation; https://www.cff.org/

U.S. National Library of Medicine and National
Institutes of Health Reference page
http://www.nlm.nih.gov/medlineplus/cysticfibrosis.html

———————————

Tracy

In the fall after the trial, Wayne Thomas' employment transfer request came through, and the Thomas family moved into a split-level home on the outskirts of Washington, D.C.

Tracy enrolled in the Kendall Demonstration Elementary School,* which was part of, and located on, the campus of Gallaudet College.* She was an eager student whose hunger for intellectual challenges and social affection, led her to take an interest in kittens and puppies. The Thomases adopted an 8-week-old Saint Bernard puppy they named Paxi; then taught the puppy to read flash cards and simple finger signs, Tracy became the most popular kid in her class. And when the Hearing Hounds Guide Dog Association formally trained Paxi, Tracy's independence grew.

For six months, Irene Thomas spent an hour a week in a psychologist's chair. Then every other week. As Tracy excelled, Irene bid her counselor good-bye, then threw a fist full of imipramine and Valium into the bowl, flushed once, and never looked back.

------

* See References and Resources

Alphabetical List of
Resources and References

Alzheimer's Association, Chicago, IL
http://www.alz.org/index.asp

American Foundation for Suicide Prevention, New York, NY
http://www.afsp.org

American Sign Language Dictionary, Sternberg, Martin L.
Collins Reference, November 1998

American Sign Language The Easy Way
Stewart, David A., Stewart, Elizabeth, Little, Jessalyn; Barron's
Educational Series, 2nd edition November 2006

Americans with Disabilities Act
U.S. Department of Justice, Washington, D.C.
http://www.ada.gov

Animal Liberation: A New Ethics for Our Treatment of Animals
Peter Singer, Avon Books, 1975

Animals and Society Institute, Inc
http://www.societyandanimalsforum.org/aboutus.html

Animals Make Us Human: Creating the Best Life for Animals
Grandin, Temple and Johnson, Catherine
Houghton Mifflin Harcourt, January 2009

Braille is Beautiful Curriculum Program
Teacher's Guide and Student Workbooks
National Federation of the Blind, 1998

Cystic Fibrosis Foundation, Bethesda, MD
http://www.cff.org/home

Dog Body, Dog Mind: Exploring Canine Consciousness and Total Well-Being, Fox, Michael W.
Lyons Press, July 2007

Dog Listener, The; Fennell, Jan
Harper Collins, January 2004

Dog's Mind, The ; Fogle, Bruce
Howell Book House/Maxwell Macmillan, 1992

Earthlings, Nature, Animals, Humankind, Make the Connection
http://www.earthlings.com/index.php?option=com_events&task=view_detail&agid=77&year=2009&month=09&day=21&Itemid=1

English Braille, American Edition
American Printing House for the Blind, Adopted 1959 (1972 Edition)

Essential Elements in Early Intervention: Visual Impairment and Multiple Disabilities
Edited by Deborah Chen, Ph.D.
American Foundation for the Blind Press, 1999

Everything Sign Language Book: American Sign Language Made Easy,
Duke, Irene
Adams Media Corporation, December 2003

Factory Farming and Concentrated Animal Feeding Operations (CAFOs) http://en.wikipedia.org/wiki/Factory_farming

Florida School for the Deaf & the Blind, St. Augustine, Florida
http://www.fsdb.k12.fl.us

Gorillas in the Mist , Fossey, Dian
Marina Books, October 2000, Houghton Mifflin, 1983

Gallaudet University, Washington, D.C.
http://www.gallaudet.edu

Johns Hopkins Bloomberg School of Public Health
Global Clearinghouse for Information on Alternatives to Animal Testing, Baltimore, MD
http://altweb.jhsph.edu/pubs/books/humane_exp/reference

Kendall Demonstration Elementary School
Laurent Clerc, National Deaf Education Center
Gallaudet University, Washington, D.C.
http://clerccenter.gallaudet.edu/x15175.xml

Light in My Darkness, Heller, Helen
Doubleday, 1927, Reprinted by Chrysalis Books, 2000

Minding Animals: Awareness, Emotions, and Heart
Bekoff, Marc (Author), Goodall, Jane (Forward)
Oxford University Press, January 2002

Miracle Worker, The; VHS with voice-over scene descriptions
Anne Bancroft, Patty Duke, 1962

National Alliance on Mental Illness
Mental Health Support, Education and Advocacy,
Arlington, VA   http://www.nami.org

National Institute of Mental Health, Suicide Prevention
U.S. Department of Health and Human Services, Bethesda, MD
http://www.nimh.nih.gov/health/topics/suicide-prevention/index.shtml

National Institute on Aging,
Alzheimer's Disease Education & Referral Center
U.S. National Institutes of Health
Silver Spring, MD
http://www.alzheimers.org

National Institute on Disability and Rehabilitation Research
Richmond, VA   http://www.adata.org/whatsada-history.aspx

On the Origin of Species By Means of Natural Selection
Preservation of Favoured Races in the Struggle for Life
Darwin, Charles (Author) 1809-1882
Various publishers through 2008

Sign Language Learning Cards with Braille
School Specialty Publishing, January 1999

Society & Animals Forum, Grove, MD
http://www.psyeta.org/index.shtml

Suicide Awareness Voices of Education (SAVE), Bloomington, MN
http://www.save.org

Story of My Life, The, Classic Bound Edition, Keller, Helen
Doubleday & Company, 1954

There Are Men Too Gentle to Live Among Wolves, Kavanaugh, James,
Nash Publishing, Los Angeles, CA, Canada, 1970

Tackle Climate Change
http://www.tackleclimatechange.co.uk/2007_08_19_archive.html

TRAFFIC International, Wildlife Trade Monitoring Network
Wild vs. Farmed Salmon: What's the Catch?
United Kingdom
http://www.traffic.org/home/2007/3/7/wild-vs-farmed-salmon-whats-the-catch.html

U.S. Food and Drug Administration, http://www.fda.gov

Union of Concerned Scientists
Citizens and Scientists for Environmental Solutions, Cambridge, MA
http://www.ucsusa.org/about/CAFOs Uncovered
http://www.ucsusa.org/food_and_agriculture/science_and_impacts/impacts_indu
strial_agriculture/cafos-uncovered.html

* * *

To benefit those readers interested in pursuing further information on any of the referenced resources, the author has made every effort to provide accurate Internet addresses and other relevant information, and welcomes reader feedback with updates, omissions, editorial or other errors. However, neither the publisher nor the author assumes any responsibility for errors or changes that occur after publication. Further, neither the publisher nor the author has any control over, and does not assume any responsibility for, third-party websites or their contents.

* * *

Read on for an exciting sneak preview of Gail Hallas' new novel

The Burner
by Gail Hallas

Carlyle Neuse takes a night-shift job at Sunny Palms Nursing Home where he befriends patients in the locked psych ward. Soon the entire nursing home burns to the ground. Eleven people are dead. Carlyle is thrown into prison for arson and murder, where he's tortured by inmates, guards, and the jail psychiatrist.

Somewhere three patients and a 12-year old girl know the truth. Can Carlyle find any of them before it's too late?

Or are they all dead, too?

One of Hallas's great gifts in this, her second novel, is making you constantly question what kind of story you're reading. Is this medico-legal thriller actually a mystery where the revengeful orderly and cruel nurse plan multiple murders? Or are we looking inside the mind of an eccentric nursing home patient in the midst of her harrowing psychological collapse?

Both of these possibilities seem equally plausible at various times; and it's that uncertainty that keeps you up all night long, propelling you through page after page until dawn to find out.

Coming soon from Amazon.com
Paperback, Kindle, and Audio book

The Burner

Prologue

At first, the old woman thinks she can't get the match to light. From her chair, she saturates three crumpled napkins with nail polish remover, and shakes the rest of the bottle over her bed, creating wet spots on the worn blanket. On the way back from the bathroom an hour ago, she had loosened the sheets from a nearby bed and tucked a corner under her own mattress. Surprising how much she can do when the aides leave the room for a minute, she thinks as she scrapes the match again.

Suddenly, the fire is in front of her, small at first, then licking across the entire top of her bed. In the next instant, flames grow and travel along the sheet she had bridged between the two beds. There is a whoosh, a flash, and she smells her hair singe.

The old woman's hands tremble now as she wrestles a key into the lock at her waist. Hot metal stings her fingers, and she gropes to wrap her skirt around the buckle. The belt releases with a click and she rises from her chair. Looking around the room, she can't believe that the beds near the windows are already ablaze. She heads toward the hallway, but trips on the leg of her chair and falls.

Lying on the floor, the old woman feels hot particles settle on the bare skin of her arms and legs. She sees the ceiling cave in halfway across the room, then it drops, creating a wall between her and the two patients near the windows. She opens her mouth to call for help, but a chunk of plaster lands heavy on top of her, cracking four ribs and crushing her jaw. A billow of soot catches in her throat, and black ash burns her eyes. Then she feels nothing.

Chapter 1
1973

The school bus came to a slow stop in northeast St. Petersburg, the vehicle's worn brakes ringing painfully through the open window of Sunny Palms Nursing home. The August sun cut morning shadows across the floor of C Ward. In her chair, Helga Weis flinched and opened her eyes. She lowered her head and rubbed the spot on the back of her neck where the metal frame had left a crease.

Helga's mouth felt dry, and she turned toward the nightstand beside her bed. Staring at the plastic drinking glass, she studied the lines where the water had evaporated into powdery mold at the bottom. On the outer rim, light reflected off fragments of dust where sticky lip prints were wrinkled and thick.

The bus's brakes screeched again, and Helga looked out the window. Shimmering sunlight made her squint, calling up images of bright lights from a long time ago, back in Wurzburg, Germany. She closed her eyes. The glare had been from the front of a truck then, lighting up wide cracks around the door in the room where she and her sister Anna had crouched. A man had kicked in the door, and Helga heard people scream as they ran from the room. Helga took her sister's hand and started to stand up. Anna pulled away.

"I want mama," whispered Anna.

"Mama's dead, Anna. You know that." Helga reached for her sister again. "Come on. We've got to get on the truck."

Everyone else was gone now, and Helga heard people shouting and climbing onto the truck bed.

Helga Weis was in her mid-teens then, five years older than Anna, and she knew that if they were to live, they had to leave with the others. In a quick move, Helga wrapped her arms around Anna's waist. She carried Anna to the door, and smelled her sister's terrified breath in her face. Just then, the ribbon from Helga's hair fell to the floor. She stooped to pick it up, and Anna wiggled free.

"Don't," Helga said. "Come, we have to go."

"I'm scared. Please, Helga," Anna begged. "Please don't make me go."

Then Helga heard the truck's engine roar. She clutched Anna's arm and pulled her outside toward the truck.

"Hurry, Anna. Here, put your foot in my hands and climb up. Quick. Step onto the bumper. Grab the wooden stake. Hurry."

Anna jumped back. "You first." She motioned Helga toward the truck. Helga frowned, then reached for the stake near the bumper and hopped on one foot. She stepped off the ground, and when she turned to take hold of Anna's hand, her sister was just out of reach. She saw Anna move toward her, then stop. At that moment, a man on the truck bed seized Helga and pulled her over the railing. She landed on top of someone's legs. A baby wailed. The truck lurched once and rolled forward. Helga scrambled to the rear of the truck and looked through the slats. She saw Anna reaching out. Then a bomb exploded near Anna, and all Helga could see was a dense cloud of gray smoke.

Now, with the sun's glare outside C Ward, and from a distance of 38 years, Helga still hears the echo of men's boots clacking on the stone street where her family had lived. The men pushed her parents out the door and Helga hears her father beg the men not to hurt her mother. She hears a gunshot. Her mother screams. Then another shot. Helga never saw her parents again.

Two weeks later, a truck came to save Helga and Anna and the others hiding in the room.

Helga recalled only bits and pieces of her trip to America, of living in an orphanage in Fort Myers, Florida. She found a job at the Lee County Printing Press, where she emptied wastebaskets and vacuumed floors late at night. But images haunted her, and when her mind snapped, they took her to Chattahoochee State Hospital in Tallahassee, and put her in a padded room so she wouldn't hurt herself.

Years dragged on, ran together. Helga forgot who she was. She rarely talked. Then one day an employee of the hospital found her with gashes on her wrists, cut with a spoon she had bent back and forth to make a sharp edge. They sewed her up and she didn't remember doing that again, but her memory was blurred and she couldn't be sure.

Things came into focus now as Helga opened her eyes in C Ward of the nursing home. There were two women sitting nearby, and a scorching sun bounced off the school bus on the other side of the window.

Chapter 2

Across from Helga, Tess Oliver sat in a vinyl chair that was two feet from the bathroom she shared with other patients in C Ward. On her lap was a book. Tess slid her finger, snail-like, across the page, stopping every once in a while to rest her eyes.

...He opened his mouth and taught them, saying blessed are the poor in spirit: for theirs is the kingdom of heaven. Blessed are they that mourn; for they shall be comforted. Blessed are the...

For seven decades, Tess Oliver had read from the same Bible. Though it had once been gleaming white, now the book was soiled, a dozen pages missing. Tess knew the story behind every discoloration and rip — most of them from when Daddy'd been drinking and acted crazy. It was those times that she had sought God's comfort by running to the woods behind the house, the Bible tucked close to her chest.

Tess had read *The Song of Solomon* long before she understood its meaning. But she had always known that God meant the words to be beautiful, and in her child's mind, her hunger to learn and to read gave her the resolve she needed to turn to her Bible again and again and drown in the pleasure of new life that the Lord promised her.

Sometimes, after little Tess returned from the backwoods, she'd find her father waiting, his anger still ripe. He would switch her arms and legs until she fell down, brown pigtails sopping up mud and chicken droppings.

"Get to your room," Daddy would snarl, lashing a final stroke against her thighs. Often he'd yank her Bible out of her hand and kick it, sending fragments of paper into the air. Tess would scurry to pick up the book and run into the house.

...Blessed are the meek: for they shall inherit the earth. Blessed are they which do hunger and thirst after righteousness: for they shall...

Outside the ward, a cloud floated in front of the sun, dimming the room and making it hard for Tess to read. She lifted the Bible and laid it on the bed next to her. It took her five and a half minutes to tug open the

369

nightstand door, find her magnifying glass, and settle the book back onto her lap, each movement slowed by a wide strap that was wrapped around her belly and the chair.

...*Blessed are the merciful: for they shall obtain mercy. Blessed are the pure in heart: for they shall see God...*

"I shall," Tess whispered. Her eyes lifted from the page and focused on the air in front of her. Tess Oliver *was* pure in heart. Pure as new fallen snow, silent and chaste. She smiled now, pleased with her exemplary life. The virginity she had guarded with care.

Except for Daddy, of course.

Sometimes, when Tess had run into the house with her skin tingling from the switchings, wash herself and hide the Bible under a pile of clothes in the chifforobe, Daddy would come in and take her panties off. He would touch her down there, hurting her sometimes, and then lay his heavy body on top of her.

Tess's fingers flipped to page two hundred and twenty-five of her book. She moved her magnifying glass along the page.

...*Honour thy father and thy mother: that their days may be long upon the land which the Lord thy God hath given thee...*

Tess never knew her mother, but someone had told her that she was the prettiest woman they'd ever seen. And Phillip would have been one year younger than Tess if he'd lived. But Momma died giving birth to Phillip on the same bed Tess and Daddy later shared.

Tess fidgeted in her chair now, feeling the drench of thin fabric between her back and the cushion. She tried to change her position, move a little, but the belt got in the way. Her elbows were too short to reach the armrest, and her feet hung an inch above the floor. But she had always been small. At 18, she'd had to stand next to the younger children for class pictures that spring day when she graduated from twelfth grade in front of the wood-frame schoolhouse where Daddy was too sick with the flu to come to see her get a diploma like most of the other parents did. Within a week, her Daddy was dead.

That summer, Tess cleaned the old Remington stored in the woodshed and taught herself to type. She got a job at the First Baptist Church, a one-mile walk down the gravel road, where she wrote letters and copied sermons for Reverend Greene.

Tess went through four ministers the first seven years she worked for the church. When the funds came in and they finished the new chapel and the side buildings, Tess started teaching Sunday school to some of the slower-learning children.

She was happy then. God was good.

...Blessed are the peacemakers: for they shall be called the children of God.

Tess Oliver closed the book and slept sitting up.

Chapter 3

Glorie Harper wiggled her toes on the footstool. Heel depressions in the worn tapestry had deepened over the years, dulling the fabric to the color of a dirty penny, and transforming the cushion's stuffing into crumbled cement. Glorie gazed down the length of her legs. My feet are still perfect, she thought.

Now that the throbbing in her head was letting up, she could think of Charles. Charles. He had given her the footstool on their second wedding anniversary. "To preserve the beauty of your feet," he had said. "So you can continue to torture them with your dance."

It was true. Ballet had tortured her feet. Her legs. Her body. Glorie had loved it. Her favorite position was the Arabesque Penchee' – a movement, smooth, poised, sensual. Her limbs had been supple, arms outstretched, fingers relaxed in mid-air, torso arched forward. She loved feeling her leg muscles tighten, toes pointed at an angle paralleling her arm. Perfect.

As a child, Glorie had rehearsed the movements endlessly, and by the time she was twelve, she could spin like a top, graceful, unstrained. She had all the physical traits required for ballet: small torso with long limbs and a swan neck. She was flexible, willowy and strong; and she had the emotional feeling for rhythm to express the music's moods.

Then it was the summer of her fourteenth year. Glorie had just finished the starring role in the production of Igor Stravinsky's *The Firebird*, where she pretended to be on the stage at the New York City Ballet, rather than in the small theatre in St. Petersburg, Florida. That's when she realized her body wasn't her friend anymore.

Glorie had grown four inches in height that summer, making her five feet nine. The teacher said she was too tall for ballet, but they would try to put her in minor secondary parts. She auditioned to dance as a sugar plum fairy in the local production of *The Nutcracker*, but they gave the part to a girl named Martha, who was just the right size. Although she continued to practice dance, Glorie made up her mind to study on Broadway as well.

"I am going to be an actress," Glorie had told Charles Harper an hour after they met on the train to New York City that spring day just after she turned nineteen. Throughout the ride, Glorie and Charles talked easily, sharing their dreams. By the time the train pulled into Penn Station, Glorie was head over heels in love with the young writer who carried a nine-hundred-page manuscript in his suitcase.

The first few months in New York, Glorie read radio commercials for Phillip Morris and National Cash Register. A Ladies Home Journal ad showed her holding the new big-eyed doll called Kewpie. The publicity paid off. A call from Fanny Brice led to an audition with the Ziegfeld's Follies. Glorie's height and long legs placed her center front in the chorus line, where she danced and kicked and swung suspended from the rafters above the audience. Glorie was happier than ever.

Charles and Glorie were inseparable; and he proposed the night they celebrated the publication of his big story on women strikers from the Shirtwaist Manufacturing Company in the New York Evening Journal. They were married a week before Christmas that year, and spent a glorious honeymoon in their small apartment where he wrote and she rehearsed parts and practiced dance.

After eight years, Glorie and Charles returned to Florida. They were well off now and didn't need or want Manhattan anymore. With Glorie's mother so sick, and the baby due in a few months, Glorie and Charles settled into a big house on the north side of St. Petersburg, two blocks from the Fourth Street buses that took them downtown to see a ballet or a play.

Charles was into his fourth book when Glorie gave birth to their daughter. Little Jennifer Harper had the best genes from both parents: her father's dark eyes and long lashes, and her mother's soft blond hair.

One afternoon when Jennifer was three, the child danced and played in the backyard. Glorie prepared supper. Using a two-pronged fork to transfer bacon from the pan, she drained the strips on folded newspaper.

Through the window, Glorie watched Jennifer. The child pranced across the lawn, arms raised as she sprang free and easy into graceful saute majeur ballet leaps. Glorie cheered and clapped her hands. In the next instant, a white bull terrier came from out of nowhere, trailing a short chain across the yard. Before Glorie could move, she saw the dog charge Jennifer and knock her to the ground. Glorie snatched the bacon fork and ran outside. By then, the terrier's jaws were around Jennifer's throat. Glorie screamed, kicked the dog, and then dropped to her knees. She punched the fork tips into the tight muscles of the terrier's neck. The dog released the child, yelped and rolled over, exposing its broad chest. Glorie hovered over the dog and buried the fork deep inside its soft belly, spewing blood into the air. She removed the fork. Then she raised it high and buried it again. And again. And again.

Twenty minutes later, Charles pulled into the driveway and found Glorie sitting on the ground, rocking Jennifer in her arms. There was dirt on Jennifer's neck, and Glorie's dress was sopping with blood. Nearby, a dog lay dead.

Glorie was hospitalized for three weeks; and after going home, she stayed in her bed for a month and a half. She didn't remember Jennifer's funeral. "It's a nervous breakdown," the doctor said. "We'll have to be very careful, very gentle with her, Mr. Harper." The doctor shook his head. "These things take time," he said, "but I think your wife will come out of it."

Now, sitting next to her bed in C Ward, Glorie kicked one slipper off with the toe of her other foot. She propped her naked heel on the footstool and rotated her ankle. Then she looked up and saw Tess Oliver. Glorie moved her eyes the other way. She saw the new patient. The one who didn't speak. Greta? Elga? Helga? Yes. Helga. That was it. Glorie watched Helga sitting stiff as a mannequin, eyes blinkless, hollow, like nighttime windows on a house where no one lived.

Glorie rubbed her hands over her face. "What time is it?" she said out loud to no one in particular.

"Eightish," said Tess, whose perception of time was fine-tuned from years of studying the noises in the hallway.

"Oh." Glorie twisted at the waist, opened the door to her nightstand and removed her pocketbook. Reaching inside the bag, she found a worn pencil and a notebook with thin wire curled around the top. There were still two pages left. She wrote for a while, proud of her fine penmanship. Then breakfast came and Glorie was glad because her fingers had started to cramp.

While they ate, Tess asked Glorie what she was writing about.

"A note." Glorie punched the crust on top of her oatmeal with a spoon. "To the man who works here. The one who just started." Glorie watched a stream of milk slide into the crack she had made in her food.

"You'll see him tonight," Tess said. "He comes in at eleven."

"Oh." Glorie frowned. "But I was rude."

"Rude?"

"Last night. I want to apologize." Glorie didn't think apple butter was supposed to look like this. She smeared a brown layer across her damp toast and watched yellow grains come to the surface.

"You weren't rude."

"I slept."

"He didn't mind," Tess said. "He stayed near you to make sure you were all right."

"Oh." Glorie paused. "Was I?"

"Were you what?"

"All right."

Tess moved a clump of oatmeal around in her mouth, chewing unhurried, making it last. In general, Glorie had been all right last night. At least more so than *she* had been. Or Helga, for that matter, perched then, and now, somewhere between hither and yon, and talking to no one.

Tess reached for her coffee. She turned the cup around two full rotations in a steady movement, inspecting the rim until she found a small place that was unchipped and clean. She sipped the coffee and put the cup back on her tray. "Yes," she said. "You were all right."

The two women talked in spurts, sometimes inviting Helga to join in. Helga looked in their direction once with a stiff roll of her head, but when Tess spoke to her, Helga turned away, wooden and slow, and fixed her eyes on an empty space directly in front of her.

The nurse's aide came to collect meal trays, and Glorie wanted to ask for some water. She waved in the girl's direction and started to speak. The girl waved back, moved into the hall and was gone. Glorie spoke to the air. Then she looked down at her bare foot, wondering whose it might be.

Glorie tried to finish her note, but her handwriting had changed; now the words seemed too big for the page. Fatter than before. Her pencil dragged wide gray strokes onto the paper and she hung her head close, watching her fingers move. Had she told Jennifer of the time she'd lived in New York? About the auditions for months until she finally got her first part in a musical? Of eating pancakes made with flour and water at first, because she and Charles spent their money on something else and neither of them minded a bit at the time. Did she tell Jennifer? Yes, she was sure she did. In her last letter. Of course. If you need money, Jenny, call me or write, she had said. Glorie relaxed in the chair and closed her eyes.

Jennifer always returned money Glorie lent her, the very next time she got paid. Even though Glorie told her not to worry about paying her back. But Jennifer was like that. So much like Charles. And oh, how Jennifer loved the subway. The subway. Trains. The train where she and Charles met... Glorie raised her head and watched the day change on the other side of the window. Clouds blocked the sun now. Rain? ...the subway and the delicious pace of Manhattan.

We'll travel together, Mom. As soon as you're well. We'll go first class, Mom. Just the two of us, okay, Mom?

Glorie hadn't planned to stay long with these people. Soon she'd find a place of her own. Or stay with Uncle Harry who lived in Savannah where she sometimes did shows.

Glorie's pencil scribbled off the bottom of the page and scratched the skin of her leg. Her head throbbed again and she had to go to the bathroom. She tried to stand up, but something tugged against her bladder and she fell back, scorching the skin of her stomach. Jennifer, quick, catch the letter, honey. Before it falls on the floor.

Musty vapors stung Glorie's nostrils as urine spilled onto the chair and splashed in yellow pearls underneath. A small roach darted across Glorie's bare foot.

The nurse. A mess? She didn't mean to make a mess. Glorie stretched past the armrest with her hand and grabbed for her papers. The nurse pushed her backward and Glorie hit her elbow on the arm of the chair. A bolt of pain screamed up her arm and into her neck. The water glass on the nightstand tipped over, fell to the floor, rolled under her bed and stopped when it hit the wall.

Wet. But it was an accident. Don't. I won't... Where was he?

"Chaaaaarles."

Glorie's hand went up, but the nurse was already removing her gown. Glorie looked down at her nakedness and saw the rash that sprinkled her skin. Her body looked different than it was. How come? Because this wasn't her body, that's how come. She looked at her brown nipples pointing down, limp over horizontal folds in her belly. Her behind hung down, too, between narrow thighs where she felt the skin wobble as the nurse pulled her to stand. Behind closed lids, Glorie's eyes burned like hot coals. She tripped over the lip of the shower stall and then felt cold tiles shocking her bare feet. For a time, she felt the water -- neither warm nor cold -- splash over her skin. Glorie wasn't sure when the water stopped, but she found herself lying in a puddle, icy, and she couldn't seem to get out of it.

She must have slept then, because the next thing she knew she was hearing the familiar sound of her husband's breathing next to her. In the dim light Glorie saw the bulge of his vein pumping along the side of his neck. She watched it for a while without waking him. Then she eased herself out of bed and went into the kitchen. She returned with a glass of warm milk and Charles woke up. They talked for a while, voices hushed, as if they were in public surrounded by other people, instead of in their own bedroom with no one around. Charles said he'd felt tired lately.

"It's just the time of year, darling," Glorie said. "In the winter, everything slows down. Even people. I feel sluggish myself." Glorie stroked Charles's cheek as she spoke, and convinced him he was fine. They talked about taking the bus downtown tomorrow. Get tickets to the Sunshine Players Theatre. "Then we'll go to the drug store," she said. "Buy some vitamin tonic for you." Charles nodded and they fell asleep in each other's arms.

In the morning, Charles had said he wasn't hungry, and his voice sounded strange to Glorie. Like there was sand in his mouth. When Charles grunted and grabbed at his chest, Glorie dropped her teacup on the floor. Was it the noise that made Charles wheeze then? His eyes rolled up into his head, and all Glorie could see were the whites. Then he was dead.

For a long time Glorie cried. She felt weak now and ached all over, but she couldn't seem to stand up or get out of her chair. Was there something wrong with her mind? Tess would know. But she couldn't seem to find Tess.

Glorie's foot was getting cold. She tightened her calf muscles and forced her toes downward to a point. She watched the skin stretch along the front of her leg and over the arch of her foot. Tiny blue veins meshed with the puckered ivory of her instep in a graceful line that revealed fine bones in her ankles.

378

Glorie smiled. She leaned into the canvas strap at her hips, picked a wet pink slipper from the floor, and slid it over her foot.

. . . to be continued . . .

About the Author

Gail Hallas, RN, PhD is an author, artist, public speaker and registered nurse. Her writings have been published in over sixty publications, including professional journals, children's picture books, healthcare academic texts, fiction and nonfiction books, many in print, Braille, voiceover and music. She has won numerous national and international awards and recognition for her research, writings, and advocacy for healthcare consumers, disabled and disadvantaged children, and animals.

The lay version of her doctoral dissertation published as the feature cover story under the title of *Why Nurses are Giving it Up* in **RN Magazine**, which was based on her research project, *Analytical Study of the Nursing Shortage and the Problematic Stressors of Individual Nurses.*

Hallas worked in clinical nursing, infection control, pediatrics, psychiatry, staff development administration, and education. She has owned her own healthcare consulting firm for the past 18 years, leading seminars and workshops for hospital administrators, physicians, lawyers, judges, business owners, nurses, emergency medical techs, social workers, and other professionals. She was among the original 400 students trained by the Department of Justice (DOJ) and Equal Employment Opportunity Commission (EEOC) to teach compliance under the Americans with Disabilities Act (ADA) to employers, government agencies, and public accommodations.

She has written numerous articles, monographs, and texts on how to comply with the ADA for businesses.

A strong advocate and representative for disabled children and adults, Hallas has won disability discrimination cases with a large department store on behalf of a 9-year-old girl with spina bifida; as well as an entertainment complex for discrimination against wheelchair users, and other actions. She was a student of Braille, St. Petersburg, Florida, and Reading for the Blind, Austin, Texas, and teaches beginning Braille to both blind and sighted children and adults. All of her recent children's books contain Braille transcription of the print version, and musical narration or songs of the story, so that a family can read together no matter what their visual level.

Hallas was former guest faculty for National Judicial College at the University of Nevada-Reno, and the University of New Mexico Law Center, Albuquerque, where she taught the newly enacted Americans With Disabilities Act (ADA) to lawyers, judges, and court administrators. She wrote Chapter 7 *Reasonable Accommodations for People with Disabilities under the Americans with Disabilities Act*, for the National Judicial College's teaching text, **Understanding the ADA for Judges and Court Administrators,** University of Nevada, National Judicial College, American Bar Assoc., University Press, Reno, Nevada.

Hallas founded several nonprofit organizations for nurses, people with disabilities, and at-risk children. In 2001, she founded a charity organization that serves children who are disadvantaged, disabled, and at-risk. In partnership with the County Sheriff's Office, she developed and conducted classes to teach female inmates creative writing and illustration for children's picture books, and how to transcribe their work into Braille. She runs her nonprofit charity organization, and spends most of her time writing novels, children's book, management journals, and nursing and dog-care how-to's. In addition to completing her novel *The Burner*, about racism and ageism in the deep south, Ghigna Hallas is currently completing several non-fiction works. *The Diary of A Saint Bernard: Looking Inside a Dog's Heart; How to Recruit and Retain Staff in Long Term Healthcare; Braille Behind Bars; and Riddle Crimes from Father Goose: A Memoir.*

She lives in Florida with two 170-pound Saint Bernards, and is happy to hear from readers.

Website
www.gailhallas.com

* * *

Author's Note

While all of the accuracies and good stuff in this book are due to the expertise of my colleagues and writing peers, as well as hundreds of supporters and others too numerous to list, I fully acknowledge that any errors or omissions in my writings are solely my own. I hope my goofs are insignificant.

NO OTHER MEDICINE is a work of fiction. Literary perceptions and expressions in this story are based on my experiences. Names, facilities, characters, places, and incidents are either products of my imagination, or, in the case of places, businesses, entities, agencies, organizations, corporations, or locations, they are used fictitiously, and mentioned to promote conceptual awareness for readers.

I have tried to tell a story that is interesting, entertaining, educational, and informative – and one that can make a difference. I hope I have succeeded.

Acknowledgements

My heartfelt thanks to Jack Hallas, my late husband, my nursing professor (biophysical science) – and strongest supporter of all – for his patience, his never-ending loving advice, editing insight, and expertise, who grinded through the manuscript from the day of its inception to offer suggestions on discourse, dialogue, and dangling participles. I just wish he were here to celebrate the finished book.

Captain Ed Engemann, colorful mountain man, beach walker, and acclaimed advocate for any underdog who needs advocating for, thank you for listening to me ramble on for fourteen days straight, as I read the entire manuscript aloud to you while you drove across the country from Florida to California. Thanks Ed, for your undying faith and support.

I'm grateful to all the students in my writing class, for your endless encouragement and support. Especially Carolyn McDonald, Paul Elliott, and Barbara Bender, my assistants during an entire 18-week grueling course. And to Sonia Roberts, Donna Thewlis, Jim and Rosie Bolla, Celeste Williams, Carmelo Santos, Chuck and Olga Wood, Nellie Bright, and Velma Roberts.

To Lawrence Oliver, New York playwright, actor, and author, who read the complete manuscript and texted his comments day after day, piece by piece – even during breaks from his Chief of Detectives Blue Bloods role, leaving Tom Selleck in the other room. Without his assistance, I would have had to sleep instead of work all-nighters while he listened and advised me from across the country. Thank you.

To BethAnne Algers, nurse extraordinaire, whose opinion I value immensely. Not only did she make corrections in medical issues, in grammar, spelling, and syntax, but she even offered actual suggestions — unheard of in this business. My heartfelt thanks.

Thanks to Coach Chuck, the original Sang Froid, who is always there for me whenever I need a strong shoulder, soft words, and hard reality checks.

I am grateful for my Capitol Doo Wop Cop, who still believes in me, gives me support and encouragement; and listens patiently when I need a friend — no matter how maddening I am. Thank you, Jimi.

Gerri Fleetwood, RN, who stayed up all night to read the manuscript, and then generously shared her nursing insight as we walked together on the beach, never complaining once when my Saint Bernard splashed wet sand all over her feet. Thank you for being at the right place at just the right time.

Thank you Gary, Jim, Barbie, Paul, and Sam for proofing the second edition of this manuscript.

~ ~ ~

Raves for
NO OTHER MEDICINE

Suspense, drama, and wonderful courtroom scenes. The protagonists have you cheering and hissing. The author's medical knowledge and love for children shine brilliantly throughout this book. Watching eagerly for more from this author.
- D. Banner, Former Science Professor, Kansas City

Rich characters and real medicine. Strong action and drama come from a vast well of experience. A storyteller in the grandest tradition.
- L. Oliver, Author, Playwright, Actor, New York City

Brings to life passion and horror that do exist in the field of healthcare. Deep insights into characters. Truth is that such characters do exist not only healthcare, but all professions. This is a must read!
- V.R.,MBA, HCM, Business Admin., 1,300-bed teaching hospital.

Brings readers into the thick of it with authenticity and passion. A must read for anyone who's ever had a blood pressure cuff wrapped around their arm.   - B. Algie. RN, Infection Control Nurse, Tallahassee, FL

Masterful! Captivating! Reality slaps you right in the face.
- J. Bethel, Retired Law Enforcement, Washington, D.C.

Unbelievably accurate! Impressed with the reality and quality of the characters and situations.   - Gerry F., RN, Lawrence, MI

Most moving book I have read. (And I'm an avid reader.) The author has used her experience to create a most plausible tale. One can only hope that Dr. Fossari is a fictional character.
- Capt. Ed Engemann, U.S. Merchant Marine (Ret.), Highlands, NC

Until one has loved an animal,
a part of one's soul remains unawakened.
– Anatole France, 1921

Eternity is longer than time,
a mind is stronger than matter,
thought is swifter than wind,
and genius is more potent than gold.
– Edward Miner Gallaudet, 1870

~ ~ ~

Dedicated to the real-life inspirational heroes of this story
My baby daughter, Nicole Marie
Connie Smith
Arnold Dunn, M.D.
Alicia Taylor
Gary Moses
Georgette Weaver

And for Chuck,
– the original Sang Froid –
with love and admiration.

~ ~ ~

This book is also dedicated to
all the nurses,
the doctors and the hospitals
truly committed to the healthcare profession.

Most of all it is dedicated to
the thousands of patients who,
over the years,
have taught me so much —
about life and death,
love and hate,
kindness and cruelty.
They also showed me the tragic effect
that human indifference can have
on the plight of all living animals,
both human and nonhuman.

~ ~ ~

I pray this story makes a difference,
and offer its message with hope that it reaches
those with the power to make significant
positive changes in our nation's healthcare system.

And that they will.

Made in the USA
Lexington, KY
05 February 2017